Terry Endacott gained an MA from the University of East Anglia. He worked for many years in education before leaving the profession to devote more time to writing, playing music and travelling. His writing genres include imaginative fantasy for both adults and older children.

To family and friends.

Terry Endacott

PUDDLEHOPPERS 2
CLOUD JUMPERS AND
THE HAIR EATER

AUSTIN MACAULEY PUBLISHERS™

LONDON · CAMBRIDGE · NEW YORK · SHARJAH

A CIP catalogue record for this title is available from the British Library.

ISBN 9781035843282 (Paperback)
ISBN 9781035843299 (ePub e-book)

www.austinmacauley.com

First Published 2024
Austin Macauley Publishers Ltd®
1 Canada Square
Canary Wharf
London
E14 5AA

Chapter 1

"Ca-Bang-Boom-Bang!"

The building shook and crumbled as if a person with a sledge hammer had hit it. Some roof tiles flew up in the direction of the outer atmosphere as if they thought they were space rockets reaching orbit. While a huge explosive gust of grey wind gathered pace and pushed high in to the air before spreading outwards like a mushroom cloud. It was uncertain where the debris from this explosion would land. No doubt some of the fragments would land far, far away. If anybody picked them up and wondered how they got there, they would never guess it came from that explosion. Well, I don't think they would anyway.

"What on earth was that?" Police Sergeant Muddle asked himself as he held on to his helmet with both hand.

His blue hat wanted to leave his head with the strong gust of wind that accompanied the explosion. He turned in the direction of where it had come from and saw the rising cloud of smoke. It reminded him of when he burnt the toast very badly in his kitchen. He normally had a dark cloud of smoke rising from the stove at that point as well. He was soon dashing off in the direction of the explosion on foot.

As the dust settled, workers began to emerge from the destroyed pickle factory. As you can imagine, they were covered in a layer of grey dust. Each one emerging was coughing and spluttering like cars back-firing. Each one eventually leaned for support against the car park wall. Gasping, like goldfish in a bowl for air. To tell you the truth, each was glad to be still alive.

Within a few moments, the army of ambulances and fire engines arrived. Their blue lights flashing and their sirens whirring. There was a look of horror on their faces as they observed the demolished factory with its thick treacle smoke still coming out of the broken windows and now non-existent roof.

"What on earth happened here!" The chief fire officer commented.

His men straight away rushed in to the building to see what they could do to help. They gave little thought to the danger that may be ahead of them.

"It was the pickling machine! It exploded!" said a shocked voice from a stumbling figure emerging from the doorway. A doorway that didn't have a door any more. Come to think of it, there was not much of a building around it either. The voice belonged to Jules' mum.

"I was putting in some more onions and pressed the button to begin the process to turn them in to pickles and, suddenly, there was an almighty rumble. When I looked, the machine was beginning to rock from side to side on its elderly legs. A few moments later smoke was pouring out from the machine in every direction. I just turned to everybody and said, 'RUN!' Then there was an almighty explosion!"

"It was her! She's the one to blame!" An aggressive voice boomed out.

Everyone turned around to see who was shouting and who they were blaming. Worried it could be them.

It was the pickle factory owner himself. He was the one shouting very loudly and pointing his finger. He was aiming it at a very sad looking grey dust covered figure. A figure, where you could only see two very frightened eyes looking back at him in horror and shock at what he was saying.

"Me?" Was all the grey figure could reply. Surprised she had been picked on by the boss. Why her? Yet, there was no doubt he was definitely pointing at her. Goodness knows how he could tell one grey figure from the next but he had.

"What do you mean? Her fault. Explain yourself!" asked the surprised chief fire officer. It was as if he was talking to a lower ranked soldier who had spoken out of turn. Mind you he had been in the army.

"She's the one to blame!" He repeated his accusation. The finger still pointing her way. "She just admitted it herself! She was the one working on that pickle machine that exploded. She overloaded it with far too many onions. I've told her time and time again not to put so many onions in that machine. And what does she do! Put too many onions in the machine. No wonder the machine exploded. "It's all her fault, I tell you!"

"But, but I have never put too many onions in the machine. Never! And you've never told me I have!" A shocked Jules' mum stuttered as she spluttered.

The explosion was bad enough but then to be accused of causing such destruction. Her heart sank.

"Listen to her lying! You should take her down to the police station, Sargeant Muddle."

The Sargeant had just arrived on the scene with his notebook out and pen ready.

"Book her now. My factory manager will back me up on this! He knows what she is like." The owner looked at his factory manager with a threatening gaze as if to say, 'If you don't agree with me, you are going to lose your job!'

After a few moments' hesitation, everyone turned to look at the stunned factory manager. He was now put on the hottest of spots. You, like me, know there was only one thing he could say. That is if he did not want to lose his job.

"Yes, that's right! Mr. Brian has told her many times before! She knew the consequences of putting in too many onions. Now it's happened again, hasn't it? It's all down to her."

Every one turned to look at Jules' mum as if she had a head with a lot of poisonous snakes coming out of it. They all seemed to be agreed she was the cause of the explosion.

"But I never..." She was too shocked to try and defend herself from those cruel accusations.

Moreover, why had they blamed her? She had worked at the pickle factory as a good employee for many a year now. Always arriving on time and doing a good day's work. She was never off sick and always did what the factory manager asked. What is more, she needed that job and the very little money she took home each week. Why blame her?

She turned towards the factory manager. Aghast at what he had said. She had always got on with him very well. She could not believe he was now telling such lies about her. Accusing her of causing the explosion. He knew that wasn't true. One thing for sure, it was going to get her in to a lot of trouble. In fact, so much trouble, it would all be piled up as high as a bonfire ready to light on bonfire night.

He could not meet her terrified gaze. He was probably too ashamed of himself. He knew the truth but dare not go against Mr. Brian. For there would be only one outcome. He would lose his job. That is if he had a job now anyway. For come to think of it there was no pickle factory behind where he was standing.

A wicked smile of success appeared on the factory owner's face. He knew no one would doubt his word for he was the town mayor as well as owning the factory. Mr. Stanley Brian welded a lot of power in the local community and he was used to getting his own way. And if you lived in the town there was only one way, his way. If anyone was going to disagree with him, they were not going to do it aloud. Not if they had any sense that is. For he could bring a lot of problems down on someone's head if they opposed him. The mayor ran the town as if it was his little fiefdom and everybody cow-towed to him.

"Well, then, Police Sergeant Muddle. I think you better take her to the police station and charge her," the factory owner smirked with success.

The police officer looked at Mr. Brian in surprise that he had brought him in to this discussion. He thought his priority was to help those in distress coming out of the factory not to arrest someone.

All around there were people lying on the ground, struggling with their breathing and with wounds. Ambulance staff and first aiders were doing their best to look after the injured. Firemen were hosing down the building, while others sealed off the building from anyone entering. Surely, dealing with this was the priority now.

"Well, what, Mr. Brian?" asked the confused policeman.

"Are you going to arrest this woman or are you not? She's the one who caused the explosion and needs to be put in prison for her negligence," he continued with his verbal assault on Jules' mum. Even though she still had cuts and bruises that needed to be attended too.

"She needs to be arrested at this very moment and made to pay for what she has done to my pickle business. It's downright scandalous to say the least! You must arrest her! I insist!"

All heads turned back towards the police officer. What would he do? In truth, he felt he had no choice but to take Jules' mum down to the police station and book her as requested by the mayor of the town. You can never disagree with a mayor, can you? They must always be right, mustn't they?

"Right then, Mrs. Appleyard, let's be having you," he went over and grabbed her arm. "It seems like you have a lot to answer for. I think we will take you down to the police station and take a statement from you."

"But, officer, I haven't done anything!" She protested. "I am not to blame for the explosion! It's untrue what Mr. Brian is saying! For some reason that I don't understand, he is making it up about me!"

"What? Are you calling me a liar now!" Mr. Brian came up to her and shouted right in her face. "Did you all hear that? Me! Mayor of this town! Being called a liar! How dare you say that about me? I am renowned for being an upstanding member of this community. I would never lie! Everybody knows me and knows that it is untrue what you say."

"Well! Mrs. Appleyard, I think it does look like you are to blame for this damage. You should be grateful no one has died or is seriously injured due to your negligence," He looked at her sternly as only a police officer can. "Let's get you down to the police station before you cause any more trouble!"

*****

"I don't know what you have been up to Rogers. But you must go home right now and have a bath. You smell terrible! I told you, you eat far too many garlic sandwiches," The mayor's wife in her Rolls Royce was winding down the window quickly to let in fresh air. Yet, she soon discovered that with the car window open, the smell was even worse.

Yet, she never thought to reconsider that perhaps it was not him. For there seemed to be a terrible smell all about the town.

"I'm sorry Madam! I will drop you off at the town hall and then rush home and have a shower."

Even he had to admit the smell was awful. And as the mayor's wife said it was him, who was he to disagree with his boss's wife.

"I will get back as soon as I can to take you to the hairdresser!"

*****

It was not long before the pickle factory explosion became the main news in the town. It was on the local radio and television. The newspaper sellers had the headlines on their street hoardings. Everyone was talking about the explosion in the biggest factory in the area.

The mayor, as we have said already, was also the factory owner. He was soon appearing on all the media networks with his best 'pretend' smile. Of course, dressed as a Hollywood movie star for his TV appearances. Making sure he proportioned blame for the cause of the explosion where he thought it lay. That was with the worker who had been working on the pickle machine. Ensuring that everyone understood she was to blame. Going on about how he had told her time and time again not to overload the pickling machine.

"It was down to Mrs. Appleyard not being careful in what she was doing. She overloaded the pickling machine with onions. I have told her many times before to make sure she did not do it! And now look what's happened. She has to take full responsibility. My poor old pickling factory!"

He was not far off producing tears. I will leave it up to you to decide if you think they were real tears.

"Do you think she'll be sent for trial?" The local TV reporter, Robin Biggs, posed the question to him.

"Of course, she will! She'll get life in prison at least, I should think," The harsh mayor responded with his usual sharp retort. "She's ruined my factory and where will we all get our pickles from now?"

"And what will happen to those who work at the pickle factory while you are repairing the factory and machinery, will they receive any wages?" The TV reporter probed.

"Of course not!" Hissed the mayor. "How can they, when there is no factory? They will be unemployed until we get the factory up and running again. And, of course, that is all due to that silly woman!"

"Do you think this awful smell in the town is due to the explosion at your pickle factory, Mayor?" Even Robin Biggs was covering up his nose at that point as he posed this question.

There was not a person in the whole town who could not smell the terrible odour. No matter where you tried to hide yourself from it, that awful stench followed you around like the smell of a bad farm egg that had been squashed in your pocket. Only this smell seemed to be getting worse and worse. What was happening to the town?

"I have no doubt about it. She's to blame!" He carried on his rantings. "They should lock her up and throw away the key. My poor factory! I have built the business up from pickling onions in the back garden shed of my small terraced house to being the rich man I am now. Look at me, I am one of the richest men in the town!"

He took a handkerchief from his pocket and feinted crying.

"Boo-hoo! Boo-hoo!" Yet, as soon as he saw the TV journalist and his cameraman had stopped filming, so his crocodile tears terminated just as quickly as they had started.

"Right. Make sure you get that out on the television news tonight. Remember, I always give your television station first coverage on any events or news in the town. So, I expect this to make your headlines!" The mayor seemed to be threatening the TV interviewer in his usual dominating way.

The TV interviewer, was somewhat surprised, how suddenly, the tearful Mr. Brian had stopped his crying once the camera had ceased rolling.

"I am sure the editor will want to use this interview footage, Mayor," He responded politely, knowing he needed to keep on the good side of the mayor. He often needed interviews from him. There were also times when he provided free tickets for various events in the town. These he did not want to lose out on.

"Thank you for your excellent interview," He added politely.

*****

It was not too long before everyone in the town was blaming Jules' mum not only for the explosion at the pickle factory but also for the terrible smell that was everywhere. Whispering behind her back as she passed by.

"She's the one to blame!"

Many people had taken to wearing pegs on their noses. Saying they couldn't put up with the pong for much longer. There were calls for the town council to do something about it or they would be voted out.

Those with more money in their pocket had decided to book hotel rooms in other nearby towns. Their intention was to stay there until the smell had gone. Of course, they found that they were not being welcomed in these surrounding places where they had sought refuge.

For the obvious reason that they brought the stench with them. It stuck to you like glue. Those fleeing would be politely asked to shower and take their clothes to the local laundry to be laundered. This, those who had deserted Boreham Wood, were more than pleased to do. They were only too happy to get rid of the smell on themselves.

There were even attempts being made to ban people from going to "that smelly town" as they were calling it now. That is until the smell had gone. The mayors of those surrounding towns, were also thinking of diverting traffic around that smelly place. For even those cars that passed through the town, carried the smell back with them. Things seemed to be getting out of hand.

*****

"I'm bald! All my hair has gone!" The Mayoress was the first to wake up that day with all her hair having disappeared.

She had gone to bed the night before, having washed it in a lovely peach and lavender hair wash. Almost every hair had one hundred brushes carefully given before she laid her head to rest on the lush purple pillows. Yet now, it was not there. She looked aghast at her husband.

"What has happened to my hair! It's gone!"

He looked aghast back at her. It was true all her hair had gone somehow during the night. But how?

"I don't know, my darling sweety pie. It was there last night when I turned out the light."

"I know it was there last night when you turned out the light. You silly man! But it's not there now, is it? I'm bald! What am I going to do?"

There was no sign of any hair in the bedroom or bathroom. No sign of someone breaking in to take her hair. But why would they? Who has ever heard of someone breaking in to a house and stealing hair? It seemed a mystery.

The Mayoress had long permed hair and had given it a slight tinge of auburn. There was never a hair out of place on her head. To be honest, no hair dared be out of place on her head!

The mayor could only look horrified knowing he was going to be in for a bad day and more.

"Rogers!" She yelled so even the near neighbours could hear her. "Drive me down to that wig shop in the town right away!"

*****

"My hair! It's all gone!" Ann Lillie, a famous model living in the town, screamed. She was doing an important photographic shoot that day. "It was there last night! What has happened to my hair! I'm as bald as my dad!"

Her petrified husband looked stunned. "How can hair just disappear overnight! It doesn't make any sense! Are you sure it is not under the pillow!"

He started looking under the pillows and blankets before going to search for the missing hair under the bed. He seemed to be under the impression it had somehow fallen out and he would be able to find it and stick it back on.

There was no sign of a break-in in their house. But, once again, why would anybody steal her hair. There was no sign that her hair had fallen out. It was a complete mystery.

She was famous for her long flowing blonde locks bristling with curls. It bounced from side to side as she walked along. It gave her such pride and confidence. But it had gone!

"Quick! Ring up the wig shop in town and get them to bring me a wig!"

*****

Billy Wise, the famous footballer who lived in the town, stretched and yawned as he woke up for another day. He went to scratch his hair as he did every morning before putting his hands back under the warmth of the blanket. It was then he sat bolt upright. His eyes opening as wide as the wheels on his latest large free sponsored SV.

"My hair! It's gone!" He had woken up with the smoothest head you can imagine. It looked and felt like a baby's bottom.

"How did that happen? I didn't have a lot to drink at the pub last night as far as I remember!"

He looked all around him there was no sign that the hair had fallen out or had been cut off. There was no sign of forced entry in to the house by fans who then cut off all of his hair with the intention of selling it on e-bay!

He desperately looked up the telephone number of the wig shop in town. He couldn't go to the match today looking like that!

The wig shop could not believe its luck. There was so much business coming its way all of a sudden. For years, it had only a few customers stepping in to the shop or asking her to come out for a private fitting. Yet, now the telephone was ringing all the time. And it appeared to be always the same story. A story that didn't make a lot of sense. Her customers had woken up in the morning without any hair on their head and there was no account as to what had happened to it. Each of them had heads that were shiny and bright as if someone had polished them. Not that she minded. Money was rolling in to her coffers.

*****

Poor Jules, this was not the start to the summer holidays he wanted or expected. Things seemed to be going from bad to even worse than worse.

Sadly, as last year, his mum had explained to him very gently that they would be unable to go away again for this summer holiday. He had been hopeful all year, that this year they would get away somewhere. Not to Spain, or France, or Italy but may be to St. Albans or Barnet. Towns very nearby to where they lived.

That was all he wanted to be able to say to his friends, "Yes, I went on holiday! We went to Bedford or Milton Keynes!" Rather than having to say he had stayed at home again.

There was no doubt his friends, who all had gone away to strange and exotic lands, would come back full of exciting adventures and stories about their holidays and where they had been. They would talk about the places they had seen and the people they had met.

While he would have to sit through hours of looking at amazing photographs. Each one making him sadder than a poke in the eye that he could not go to such lovely places. Not that he was jealous. He wasn't the jealous type. But he wanted his own photographs to show them of his holiday as well.

It would not be so bad if even one of them had stayed at home so he had someone else to go around with. They could do things together. But there was no such person. Absolutely, no one. It was as if every one of his age had left the town for the summer. He was in a 'same-age' desert.

"But, I thought our Uncle Gideon left us a lot of money last year before he went back to Alaska? He said it would keep us going for a long time," Jules replied to his mum fighting back the tears.

"He did!" His mum retorted. "But it only paid off the existing debts we had, I am afraid, Jules. You know how we were struggling to make ends meet. And I never get paid too much from the job at the pickle factory."

She looked at him only wishing she could take him somewhere on holiday. Even if it was for a few days. Just so he could say he had a holiday. She knew he found it difficult when his friends came back from where ever they had been abroad and told him all about their adventures. When they asked him, what he had done during the summer? He could say only that he had stayed at home again this year and nothing much happened.

"And I am afraid, since we spent Uncle Gideon's money, sweat heart, we've been living on my little salary. And, as you know, that doesn't go that far and our debts are mounting again!"

"But didn't Uncle Gideon say he would send us more money. And he told us to ask if we needed anymore! I am sure he would help us out if he knew!" Jules really got on well with his Uncle Gideon and knew what a good man he was. His uncle, who had no family himself, had promised to help Jules and his mum as he had a lot of money and nothing or, no one else to spend it on.

"He did!" His mum gave her son a teddy bear cuddle. "But I don't know what's happened! He's not been in touch. We've not received any money from him over the last year at all!"

"But why don't you write to him and ask for some? He said you could if we needed it!" This seemed the obvious answer to Jules.

His mum almost in tears responded. "I have written to him, Jules! And there has been no reply I am afraid! Not one letter!"

Both gulped. There was quite a long silence.

"To tell you the truth, I am worried about what has happened to him!" His mum continued. "He was so keen to keep in touch with us. But I haven't heard a thing!"

*****

Jules had been trying again to beat his own world record for going around the new adventure trail the local council had set up in the park. He timed himself going around the course and each time tried to improve on it. What pleased him, was that almost every time he did it he got better and better. He even timed other children going around the course and knew his time was far better than theirs.

It was while he was in the park, he realised the smell that had lingered for quite a long time now in the town was actually getting worse. It was awful and once it got up your nose it seemed to sit there and refused to move. It seemed to affect everything you ate and drunk. So, all the food tasted like a fresh squirt from an angry skunk had been put on it.

"Er, aren't you Mrs. Appleyard's son?" A mum with her young daughter called to Jules. She was looking up at him on the adventure trail walkway.

"Yes! That's me!" He replied. Not too sure why she wanted to know. She had seen him many times in the park and never said anything to him before. She normally took her daughter around the younger children's apparatus. That is when she was not looking at her phone.

"Well! You tell your mum from me that I'll give her a mouthful when I see her next!"

"What do you mean?" Jules felt a little confused by her statement and a bit upset. Why would anybody want to say something horrible to his mum? She was the nicest mum in the world.

"Well, she's the one to blame for this rotten smell in the town isn't she? If she had made sure she had put the right number of pickles in the pickle machine and not overloaded it then none of this would have happened!"

Jules had no idea what she was going on about. What had his mum to do with this rotten smell that was about the town. It just didn't make much sense to him. But then again he was not aware of what had happened at the pickle factory.

It was then that another mum joined in.

"Yeah! You can tell her from me too!" The mum put her small boy on the kiddies roundabout as she called over to Jules. "I've had enough of this horrible stink she has put about the town. I hope she gets a stiff sentence in jail for what she has done!"

"And me too!" Another mum added. "My husband has not got a job now due to your mum and the pickle factory closing. She's got a lot to answer, that's for sure!"

Now Jules was alarmed. What were they talking about his mum and a prison sentence. He wanted to find out more. Yet, knew these mums in the park were not the ones to find out from. He needed to get home and try to find out from his own mum whether or not there was any truth in what they were talking about. It sounded so bizarre. His mum never did anything out of the ordinary so how could she have caused this terrible smell. They must be confusing his mum with someone else he thought.

Jules jumped down from the skyway and started to make his way home. To his surprise he found that people as they passed were pointing over towards him and whispering behind their hands. He was growing more and more alarmed as each step took him nearer home. What did all this mean? And to make matters worse he had to admit the stink in the town seemed to be getting worse.

*****

Jules stopped in his tracks when he arrived at his house. He could not believe it. There were a host of media people with their microphones and cameras waiting outside their gate. Alongside, were a few TV satellite vans as well. Just away from them stood a group of local people interested to find out what was going on.

"What is all this about?" Jules thought to himself. He was a bit frightened by everything that was happening as he knew it was all to do with his mother. He only wished he knew what it all meant!

He decided to go around to the back of the house and get in that way rather than try to push his way through the journalists and camera men. They would soon cotton on that he was the boy that lived in that house and try to get him to answer some of their questions. Questions he would not want to answer even if he could.

"Mum!" He called out as he entered the house.

"In here, Jules!" Came the comforting reply.

His mum was in the house at least. He was sure that she would be able to explain what was going on.

He made his way through to the living room only to find his mum on the couch crying a bucket load of big, wet tears. He had never seen her looking so pale and frightened. It was not like her at all. Normally, she kept all her worries deep inside her in a box under lock and key and never gave in to breakaway tears.

"Why are you crying, Mum?" Jules sat down next to her on the couch and put his arm around her to try and give a little comfort. Even he could feel her shaking. "What's wrong?" He was frightened now as well! His mum was never like this. "Please, mum, tell me what's wrong!"

And so, it came out. All that had happened that day. How the pickling machine had started going crazy and blew up. How the factory is ruined and how Mr. Brian was blaming her.

"But I had not put too many onions in as he says I did." She spoke between her crying. "I've been doing that job for years and years. I know exactly how many onions to put in the pickling machine each time to make sure it worked properly." She tried to explain to Jules. "How could he blame me for that explosion. And now they are saying I am too blame for the awful smell in the town too! They believe the awful smell is coming from the explosion at the factory!"

Again, it was all too much for her and she broke down in to a rumble of tears again. She was hugging Jules so tightly he thought he was going to pop out the top of her arms like a cork top out of a fizz bottle at any moment and hit the roof. "You need to tell them mum!" Her son tried to console her. "They know you are such a lovely person and would never do anything like that!"

"They won't listen to me!" She gasped in despair. "I've tried to tell them time and time again. But that mayor keeps on saying I'm the one to blame. It is him who they believe and not me!" His mum burst in to tears once more! A river was almost running through the house. Jules didn't know what to say.

"And even worse the police have charged me with causing the explosion at the factory. I will soon need to appear in court! Me, a criminal! I have never broken any law in my life! I cannot believe all this is happening to me. I expect to wake up at any moment and find this is all an awful nightmare I am having!"

Jules could not believe what he was hearing. Surely this could not be happening to his mum. Not his mum. His mum was the best mum in the world.

"Things are going from terrible to even worse!" More tears flowed as she took in the enormity of what had befallen her that day.

This was beginning to look like it was going to be the worst summer holiday ever for Jules as his world crumbled more and more around him. There appeared not a lot he could do to help his mum either. He was still too young to get a part-time or full-time job and the law said he still must go back to school in September. Yet, how were they ever going to survive in these present circumstances without any money coming in. And there seemed to be so much hostility towards her in the town who was going to give her a much-needed job.

Chapter 2

The previous summer, Gideon had fallen asleep quite easily on the airplane taking him back to Alaska. He was relaxed and needed to get some rest before arriving at the airport. Then he had to undertake that arduous journey back to the oil-drilling site. His two companions, Vic and Doug, either side of him were also snoring away quite happily.

All of them knew they were in for another busy year drilling somewhere in the frozen north. They would again be isolated, eating food from tins and facing bitter weather day in and day out. It was part of their job. Yet, they were used to it by now and received an incredibly well-paid salary for the many inconveniences they put up with.

Little did Gideon realise when he returned to Alaska with his two work companions and, firmly established friends, that they were being followed. They never looked behind them once. Why should they? Who would want to follow them? They weren't spies on a secret mission or anything. They never looked to see if they recognised any faces popping up again and again behind them as they made their way to London airport and later on to the airplane. It never crossed their minds. Why should it?

Yet, they were being followed. Every step of the way. But if they had looked over their shoulder, they would not have seen a single sign of someone following them. Likewise, if they had set up a trap for someone following them, they would have found it fruitless. Those who were following the three companions were far too clever for that. Gideon and his two companions would have sworn on the bible that there was no one on their tail.

Jules's uncle's first concern on reaching Alaska was to rebury the three troublesome puddle hoppers deep in to the ground where they had been found. The intention was to let them remain there forever and a day. After the problems they caused when they escaped in Boreham Wood, he didn't want that to happen again. Once they were interred in the ground they were going to remain there beyond time. That was his and his companions' intentions. Those three evil puddle hoppers had already nearly caused a major disaster. The three men did not want themselves to be the cause of a similar future catastrophe.

On the flight, as far as the three men were concerned, the three puddle hoppers were safely frozen in the airplane's hold below the flight-deck. The intention was they would remain there until the airplane reached Alaska and landed safely. There was no chance they could escape.

What the three of them did not know, was that there were vigorous attempts being made to get at the three frozen creatures. Every door underneath the plane was being tried by those who wanted the three puddle hoppers free. Fortunately, for those on the airplane each attempt was unsuccessful. Not that the three sitting above knew of any such rescue attempts being made.

"Are you three ready for your dinner now?" The air hostess asked as she woke Gideon and his two friends up from their sleeps with trays of hot food.

"That sure smells good!" Vic replied with his nose fully in smell mode up in the air.

"Food! I am more than ready!" Doug followed suit.

Gideon took a few moments to wake up before his eyes fell on the trays of enticing food coming their way. "Um! That looks good!"

None of them realised that from the outside of the airplane they were being observed. Furthermore, those observing them were the same who had been following them since they had left Boreham Wood. It was they who had tried to see if there was any way in to the hold of the airplane and realised there was not. They were not happy about that but what could they do. Their plan had not worked. These pursuers would have to wait for another chance to help the three bad puddle hoppers escape.

And who was it who was trailing the three companions? Who was it set upon releasing their three prisoners? It was none other than the puddle hoppers creature cousins, the cloud jumpers. Whereas, the puddle hoppers live in puddles, the cloud jumpers live on the clouds and are able to jump from one to the other like monkeys do in the trees. Landing with ease on one soft white mass after another in a cloud filled sky.

These cloud jumpers not only live on the clouds but are able to eat clouds as well. It formed the natural resource for many things in their lives. Things you will soon be finding out about as the story unfolds. By eating cloud, they were as light as the clouds themselves and could travel anywhere around the world on those moving white ships. Another skill they had learnt over time was the ability to use the lightness of the clouds themselves to lift things up in to the sky. In the same way as balloons filled with helium can lift things up in to the air.

Little did anyone know that the cloud jumpers had observed all that had happened below in Boreham Wood during the last summer from the safety of their clouds. They saw how the three evil creatures nearly imprisoned a whole town. They were whopping with joy at what they were observing. For the cloud jumpers are sworn enemies of the puddle hoppers even though they are so closely related as a similar species.

On the other side of the coin, the puddle hoppers consider the cloud jumpers are quite unpleasant creatures. They say of them that they are always intent on causing trouble where ever they go and leave destruction and sorrow in their wake.

If cloud jumpers come across any puddle hoppers, they will roll up some cloud until it is like a strong string and tie it to the puddle hopper's feet and dangle them upside down, pull them up in to the sky and then drop them on their head. Not a very nice thing for a puddle hopper to have happen to them I am sure you agree.

As you can imagine the cloud jumpers are very light creatures. Eating cloud makes you as light as the cloud itself. In every sense, they look similar to puddle hoppers but it is obvious they are going to be mainly white so as to blend in with the clouds. However, like puddle hoppers, if need be, they can also change their colouring to fit in with their surroundings like chameleons. Sometimes they are in dark grey clouds and take on a dark grey complexion. Other times the clouds are tinged with sun rays and they will take on pinks, reds and blues for example. But they always have a very pale white tinge to their colour.

Hence, that is why when people look up in to the clouds they never spot the small creatures who are possibly up there. It helps that their skin colour almost always matches their surroundings. Another important adaption for the cloud jumpers is that from a great height, they have adapted their eye-sight to see like birds of prey. They can see even very minute things on the ground such as a worm popping its head out of a tiny hole. Not much below is missed by them. Come to think of it there could be a cloud jumper watching you right now!

However, sometimes they are spotted up in the clouds from down below by people with incredibly good eye-sight looking up as they jump from cloud to cloud. Most people, generally, do not see it as it happens so high up and so quickly it is almost unobservable to the human eye.

Yet, if they are spotted, the person who spots them just comments, "It must have been a sun ray that was breaking through the clouds at that moment. What else could it be!"

The cloud jumpers have many different names for the types of clouds they come across in their travels. In a similar way to Eskimos. Who have lots of different names for the types of snow they encounter in the far north. Hence, various colours of cloud have their own name. But it does not stop there, for all this variety of clouds have very unique tastes and, of course, they have different names for each taste as well.

They will probably tell you that the dark grey clouds have a strong flavour like over-brewed tea. While the pink early evening clouds have a really sweet, sugary, tingly taste. If these creatures climb up on to the very highest of clouds in the sky, these taste of a light watery fragrance. Whereas, the fog we often have to plough through, always has a gritty taste of grass or salt sea air. So, as you can see, many assorted names are needed to describe the many different types of cloud there are in the world in which they live!

Yet, these creatures do come down to earth to do their bits of mischief. Mischief that the puddle hoppers think is often cruel and hurtful. These cloud creatures particularly like the fog. For it allows them to play all sorts of tricks on people as they are making their way through the heavy condensed low cloud. The cloud jumpers end up laughing incessantly as they roll up fog in to small compact balls and throw them at anyone who is unlucky enough to be passing by.

They watch with great frivolity as the person who they hit tries to work out what hit them. For the fog-ball quickly evaporates in the air as soon as it strikes home. Leaving their victim bemused as to what just happened. Moreover, these creatures from the sky like to make spooky noises as people pass by. Camouflaged in the greyness of the fog they can see it frightens the person they are playing the cruel trick on.

Another one of their tricks is to make very fine string out of the cloud and lay it low to the ground between the trees. People passing by then trip over it and when they look to see what made them trip over there is nothing to be seen. For the perpetrators have quickly taken it away.

*****

"Can all passengers please make their way to the passport control!" An authoritative voice pointed out the direction they had to take. It was a message for all those passengers arriving in Alaska from London.

Gideon, Doug and Vic duly followed those passengers in front of them as the whole group were directed from the plane to the airport terminal. People were moving rapidly across the tarmac as the weather was already bitterly cold.

Gideon nodded a "hello" to one of the baggage handlers as they drove up to the plane ready to commence unloading the passengers' bags and take them over to the luggage collection point.

The four baggage handlers started to unload the bags from the plane hold on to the baggage truck. Two men were inside the hold, grabbing the bags and pushing them towards the main door. While their two colleagues were lifting the bags down on to the trailer from the plane and placing them in to the supportive meshed cage.

All four men were intent on doing what they had to do as quickly as possible so they could get out of the intense cold. Hence, they never noticed a group of small white characters leaning over the side of the plane and trying to identify Gabriel's bag. A certain bag with three small creatures in. This was so that they could hoist down cloud string and pull it up to them. They would then have the containers with the three evil puddle hoppers they so wanted.

Suddenly, there it was before them. The bag they so desperately sought. The cloud jumpers quickly agreed it was the one they had seen Gabriel carrying. Straight away they sent down a cloud string to go underneath the case, so they could pull it back up. Sadly, from their point of view, the baggage handlers were just as fast. For as the cloud jumpers began to lift the bag up towards themselves, two more bags from the plane were thrown on top of it.

Hence, trapping the case in the trailer cage under other luggage. The sky creatures were annoyed with themselves for they had missed their opportunity again. Soon an argument was taking place amongst the small creatures as each blamed the other for not being fast enough to pull up the case they so sorely wanted. They had been so close but failed.

Once more, they would have to play the waiting game.

*****

"That should do it!" Gabriel asserted.

"We've buried them deep and proper this time!" Vic agreed.

"No one will have any trouble from those three after this. They will be interred there forever and a day!" Doug gasped.

"After all the trouble they caused last time they got out of their lead coffins, I hope this time there is no one as foolish as ourselves who is going to release them!"

"Well, we have written warnings and put danger signs on their boxes. Only fools in the future would not understand the idiocy of opening up the containers." Gabriel added.

The three workers had returned to the site where they had originally found the three evil puddle hoppers to rebury them. The company had already started the process of exploiting the rich oil seam the three men had discovered last year at the same spot.

Hence, Gabriel and his companions were able to use some of the firm's plentiful and expensive equipment now based there to help with the reburial. The oil company was busy erecting a new, functioning oil rig with its accompanying pipeline across to the main pipeline that goes all the way back to the USA from Alaska.

Fortunately, for these three, the main drilling site was now a little further to the east of where they had originally drilled to see if there was oil in the area and where they discovered the three evil creatures buried. This allowed them to get on undisturbed with digging this new deep burial grave right where it had been before. Workers on an oil rig site are used to seeing other men digging holes around the work place for various reasons such as soil samples and bases for buildings. Hence, no one who saw them thought anything of it.

The three men then covered up the deep hole they had dug so the ground looked as flat and natural as when they had first arrived in the valley.

It was fortunate for the three of them that they had been told to report back to the very same site they had wanted to be at by their manager. For this was the site where they wanted to rebury the three evil puddle hoppers. The place where they had originally found them.

The accommodation vehicle they had used while digging for oil, was still there when they got to the burial spot. It had been used by the company to provide short term accommodation for some workers until more of the container homes could be built. The company did not like to see expensive equipment just sitting around idle when it could be serving a purpose. Hence, now the workers accommodation was completed the vehicle would soon be taken away to be repurposed.

Gabriel was surprised to receive a text about what and where his next job was to be. His boss normally told him personally. This time he was being sent on a mission by himself further north to search for oil. Unfortunately, the other two were needed to replace two drillers who had been sent to hospital following an accident at another potential oil site. It meant Gabriel was expected to use the drilling equipment by himself for the forthcoming venture. This annoyed him a bit.

Being stuck in the frozen north in winter by yourself was dangerous to say the least. To be honest, the company knew that too. If something happened to him while he was there, how was he going to call for help? Plus, operating that heavy drill by himself was not going to be easy. Especially, if the weather turned nasty which, it often does, in the heart of the artic region. It shows how much esteem the company had for Gabriel as they would not be able to ask many of their oil drillers to undertake such a task all by themselves.

"You know I'm going to be up on the very edge of the artic circle don't you!" He barked at his manager about sending him up to do a possible search for oil all by himself.

"You'll be okay, Gabriel. You're one of our best oil explorers. You're a tough old boot!" Came the harsh reply.

"But if something goes wrong I would have no one to call for help! And what happens if the drill work becomes a two-man operation at some point!" He tried to explain his concerns.

"Gabriel! You've done these oil searches thousands of times, it will not be a problem for you!"

Gabriel breathed in deep. He seemed to be fighting a lost cause. He might as well accept that he was being sent up there alone and that was that!

"Now have you got all the equipment you need!" His boss asked.

"Yes! That's all sorted!" It had taken quite a few days for him to gather what he would require on this remote site he was being sent to. He had grumbled to himself that it was all right for the company to try and ensure that all the equipment is being fully utilised. However, that makes it really hard to get the necessary equipment you require for a new job. Everybody says, "But we are using that" or "We need that!" It became quite frustrating for him but he gathered it all in the end.

"What you can do for me!" Gabriel continued talking to his boss. "Is to make sure you forward that money I have asked. Ensure it is sent to Mrs. Appleyard, my sister-in-law. I know she will need it. I have written letters to accompany the money as well. And if there are any letters sent to me, if you can make sure they are forwarded on to me at the drill site. They may be very important!" He emphasised.

"Will do!" The boss said nonchalantly. "No problem, Gabriel!" Yet, he was not writing anything down as a memory aid. So, it was not surprising that with everything else he had to do, he forgot. As we found out from Jules's mum, over that coming year he was away, they received no communication or money at all from Gabriel. While, her letters were not forwarded on to him either. Hence, the reason Jules and his mum were struggling financially! The extra money her former brother-in-law had the intention of sending, we know would have been more than useful. However, it never arrived.

Gabriel was able to claim the accommodation vehicle with the drilling rig on the back they had used the previous year. He knew it was a good piece of equipment and would not let him down. This became especially important, as he had not gone far when the weather deteriorated and continued to get worse as he neared the artic circle. The winds blew the huge mounds of snow about. Often hiding the tracks he was meant to be following. He became totally dependent on the satellite navigation system he had with him to keep on track. For trails that were meant to be there were covered over.

Finally, he reached his destination and was soon setting up a base to start drilling for oil. The snow continued to fall heavily and he knew he would have to wait days before he was able to commence his work. Sitting back in his quarters, unable to use any form of communication to get in touch with his company or the outside world due to the weather, he knew that this winter was going to be a lonely time for him. He was longing for the next summer to come so he could return south with his findings on the oil in that area.

*****

The cloud jumpers had quite a difficult time getting the three evil puddle hoppers out of the deep hole they had been buried in. Gabriel, Vic and Doug had tried to ensure no one would ever get them out of there. From above in the clouds they were able to watch the three men bury the containers deep in the earth from whence they had come. They grew more concerned as they saw how difficult it was going to be for them to release the three evil creatures. The three evil creatures they so wanted to help them in their fight to get revenge against the puddle hoppers.

No workers seemed to take any notice of the ever-increasing depth of the original oil hole on the site that appeared again. The cloud jumpers ensuring they only dug when they were sure there was no one about. Eventually, they reached the depth where the three containers were buried. The containers were theirs now to do with what they wanted. They had waited patiently for this moment to arrive and now it had come. They could get on with the next stage of their plan.

*****

Once, the cloud jumpers had released the three puddle hoppers from their containers and frozen state, they used cloud string to lift them up to their cloud home. There they secured them with more cloud string to ensure that if they were not going to help the cloud jumpers with their plan they would be able to return them back to the buried place they had obtained them from. Those three blue skins shone brightly with their rubbery exterior standing out against the white cloud background.

Besides that, it was surprising how much the two species looked alike. Both were a similar size of half a metre, had pointed ears with turned up noses. Their skins looked quite shrivelled up but flexible. The cloud jumpers had very little flaps of skins between their fingers whereas the puddle hoppers did. No doubt, David Attenborough would say that the puddle hoppers needed these excess bits of flapping skin between the fingers and toes for moving through the water in the puddles.

Being closely related species they still spoke a single language they both understood. Of course, they had different accents like the Australians and Canadians but both of them could understand the other when they spoke.

"Why are we tied up?" Trud asked his captors after waking. He was the slightly older one and had the tuft of hair on his chin that gave him an air of being distinguished.

"If you want us to help you, you shouldn't keep us tied up!" Surr added with what seemed like a mild threat. But it was not as if they had anything to threaten the cloud jumpers with. He was the chubbier of the three and was already wondering how the three of them were going to get moss to eat up there on the clouds. He was aware moss did not grow on clouds.

"We want you to help us get our own back on the puddle hoppers for what they have done to us!" Castor, one of the cloud jumpers told them. He stood at the front of a crowd in front of these captives. His white body glowing with the sun on it. He appeared to be the chief of this tribe.

31

"But we are puddle hoppers ourselves, aren't we? Why should we help you against our own kind." Rak commented. He was the youngest of the three and appeared to be the thinker. His face often taking on different screwed up features a bit like a squirrel to show he was contemplating matters.

"Well! We saw what happened to you three last summer. Although, you may be puddle hoppers, you are not like them at all. You are more like us!" Klaxon said in his high pitch voice that all these creatures spoke in. He was a duller colour to Castor and his eyes were more protruded than those surrounding him. He was another of those who stood at the front before their three tied up hostages. He was known far and wide as a wise counsellor to the chief.

"We saw the way your own kind treated you! Ha! Instead of helping you to imprison humans they joined them to fight against you! And even locked the three of you up. Your fellow puddle hoppers then helped them return you to your frozen state in the far north ice country. You can't say much for your own species can you! You are far better off with us and you know it!" Vendor, who appeared to be another counsellor to the chief, bluntly laid out the facts for them. He had quite a mottled skin with his whiteness having blotches of grey. Yet, although, he was closer in height to the chief, he did look incredibly strong.

The three puddle hoppers nodded in agreement with what they had heard. What else could they do. It was all true. They knew the other puddle hoppers were not their friends. They did not help them in any way to try and destroy the humans. The puddle hoppers in Boreham Wood seemed to accept the humans living about them as friends. Even though their race were over-running the world. "Why didn't you help us then!" Surr gasped. "If you could see what was happening. You were there. We could have done with your help! We may not have failed if you had helped us back then."

"Unfortunately, you were already being imprisoned by the time we knew what was happening. It was far too late to try and help you." Castor shook his head in sadness. "If only!"

"We didn't have any idea what your plan was. So how could we help." Kloxon continued to explain.

"Have you got a plan!" Trud asked.

"Oh! Yes! We have a plan! And I think it's a good plan!" Ventor nodded. A slight twinkle of a star in his eye.

"And we want you to help us undertake it! We think with your help we could achieve all the things both of us want to achieve. We can get the better of the puddle hoppers and seek the revenge we want." Castor proposed.

A rousing cheer went up from the other cloud jumpers surrounding him.

"That sounds good! But how can we trust you?" Rak answered. "And what's in it for us?"

"Likewise! How can we trust you?" Kloxon replied. "You could easily disappear in to a puddle and never be seen again!"

"If you help us, we will make you members of our cloud jumper community. You can use the cloud ropes to come up and down from the clouds like us." Castor smiled. "You will be among friends here!"

"What we intend to do in the future, is something we know that fits in with your own ideas. You will be able to join us in doing all sorts of bad deeds on those we choose to between ourselves!" Ventor added.

Those cloud jumpers standing behind the leading group nodded their agreement. There was no doubt these cloud people were as bad as the highway man on his horse waiting for his next victim to come along the road to hold up.

"So, you see we can help each other with our plans in the future. You have got to remember, we are similar in many ways, you and us! Both like to do evil things. Are you interested?" Celeste added. Celeste was the chief's wife. She, like all cloud jumper women, had narrower face features, longer eye lashes and a lot more hair on their head than their male counterparts.

"We will need to talk about it amongst ourselves!" Trud responded rather coyly.

The other two puddle hoppers agreed with Trud on that matter. There was a need for a discussion amongst the three of them. Hence, they went in to a huddle to discuss the proposition they had been offered. In a sense, they had no choice but accept. They all knew that. For if they did not agree they would be returned to their imprisonment for eternity. Not a very endearing thought. Tied up as they were there was little chance of escape for the moment. Yet, if they did agree there would be the opportunity of sweet revenge on their fellow kind for what they had done to them. Hopefully, they would get revenge on the humans as well. How sweet that would be!

Moreover, once these goals had been achieved, they would be given the opportunity to help the cloud jumpers do further devious deeds. That sounded like something they would enjoy to say the least. And if they did not like the arrangements, they whispered quietly to each other, they could escape and be free to do their own evil work elsewhere. Besides, it sounded like fun to be flying high above on clouds. It could be quite an adventure for the three of them.

"What have we to lose!" They all agreed.

The three of them turned towards their captors soon to be colleagues. "We will help you!"

*****

"They've gone!" Shouted Gabriel upon his return to the oil drilling camp he had left months ago after a long, hard winter further north.

The weather had been atrocious at his winter site. More than atrocious. No one had been able to get in or out from his isolated drilling site. It had nearly driven him mad being totally isolated for so long. Towards the end he was nearly talking to the wall as there was no one else to talk to.

The weather even stopped any chance of radio contact with his boss. But now back at the base he had left, he was hoping for a relaxing period to recover. Only to find to his horror what had happened while he had been away! The puddle hoppers were not there any longer. They had gone!

He could not believe his eyes. Doug, Vic and he had dug the hole for those three evil creatures so deep the three of them believed they would never be found!

However, within only a year the three creatures had gone! Disappeared!

How could it be!

"But how! There is no way they could have escaped by themselves!" He contemplated.

Yet, there it was the hole they had filled in now empty with the vacated caskets lying beside it. The mount of frozen tundra they had used to put in the hole piled up next to it like a small mountain.

Drill workers were passing by as if the hole was not there. They assumed someone else knew about it and was dealing with it. They had no idea why it had been dug. Why would they? They had their own jobs to get on with!

Gabriel telephoned Doug and Vic at the drilling location they were now working at to see if they knew what had happened to the three puddle hoppers. They were just as exasperated and worried as Gabriel was. Neither knew anything about the disappearance of the three evil puddle hoppers. They had not even left their present drilling site since arriving there late last summer. There was too much work for them to do.

Gabriel talked to the managers, staff and anyone he could find around the area where the three creatures had been buried. Trying to discover if they knew what had happened at the burial chamber. No one saw or knew a thing. Yet, one thing was for sure. The three evil puddle hoppers had escaped and were probably on the loose somewhere. That was bound to mean danger where ever they were.

"Oh! My Goodness!" It crossed Gabriel's mind. The one place they would likely to head for was the home of the puddle hoppers in England. He realised they would probably be set on getting their revenge. What was more, Jules and his mother could be in great danger as well! He straight away knew he had to get back to England as soon as possible.

*****

"What do you mean that the money and letters were never forwarded to Mrs. Appleyard!" Gabriel was astounded to hear the news. When he reached the company's Head Office before departing for England and another well-deserved break from the oil drilling business, he decided to check up on whether the requests he had made to his boss before he went north had been carried out.

"Well! I forgot to remember to check with the accounts department about sending it." His bright red-faced boss explained. "I'm sorry! It was my mistake!"

"And look! All these letters that were sent from Mrs. Appleyard are just sitting here! Why weren't they forwarded on to me!" He held the cache of letters from Jules' mum up in his hand and brought them down with a thud on the table. He was like an angry elephant thumping the ground as an over eager tourist got between it and its young.

This might have been his boss sitting before him but Gideon was so enraged he forgot about protocols and let his anger fly.

"They were depending on that money in England! Goodness knows what problems you have caused by not ensuring the monies and letters were forwarded on!" Gabriel was getting angrier and angrier as he spoke. How could his boss forget to sort it out. It was so important they were sent.

His boss had never seen this side of him before. But in truth, he knew, himself, he was more than well deserving of this angry backlash. In his own head, he was saying to himself, "Why didn't I write it down. I had promised. And I knew he was going to be up there in the back of beyond for a long, long time. It was the least I could have done!"

"I know it would have been difficult, if not impossible, to get these letters to me where I was!" He gasped. "But, come on, you didn't even try!"

The boss was suitably reprimanded. "I have no excuse, Gabriel! I can only say I am sorry and ask you to accept that apology! I have learnt a powerful lesson from what has happened. I know it doesn't help you now but I will ensure I never do it again!"

Gabriel could see that the boss was truly sorry and what was done couldn't be undone. He had made his point very strongly and forcibly. Not everyone gets the chance, or would even dare, to rant and rave in such a way at their boss as he had done.

"Well, when I get back to England, I hope everything is okay or I will be coming back to let you know what I think of you and what you have done!"

"I understand, Gabriel. I sure hope everything is fine when you get back there. I must admit I feel quite guilty. And if there is anything I can do to put this wrong right, let me know!"

Gabriel realised there was little point continuing this ranting and left his boss's office knowing he had said his piece and made his point. His only concern now was to get back to England as soon as possible. The letters he had never received but now could read, told him of the dire financial situation Jules and his mum were in. If only he had known, he could have tried to help.

He remembered saying to them, "If you need any help, in any way, especially with money just let me know. I have all this money and don't know what to do with it and you are the only family I have got."

And what has happened? He had let them down. Maybe, not directly his fault! But he had let them down! Moreover, to add to that, he had a hunch that is where he was going to find the three disappeared puddle hoppers. What's more, he was sure they would be up to no good. Would he reach there in time!

Chapter 3

"See you in a while, Mum!" Jules called out.

He was going to do the little shopping they could afford on the very limited budget they had. He would take the short list of things his mum had written down with him. However, the truth was that there were so few items on it, it would not have been a problem for him to remember all of them in his head.

There was another problem why he was going to the shop. His mum was too terrified to go out at that moment. She feared if she entered the street, someone would be shouting at her about the factory explosion or the smell. So, she was only going out when it was really necessary.

"You're the one to blame for that explosion!" Someone would shout.

"Yes! And now the factory is closed because of you!" Another housewife would yelp.

"Why didn't you do your job properly!" One would cry with frustration.

"And what about my husband now! He's got no work! And we have no money coming in! You've got a lot to answer for, lady!" Another housewife would yell even angrier.

"Are you going to pay for our rent and food! Someone has to!" So the ranting continued.

"And what about this awful smell we now have!" One mum waved her arm in anger at Jules's mum. "That smell is on everything. All the clothes, all about the house, even when you eat your food it tastes of that awful smell! We can't get rid of it! And it's all your fault!"

"My husband even ate the cat's dinner when I was preparing it for the cat, thinking it was his meal!"

"I can tell you he isn't happy with you woman!" When this mum explained her story, all the other mums laughed. Yet, that soon turned back to angry stares at the one they held to blame.

So, you could tell why she didn't want to go out anymore. It was as if she was in a castle with the drawbridge drawn up so no one could enter. A castle that was surrounded by enemies. All she could say time and time again was, "I am sorry and it wasn't my fault. I'm not the one to blame. What you are being told is not the truth. You've got to believe me!"

She wondered why those who were there at the time of the explosion were not sticking up for her. The trouble was they were probably thinking of their own jobs. No doubt, if they suggested things were not quite as the mayor and factory owner had said then they could lose their positions. Hence, it was best for them to keep their mouths well and truly closed.

They had all listened to the mayor talking about the explosion on the TV and read about it in the newspapers. It was obvious they would come around to believing his version of events. Why shouldn't they if they wanted to keep their jobs! For he was the mayor and the factory owner after all. Surely, he always told the truth. Didn't he!

*****

"I'm bored, Michael!" Bill sat on the park wall with his head held between his hands. His screwed-up face gave away the story of his boredom. "What are we going to do! We need to do something!"

Bill had so much hair growing out the top of his head he looked like a sprouting water fountain that was being lit up at night. For it was a strange mixture of different coloured ginger hair that flowed out of it. This came down below his 'lost for ever' ears and carried on gushing down his neck. At the front the hair hid most of his spotty face and red cheeks.

While, if you were to look further down, you would notice that his clothes not only had the town smell everyone was complaining about but this was mixed with a dangerous combination of dirty, unwashed for weeks, clothes. Clothes that had more tears and holes in them than there were holes in a sunken pirate ship at the bottom of the sea. As for his trainers, they were fashionable when Tony Blair was prime minister and showed their age with each dirt and mud stain.

"We've been sitting around this park for weeks and done nothing! Absolutely nothing!" Darren, who was the newer member of the gang added. He joined when he lost his job as a trainee chef for putting sugar instead of salt in to all the dishes.

The chef was not pleased as customer after customer began to complain.

That night, as the proud chef told his waitresses and waiters to take out his wonderfully prepared food to the adoring waiting customers, he prepared himself for the usual excellent compliments to be paid. Compliments he always modestly received. Yet, little did he, or they, know there was going to be a great shock in store once those served started eating their food.

His distraught staff were soon running back in to the kitchen telling the chef everybody seems to be choking on the food and saying it tasted horrible. The chef's expectant smile soon turned to total horror. Yet, after he had tasted it himself, it didn't take long for the chef to realise what Darren had done and within nanoseconds gave him his marching orders.

Obviously, Darren was going to struggle to get another job as the job centre pointed out to him after such a catastrophe. So, here he was now, out on the streets with the other two losers he was now friendly with.

He wasn't a bad looking boy, with his short dark hair, big ears and huge cheeks that seemed to pull his mouth apart from one side to the other. The money from his job had provided him with a reasonable revenue to buy some decent clothes and these were still quite presentable. Although, they were getting more and more ragged as the weeks passed since leaving his job. He was not going to wash them and nor was anybody else at home going to do that job for him.

Both of these boys were easily led and Michael Duranty was just the one to lead them astray. Not that they didn't want to be led astray. Michael was known as the 'wild one' ever since he was bouncing on his mum's knee. Although, not particularly tall, strong or bright, he nonetheless, believed he was all of these things. He had always wanted his own gang and so tried to find boys that were easily led to follow him.

Hence, it was, that Darren and Bill had fallen under his spell at that moment in time. Many had done it before and, in one way of another, managed to leave him. Mainly, when they got themselves in to big trouble, ended up in hospital or police custody.

He always regaled potential new members to his gang with tales of his own daring-does. Hoping the future candidates would see him as some sort of leader and hero. His favourite one to tell them was about the time he took on four youngsters, the same age as him. They were from another nearby gang. These gang members produced their knives and were threatening to stab him for entering their gang's territory.

"But you said it was three gang members who attacked you last time!" An existing member of his gang commented as he told the tale to someone who was thinking about joining the gang.

"No! You are mistaken, I said four!" He corrected his gang member with a threatening look.

Hence, the sub-ordinate looked down in submission rather than confront his leader.

"As I was saying, there I was standing there, with these six burly gang members from across the other side of town. All with their knives out and threatening to stick them in me for being in their territory!"

"Ay! You said four gang members with knives last time!" Another of his existing gang popped up as Michael tried to carry on with his story.

"I am afraid you've got it wrong as well! I definitely said six gang members with knives!" He again gave the interrupter a stare of "Don't argue with me or else!" look.

Once again, the gang member took to looking down at the ground as he submitted to his boss.

"Right, I will try to finish this story then! If I can do it without any interruptions, thank you!" He looked from one gang member to another. Daring them to say anything.

All stared down at the ground in a subservient fashion.

"As I was saying, I was standing there with eight massive gang members from across the other side of town each with cutlasses, threatening to kill me for being in their territory. While I stood up to them and threatened them back with my little dagger. Daring them to try and come near me! And do you know what none of them would!"

You only had to look around the existing gang members and the potential new ones as well to see they were all putting their hands over their mouths to cover up their sniggering at his ever-growing fantasised story.

Michael was a medium sized boy with a thin pencil shape to him. He was quick and shifty like a rat in a run, and would be as aggressive as a lion with a thorn in its paw to anyone standing in front of him. Even if they were trying to be nice. The trouble was he felt he couldn't afford to let people see he was nice. To be nice, he believed, in the gang's eyes would be bad. They may consider he was getting a little bit too soft. He had to be seen to be as tough as old boots. A strong leader.

Hence, it looked as if he was almost about to shout at you. At the same time, he took such an aggressive stance you thought he was going to hit you at any moment.

Yet, his brain and physic did not match his view of himself or his grand intentions. It is sad to say he would always end up being the loser in one way or another at anything he attempted.

On one occasion with his little gang he had tried to rob a toy shop. His intention was, as it was just before Christmas, to sell the toys on a market stall belonging to a friend and make lots of money. The trouble was when they attempted to break into the shop at night through the back door they were surprised to find it already open. They were even more surprised to find the owner was in the front of the shop.

He was putting up his Christmas decorations. The owner was a big burly man. Hence, they would have struggled to overcome him. So, they ended up telling him they were interested in buying toys from him and that is why they had come in to the shop through the back. They ended up having to buy a number of toys they really did not want.

Another time, he took his gang to the house of the mayor of the town. The intention was to break in. They all got in the open bedroom window only to find it was the mayor's own bedroom and he kept a gun beside his bed. A gunshot soon put paid to their burglary as they scarpered back out of the window as quick as possible. Unfortunately, for Michael he received part of a gunshot and gunpowder stains on his back side. He could not sit down for weeks.

"You two are always moaning!" Michael groaned at his two latest companions. "Why is it always me who has to come up with the ideas as to what to do! Haven't you got a brain cell between the two of you!"

"Of course, we have!" Darren responded. Feeling irritated by his leader's comment.

"Yeah! But you're the leader of our gang! You should be leading us to do big things! That's why we joined your gang!" Bill uttered.

"Like what!" Michael yelled. "Do you want us to rob a bank! We could do, if you want. I'm up for it! We might end up in prison! Alternatively, we could end up with a million pounds!"

Both his gang members eyes lit up at the idea of a million pounds. But they knew, like their leader, they needed money up front for such a robbery. To pay for masks, booty bags, reconnoitre visits to the bank, equipment to break into the building and places to go to hide after. And what did they have nothing but a pocketful of sweets stolen from the corner sweet shop in their pockets.

Michael knew he had to come up with something quickly. In an attempt to make these two happy at being in his gang. But he was struggling to think of anything beyond the usual stealing of food from children's school lunch boxes as they made their way to school, letting down car tyres or sneaking in to the local cinema through the fire exit.

"Well, I think I might as well go home then!" Darren muttered. "At least I can sit and watch tele. There's not much happening here!"

"Yeah! That's a good idea!" Bill agreed.

"But I thought you didn't have a tele anymore at home?" Michael looked at Bill. "I thought it was taken away when your dad didn't pay the rental!"

"Oh! Yeah! I forget!" Bill chuckled. "Anyway, my dad took my key for the house away. Saying if I don't get work, he doesn't want me sitting around at home all day!"

"And that's why we're a gang! Here together! Standing against everyone else! Nobody likes us or will give us a chance. We'll show them all right! Show them they are wrong about us! We'll teach them to ignore us. Why don't they give us jobs and lots of money as we deserve." Michael tried to stir up his troops.

Well, his troop of two!

"Yeah!" Bill and Darren agreed. Their enthusiasm stirred.

The three of them needed to stick together through thick and thin. That's what gangs do!

It was at this point a little old lady started to head towards them as they sat outside the park gate busy doing nothing, busy going nowhere.

Michael was the first to spot her and for a moment didn't think anything of it.

Then with his next glance, he noticed she was carrying a bag full of shopping and looked pretty unsteady on her feet. Head bowed and dressed in a green woolly hat and gloves even though it was rather warm. Her glasses looked as if they were leftovers from old National Health Service issue stock. Her coat reached down to her knees and had enormous buttons that were fashionable in the 1950's.

She stopped a couple of times to change hands holding what was to her a heavy bag. And you could tell by the way she was dressed money was an issue.

Everything about her shouted out here was an elderly person on the bread line. Someone struggling to make ends meet.

Then with his third glance, the gang leader hit upon an idea. An idea he hoped would rally his troop and give them something to focus on. He wasn't concerned about an old lady struggling with her day to day living. He wasn't worried about an old lady with only a few pence in her pocket. He wasn't worried about an old lady who found it hard to walk a short distance let alone from her flat to the shops and back because she couldn't afford the bus fare. He was only worried about trying to find something for his gang to do.

"Right! I've got a plan!" Michael beamed a smile of contentment at coming up with an idea.

"Great!" Bill revelled in the fact of having something to do at last.

"What is it, Michael?" Darren quizzed. Intrigued as to what was planned for them.

Both thought at the same time, "It was about time their leader came up with something to do."

"Well! You see that little old lady walking towards us!"

"Yeah!" Darren's eye quickly zoomed in on her. "Michael is right she is old!" He thought to himself.

"She looks like my granny! Poor old duck! Look at her!" Beamed Bill.

Unaware at that moment of his gang leader's intentions.

"You see she's got that shopping bag full of goodies!"

"Yeah!" Darren could see where this discussion was going.

"I bet that bag is heavy for her too! Do you think we ought to help her carry it?" Bill had still not picked up on what Michael was planning.

"What we're going to do! Is when she gets here, we're going to push her over and steal her shopping bag with all the goodies in it. We can then have a real good old binge on food! That will cheer us all up!"

"You mean we'll run in to the park with it!" Darren asked.

"Yeah! And there we will share out the goodies amongst the three of us!" Their leader nodded.

"But she looks like she hasn't got a lot, Michael!" Bill added.

"You stupid idiot! Don't you understand!" Michael pushed his gang member. "She's got a lot more than us! You can't get sentimental over an old woman, she's just another horrible person in our way. A horrible person who we've got to use to help ourselves. And anyone in our gang territory is legitimately game for us!" There was fire in his eyes as he looked at his two gang members. He knew he had to convince them she was fair game. This was a target they could attack with ease to get what they wanted. Moreover, they had a right to demand anything they required from those living in their gang's territory. As far as this leader was concerned everybody in their part of the world needed to pay his gang their dues.

"Remember, aren't we keeping them safe by making sure gangs from other areas around us don't come and attack them? They depend on us and owe us!" He tried to convince them and himself about what they were going to do. "We have the right to take what we want and treat those in our area how we want. We are the bosses here! Just remember that!" He lifted his hands up and made two fists as if threatening anybody who disagreed with him.

"She'll be easy pickings!" Darren added. "And the food will keep us going for the rest of the day! And we're all pretty hungry!"

"And she'll be able to buy more food! She'll have enough money." Michael laughed. Unaware of her real financial position.

"Yeah! I suppose we have got to remember we're the bad guys around here and we need to show everybody that we mean business! That we're tough! They better do what we say or else!" Bill saw himself now as a rough and ready guy protecting his territory. He couldn't see the reality behind what he was saying.

"We better take her purse as well and we can use the cash to get a cup of coffee later!" There was a snigger in the leader's evil thoughts.

The only way Darren could undertake this upcoming deed was not to question it in his thoughts but just get on with it. He was in the gang now and had to do what the gang did. Michael would see them all right. He was a strong, tough leader to follow. "Okay, boss! Let's get it done!"

After all this contemplation, the little old lady was about to reach them.

She was puffing and panting with the weight of the shopping even though there was not a lot in there. Her shoulders lurched forward, it is unclear whether this was due to her age or the weight of the bag. This elderly person had been looking down at the ground as she went along so she had no idea of the three older teenagers sitting on the park gate in front of her. Watching her every move. Her feet shuffled from one step to the next as she plodded along at a pace even a snail would have beaten.

The three older teenagers had a quick look around, there was nobody about. Perfect! For what they wanted to do. They got down from the gate and stood in front of the little old lady who was still unaware of their presence as she got ever nearer to them.

It was right in front of them she stopped to change hands with what seemed to her heavy shopping. When she looked up she was surprised to see the three, what appeared, massive figures standing there in front of her.

She smiled as she courteously asked. "Hello young men have you come to give me a hand with my heavy shopping? That would be very nice as it's a real struggle for me!" These words were inter-laced with efforts to get her breath as she was truly tired.

Not that this worried her attackers.

"Help you!" The gang leader laughed. "We wouldn't help you, you silly old lady! We're here to rob you!"

"Yeah!" Grimaced Bill. "What you got in that bag we could eat!"

"You better hand it over or else!" Darren threatened her as if he was confronting an enemy gang member.

"But this is my shopping for the week! It's all I can afford! And I've just carried it all the way from town! Surely, you wouldn't rob a little old lady like me?" With a tear of fear in her eyes, she struggled with the pain in her back to stand up a bit straighter and look these three hooligans in the face.

"Of course, we will!" Michael continued. "Don't you get it! This is our gang territory we can do what we want here!"

"And you need to pay your dues to us for keeping you safe from other gangs!" Bill shouted at her.

Darren was beginning to get an adrenalin rush.

"You are lucky the gang in your territory is not as cruel as some in other areas! They would beat you up as well for answering back!"

"Well! You're not exactly Robin Hood stealing from the rich to give to the poor!" She managed to say before Michael had built himself up to start the robbery.

At that point, he pushed her over on the pavement and watched as she tumbled down on to the ground. Finally, banging her head with a thump on the hard tarmac. The three of them showed no sympathy for her as she groaned and began to try to sit up from her fallen position.

They were more concerned with what was in the shopping bag.

"There's hardly anything in here!" Bill exclaimed as he looked in the bag she had been carrying.

"I don't think carrots are what we want to eat! Or potatoes!" Darren added looking inside the bag with his other gang members.

"Please, that is all I have to last me all week!" The little old lady squeaked as she used her two arms to sit up straight on the cold pavement and look up at her three attackers.

By then the infuriated Michael was angry with her! For the bag was going to give them little in the way of nourishment to keep them going all day. This was not what he was hoping for anyway. Hence, he believed he needed her purse now. Surely, there would be a lot of money in there they could take and use to buy food and other things they needed. She had been to town so, more than likely, had been to the bank as well and withdrawn a lot of money for the week.

"Well! We'll have to have your purse, you silly old bag! Your money should provide us with enough food and other things we need at this moment!" At which point he commenced to start to search her pockets as she was sat on the ground before him.

*****

It was while this robbery was taking place, it so happened that Jules was on his way to the shops to buy the food for his mum. He came around the corner towards the park and saw what was taking place at the entrance to the green space.

"What on earth is happening?" Was his first thought as he saw Michael pushing over the little old lady while the other two grabbed her bag and started to take out her purchases.

He could not believe what he was seeing. He watched as the little old lady sat up and then Michael began to search her pockets. It took him a few moments to realise that the woman sitting on the ground was the little old lady he had helped the summer before with her shopping after being knocked down by a car. Now she was in trouble again but, this time, being robbed. He knew even though the odds were stacked against him with three older hooligans he had to go and help her. It was what he had to do.

Without thinking any more about it, Jules found himself running as fast as he could, to try and reach the robbery before the thieves could do any more damage to the woman on the ground. He knew if he did not get there quickly they would run off with what they had taken. Leaving her with nothing.

"Hey you three!" He shouted as loud as he could at them as he got closer. Trying to sound aggressive and threatening at the same time.

As soon as his voice reached them, the three thugs stopped what they were doing and turned towards this fast-approaching help.

"Leave her alone! She's only an old lady!" He carried on. Getting closer all the time and not slowing down as he got nearer to them.

At first, the three attackers were all set to run off as fast as they could. They assumed they were in danger of being caught, or handed over to the police or of even getting attacked themselves.

There was a moment of fear as they stood up and looked towards this nearing opponent. They were expecting to see a huge number of older and larger men running towards them.

"Leave her bag alone! That's all she's got! You thieves!" He carried on shouting as he closed in.

After only taking a step in starting to run off, Michael was the first to stop. Suddenly, realising that this approaching saviour did not pose any real threat to them. For a start, he was younger than they were. He was alone. He was smaller than they were and had no weapons that could be seen with him. What was there to run from. What was there to stop them from carrying on doing what they had been doing. What was there to stop them from dealing with him as well! After considering the options, Michael stood tall and threatening. Knowing he was the king of the situation.

As soon as their leader had stopped in his tracks to face Jules, so did his two gang members. All three of them turned towards Jules and were ready to meet him. The moment of fear and cowardly running off had turned in to a cocky certainty that they were now again in charge of the situation.

Jules stopped right in front of them.

"Get away from her! She is a nice old lady and doesn't deserve what you're doing to her!" He faced them with courage.

But as he weighed up their size and the fact that there were three of them, he began to realise the odds were not on his side. With embarrassment, he suddenly did not feel so confident about trying to intervene. In fact, he felt quite vulnerable himself as to what they could do to him as well as the old lady.

"And what are you going to do about it?" Michael took a step towards Jules and raised his fists near his face.

His two companions, again with rising confidence, were soon closing in on Jules as well. Raising their fists to him in a similar fashion to their boss.

"Come on!" Jules was the one now under threat! "You shouldn't be picking on a little old lady like that! You can tell she hasn't got a lot of money or anything worthwhile you stealing!"

"Who says we were stealing!" Michael gave his adversary a push. Not too sure at this stage whether Jules would strike him back. So, he stood ready to receive some sort of physical reaction back.

Jules was pushed but it wasn't a strong enough push to knock him over. It was more a threatening shove. Perhaps, even to test how he would respond. It gave his three aggressors a confidence boost when he did not react in any way. Hence, they began to feel this smaller lad in front of them was going to be a push over to deal with.

"And instead of picking on a little old lady, perhaps, we'll pick on you instead." Bill gave Jules a far bigger push. "How do you like that!"

This time it sent the younger boy tumbling backwards. He stumbled before regaining his balance and standing up to face them once more.

"You'll get in to trouble with the police if you steal from this old lady!"

Jules was desperate to try and think of a way to make these thugs leave not only her alone but himself too. He could see they were now about to start on him. He was terrified at the thought of what they were going to do. Then he began to realise that after dealing with him, they would continue their assault on the old lady. There was nothing he could do about that. Even though he was bravely standing up to them. It would all prove meaningless in the end.

"Ha!" Darren laughed. Now confident that this pitiful boy in front of them would not give them any aggravation. He gave him a far more powerful hit in the stomach that took the wind out of the boy and sent him rolling over on to the floor amidst coughs and splutters. "Do you think we're worried about the police!"

"Yeah! This is our gang's territory here and we run it!" Bill gave the boy on the ground a kick on his thigh. "The police better not to turn up here or else!"

Jules gave out another sigh as the force of the kick hit him. He wondered what was to come next. Yet, it did cross his mind that at least they were leaving the old lady alone at that moment.

It was then the boy on the ground heard the roar of motor bikes in the background. Even though his focus was obviously on what was happening to himself.

What he didn't realise was that a large group of Harley Davidson bikes had come around the same corner he had come around only a few minutes earlier. They were seeing a similar scene to the one he had seen. Except, instead of the little old lady being attacked and stolen from, now it was him who was receiving a beating.

There must have been ten bikers, dressed up in their old, beaten leathers, dirty, greasy Levi jeans and well-worn cowboy boots on. On the back of their leather jackets were the name of their tribe. 'Hawker Hunters.' Most had cow horn handles on the bike and dangling leather strips.

One had a crash helmet with Viking horns coming out of the sides, while another was wearing a cowboy hat John Wayne would have been proud of. Towards the back one was dressed as a red Indian medicine man with a buffalo hat on. All had beards at various stages of growth and ear-rings that pirates would have been boasting about. They looked a tough bunch of riders.

The sound of their bikes was overwhelming as they came closer, even though Jules had not realised it. His mind was tuned in to what was happening to himself. The bikers seemed to look at what was happening outside the park gate and it appeared they did not like what they were seeing. There was a quick wave and a nod between them before they altered their direction and made their way over to where the three gang members were undertaking the robbery and beating up.

Even the three thugs stopped attacking Jules as the bikers neared. Unsure what it meant in relation to what they were doing. Each of the bikers giving short bursts on their accelerators as they neared. Each accelerator roar sounded threatening. Michael wasn't too sure what the newcomers wanted. He realised he didn't know them at all and wasn't too sure whether they were only interested to see what was taking place or were they going to interfere in some way.

Once in a semi-circle around the event happening outside the park, the Hell's Angels turned off their bike engines. They faced the three attackers who in turn had stopped what they were doing. There was an uneasy silence. The gang members looked at these newcomers unsure what their intentions were. None of those five there before them had any idea what the arrival of this large group of bikers meant. What were they going to do if anything.

"Oi! What do you three think you are up to?" One of the Hell's Angels grunted. While taking off his helmet and wiping his nose on his sleeve. He nodded towards the old lady and Jules.

"Us!" Michael replied as if surprised the Hell's Angel was talking to him.

His interlocuter nodded. "Who else would I be talking to!"

"Oh! This is our gang's patch! We're just doing a bit of business!" he said as if he had a right to be doing this in their territory and this group of riders should not interfere or else. "You know how it is!"

"With a little old lady and a boy? I don't think I do know how it is!" He shook his head and nodded towards the two of them. "Isn't there someone a bit more suitable for you to pick on!"

"We know what we have to do!" The gang leader replied. Still uncertain what this group of bikers' intentions really were. "We have this situation under control!" He seemed to be under the impression that the bikers were there to help them.

"Yeah! They deserve it" Bill urged, flexing his muscles at their interruption. "This is our territory! We can do what we like here! We're letting them know who is the boss around here!"

Darren cowered a bit at his other gang member's assertive replies. He could see that there was a good chance that these bikers were not happy at what the three of them were up to. Yet, it was too late now for him or them to get out of this mess. The situation had turned. From them being the powerful aggressors they were the ones who could be about to receive some sort of beating.

The biker looked at his comrades. They all nodded at each other in agreement. What that agreement was Michael and his two gang members were about to find out. Each of the new interlopers put their bikes on their stands and those with helmets removed them. The whole group seemed to be moving with the same intention.

"Well! To tell you the truth, you three idiots, we don't think you should be robbing a little old lady and beating up such a young boy. We're of the opinion that if this is your gang territory, you're not too nice a gang. And we think we're going to do something about it!"

"I don't think you need to concern yourselves with us, lads!" Michael was now frightened at what was going to happen to him and his colleagues.

"We'll just leave these two alone if you want and walk away!" Darren took a deep breath and hoped that would appease these new actors upon the scene.

"To tell you the truth, I think it's far too late for that!" One rider barked as he got behind the three terrified gang members.

The other bikers all nodded in agreement and started walking towards the three now frightened gang members. The three knew it would be useless to run and there was no way they could stand up to this larger group. All, who seemed far bigger and stronger than themselves. It was not difficult to see it was not looking too good for Michael, Bill and Darren. Not good at all.

One Hell's Angel helped up the old lady, asked her if she was okay and started dusting her down. Another grabbed her shopping bag from Bill and returned it to her. A third member was helping up Jules and checking he was okay after the cruel beating he had received.

While the rest of the bikers were now fully gathered around the three frightened cowards and shoving them between themselves as if they were playing a game of ping-pong.

"We're very sorry for what these idiots were doing to you!" The leader of the Hell's Angles group spoke to the old lady and Jules. "Are you both okay?"

"Thanks to you! Yes!" Replied the timid lady. "You have been most kind helping us. This young boy only came to try and protect me. Then they started picking on him! They were stealing my weekly shopping and searching for my money. Money that has to last me for the whole week! How wicked are they!" There were tears in her eyes.

"Yes, they are!" Almost all the riders replied. They were used to seeing cruel things but even they could see how low these three gang members had fallen.

"Well! I don't think you'll need to worry about them anymore!" The leader of the Hells Angels replied.

"Yes! We'll take care of them for you!" Another added.

"It will be our pleasure!" Another voice reiterated.

With that the Hell's Angels group forced the three gang members to come over to their bikes. When the Hell's Angels group had all got back on their machines, they started up their engines and soon the loud revving commenced again. The three frightened attackers were thrown over the petrol tanks of three bikes with their legs dangling one way and their heads and arms dangling the other. They were then driven off by the gang to be appropriately dealt with.

"Are you okay?" Jules asked the little old lady once the sonorous sound of the bikers had gotten far enough away in to the distance for them to hear themselves talk.

"I'm fine! Thanks to you and those bikers!" She replied with a little smile creeping across her face. "You've come to my aid again as you did last year! You're very kind!"

"Oh! You remember me from last year then!" He smiled. "I didn't think you would!"

"Why wouldn't I?" She pulled on her coat to straighten it. "Do you think my memory is going?"

"No! No!" Jules was suddenly afraid he may have upset her. Not noticing the creeping cheeky smile growing on her face. "I just thought it was quite a long time ago!"

"Well! I suppose it was, wasn't it!" She agreed. "I dread to think what those yobs would have done if you had not turned up! They were not concerned with the fact that they were dealing with a timid old person. There only interest was in what they could get from me. I could have been seriously hurt not that they were worried. They were really awful thugs!"

"Well! I didn't prove much help did I! If the bikers hadn't turned up, I dread to think what would have happened to me as well as you!"

"But you were brave enough to stand up to them! Even though you knew you didn't stand much of a chance. And it gave us just enough time for the Hell's Angels to arrive and really put a stop to what they were up to!" She steadied herself. "I can't thank you enough!"

"There's no need to thank me! I'm more than happy to have helped!" Fortunately, there was little pain from the thumps he had received. If he touched those parts of his body, there was a soreness but nothing else. "Would you like me to carry your bag home for you again!"

"Would you! That would be most kind! After what happened I could do with some help."

She leaned across to Jules and gave him her bag of groceries. He was amazed at how light it seemed. They both started walking in the direction he remembered they had taken the last time.

"Do you still live in the same place?" He quizzed.

"Oh! Yes!" She replied. "Do you remember where it is! It is not far! It is just around the corner."

What he could remember from last year was when she said, "It was just around the corner, around the corner never seemed to come!"

"You know!" He added "I know this town really well! But I had never been to your flats before last summer and never been able to find them since."

"Well! Isn't that interesting!" She replied turning in to another road.

"That's funny!" Jules thought to himself. "This bag of groceries is getting to feel really heavy again. I remember that happening last time. Even though when I initially picked it up, I thought it was as light as a feather!" After a few moments he continued. "Do you know what!"

"What's that!" His companion asked.

"Well! Isn't it funny, the last time I helped you it was almost exactly a year ago!"

"Is that so! I wonder how that can be!" She exclaimed.

"Yes! Right at the start of the school summer holidays!"

"And if I remember right, you weren't going away at all for your summer! Is it the same this year?"

She looked at him with concern.

"Afraid so! We are even in a worse situation than we were last year. I would get a job if I could to help mum out! But I'm still too young for that!" He shook his head in worry.

"So, all your friends have gone away and you've been left to twiddle your thumbs I suppose, until they get back!"

"Yes, that about sums it up! Of course, I'll have to try and help mum as much as possible! Believe it or not, it looks like she has lost her job as well! Goodness knows what kind of mess we will be in from now on!"

"Oh! Dear!" The old lady stopped and looked at him. "This sounds a terrible mess for you both."

Jules took the opportunity to change his hands for holding the bag. He could not believe it the bag that once seemed so light was now exceedingly heavy and he was struggling to carry it.

They had turned quite a few corners since leaving the park and he realised again he had no idea where he was.

"Have we got far to go?" He puzzled. "I've kind of lost my bearings again!"
"No! Not too far! Just around this corner!" She answered.

He knew about her "around the corners" as he changed hands again. It was difficult to miss the red lines caused by the bag on his palms.

"Oh! Dear! Is the bag getting too heavy for you?" His aged partner asked.
"Don't you worry, we're nearly there!"

"No! No!" He responded with an attempt to sound like he was able to cope with this light bag of groceries without any problem. How could he not. He knew when he picked it up it was very light. The trouble was now it wasn't light. In fact, if the truth be told, somehow it was quite a weight.

He put the bag down in exhaustion. "I think I do need a few moments before we carry on! Obviously, I'm not as strong as I thought I was! Your bag seems to have got heavier and heavier! Are we nearly there? I have no idea where we are!" He looked around him not recognising any buildings in his very own town. The town he thought he knew so well.

"Well done and thank you once again!" She grabbed his arm to thank him. "We're here. There's my flat over there in that tall building!"

When Jules looked at where she was pointing, he could not believe he had not seen it before. How could he have missed it. For there in front of him stood a tall tenement block of flats. It crossed his mind that surely he would see these flats from other parts of the town. It was so tall, yet, he can truly say he had never noticed it before. How odd.

"Shall I help you take the shopping bag up to your flat?" He asked.

"Oh! No!" She replied. "I can manage from here, dear! You've already helped me far more than I can tell you!"

"Are you sure you can manage your bag? It seems really heavy now!" He struggled to lift it up for her.

"I'll be fine!" And she took it from him far easier than he imagined she would. The weight didn't seem to cause her much of a problem at all. "Let me give you this for your troubles!" She began to take a few pennies out of her purse to give him as a way of saying, "Thank you!"

"No! Put that away! I did it because I wanted to help you and I certainly don't want any money for it! Anyway, us two are getting to be like old friends!" They both laughed.

"Do you think you can find your way back from here?" She asked him.

"Of course, no problem!" He retorted with confidence. Yet, in truth, when he thought about it, he had no idea where he was or how he got there. And come to think of it, last year when he left her, he struggled to find his way back home. "Well! I hope you have a lovely summer! Once again, I can't thank you enough for all you have done for me!" She tapped his arm again in recognition of his kind deeds.

"My pleasure!" He smiled at her. "You take care. And I will look out for you to see if I can help you with your shopping!"

With that, he turned and started to make his way off. Pleased with himself for doing such a good deed. Yet, something made him turn around to watch her go. When he did, to his surprise he could not see her at all. She wasn't anywhere between him and the tenement block. She couldn't walk that fast and be in the building already, that was for sure. Yet, when he thought back to last year, he remembered the same thing happened. She disappeared once he had turned his back on her. How odd!

Chapter 4

Well, to Jules total surprise he was lost again! In his own home town. A town that he knew so well. He made his way down numerous streets he didn't know and whose street names he had never heard of before. This seemed to him so strange. How could it be. He had walked the whole town time and again but never come across this set of roads. They were even reasonably close to his own home. It didn't make any sense.

He decided to keep on going down road after road in the hope that eventually he would find a street that he knew. Surely, he was bound too. There can't be so many roads he didn't know. It was just a matter of time and patience and he would soon find out where he was.

Once again, his thoughts went back to last year when he found himself lost after helping the old lady. In the end he found a street he knew and from then on there was no problem finding his way home. Yet, he had looked for these streets he was now lost on numerous times during the year since and he could never find them. He had searched the skyline for the high tenement building where the old lady lived and could find no such place. This was all so confusing and odd.

The next thing he knew, Jules was coming around a corner and there it was. To his total surprise he was standing at the roundabout at Gateshead Road and there before him was where the puddle hoppers had their puddle homes. How he had got there he had no idea but he was pleased to be back on a street where he knew exactly where he was.

Jules was surprised to see some of Farmer Wicks Friesian black and white cows roaming around the field where the puddle hoppers had their homes. This field was often left to grass all year and then cut for hay towards the end of the summer. Perhaps, the farmer was short of feed for his cows this year.

It was then Jules saw a flash of green-blue move near the fence on the far side of the field. Most observers would write it off as an optical illusion or a shadow. Yet, Jules was aware that the puddle hoppers lived in that field and what he saw there was about the same size, same colour and same type of movement as a puddle hopper.

Next, he was aware of a cow ferociously baying at the smaller creature from only a few feet away. Somehow or other the puddle hopper must have annoyed the large beast and it was now ranting in anger at it.

The small figure tried to dodge this way and that to get away from this mighty foe but all to no effect. The cow was ready to block its every move with a lowering of the head and short charge in any direction the puddle hopper chose to go.

There was no puddle nearby for it to slip in to and escape either. The puddles were more in the central part of the field and, obviously, there was no other member of the tribe around to realise the danger their fellow creature was in. The puddle hopper seemed to be in a predicament. A predicament the puddle hopper could not get out of. While the cow was slowly edging nearer and nearer to it. You could see the terror on the face of the figure facing the aggressive animal.

Jules knew he had to act to help save the puddle hopper from the cow that had taken umbrage. He hopped over the fence quickly and started to run towards the part of the field where the altercation was taking place.

"Hey! Hey!" He shouted as he closed in on the cow. "Leave the puddle hopper alone, you great oaf! Go on! Away with you!"

As he got nearer to the beast he clapped his hands and made jeering sounds to frighten it off. In truth he knew that this hefty cow was much bigger and weighed a lot more than he did. If he had to confront the beast, he would come out the loser.

The cow turned towards him and you could tell it was not very happy at being disturbed from what it was doing. Goodness knows what the puddle hopper had done but the cow was obviously very annoyed. But, as Jules came nearer and nearer, the bovine farm animal mooed before leaping away from the smaller being and the approaching human. It was not very happy but it ran off to join the rest of the herd in another part of the field.

Both the puddle hopper and Jules watched the cow settle down alongside the others in the herd and within a few moments it started to eat some of the long grass that was right for chewing on. Soon the cow was so calm it was difficult to realise it had ever been so aggressive.

"Well! The cow certainly took a disliking to you!" Jules joked.

The puddle hopper was still in a bit of shock and could only nod her head in agreement. "I guess I owe you a great big thank you!"

"What caused it to set upon you like that? These Friesian cows are usually quite calm and friendly animals." He continued. Expecting his interlocuter to answer his question.

But before he knew what had happened the green-blue creature had pushed him backwards.

"Hey! What's going on!" He asked. But before he had time to explain who he was, he was tumbling backwards in to a puddle and disappearing downwards. Landing with a thump at the bottom of the recess under the puddle. Of course, he had been in a similar situation before. But he had no idea why he had been shoved in to a puddle this time after helping save this creature. And he was not too sure if he was a prisoner or what?

He tried to push his way out of the puddle above him and found, as he suspected, it was an invisible tough wall. There was no way he was going to break out of that puddle. He knew that from past experience.

He sat there and looked up at the puddle hopper looking down at him.

"Why have you done this to me?" He pleaded. "I only helped you!" She didn't reply to him.

"I'm a friend of the puddle hoppers!" He exclaimed. "I helped last year with those three evil puddle hoppers! I came in to your tribal homes! You must remember me!"

She looked at him carefully but then shook her head as if to say, "No, I am afraid I don't!"

Nothing seemed to be working in getting her to change her mind. Perhaps, he thought, she could not speak English. However, she had thanked him for saving her before she pushed him in to the puddle.

Perhaps, she had got very limited English. Even so, why would she imprison him. It didn't make sense.

It was then he heard another voice above. He looked up and could see there were two puddle hoppers talking now. They were speaking in their usual high-pitched voices where sounds all ran in to one another. He assumed it was a discussion about him taking place above. All he could do was to await the outcome of what was being said. There was pointing down at him and shaking of heads. Yet, it made little sense to their prisoner, if that was what he was.

"Hey! Let me out!" He called. "I'm a friend of the puddle hoppers!"

It did cross his mind that things might have changed in the "puddle hopper" world. Although, they were very friendly and helpful creatures last year perhaps there had been a radical alteration as to how they view the world. It could be that they hate all humans now. They were going to be aggressive to those who lived above them on the earth.

Perhaps, they were following in the footsteps of the three evil puddle hoppers who his uncle had taken back up to the artic lands of the north to re-inter. Jules had not seen the local puddle hoppers for a while and wondered what may have brought about such a change. If there was such a change!

"Ha! I should have guessed it would be you!" A puddle hopper spoke in English as he stood on the side of the puddle and looked down in to it at the captive.

Jules looked up puzzled. It was difficult for him to see who was speaking from above.

"Of all the people for Luce to imprison, it had to be you!" The blue-green creature continued with a tint of humour in his voice.

"Prok! Is that you up there!" The human below exclaimed. A slight relief in his voice.

"Who else would it be!"

"I should have guessed! Get me out of here, Prok!" Jules laughed with quite a bit of relief.

"Get you out! No way!" The voice above continued to joke with him. "I think you deserve to stay down there for quite a while!"

"Why is that?" The boy answered. Exasperated! "I only helped your friend when she was being attacked by a cow! Surely that was a good thing to do!"

"Ha! That's what you say! I bet you were the one who provoked the cow to attack her in the first place!" he said with a slight laugh in his voice.

"Come on, Prok! You've had your fun at my expense!"

Prok's hand reached down through the puddle surface and took Jules's hand. He then helped to haul his body out of the water so that he was standing up next to him. There was a real look of enjoyment in his face as he watched his human friend brush himself down.

"Thanks!" he said to Prok who burst out laughing. "I don't think it's funny! All I did was try to help!" Yet even the boy had a growing smile on his face.

"I'm sorry for what I did to you!" Lace looked forlorn. "I should have thanked you for what you did to save me from that frantic beast. He just went wild!"

"What do you think upset the cow?" Jules asked.

"I was collecting moss and I backed in to him accidently and grabbed his tail to steady myself. I didn't know he was there. He yelped when I grabbed his tail and became angry very quickly. Before I knew it, he was chasing me across the field to this corner and I could not escape from him. Then, gratefully, you came and saved the day!"

"But why did you then push me in to the puddle and imprison me!" He gasped. "After all, I had helped you and driven the cow away!"

"Well! I am afraid I didn't know who you were at that moment and I panicked. I began to think if this strange boy goes home and tells his people about this odd creature he met down in the meadow at Gateshead Road, we could soon be inundated with curious humans searching around for us. It would not be long before we were discovered." She took a breath as she tried to remember her reasons for her actions. "So, I thought if I put you in a puddle and talked to the tribe's elders they would know what to do with you in this situation. I was only trying to ensure that our tribe and our place in this town were safe."

"That is when I came along!" Prok giggled. "I came to see what had happened to Lace. She is, what you would call, my "girlfriend" and she should have been back quite a while ago. When I arrived, she told me the complete story and asked what we should do! I thought we would have to keep you as a prisoner for the rest of your life. So, you could not pass on what you had seen and where you had seen it."

"Keep me imprisoned for life!" Their captive was stunned. "That's a bit over the top!"

"Well! You never know what you humans can get up to! We have to protect ourselves."

"Be real! Prok!" He laughed.

"That is when I looked down in to the puddle and thought to myself, I recognise that ugly looking face staring up at me! And it was you!"

They both laughed and after giving each other a warm hug began to reminisce over last year's events.

Lace listened with interest. After Prok had explained who this boy was who had helped her with the cow, it all came back to her. He was the human boy who had been party to helping defeat the three evil puddle hoppers that had escaped. She had not really looked at human boys too closely before. To tell you the truth they had all looked the same to her like empty milk bottles all sitting in a row waiting to be collected.

"I am so truly sorry!" She cowered to him realising she should have recognised his face. "But I did panic a bit about what was the best thing to do!

And I hope you can forgive me!"

"Of course! I do!" Jules smiled. "I can understand what you did and why you did it. If it had been some other boy, who did not know of your tribe's existence that would have been quite awkward. It could be really dangerous if they ran off and told the world about what they had seen!"

At that point she brought out her pet mouse and stroked it in front of Jules and Prok.

"That's a cute little fella!" Jules smiled as he gently leaned forward to stroke her pet.

"Yes! I've had it since I was tiny!"

"Ha! She's always playing with that small creature. Everywhere Luce goes, that mouse goes with her. It's like they are joined at the hip!" Prok half-mocked, half-joked.

"I can understand that," Jules was still stroking the pet. "It's great to have a pet and a friend like that! Humans keep mice as pets as well."

"He's such a cutie!" She rubbed the mouse up against her cheek! "He knows how much I love him! We are really good friends!"

*****

While her son had gone off, Jules' mum had gone out in search of another job. Whether she had been sacked, or was suspended, or laid off while the pickle factory was being repaired remained unclear to her. It made no difference anyway. All she knew was she needed money coming in to the house to pay for the bills. Bills that wouldn't go away. Gideon's money last year had helped enormously to dig her out of debt.

However, as the year had gone on the debts had started to mount up again. Now the pickle factory was closed and her weekly income ceased. She knew within weeks the debts would build up. What would she do then! She had to find work of some sort to help in this situation. No matter what it was. But where?

She tried for numerous jobs in the town. All with lower salaries than the one she had at the pickle factory and that was low enough. But she knew any income at the present time would be welcome. However, when the employers she approached found out where she had been working and who she was, no one wanted to give her a job. The mayor and pickle factory boss had made her name toxic in the town. No business wanted to fall out with the mayor by employing her.

He could make life very difficult for them. It did not help that all the pickle factory staff were searching for temporary jobs in the town as well. Until the pickling business got on its feet once again their jobs had been suspended without pay. There was more than enough choice from the unemployed, for employers to consider who they wanted to take on! Hence, why take a risk in upsetting the mayor when there was no need to by employing the person he was blaming for the explosion at his factory.

Constance was running out of hope, when she came to the scrap food factory that was opposite where the pickle factory was being rebuilt. No one wanted to work there. Awful stories were told by those who had taken jobs at the place. Many left almost immediately. They complained about the terrible pay and work conditions. Outside was a sign that read:

"Workers wanted! No questions asked!"

Constance knew this may be her only chance of a job in the town. A town where nobody wanted her. She decided to give it a go. It did not bode well that the factory was run by the mayor's brother, Grunswick Brian. She smiled to herself as she thought that she could be the only person in the world who he might not employ. She was aware anybody else who went along was given a job.

No questions asked. The problem was they did not stay too long!

"So, you want a job do you! Hum!" Grunswick looked her up and down.

"Yes, Mr. Brian!" She smiled back.

"And you worked at my brother's factory did you!" It was the first time she had ever met this brother.

But all that she had heard was more than true. Everything about him was kind of screwed up and twisted. How can I put it. Well! His face was all screwed up and snarling for a start. His back leaned forwards as he stood in front of you. It was as if he was going to fall on top of you at any moment. While his arms seemed to be like two loose hockey sticks swinging in front of him. If you looked at his large hands, they bent inwards and were always fidgeting.

It was as if they wanted to be doing something but were not quite sure what. His legs seemed the only straight bit of his body. Yet, if you looked at his feet they curled up, so the toes were sticking up in to the air. It was difficult to know how he could stand up without a wibble or a wobble.

His dark, unkempt hair and bulging eyes that peeked out through the mop above were like hidden cave entrances you could see in to. The dark clothes he wore, that people said he never changed, gave him a dour, menacing appearance. His black bow tie was just crooked enough to give him the appearance of someone who had not looked in a mirror for a long time.

He probably would have frightened himself if he had looked in it. It was difficult to ignore there was a whiff about him as well. Not the whiff that had been a problem for the whole town. This was the same whiff that pervaded the whole scrap food factory. For it had its own awful smell. It is sad to say, Grunswick Brian was not a creature you would like to meet after the sun had gone to sleep.

"Yes, Mr. Brian!" She decided not to mention she had been the one blamed for blowing up the pickle factory.

He didn't seem to realise what his brother had accused her of. This was good news as she needed the job.

"Well! We will give you a chance and see what you're made of!" He again eyed her up and down as if assessing how much work he would get out of her for the money he was about to pay her.

"You can start now. We'll see what kind of worker you are. And make sure I don't see you wasting time!" He grumped. "I don't like time-wasters in my factory!"

"Thank you, Mr. Brian!" She had not expected to start right away. Jules would be expecting her to be at home but this was an opportunity she could not turn down. So, she decided to accept the job and start work there and then. The extra money would be useful anyway. Plus, Jules would assume his mum had gone out looking for work.

*****

The cloud jumpers and their three new allies parked their cloud home above an inlet off the east Greenland coast. The three evil puddle hoppers wondered why they had stopped in such an inauspicious, miserable looking place. It was freezing cold and seemed to have continual stormy weather.

Castor explained to them that this was a very safe place for cloud jumpers. He explained that the blizzard type weather helped to ensure that human beings kept away from there. It left them alone in peace to get on with their own work.

Within moments, the three puddle hoppers were lowered down with Castor in to what looked like a small aperture in the snow-covered mountain. To their total surprise, as soon as they entered the hole in the mountain, the terrible weather ceased. Moreover, they found themselves in a huge, open cavern. Their mouths opened in awe.

Looking below they could see lots of beings, who seemed to be working very hard. Who they were and what they were actually doing was difficult to tell from the height they were at. They would have to wait to find out as they were gradually lowered down.

Finally, they reached the ground. Caster started to show them around. Even they were shocked at what they discovered was happening. For the workers who they had seen from above turned out to be human children or young puddle hoppers. What they seemed to be doing was making denser clouds out of normal clouds. Even the three puddle hoppers found it hard to believe. These workers were making the clouds very thick and strong.

Clouds that were more like a flexible material you could mould as required. This was done with a great big suction machine. Once the thicker cloud was ready, they were allowed to float off. It was then up to other children workers to gather them up and bundle them in to huge cloud-forms so they looked like other clouds we see in the sky. Ready to be used by the cloud jumpers as their travelling homes.

"These clouds are different to the normal clouds in the sky." The cloud jumpers chief explained to his three astounded guests.

"These ones we make, are far denser and more durable than they are. We can walk about on them, make living quarters inside and use their fibres for making things like string and rope. These clouds won't become rain and fall as raindrops like normal clouds either. Although, they can be blown about by the same winds as other clouds we have learnt to control these heavier clouds. So, we can steer them like ships on the sea and bring them to a stop when we want. Of course, we can still walk on normal clouds but these are a little bit more special. These clouds are perfect for us to live in and travel on." Castor carried on explaining.

Yet, even the three evil puddle hoppers were shocked by how down trodden these human children and young puddle hoppers were. Cloud jumpers were continually yelling at them to get on with their work. While the children and young puddle hoppers walked around with red eyes from crying and some were even sobbing in front of them. The workers' clothing was in tatters and they all looked so thin as if they were being fed cloud food to eat and nothing else. This, as it turns out, they were. There was not a young child or puddle hopper there who did not want to return home and see their mum or dad.

It was at this point the three visitors began to really realise these cloud jumpers had as much evil intent as themselves. They were bad through and through. These creatures seemed intent on achieving the most awful things they could. These were close cousins they felt they could work with.

Trud, Rak and Surr watched as the cloud jumpers forced the youngsters to herd clouds together and let them float up out of the mountain hole to join the other clouds. Clouds that would form part of the cloud jumpers' future travelling homes.

"We are going to take more cloud jumpers with us when we go back to England. We want to make sure we succeed in our mission. Not only do we want revenge on the puddle hoppers but we want to capture enough children to bring back here to carry on the cloud-making work. You know, these young children and young puddle hoppers don't seem to last too long before they give up and die. They die as quickly as butterflies that have been kept in glass jars."

"So, we need to keep a steady supply of them coming back here. We hope you three are going to help us do that! As well as help us on the other part of our mission. We need to work together to ensure that the puddle hoppers take the blame for all the children's disappearance! Then the humans will turn on them. What a wonderful plan! We can watch the turmoil from above! Ha!"

The three future accomplices nodded in agreement. They were more than happy to do that. There were smiles on their faces at the likely revenge that could be soon unleashed. It felt good to them knowing at long last, they were going to get their own back on the puddle hoppers in Boreham Wood for all they had done to them. Revenge would be sweet!

*****

Prok invited Jules to join him again in the main puddle cavern where the majority of the clan lived. It would be a chance for him to re-meet his father who was chief of the puddle hoppers. They had not met since last year. When the boy entered the huge space, he was greeted as a long-lost friend from those he passed as he made his way to the leader of the tribe.

Jules knew when he left last summer he could not keep on returning to these new found friends without the chance of catching other people's attention as he entered the field and then suddenly disappeared in to a puddle. However, it had not been his fault at how he had arrived back at their home this time.

After helping the old lady, it was a total surprise to him where he had ended up after being lost, Moreover, if it had not been for him seeing Luce struggling to get away from the aggressive cow he would have passed right on by. Yet, somehow, he had been drawn back to their home. Here he was, once again, unexpectedly, sitting with the tribe's elders.

At first, they talked about what the year had been like for the puddle hoppers. In return, they asked about himself, his mother and uncle. They then began to discuss other issues that had taken place recently in the town. Jules explained about the explosion at the pickle factory. However, he did not mention his mother's role in it at all.

"It is strange?" said the chief.

"What's strange?" Jules wondered what he meant.

"There has been a strange smell lingering around the tribe's site for quite a while. A smell we have been unable to work out what it is!" The chief looked at him. "Have your people smelled it? Do they know where it comes from?"

"Oh! It's really horrible isn't it? It seems to stick to anything and everything." Prok backed up what his father had said and could not resist smelling his own arm.

"Yes, we have smelled it too! It's awful isn't it!" Jules agreed with them. "Some people have said it is the remains of the fallout from the pickle factory explosion. But to tell you the truth it was around before that happened. To be honest, it doesn't smell anything like pickles any way!" Once again, he decided not to mention his own mum's involvement in what had happened with the machine blowing up.

"Some of us have even seen a strange creature lurking about at night!" Lace added.

Jules looked from one to the other and wondered what they were talking about. He had never heard of such a thing before.

"I don't think we should mention that!" The chief seemed to want to close down the subject. "Some puddle hoppers think they have seen something lurking in the shadows that somehow disappeared before they could get close enough to investigate. There has been no definite sighting."

"Well! They did add father that the smell about town seemed to get a lot stronger as they got closer to that strange creature!" Prok supported Lace's comments.

"But, if it's a calm, dark evening then smells are going to linger and seem to be stronger! There's no real evidence to support they saw something unusual or the smell was worse than at other times around here."

The chief was adamant that this line of discussion was not going to get out of hand. Obviously, he felt strongly, there was not enough evidence to support these claims of what had been seen and whether or not it was linked to the awful smell.

Chapter 5

Things had not exactly gone smoothly for the twins once they returned to Adelaide in Australia after their exciting time in England. You would think they would have learnt to be less troublesome. Perhaps, even cut back on their pranks after the way things worked out for them at their Aunt Constance's. But that was not to be the case.

Actually, it was just the opposite. Once again, leaving their desperate mum and dad in the normal state of despair. What could you do with these two terrors! You never knew what they would get up to next. After all that had happened in England, they had learnt nothing. Nothing in their behaviour had changed. The twins were still two fireworks exploding anyhow and anywhere.

However, things did not run too smoothly for them on their arrival back home. Of course, they were very excited about their adventures at their aunt's home and, although, they had been asked to keep quiet about the existence of the puddle hoppers by their Aunt, Gideon and Jules this was impossible for them to do. How could they? For it was the most exciting thing that had happened to them in their lives! Remember, we are talking about the twins.

Initially, both of them kept on saying to the other, "We must not say anything about those small creatures we had such an exciting time with. We have to keep quiet about what happened in the summer."

They knew what danger they may be putting the puddle hoppers in, if they mentioned them. They both nodded their heads in agreement. Each of them must keep silent. They knew what they had to do. Yet, as soon as their friends started asking whether they had a good time in England, they were finding it exceedingly difficult to keep their mouths closed about what had really happened.

It didn't help when their friends starting telling the twins about their exciting holidays. How they had seen wild tigers stalking prey in India, or had been sea fishing and caught a merlin who had put up a fight for three hours. Others told about being allowed to take a trip in a fighter plane and going through a force G8. Another told how they had been in a bank hold up and were held captives in Columbia for two days.

Whereas, what could the twins say. They bit their tongues for quite a while. Yet, soon their excitement got the better of them. They could not help talking about their adventures with the small creatures called puddle hoppers. They had let the cat out of the promised bag.

Although, they felt as if they had betrayed their English relations, they defended their position to themselves by saying, "Well, we are well away from Boreham Wood and the small creatures that live there. We cannot be putting them in any danger can we! Not really!"

While their friends believed those who had been on holiday and stated they had seen wild tigers, or tackled a merlin on a fishing line for three hours, or been in a fighter plane or, come to that, even having been held hostage in a bank robbery, no one would believe the twin's story about these small creatures, called puddle hoppers, who lived in puddles. Or, about the three evil puddle hoppers who had started to kidnap the local children!

"Oh! Yes!" One disbelieving friend quipped. "And did these puddle hoppers have towels to dry themselves off each time they got in and out of the puddle!"

"And did they bump their heads on the ground as they tried to get inside the puddle!" Another mocked them.

Things got even worse for Bronwyn and Seth when they told the other children about how they were kidnapped. How they were held hostages by these small creatures in a puddle. The look of disbelief on their friends' faces was obvious. They thought it was far too fetched to be true.

"And how did they get you down in to the puddles to hold you hostage then?" Another friend sniggered. A friend who did not believe a single word of what they were saying.

"Did they suck all the body matter out of you and lay you flat in the puddle!"

The twins pleaded with all their friends that they were telling the truth. They even drew pictures of the creatures and explaining how they got in and out of the puddles. Both were stunned that here they were telling the truth for once and no one believed a single word they were saying. The trouble was all their friends assumed that these two well-known liars and pranksters were trying to pull another fast one on them.

Of course, all their friends had suffered at some time or other from being the recipient of one of their jokes or pranks. Hence, they weren't too keen to fall for this obvious one about mythical creatures living in puddles and interred evil doers being buried in Alaska. These tales they were being told were far too fantastic! Adelaide had never heard or seen anything like the stories these two terrors were talking about.

If both of them had any intention of staying on the straight and narrower over the coming year that soon went out the window. It was true they did consider behaving like sensible school students for the forth coming year. However, that somehow got lost in being back home and getting in to the old routine that had existed before they went to England. Of course, that meant only one thing. Being in trouble.

Matters deteriorated rather rapidly when they got back in to the classroom. It did not help that Seth had become a very good mimic and had learnt to take off their school principal's voice very well. So well in fact that the twins decided they would use it to do a prank on the rest of the school. If only they had thought through what would be the consequences of such an action!

It was a Thursday lunchtime. It was as hot as a boiling kettle blowing to let you know it was ready for you to make a cup of tea. Bronwyn, Seth and their friends were saying how great it would be to be at the beach that afternoon. The tide was in and there was no wind. It would be perfect in this sweltering heat as well!

"It's going to be stinker hot in that class this afternoon!" One friend said taking in such a deep breath the hot air nearly burnt his mouth.

"Blimey mate! We've got history right, this afternoon. We're going to fry like chicken on a barbie in that classroom!"

"That air-con is lousy too!" Another added. Not looking forward to such a long, smelly session.

The friends slowly made their way along to the history classroom where the lesson was about to take place. Each continuing with their moans and groans about the heat as they went. But what could they do about it. Not a lot.

They might not be able to do anything about it but two others with them thought they could. Yes, the twins were beginning to play around with an idea.

"I'll tell you what Bronwyn! I saw the old principal going out in his big truck! I bet he's going to be out all afternoon. Tell you what, if we get in to the tannoy room, I could mimic his voice and send a message to the whole school, right. Maybe, I could wangle an afternoon off for us! What d'yer think, Sis? Shall we give it a whack!"

"Yeah! Let's give it a try, mate! Anything is better than being cooked as a fried egg in that classroom."

So as the rest of the school's children moved around the corridors to get to their various classes, the brother and sister managed to sneak in to the school's tannoy room unseen and hide themselves. They waited until lessons were under way and then they started to put their plan in to action.

"Good afternoon! Staff and pupils!" Seth's voice sounded like the principal of the school as he spoke on the tannoy system. Everybody was fooled. For who else would use the tannoy. "I am afraid we are going have to close the school this afternoon due to the heat. The old air conditioning system we have just can't cope! I know you will all be very upset at missing school. So, children you can all go home and we'll see you tomorrow. While, teachers, you can use this extra free time to stay in the classroom and do some marking and planning!"

Seth's voice was so like the principal's that not even the staff questioned what was being said and who was saying it.

Suddenly, there was an eruption of loud cheering from each corner of the establishment. The children were jumping for joy as they picked up their bags and clothing and were rushing out of the school as fast as they could. Before the school changed its mind about sending them home for the afternoon.

The teachers seemed to be just as happy to tell you the truth. Why shouldn't they be. The heat was just as intense for them too. Now they had an afternoon off to catch up with marking and planning. This would give them an evening free as well. Why would they complain.

It was about thirty minutes later the principal returned from his luncheon with colleagues at the Golf Club. He wondered why the school was so quiet. It was never that quiet. Even when the children were studying in their classrooms it was never that quiet. He thought it was odd as well as he could not see any children in the classrooms at the front of the school as he entered the building. Even at that point, he knew there was something wrong but had no idea what. But things were about to explode.

"Where is everyone? It is as quiet as a library reading room in here." He asked as he approached the Deputy Principal. She was marking pupils work in her classroom.

"Yes, it's very quiet isn't it with all the children having gone home!" His deputy smiled unaware of the deceit that had taken place.

"Gone home! The children have gone home?" The perplexed leader looked at her as if he had been struck by a renegade thunderbolt.

"Yes! Gone home! As you told the pupils to!" She could see her boss was looking confused by what she had said. Suddenly, it began to raise doubts for her too as to why he would send them home.

"I never did any such thing! As a matter of fact, I have only got back from an important meeting!" The "by now" very angry head of the school was getting even angrier.

The Deputy Principal stood up in horror as she began to realise the staff, plus herself, had somehow been tricked. How could that have happened!

"But we all heard you speaking to us over the tannoy system, Principal. You said the school will be closing this afternoon due to the air-con not working properly!"

The principal shook his head in anger. "How could I have done that when I have only just returned from being out for lunch!"

"Well! If you didn't give out the message over, the tannoy system, who did?" This was the next obvious question.

They both made their way to the office and started watching the CCTV footage to try to establish who had gone in to the tannoy room about the time the message was put out. It was not long before the finger was pointed quite firmly at two particular children. Yes, the twins.

What could they do but admit it. Although, they became naughty heroes to their fellow pupils, it was not so with the parents of the school. Parents told their own children to stay away from those two awful twins. They were nothing but trouble. While the principal and the School Governors labelled them as 'behavioural delinquents.' The decision was made that they would be suspended from the school until further notice!

You may be thinking things could not get any worse for the twins after pulling that prank but you would be wrong.

On their return to school, the Prime Minister of Australia, who had been visiting Adelaide, decided to visit the establishment. The pupils were to be allowed to go and wave national flags as he departed from the school. The principle had already thought about what to do with the twins. He did not want them to ruin this important visit. They were to stay with a teacher in a separate classroom well out of the way. The teacher was told for no reason could they leave that classroom until their honoured guest had left. The school did not want any embarrassing moments.

Once the prime minister had left the school building, the teacher told the twins they could go to join the children outside and watch the prime minister driving off. What harm could they do now the teacher thought. Hence, Bronwyn and Seth dutifully made their way out to the front of the school where everyone was watching the very important dignitary leave. The twins, who were at the back of the crowd, couldn't see over everybody's heads.

This left them frustrated. Hence, their eyes were drawn to the ground where they discovered there was a bank debit card sitting there right in front of them. Nobody else had seemed to have noticed it. They were all too busy watching the prime minister depart. Each of the twins nodded to the other in agreement that they should pick it up as no one was looking and put it in their pocket until later.

A quick bob to the floor and the deed was done.

*****

"Who d'yer reckon this S. Morrison is anyway, Sis?" Seth asked as he looked at the name on the bank card.

"Don't know who he is, bro!" His sister replied. "What d'yer reckon we should do with it?"

"No idea!" Seth shrugged his shoulders! "But reckon we could have a bit of fun with it!"

"What y'thinking?" She looked at him. Her eyes beginning to light up at the thought of a bit of fun. One thing for sure was they both liked fun.

"Well! We could go and buy some sweets and things with it!"

"D'yer reckon!" Bronwyn smiled like a tickled baby. "That would be buckeroo good!"

Soon they had agreed on the plan. The plan was to go to the shop and use the debit card to have a big feast of sweets. These they would eat in the park before going home. They were sure no one would know anything about it.

In the supermarket the twins did go a bit wild with getting the sweets, cakes and fizzy drinks. Perhaps, a bit too wild. They needed to get a number of hessian carrier bags to carry it all in. No one confronted them about using the debit card as it was only a small amount. All they had to do was flick the card up against the card machine and that was it. They could walk out of the store. No questions asked. Immediately, the sum was deducted from the card owner's account.

The twins left the shop double quick with their heavy bags. Both were soon to be found sitting in their local park having a real sugar fest. There was no way they would be eating their dinners that night.

"Wow! Isn't this great!" Bronwyn laid back in the shade of a eucalyptus tree stuffed full as a rabbit in a field full of delicious dandelion leaves.

"I don't think I'll be able to walk again! I'm as full as a fat bull frog!" Her brother laughed fully bloated.

While they lay there, they heard some police sirens going through the town but thought no more about it. Like most towns, it was not unusual to hear such high-pitched sounds during the day.

It was only when they arrived home and found there were four police vehicles with flashing blue lights outside their house that they began to think they were in big trouble. Not just any old trouble but really big trouble! There were policemen waiting at the cars, others waiting at the open house door. It didn't look that good. The twins were certain it would be to do with them. They were beginning to wonder what was going to happen to them this time!

"Bronwyn and Seth?" They were asked as they got to their house by a very senior policeman with lots of ribbons and glossy silver bands on his uniform.

They nodded and were ushered inside the house where a very upset mum was sitting on the couch watching them enter.

"Ah! Yes! These are the two we caught on the video!" An official speaking plain clothes officer raised his eye-brows at them both! "Did you have a lovely feast on all those sweet things you bought."

They weren't sure whether to admit to what they had done or not!

Their mum helped them make the right decision. "It's no use yer denying it you two idiots! They got yer doing it on camera!"

"We're sorry!" Both twins now knew their best approach was to look small, contrite and apologetic. They had been in this situation many times before. They knew the game. From past experience they had learnt this was the best way to be either let off or receive a lesser punishment.

"Well! You two monkeys have you got anything left of all that rubbish you bought?" The plain clothed police officer asked.

They both shook their heads.

"That came to 25 dollars you know! That's a lot of money you have stolen. And you both know it is stealing don't you!" He looked seriously at them. They both nodded their heads. "You're both in big trouble!"

"Did you realise it was the prime minister's debit card you had taken?" The more senior detective asked them.

The twins looked at each other in shock. Then after the biggest gulp ever, they shook their heads at the officer. Now they were really shaking in their boots. The prime minister himself!

Their mother let out a howl with shame and worry. She was concerned as to what was going to happen to her two little darlings. If it was in England, they could be locked in the Tower of London and the key thrown away.

At that point the detective's mobile phone rang. He began to explain to whoever he was talking to on the device, that the thieves had been apprehended and were here with him now. He explained the thieves had turned out to be two young pupils at the school the prime minister had visited.

It was they who had found the card on the ground. Then they had used it to spend the money on a bunch of sweets, fizzy drinks and cakes. The speaker on the other end seemed to laugh. Then the detective sitting opposite the twins began to say a lot of "Okay!" and "Yes, sir!" as the conversation went on. The twins could tell the detective was talking about them. He kept looking at them as if they were hardened criminals and shaking his head as if in despair.

"Are you sure, Sir!" He replied at the end. "Okay, Sir! If that is what you have decided."

He put the phone down and turned to look at the twins with a serious look in his eye. "You two are lucky! The prime minister and the bank have decided not to bring any charges against you! Given that you have got the debit card and can hand it back over to me now!"

Within the quickest instant you have seen, the twins produced the card and handed it over. They were only too pleased to be getting rid of it. It was like holding a whole bunch of fat wiggly worms in your hand once they knew it was the prime minister's.

"The prime minister has also requested that you do not mention this whole episode to anyone. Any of you!" Here, he looked from the twins to their mum and back again with a slight threat in his eyes as if he was a Spanish inquisitor.

All nodded back at him with great sincerity. Each only too pleased there was going to be no further repercussions.

"I can assure you we won't officer!" She looked firmly at her two children to ensure they fully understood!

The twins said, "No way! Our lips are sealed!"

And so the column of vehicles departed with as much haste as it arrived.

Their mum did not give them an easy time after the police vehicles had left but that was nothing unusual to them both.

You may consider these to be the only things the twins got up to over the year but you would be very, very wrong. These tales are only the tip of the enormous iceberg. They never seemed to learn. They made promises after promises and although they always had the intention of keeping them they never did! Never could! We all know it wasn't in their nature!

Perhaps, the last one that finished their mum off was when they were made to do home tutoring. After the incident with the prime minister, the school was too afraid to have them anywhere near it. Hence, their mum was having to work from home herself to be with them. In this way she could keep an eye on them. It was decided the twins would receive lessons on line from the school. Lessons that they would undertake with the teachers available for help on the internet if required.

Eventually, it got to the point where their mum needed to pop in to the office to pick up some important files to carry on with her work. She knew she would not be too long. So, she decided to take a chance and trust them by themselves for a short period of time. What else could she do. "It would not be too long," she told herself. When she left, she made them double promise not to get up to any sort of tricks and so on!

After their mum departed, a new lesson was about to commence. Perhaps, their mum would not have left if she had known what it was. For the lesson coming up was a home cookery lesson and involved the twins baking. They were meant to ask their mum to get out some ingredients ready at the start of the day in preparation for this lesson. As you can imagine they both had forgotten. The lesson involved making a cake. Are you beginning to get as worried as I am.

Hence, here they were about to start the session but without the ingredients they would need. Realising the predicament they were in, they quickly ran to the food cupboard and fridge to get the items on the list that would be required for the cooking session. They were back at the computer screen just in time for the lesson. The teacher spoke to them over the video-link and clearly laid out the order of doing things. They were given the exact measurements of each ingredient to put in at every stage.

Whether they were not listening, weren't that interested or became flustered I am not too sure but they were soon adding in huge amounts of extra ingredients compared to what they were being asked to put in. If you were kind, you would say they were not too sure what to do. Others would say they were just being the devils they were.

"Have you put in the two ounces of flour?" The teacher asked.

"Yes!" They replied in tandem. But they had not counted the amount gone in at all. Just poured in any amount from the packet. Both of them were not showing any interest in following the teacher's instructions. What did it matter about the amount you put in, it all cooks anyway. They did not seem to realise the need to stick to specific amounts or it could affect the outcome of the cake.

"The oven should be lovely and warm by now and ready for you to put the cake mixture in!" The teacher iterated. "Don't forget to use oven gloves for safety!"

They readily obeyed by putting on the oven gloves and lifting the cake that was on its tin plate in to the oven. Once the oven door was closed and they could see the mixture inside, they stood back feeling quite proud of themselves. The smells in the kitchen were very tempting and they could not wait for the cooking part to be completed. They could then get on with having some of that wonderful cake to eat!

Next the teacher asked them to sit down and write about what they had done. She would talk to them again in twenty minutes or so to discuss their written work.

"You can then read back to me what you have written and we can check to see how your cake is coming on. Okay twins?" She asked full of joy.

"Okay!" The twin smiled back equally full of joy. They were looking forward to eating the cake they had made.

"We'll save some for mum and dad!" Bronwyn suggested.

"Of course, Sis! They'll be mighty proud of us two! Our first cake!" Seth agreed. Uncertain how much he could eat anyway. The cake they had put in the oven was pretty big. He did think to himself the teacher's cake on the video looked a lot smaller.

And it wasn't long before the repercussions of the overloading of ingredients in the cake began to cause problems. Neither of them understood that it was yeast that made the cake rise. They had put in huge amounts of that ingredient. Even though the teacher's instructions suggested only a small teaspoonful was required. Of course, they had other ideas and put in the whole packet.

There was the excess of baking powder they put in as well. Far more than the teacher's list had recommended. They decided they would like to ensure it was well baked and so added loads of baking powder. Seth had not bothered to break the eggs open but put them in whole before stirring them in. While they both agreed they liked sugar in their cake. So, they decided to put in extra-large spoons of it to match their taste. Licking the spoons as they did it.

The twins then sat down at the table and were attempting to write what they had done in this home economics lesson as the teacher had asked them to do. Ready for when she came back on line.

"Blimey mate! That smells really good!" Seth put his nose in the air and smelled the wafting aroma of cake baking around them.

"I can't wait to eat it!" Bronwyn was already feeling as hungry as a crocodile in a local gum tree river full of fat fish.

"I bet it's going to be fantastic!" Seth licked his lips.

"Mum will be really proud of us!" Bronwyn smiled. Pleased to please her mum.

Then there was a mighty boom! The explosion blew the door off the cooker oven. It was loud and short. Fortunately, for the twins the door blew off in one piece. Flying across the kitchen, smashing through the kitchen window and straight on in to the garden. There it finally settled on the now scorched grass.

In fear they both ducked underneath the table they had been working at, when the cooker oven door blew off, flew across the kitchen and out the window.

Before both the children could gather their wits, there were four more horrendous bangs. Out of the cooker oven shot four eggs exploding as they hit the far kitchen wall on the other side of the room. Leaving a splattered yellow mass running down its side.

Next to emerge from the source of all this action was black smoke and a hissing sound. This was soon followed by sharp popping sounds and the appearance of a bubbling mass.

The twins could only look on in terror wondering what on earth was going to happen next. It was then from the blackened oven entrance began to crawl out the oozing splurge of a brown and black mixture spilling on to the floor. You would have thought there was a cake making factory inside the oven that could not turn itself off. The trouble was it did not look like cake at all. It looked more like a running river of horrible sludge that kept on coming.

Of course, it had to be at that moment their mum arrived back. You can imagine her face as she opened the kitchen door and looked around her at the mess. She dropped the files she was carrying and raised her hands to her mouth in horror as she had done many times before with things that the twins had got up to!

"What on earth is going on here!" She screamed in fright. "I was only away for a few minutes!"

Looking through the black smoke she could see her two children hiding under the table, the smashed window, her wall caked in egg and shell, the floor oozing with running cake and when she looked at her lovely cooker, its door was missing. Where the door had gone at that point she had no idea.

"Hello Mum!" Said Seth.

*****

"Go!" Mum gave in finally. "Yes! You can go!"

The twins had been on at their parents to let them return to England for the English school summer holidays. They wanted to stay with their aunt and cousin again as they had done last summer.

It had been so exciting last year they wanted to go back again. Hence, they had both been plaguing their poor parents about it. "Can we mum!" and "Can we dad!" These requests up until this moment had always been met with a noncommittal reply.

The twins jumped up and down for joy when it was finally agreed they could go back to England again! They were keen to meet up with their cousin and the puddle hoppers once more. They felt sure there would be adventures waiting for them as there was last year.

Their school was only too pleased for them to go as well. Saying how useful it would be for them to be in such a historically rich country. Both of the children would be bound to learn a lot there. One teacher even suggested they may consider staying in England. But only for educational development reasons of course.

Finally, mum had given in to their requests. Not only had they harassed her over going back to England but she was worn out with having to deal with the continual upheaval they caused. If it wasn't at school, it was at home or with the neighbours. Both their father and her were exhausted. The break would not only be good for the twins but would allow their parents to recuperate.

They both remembered when the twins were away last year for a long period in England, it was so quiet and peaceful. It was a period they did not have to think about what are the twins up to now? Where are they? What are they doing? They could relax and recover. Prepare themselves ready for their return.

Chapter 6

Underneath the town of Boreham Wood runs an interlinking underworld of sewers. These connect to other sewers in other towns and then on to other sewers that go out to the sea. These sewers beneath the town were a dark world where water runs along its bottom. In it are lots of horrible things from people's homes that have been washed down there. Some of the things should never have been put down there. Yet, some householders cannot be bothered to take them over to their dustbin. They just flush it down their toilets or sinks with everything else and say to themselves, "It won't matter!"

Running alongside the moving brown slush, rats and mice can be found rummaging about picking up scraps of food that have found their way in to the sewer system. They do not have to go up on the surface above ground very often as they can get enough food down in this underground world to feed themselves and their youngsters. As people infrequently go down in to the sewers to look inside this dark world or check it out, they are unaware of the huge sizes these subterranean creatures are growing to.

While, above the dirty waters itself in this subterranean world, can be found lurking all kinds of spiders and their webs making it very hard to see far in to the distance as it looks misty. In reality it is the spider webs that are in the way. Yet, not one of the spider webs doesn't have a flying insect in it. These smaller flying creatures buzz around in there, enjoying all the rotting food, the bruised fruit and the dying creatures.

However, it is only a matter of time before these small flying creatures find themselves caught in a spider's web. And through all of this lively activity flies the myriad of bats that somehow manage to make their way between everything and anything. Here they find their own insect food and enjoy the warmth coming from the decomposing wastage that heats up the sewer world and allows them to roost happily in peace.

Even though the sewer world smells really awful and, hence, council workers do not go down there unless kitted out like a spaceman on the moon, there is another stronger smell lurking. A smell that has grown more overpowering over the last few weeks. The creatures that live in this lower domain are still learning to come to terms with it themselves as there is no escape from its awful presence.

Council workers always go down in to this subterranean world in pairs as if they were boarding Noah's ark. Tied together by rope that goes right back up to the surface entrance. They only venture down there when there is a desperate reason. Telling their bosses categorically they will not go in too far for fear of what is down there. There had been rumours circulating for years about a council worker who went in to the sewers and never came out. It was said his disappearance was covered up by the council and the man was never heard of again.

The problem was that in to the sewers of Boreham Wood had moved a dark, foreboding creature. A creature that had never ventured in to that part of England before. Or, in recent times anyway. A dark looking, hairy creature that almost filled the height of the sewer itself as it moved along. No person above had any idea he was there.

It could slink around almost undetected by man in this underworld. Even the rats and mice avoided him and kept out of his way. This was a creature they had a natural fear of and hissed at whenever he came too close to them. Not that it frightened him. Not in the least.

His long straggly hair, thick in dirt and muck never got cleaned. That was probably the cause of his awful smell. Yes, you are right this was the source of the smell that was contaminating the whole of the town above and the reason why people were covering up their noses. Yet, it might be added, that the smell of his breath was even more than awful. It stank of ten sewage farms on each breath he breathed out.

His face was well hidden by the clinging mucky hair but you could see the whites of his eyes that gleamed through the glumness around them like two full moons in the night sky. His small, short ears stuck out either side but had the ability to pick up sounds quite a distance away. He would listen for movement and know where every small creature was in his vicinity. Even the movements of the spiders he was able to hear and plot. Yet, it was his own sense of smell that stands out.

For this creature could smell every single smell in a thousand smells around him. He would be able to name the smell and tell exactly who and where it was from. I need to warn you that if he opens his mouth you would be terrified by the gleaming white sharp teeth that faced you. This is probably why the local animals were all terrified of him. But you would not have to worry too much for I can tell you that he does not eat people. Or, at least, we do not think so. There may be the odd one here and there. However, there had not been enough studies of this creature undertaken or sufficient evidence to prove he did not.

Yet, he had found himself a lovely lair in this new underground world he had discovered below this town. A lair, where he could curl up and rest in peace. A place he could treat as a home. A large cavern that the workmen digging out the original tunnel system must have used as a base for themselves to meet and chat in between work shifts.

A place where their bosses would not be able to find them. The bosses would think they were working hard away at the tunnel face. For this creature it was a perfect lair. He had laid out some warm materials he had come across as some sort of nest. There he could lay and listen to the noises of water dripping and the gushing river of waste through the drain system he inhabited.

What he did snack on as he moved through these connected black tunnels were the spiders' webs themselves. Just to keep himself topped up with food. He particularly liked the big fat black spider's webs that stretched right across the width of the space. They were sticky and had fat fibres he could enjoy chewing on. Of course, there was often a lovely taste of juicy insects that had been pinioned on to the web. This gave his meal an additional flavour he adored.

There he sat in the sewer snacking on the threads of a spider's web as if it was candy floss, while the garbage laden brown, mushy sewage ran almost beneath him. You must remember that he thinks he himself smells lovely. He thinks the sewers he is living in smells lovely. He can't understand how anyone would want to live up on the land above.

"They not know what they be missing!" he says to himself with his own grunt of a laugh. "It be good here!"

While he lifted his long leg up towards his mouth so his toes reached his lips. This allowed him to begin to suck on the various pieces of muck caught up in the fur on his toes. There was no need to drink clear and clean water in his world for there was this lovely flowing sewage to provide all the drinking material he wanted.

*****

It is as night falls, this beast underneath the town begins to stir itself. He seems to know when the stars and moon appear in the sky. Perhaps, it is the change of the sounds or smells from above ground that his delicate ears and nose picks up on. He seems to know when people are going to bed.

Perhaps, he can hear the constant noise of their sleeping pattern sounds. But it is more than likely as he lifts up a sewer lid and enters the world above that he can smell what he considers the best smell in the world. A smell he goes in to ecstatic trances over. It is the smell of people's hair. He just loves the hair of humans.

"Me smells lovely hair me do!" He hugs himself in joyous bliss.

He replaces the sewer lid and slides his way in to the nearest, darkest tree and bush covering. Here he is soon lost in its darkness.

A few people pass only a few feet away as they make their way home from an evening out somewhere.

"What is that awful smell?" The lady comments. Even her expensive perfume cannot hide the obnoxious odour that comes her way.

"It isn't me! I showered two days ago!" Her partner commented panicking.

"You know, this town is getting to smell more and more like a garbage bin left open in the sun on a hot summer's day." She covered her nose up. Placing the wrist that she had put some perfume on before she came out for the evening over her nose. "I am going to complain to that mayor of ours! He's got to do something about this terrible stink."

The hair eater, for we shall call him that now, as we know what he has come above ground for, does not stir an inch. He is used to being invisible in this world above ground. He has learnt to move around unobserved.

"Um! Where lovely hair smell come from?" His nose rises higher and higher in to the air as he distinguishes one particular person's hair from the many others that he can smell around it. Do not get him wrong. They all smell lovely and he would love to eat them all. But that one is the one he knows he wants to eat more than any other at that particular moment. It had that richness of taste he really loved.

With his nose in the air, the hair eater follows the smell of the hair that he wants to eat along the walls of the gardens. Always keeping himself in the shadows to be more invisible than invisible itself. Slithering over fences and walls very low and lithe as a snake would progress.

Only his stench would give him away. But he would never know that for he does not believe he has a smell at all. His opinion is it is all the people who live above ground who have the bad smell. They need to get themselves covered in sewerage like he has. Then he believes they would all smell better.

Eventually he comes to the window where his nose tells him the smell of the hair he wants to eat is coming from.

"Ummm! Love it me do! Me want it me do!" A rousing smile spills across his hairy face and the white teeth appear. They have a job to do!

He cannot believe his luck as he hides beneath the window in another dark shadow. For the couple who live there have left their window slightly ajar. Little do they know it will be more than enough for the hair eater to slip through and do what he wants to do.

You may think that a fraction of an inch would not be enough for him to squeeze in through but, my goodness, you would be more than wrong. For this creature is able to squeeze himself in and make his bones quite rubbery so he can get through the tiniest of gaps. You could say no house is safe from him!

"Me wait good! Me no rush!" His eyes look in to the bedroom as the couple prepare to go to bed. Luckily, they do not see their observer. For they would be quite frightened to death by his hairy visage looking in at them.

"Whose turn is it to turn the light off tonight, my little sweetie pie?" The husband asks with a kind, gentle voice.

"I think it's your turn, darling duck!" Came the wife's giggling reply.

"Oh! Okay! I'll do it then, my little soap sud!" Up he gets and soon the room is in total darkness.

The hairy beast knew it always took time for his subject to get to sleep but he was prepared to wait before he feasted on their hair. His sensitive ears would listen out for the change in their breathing to know they were now in to a deep state of sleep. Then it would be time for him to slither in to the room so quietly he would be unnoticed and he could start to have his delicious meal.

Before the husband turned off the light, the hair eater had seen the woman's long bright and bouncing red hair that hung down her back. She had taken it out of its pins that held it in the day so it hung loose. You could tell she had just combed it. Probably a hundred times as recommended as a daily routine by many hair specialists. For the hair eater, red hair had a sort of fruity flavour that he enjoyed.

"Umm! Looks me good! Me love hair she got!" The hiding creature was mentally already feasting on the lady's hair in the bedroom.

The moon came out and went in countless times between clouds as he waited for their breathing to change. Yet, you would never be able to pick out this creature in this darkness then half-light. He was so well camouflaged. He was finding this couple, who he was waiting upon to go to sleep, were certainly fidgeting a lot. Tossing and turning. Perhaps, they had had too much coffee during the day and it was pay-back time?

Eventually, their breathing slowed as they entered the world of heavy sleep. They both lay totally still. Whereas, before they were shuffling around and scratching here and there. Hence, it was time for the hair eater to go and get his first meal of the evening.

With great dexterity, without the slightest murmur of a sound, he inched himself through the slenderest of gaps. Pulling his body this way and that as if he was a plastic putty creature. Until he slipped in to a dark corner of the bedroom itself. All this was done without the couple even changing their breathing. Then as slow as a sloth, but following the shadows he got nearer and nearer to his prey. The lady with the long red hair whose locks he was going to eat.

"Ummm! This be good!" He pulled his hairy fingers with long finger nails through the fresh and airy red hair. Smelling the vibrant smell coming from it. "Me ready to eat now! Red hair for me! One of my favourites!"

Lifting himself up by her side, so you could see a dark ghostly figure leaning over the lady. He started nibbling on the soft delicate ends first. Chewing each delicious mouthful with ecstasy written all over his face. That is if you could see it. He had perfected how to eat without making a sound. His razor-sharp teeth could bite through a number of strands simultaneously without as much as a moment of strain. Each mouthful moving closer towards the roots of the once long beautiful hair.

If the lady woke up now, she would scream the world down with fright. But no one ever woke up! It was as if the creature had hypnotised them to stay asleep. To stay asleep and not realise what was going on while they slept so peacefully. Often the victim had a set smile on their face. Not even the increase in that awful smell right next to them seemed to register alarm. They slept through it all like a new born baby with a rubber sucker teat in its mouth.

"Me much like! Me much like!" He whispered to himself with uncontrollable joy.

Her once long red hair that had stretched down her back now had only short bristles sticking up. The hair eater having consumed the lot. Food for his stomach. Food he needed to live.

Yet, now was one of his favourite moments in this ritual he played out most nights with someone's hair. For he was down to the remaining tufts. Using his sticky tongue, he wet the tufts and numbed the nerve endings. When ready, he then pulled his sharpest teeth across the head and all the remaining tufts were removed instantly.

For his teeth were like a razor on a man's face cutting off the day's bristle. Hence, he left the person's head not only bald but as smooth as a baby's bottom. The person would wake up in the morning with a real shine on their head. Not that they appreciated it.

Some uncaring people, who do not understand how sad it is to lose all your hair, even say, "Hey! What's the problem it will grow back! Don't worry!"

Before he departed, the hair eater would then lick up the last bits and have a final chew. There was disappointment he had no more hair to eat on this woman's head. It was all over! It had all gone! He felt quite upset. He had been enjoying it so much.

With a grump, he rubbed his stomach after such a fine first course for the evening.

"Umm! Me enjoy!" He quietly asserted before turning away to slither like the snake back along the floor and up to the window. With the same careful breathing in here and breathing out there he managed to squeeze his body back through the slit in the window. So, in the morning the couple would believe it was impossible for anything to have come in that way. Let alone something that would steal the wife's hair. If only they knew!

Once back outside and sitting beneath the window he could afford again to relax. First mission of the night accomplished.

"That be good! Me good! Me like!" He continued to say as he disappeared back in to the bush and shrub cover. There, once again, he put his nose in the air to find the next victim for that night! The hair eater had to eat and eat he would.

You would think he would only go for red headed people as he liked red headed people obviously. However, you would be wrong. Definitely wrong. For during the evening he would want to vary the types of hair he would eat. For just like you or me for a meal he would want different types of food. None of us would eat potatoes and nothing else. Or cucumber and nothing else. No, we have a variety of different things we eat in any meal. Well, it was the same with the hair eater.

He would enjoy next perhaps a less sweet tasting hair, such as blond hair. Or a more bitter tasting head of hair such as a dark brown colour. Sometimes, an older head of grey hair was enjoyable as it gave a chewy mature taste to the bite. Children's hair was a real treat, it was like having a young lamb's meat or a piglet's chops. Children were funny as they often didn't even realise their hair had gone the next morning. They would think they must have had a really short haircut the night before and could not remember it at all.

Other times, this night visitor would go for short cropped hair as it was like a freshly cut lawn and his razor-sharp teeth would cut long strips off in a line like a lawn mower cutting the grass one way first then the other. This hair often tasted of salad such as lettuce or celery. Another type of hair he particularly liked was hair that had been dyed. The colours of the dye often giving each mouthful of hair he ate a real alternative taste to normal hair. Yet, dyed hair often left him with burps. This he never understood why.

Of course, some hair he would save for later to snack on. Wrapping it up in old newspaper like fish and chips from a fish and chip shop. The smell was like a fragrance of fresh flowers to him. This he would keep in his lair until he was ready to eat. It made a change from spider's webs.

Once more hidden amongst the undergrowth, he was able to raise his nose up in the air to find his next meal. There among the thousands of smells entering his nasal entrance, he would begin to isolate particular hair smells that he liked. Choosing one, then the other until he decided on what hair was to be his next meal.

"Hummm! That smell good! Me want that one!" His long tongue running over his wetted lips as he imagined eating what he could smell.

With his usual care he began to move through the hedge cover in and out the shadows slowly and carefully. Always ensuring he was hidden from the view of any human onlookers. Getting nearer to the man's short dark brown hair he so fancied eating next. His taste buds getting more and more aroused.

"Can you smell that?" A man's voice utters to his female partner as he draws close to where the hair eater is hiding.

"What can it be! It's like ten thousand dead cats piled high and left by a dustbin for a week!" His partner replied.

"This town is getting to smell worse and worse as the days go on! And no one seems to be doing anything about it!"

"It's all to do with that factory explosion! The mayor says it will go eventually!"

Each looking over towards the right place where the smell was coming from. It was, as if they knew, something strange was over there but were unwilling to accept it. Obviously, it was the place where the hair eater was hiding. Yet, he was so well hidden amongst the shadows and undergrowth he was unobserved.

Frozen to the spot as he always was as people passed, he stayed still until they had moved on. Then and only then, when all was still and quiet again would he slowly wend his way towards the smell he so desired. Slow footstep followed by slow footstep, with his nose raised in the air picking out that one smell amongst all the others around him as the one to follow.

*****

Finally, at the end of the evening having gorged on five people's hair, the very full-up creature began to make its way back to the sewer entrance he had crawled out of many hours ago.

"Hmmm! Me full-up now! Me eaten much! Me need sleep!" He burped and burped and held his stomach as it erupted with all the food he had eaten swilling around. Rubbing the last vestiges of dried elderly man's hair from his mouth that he had as his final meal, so the miniscule bits fell on to the ground. There is no doubt if a Sioux Indian had been on his trail there would have been enough tiny bits of hair remaining on the ground where he had been that night to allow the expert tracker to trail his every movement over the course of the evening of stealth.

"Hey! What are you up to?"

A voice loomed large as the hair eater broke his cover to cross the road.

The creature turned to see on the other side of the road a policeman standing there watching him slip from one shadow across the street to another shadow on the other side of it. The hairy creature had not spotted the policeman at all. The beast was normally so well versed in what and who was around him that it was odd how he missed this watchman of the night.

He had even missed the slight breathing the man was making and the smell of his fusty clothing. The hairy eater had mistaken the breathing for a nearby cat that had leapt on to the wall between them and the fusty smell was blown by the wind in the other direction.

Yet, the main reason he probably missed the man in blue was that the officer had been himself hiding in a shadow without moving. The reason Sargeant Muddle was hiding was that he was keeping an eye out for a house thief. He knew this thief was robbing properties in the area. This was a particularly clever robber, who left no clues as to who he could be but managed to take the valuables of numerous well-to-do people almost unnoticed.

The hair eater could kick himself for missing the policeman in the shadows. He had dropped beneath his own standards of being extremely cautious when hunting after dark. It had been a long, long time since he had been spotted by a human being but this was an important reminder to be far more vigilant in the future.

"Hey! You! Where you going? Come here!" The tall man in his very important blue uniform called out. He was used to people doing exactly what he said. The three stripes on his arms often gave him an authority that none would argue with normally.

However, this dark creature he was observing seemed to be taking no notice of the booming voice he was shouting with. Obviously, the man in blue thought he was on the trail of the thief who had done so many robberies. A law-abiding citizen would stop as he requested. It did cross his mind that this person moved very oddly and they seemed to slip quickly through those shadows as a fox on the prowl.

Yet, he did not for a moment think it could be anything but another person. Moreover, he felt sure it was the person he was after. It was more than likely that such a successful thief would be able to slide easily, almost unobserved, in the night as the person he thought he had been observing could do.

"I'm an officer of the law! I demand that you stop!"

The shadow seemed to move away even faster from the sergeant as he shouted more at him.

The hairy eater's rush to get away was followed by the officer raising his whistle to his mouth and giving a full long blast on it. Such a loud call woke up a lot of sleeping people in the vicinity who wondered what was going on.

The shadow in front of the policeman slithered over a fence and faded in to the darker world of a garden. Before slinking over two more garden walls without making a sound. Even though he was moving far faster than his pursuer could run.

"I know you're in here somewhere!" His follower called out in to the first garden the creature had disappeared. He thought he had cornered the thief he was chasing. Not realising his prey had already departed over a couple of other garden walls.

He began searching every inch of that space before looking over the fence in to the next garden. He was puzzled how this person he was following had somehow disappeared.

By this time the hair eater had climbed over the fence on to the street where the sewer cover to his underworld was. He made sure no one was about for he did not want another mistake. With his usual skill, the creature lifted the cover in absolute silence and slipped in to the underworld before replacing the lid above him without a sound. All of this, the police officer was totally unaware of.

"Me be safe now! Me be safe!" A smile crept over the creature's face.

While above him the man in blue continued his search. Certain he had the thief somewhere very close to him. This was a chance he did not want to miss. He had been after him for weeks and now he believed he was so close. So close.

"I'm going to get you! I know you are in here somewhere! I saw you enter the garden!" The policeman had a hint of desperation in his voice.

Yet, if he had considered the strong smells that were emanating from the garden, he would, perhaps, have questioned his own determined opinion. For there was something very odd about the smell he had been following since he had spotted the moving figure. In his own head he was so convinced the figure he saw had to be the thief he never reconsidered that the movements were odd for a human being. Or, that if anyone smelled that bad, he would immediately pick it up at the various houses where the burglaries had taken place. Moreover, if he had trusted his nose, it would have led him over the garden walls and to the sewer where it disappeared down. However, the sergeant was not used to trusting his nose in the matter of tracking thieves.

*****

"Aghhhhhhhhh!" There was a look of horror on her face as she finally looked in the mirror. The cold breeze coming in through the slightly ajar window seemed to be very cool on the top of her head. When she felt it, she wondered why she couldn't feel any hair. Yet, her mind would not let her believe no hair was there. That could not be! Her mind only suggested she go and look in the mirror to find out why she could not feel any hair on her head.

It was when she looked in the mirror, the look of fright pulled her face down so low her bottom jaw nearly hit the bathroom tiles. For it was true she had no hair! It had all gone over night. How or why, she had no idea. It was all there last night and now she did not have a trace of hair on her head. It had all been removed so only a very shiny skin surface remained.

"My beautiful hair has all disappeared!" She screamed so loud you could hear her two blocks away and wondered what on earth was going on!

Her husband leapt out of bed still somewhere between sleep and awake and not too sure what was going on. But on hearing his wife's scream he knew he had to be doing something and after finding his bearings and where his wife was, he dashed in to the bathroom.

"My Goodness!" Was all he could say as he viewed his wife standing there with even less hair on her head than him. And that was saying something!

They looked at each other in a state of shock for a few moments while his wife carefully passed her hands over her new shiny head. Still both disbelieving what they were seeing.

"But this is what has happened to others in the town! It has been on the news! People have been waking up bald!" She bellowed. "And now it has happened to me! How could that be! The windows were open only a fraction so no one could get in. Nothing could have got in through there could it?" She looked at her husband in disbelief.

"Well! No!" He scratched his head. Feeling at the same time that his hair was still there. Although there was not a lot of it. "But they say it grows back to normal!" He tried to calm her down but, perhaps, it was not the best thing in the world to have said.

"Grow back! Grow back! I will be bald for weeks! What am I going to do!"

"Well, we can get you a wig in the meantime! That will do!"

She looked at him in dismay! He had no idea about the horrors of trying to wear a wig for months.

"What on earth could have taken my hair in the middle of the night! I didn't hear, see or feel a thing! Did you!"

"No! Of course not! Otherwise, I would have done something to prevent it happening!" He replied with vigour. Knowing he had not heard a single sound or seen a single thing.

Each in turn of those who had lost their hair that night woke up and was greeted with the shock of their lives. None had heard or seen anything and no one could explain how their hair had disappeared.

One boy scratching his head in the morning said to his mum, "I thought I was dreaming mum, about Dad's lawn mower going over my head as he was cutting the grass. I thought I had imagined that he did not see me as I was laying there.

But you know, mum, it must have really happened!"

His mum screamed as she looked at her son's bald head.

A lady who had dyed her hair pink for a party, woke up and felt her head and yelped in horror at her hair's disappearance. "Someone stole my hair at the party last night while I was not watching!" She screamed while a lady with long curly afro-styled hair woke up and when she felt it had all gone, screamed as she looked at herself in the mirror, "Ah! I've become my Grandad!"

Some conspiracy theorists suggested that the people losing their hair, was due to too much chemicals being used in the shampoos. They suggested soon everybody would lose their hair! This caused a lot of panic and all the hair shampoo companies had to reassure the public their products were safe.

Others put forward the idea that there was something in the water that was causing this to happen. They suggested everybody stops drinking tap water! Once again, the water companies had to pacify the public by reassuring them there was no problem with the water.

Another alternative theory was that radiation was leaking out of the sky and affecting people so some were now losing their hair! They suggested everybody stay at home indoors. Or, if they had to go out, it was best they wore something made of steel, like a saucepan, on their head to protect them from these rays.

The prime minister had to do a national broadcast to say this was untrue. The sky was not leaking any radiation. He assured people they could go out and did not have to wear saucepans or anything else on their heads.

*****

"When are you going to prosecute that evil woman!" The mayor shouted down the telephone at the Chief of Police.

"She blew up my factory and you haven't locked her up in jail yet! What is going on! I thought the police were here to protect us! You should be doing something before she sets another place on fire! I only took her on as I felt sorry for her! Through the kindness of my heart. If I had realised she was a danger to everyone else in the building, I would have never let her work at my factory."

"But Mayor! You have got to understand we have to let the legal process take its natural course." The Chief of Police tried to appease his boss. Knowing full well that he was up for re-appointment in a few weeks and this could cause the mayor to look for someone to replace him. "Don't worry! She will soon appear before the judge and jury and I am sure she will get what she fully deserves!"

"But when will that be Chief Inspector? You should be pushing the judge to get this case heard immediately as it is of such importance to the town. Then she would get the prison sentence she truly deserves!"

"We are issuing a writ today, mayor, stating she caused the explosion by wilful negligence and has brought about major environmental issues for the town with the ensuing horrible smell."

"Good! I hope you will brief the media on the writ you are issuing!"

"We certainly will, mayor!"

"Then everyone will know who is truly to blame for this catastrophe!"

*****

Constance had received the writ from the public prosecutor informing her that she must appear before the court in a week's time for causing the explosion at the factory through sheer negligence. The letter stated that her action further provoked an environmental health problem right across the town and has caused major medical issues for many people.

She cried on opening this letter from the prosecutor. Of course, it was not unexpected. She was aware how the mayor was attempting to blame the whole explosion on to her. He was using his many connections in the police department and town hall to manipulate those officials to ensure she would get the maximum sentence for the deed. She felt certain with the mayor's encouragement the judge would pin a very heavy sentence in jail on her.

Even though she knew she was innocent. But her greatest worry was what would happen to Jules during her imprisonment. Would he be put in to social care while she was incarcerated. That was the last thing in the world she wanted for her son. He did not deserve that on top of everything else that had gone wrong in his life.

It was unfortunate that the letter telling her to appear in court arrived the same morning that she was due to start the first full day of her new job at Mr. Brian's brother's food factory. As you got nearer to the building the bad smell that lingered around the town gave way to an even worse stink that hung over the factory belonging to Grunswick Brian.

You could not but help see the continual dark shadow that seemed to engulf the whole place. Yet, there was not a cloud in the sky. As Constance entered the factory, a cold shiver ran down your back.

Constance entered this dull, forbidding place and made her way to where she had been told she would be working. She looked up and could see the overbearing figure of Grunswick sitting in his office looking down at the factory floor. He was ensuring he kept an eye on everything that was taking place below. Anything untoward happening or anybody not getting on with their work, you could be certain within a few seconds, Grunswick would be there sorting it out.

"Production must not be held up at any cost!" That was his philosophy.

In the gloom, she could see all the other workers working. Yet, none of them looked up at her or attempted to greet her as she passed them by. Smiles were in short supply. It was obvious the strict rules had to be adhered to and it forbid anyone to stop working and welcome her. Their heads were bowed down in the semi-darkness and it appeared the work they were undertaking was all that was on their mind. Or, should it be said, was allowed to be on their mind.

"So you're the new one!" A dark figure that fitted in with the dark gloom spoke to her. "You sit there and you have to get all those onions cleaned and cut in half-an-hour! After that, I'll have another job ready for you! Do you get it!"

She nodded and looked at the huge beast of a man standing over her. The colour of his skin was almost a pale grey and his clothes seemed to be like all the other supervisors in the building a sort of oily green colour. She had not noticed before but there were many supervisors. There was one at almost every group of five or six tables.

They watched intensely every movement of the workers they were responsible for. In case anyone was not working or wasting time. Their greasy hair matched their slippery features and each one's face looked almost an exact copy of the others. It was as if they were clones. They each had wide facial features and monkey-style mouths that could not attempt a smile even if they wanted to.

Sitting down she set about her work. She was surprised there were other bits of food waste stuck on to the actual onions. These she had to knock off with her knife. Hence, it was not hard to tell that these onions were not fresh but had more than likely been disposed of by cooks in restaurants or were leftovers from people's meals.

These onions certainly had not been gathered freshly from fields. There was no soil to brush off them. They smelled to Constance as if they had come from street bins. There was definitely a need to wash them down and check to see if they were presentable before being put in to a carton ready for re-selling!

"Come on! You are going to have to do better than that if you want to carry on working here! We work faster than that slow pace you have been going at!" Her own supervisor reached over her, his breathe as bad as the awful smell outside. "You'll never get that bag of onions done by later tonight at that speed. Get a move on! Or you'll be leaving here without a job and no pay for what you've done!" Saying that he picked up one of those old, almost brown onions and put it in his mouth and ate it.

Constance could not believe what she saw! There was no way she would eat that awful looking food. It should all be put in pig's swill as far as she was concerned and not to be re-used for human consumption.

It was then she stopped picking out the onions from the smelly bag and took a moment's break to smell her dirtied hands. Almost immediately, the phone near her desk rang. She didn't think anything of it as the supervisor for her section made his way over to the desk and answered it.

"What!" he said. "Hey you!" He pointed over to Constance.

"Me!" She replied.

"The boss says he can see you sitting there not getting on with your work! You better stay on and work an extra hour at the end to make up for it!" All this was said in an angry voice as if her taking a few moments out from working reflected badly on him.

She looked up and, sure enough, there looking down at her with his aggressive face still apparent was Grunswick. He was just about to put the telephone down.

"I knew this job was not going to be easy!" She thought to herself but she needed it and the money that came with it as well.

"Sorry!" she said to her over-seer and mouthed it to her boss up in his office as well.

After cleaning up the onions she was then told to repack them as new in containers for re-selling. It did not take her long to realise that the packets she was preparing for resale were the same ones that were being used by his brother to make pickles from!

It came as quite a shock to her that the other brother was not using fresh onions at all but these horrid recycled ones that she could see were really unfit for human consumption. Yet, on his jars Grunswick was putting the statement. "All freshly dug up from the local farms near you!"

Having to stay on and work late to make up for lost time, Constance was surprised that, under the cover of darkness, the containers she and others had filled were being shipped out. While, in contrast other lorries were beginning to arrive full of unwanted scraps of food. Food that smelled awful. They were full of unwanted waste food that Grunswick would clean up and resell as new and fresh.

Jules's mum really did not want to work at that place but she had no choice. No choice at all.

Chapter 7

"Twins! I've got no idea what's happening at this airport but I can't get near the ruddy place!" The twins' mother was driving them to the airport so they could start their journey to London.

Both the twin's father and mother had given in to their request. The truth was they both needed the break from these two walking disaster areas. Where ever they were there was sure to be a problem. It is true some of the time the problems were not of their making but still they seemed to attract catastrophe in the same way magnets attract small iron pieces.

Her intention was to see the twins on to the plane, wave them goodbye and then go for a meal with her husband as they looked forward to a well-deserved break from the two children they, unfortunately, had to call their own. However, at that moment, the roads in to the airport were jam-packed with cars and coaches.

There were plenty of car horns going off in frustration. No doubt, lots of people panicking as they had planes to catch or people to pick up. Yet, all the cars were getting nowhere as they sat in the queue that had not moved for quite a while.

"Look it'd be better if I drop yer here and yer both walk in through that door and straight down to where you catch the plane." She turned to look at them in the back of the car. "I am not moving anywhere in this car at the moment and by the time I get parked up pets, you'll miss yer plane!"

"Yer! We remember what to do from last year!" Bronwyn chirped up. "We'll be okay if you leave us here!"

"We can do it!" Seth nodded in agreement. "No sweat!"

"You've got yer passports and tickets on yer! So, there isn't going to be a problem! Just walk through that big door!" She pointed at it.

The traffic was still stuck and nothing had moved for such a long time it was beginning to look like she was sitting in a car park.

"That's no problem, mum! We'll just get out here!" Seth was already opening his door. He didn't have to worry about any passing cars as nothing was moving.

His sister and mother soon joined him getting the bags out of the back of the car. Their mum checked they had the right documents at hand and then it was hugging time!

"Now you two look after yourselves! Promise! Make sure you say 'hello' to your aunt and your cous' for me! And have a lovely time!"

"We will Ma!" they said together.

"And I look forward to seeing you in a few weeks!"

By now the twins were already giving their final hugs and kisses. They were soon starting to pull their cases along the path as their mum waved them off. She did not have to worry about getting in the car and driving off as there was still no movement in the traffic.

She did think about taking a chance that as the traffic was not moving she could leave the car and go and see the twins off in the airport. Yet, she realised, it would be just her luck the cars would start moving again while she was in the airport!

It was probably as well she had not gone in to the airport to wave goodbye to the twins, for a police officer outside the entrance ordered her back in to the car. The twins made their way through the grand door in to the departure lounge. They knew they had to go straight ahead to the Qantas desk. That is what they had done last year. Yet, the terminal was so busy, it was impossible to see through the mass of people in front of them.

"Cor! Kuala nuts! What's going on here then!" Seth wondered. "It's so crowded, it looks like they are sardines in an overcrowded sardine can!"

"Look at them! I wonder who they are!" Beth pointed towards the middle of the hall.

It was there she had spotted the ladies Australian cricket team and their entourage. They were at the centre of all that was going on in the terminal at that moment.

"Of course!" Seth nodded his head. For the penny had dropped. "It's the ladies Australian cricket team and they are on their way to play against England. That's why it is so busy!"

"Wow! They'll probably be on our plane then! How exciting, broth!" Bronwyn got quite excited about the prospect of famous people being on the same airplane as themselves.

The whole team stood there in the green blazers and grey flannel trousers looking exceedingly impressive. Each wearing a white shirt. Their brown shoes looking as if they had never been worn before as they glistened in the sun. You could tell they were happy or excited as they were laughing away and chatting not only amongst themselves but with anyone else who wanted to speak to them.

These, were mainly the media coverage teams, who had been sent along to get interviews at their departure. Everyone in the terminal was having to squint their eyes at some point as the camera crews' flashlights came on and went off in an instant. Each trying to get that perfect picture for the papers, radio and television that evening or the next day.

You could tell the managers and coaches of the team were getting a bit annoyed at the whole media show that was taking place around them. For the players in the squad were not making their way to where they needed to be for departure. They had become bogged down in this media circus. Those in charge of the players were trying to usher them along but with little effect as each player or group of players was involved in some sort of interview or discussion.

The twins, of course, were fascinated by all that was going on around them! They had never seen such a media scrum before as each vied with the others to get the best interview and film footage for their channel or newspaper.

They listened while some of these media people talked to their bosses back at the Head Office where ever that was. Their conversations entailed finding out what their media teams had gathered so far. Then there were discussions as to who they think they should interview next and the questions they should ask.

"Do yer think we should try and get through?" Bronwyn posed the question.

"We better! Or we might miss the plane and mum and dad would not be too pleased with us!"

They were about to set off when both of them were stopped in their tracks. They could not believe what they were seeing coming towards them through the main entrance. They were frozen to the spot.

"Is that what I think it is?" Seth finally asked his sister.

"I think it is but I can't believe it is either!" She responded just as amazed as her brother.

"Out the way! Out the way! Let us through! Let us through!" Shouted the man as he came in through the entrance. He appeared to think he was the most important person in the world as he called out to be given priority. The thing was, he was being given the priority he wanted. The crowd splitting apart to let him and who he was with through. Everyone turning to look at what was with him.

"It's a kangaroo!" A smaller girl called out. Saying what everyone was thinking.

"It's a bit small for a kangaroo!" Her dad replied.

"It's a roo, all right!" The man with the creature pointed out righteously. It was as if he expected everybody to know that. "It's a baby kangaroo! So please make way for us! Let us through! We have an important engagement with our ladies' national cricket team and the traffic has held us up!" His arm was moving people aside. He appeared not to realise that the traffic jam outside had caused a problem for almost everybody there not just himself.

The zoo keeper was pulling on a lead that had a collar attached around the young roo's neck. You would have thought he was taking a dog out for a quick walk. The keeper seemed full of self-importance wearing his blue uniform and peaked cap with a 'Zoo Keeper' badge written on it.

He was pulling the roo a long with such force the small creature was unable to hop at its natural speed to keep up. Hence, it was being forced to shuffle along as an alternative. After every other step, it seemed as if it was almost going to tumble over as it was dragged behind by its far more powerful but quite inconsiderate carer.

The roo itself was a perfectly formed miniature kangaroo with its brown fluffy coat and white napkin frontage. It's bob of a black nose standing out between the dark eyes that looked with concern from side to side at the crowds now around it.

The roo, at this point, was not standing too far away from the twins. Who, in turn, were staring back at it totally mesmerised.

Seth was the first to stroke it and say, "Hi ya, mate!"

Soon followed by Bronwyn. They both gave the small creature a warm cuddle as the keeper searched the hall to figure out where he should be. The roo rubbed it's head up against the twins as if it was forming a friendship. A much needed friendship in this noisy, crowded space. The twins fell in love with the creature immediately.

The keeper looked around the hall and spotted the ladies Australian cricket team. He knew that was where he should be. Without even looking down at his small companion, he started pulling the creature towards the centre of the hall where the players were still holding court. Pulling the small animal away from the hugs of the twins until the roo was beyond their reach.

"That's a lovely roo, Sis!" Seth smiled.

"Shame he's with that horrible keeper!" Bronwyn moaned. "Did ye see the way he was treated. It isn't right broth!"

"Yeah! Not good! That man is bit of a rat's arse!" Seth added.

The keeper and roo made their way over to an official with the cricket team. After a few moments of joviality, they were directed to wait beside where the players were still chatting to the media. The reason the roo was at the airport was so the players could have a team photo taken with a young kangaroo as a good-luck mascot for the coming tour. The media knew tomorrow morning's papers and channels would love such a cuddly creature alongside the team.

While the keeper kept his eye on the team official, waiting for his call to bring the roo over for the photograph, the twins took the opportunity to make their way over to their new adopted friend and started to share a banana with him.

"Yeah! You like that mate! Don't you!" Bronwyn smiled as the small creature tucked in to the fruit.

Both twins cuddled the creature and tickled it's back. The roo seemed to enjoy this personal, sensitive attention he was receiving from his new found friends. You got the feeling he did not get it from the keeper at the way he was tugged along on the lead. Sad to say, as well, in the whole time they had been at the airport, he had showed no sign of any warmth towards his traumatised ward.

"Hey! What are yer two doing down there!" The zoo keeper snapped at the twins as he looked down and realised finally they were cuddling the baby kangaroo who was under his remit. "You shouldn't be doing that! He might bite you and then I'd be in big trouble. Get away you horrible children!"

"We only gave him a stroke, mate!" Seth looked forlorn at the guard who in truth wanted them not to be anywhere near his kangaroo.

"He's a real beauty! He wouldn't hurt anyone! And I think he likes us!" Bronwyn continued to stroke him.

"Get away you horrible brats!" With that the frustrated keeper put himself between the twins and the animal ensuring that they had to move away. They had to move away quickly as well as he cruelly tugged on the roo's lead at the same time causing it to choke.

It was at this point, the cricket team official called for the keeper and his ward to come over and have the photograph taken. With one mighty pull, the poor roo was forced over towards the waiting team. The poor creature nearly choked again as the collar was tightened around its neck.

The cricket team were now assembling themselves in to two rows. They were carefully following the official photographer's artistic directions as to how he wanted to set them up. Of course, the roo was going to be centre stage. The frantic keeper was forced to leave the roo's leash with a player sat behind it while he was forced to sit in the wings and watch.

"You know Sis, he treats that baby roo real bad!" Seth shook his head in dismay.

"If only we could do something to help it!" Bronwyn sighed.

But what could they do.

Being the twins, they now set about trying to get in to the picture the photographer was about to take with the ladies' national cricket team. Ensuring that everyone in Adelaide would see them the next day in the newspapers and on the national TV stations.

A few times the camera man delayed taking the picture due to two children turning up in his viewer. Each time he tried to re-take it, they somehow reappeared somewhere else. In the end he gave up and took the photo anyway.

He told himself, "It brings a bit of reality and cuteness to the photograph by having two children in the background, I suppose."

Yet, by this time the twins had eyes only for the roo. To them there seemed to be nothing else happening in the terminal.

"We should try and help that poor creature Sis!" Seth nodded his head.

"Yeah! But how can we when we're leaving the country!" His sister posed the real reason why they could not help it.

Seth thought for a moment.

"We could take it with us!" Seth said it even though he knew it was never a possibility. Or was it?

The twins looked at each other and smiled. A wicked kind of smile. A smile, that if you knew the twins you knew meant they were up to some sort of trick or other.

They quickly made their way over to the nearest cuddly toy shop. There are lots of these shops at airports as people realise suddenly they have not got a present they had promised a child at home. Hence, these travellers rush in to get something, almost anything, their precious one at home would like. When they get home and they give the child what they had bought in a rush, they make up a storyline of how they had spent hours looking around the shops to find the perfect present.

It wasn't long before the twins eyed what they were after. They nodded to each other and looked about to ensure no one was looking at them. When they were sure, they quickly slipped a stuffed kangaroo in to one of their rucksacks without being noticed.

You may have guessed that the stuffed kangaroo was about the same size as the roo who was with the keeper in the airport terminal. It was also a very similar colour as well. In fact, you could say, it would be easy to mistake the stuffed toy for the real roo. Except of course, the stuffed one did not move at all.

The zoo keeper was busy talking to a very pretty young lady reporter about his wonderful, precious little roo and saying how much he loved it. The young cub reporter who loved animals was asking him very interesting questions that had her interlocutor having to concentrate on what he said in reply. Hence, he was not watching at all as two little people sneaked up close to him, undid the collar on the small creature and placed it around the neck of the stuffed toy instead.

The roo did not seem to mind what was going on. To be honest, it seemed the young kangaroo was only too pleased to go along with the two kind, gentle children who it had made such good friends with.

They quickly placed the roo in to one of their backpacks and, once more, sneaked back in amongst the legs of the surrounding adults until they were a fair distance away. Pleased with their work, they did high-fives and tried to reassure the young creature they had taken that it was in safe and kind hands. Both children knew they had to get out of the departure hall as soon as possible, before their kidnapping was discovered. With this in mind, they made their way over to the Qantas departure desk and started the "boarding the plane" process.

"Can I take a picture of the baby kangaroo with yourself!" The young cub reporter asked the keeper. "It would be useful to accompany the article I hope to write on you both!"

She got out her camera and looked down at the stuffed toy before her.

The keeper smiled in preparation. Straightening his hat on his head.

"Excuse me," she said politely with a somewhat puzzled look.

"Yes." The enamoured keeper smiled, by now very much in love with the adoring young reporter. As he had his eyes focused only on her, he had not bothered to look down at his ward for a long, long time. He was totally unaware of what had happened in the meantime. He had no idea he was standing there with a stuffed toy kangaroo beside him. He was convinced he was one of the stars of the moment with the small creature all adored under his wing.

"I don't like to say anything. But isn't that a stuffed toy kangaroo you're holding? Um... Not the real thing."

"Ha-ha! Don't be silly! Of course, it's a real kangar…" He looked down in a state of shock! "Where is it! What has happened to the roo? My goodness! Who's taken it? It's a… it's a stuffed toy. I've been tricked! It's been taken."

Within a few moments a cry had gone up around the hall that the kangaroo was missing and asking everyone to search for it. Soon people were searching their bags, looking behind cases and anywhere they could think a small creature like a young kanga could hide.

"It must be somewhere!" Called the keeper in despair. He was beginning to get worried as to how he would ever explain the loss of the roo in the airport terminal to his boss at the zoo. "Find that roo! Where is my roo?" He cried in terror.

The hall became even more chaotic as the tannoy system announced it was time to board the Qantas flight that was leaving for London. This was the moment all the travellers in the terminal had been waiting for. Everyone in the hall transferred their interest away from the roo to gathering their luggage and saying the final farewells to loved ones. There was a real excitement about the place.

No one noticed the small twins shilly-shallying between taller adults unobserved as they made their way to the gate for the plane. They managed to skip through passport control and the x-ray machines unobserved in the melee that was going on around the ladies' national cricket team. All normal rules for boarding airplanes seemed to have gone out of the window. Of course, this was to their benefit.

Yet, the zoo keeper in despair kept on calling out for his lost kangaroo as people departed.

"Where is he! Where is he!" His voice getting ever more dramatic as each moment passed. The keeper seemed to realise that once the crowd in this terminal had disappeared, the chances of him finding his baby kangaroo would diminish quite significantly.

Most people were not taking much notice of him by now. There was too much going on around them as loved ones began to depart.

"We've done it, Bro!" said Bronwyn as they were finally shown to their seats on the airplane. Being two younger people, without adults, the cabin crew on the plane were taking particular care looking after them. They helped the twins find where they should be seated and got them comfortable for the long flight ahead.

Of course, when asked by the sweet flight attendant if they wanted their backpacks to go up in to the hold above their seats, both shook their heads in fear of the roo being spotted. They said they were sure their bags would fit easily under the seat in front. The Qantas crew member smiled and left them to sort out what they needed from the backpacks! Little did she know the real reason they needed the backpacks on the floor beside them.

Chapter 8

The letter was waiting for Constance when she arrived home from work! She was exhausted and smelled of the rotten food she had been working with. All she wanted to do was have a shower and a rest before she did anything else. Jules had put the letter on the mantlepiece for her.

He must have noticed that it was from her sister in Australia. But his mum was always receiving letters from her sister as she, likewise, was forever sending them the other way. Yet, there was very little chance he could have guessed what it said inside.

"Do you want me to make you a cup of tea?" Her son asked as he saw her drag herself through the door and struggle to take her coat off.

"Oh! Thanks, dear! I would love one!" She smiled. She was so lucky to have such a lovely son. So kind and sensitive to anyone and everyone. "I'm going to have a quick shower!"

"Okay! Mum!"

She was about to make her way out of the living room to go upstairs to the bathroom when she changed her mind. "I'll open my sister's letter and read it first!" Constance thought it might cheer her up and revitalise her for the evening ahead.

"Oh no!" Were her first words as she read what her sister was writing about. She covered her mouth in surprise and shock.

"What is it?" Jules ran in to the room expecting to find his mother had fallen down or in some sort of catastrophic scenario. Yet, there she stood speechless and looking at her sister's letter. "What's wrong mum?"

"You better prepare yourself for this!"

"What, mum?" He looked at her confused. What on earth could she mean. Prepare himself for what!

"The twins are coming to stay with us again!"

"You mean Seth and Bronwyn!" The breath was almost sucked out of a stunned Jules. The thought of his two tearaway cousins being there once more and wondering what tricks they would get up to next quickly ran through his startled brain.

"Yes! They are on their way here already!"

"On their way already!" He seemed to be repeating his mother's comments as he took in this piece of information.

"I wish my sister had asked me beforehand! It is a bit more difficult this time I am sad to say!" She uttered.

The realities of what this meant was beginning to hit her.

"I have got a lot less money coming in at the moment compared to last year. So, I have no idea how we are going to feed them. And if I remember right, they do like their food! And I have this rotten job!"

"We'll cope mum! I'll eat less!"

"No! You will not! You don't eat enough as it is! You're as thin as a garden rake with wood rot anyway!"

"No I'm not!"

"Yes, you are sweetie! You are always on the go! Burning off energy! You're like a little rocket ship whizzing around through outer space!"

"Well! We can get cheaper food while they are here!"

"Yes, I suppose so! We will have to go to the cheaper supermarkets. It may mean a bit of a longer walk there and back! But we'll save lots of money by doing that! We have the problem of how we are going to entertain them without any spending money also!"

The sigh his mum gave showed how worried she was by the prospect of these two arriving at the present time. Of course, she wanted them to come. She loved having them but how was she going to provide for their needs during their stay was a big question that had to be answered.

"Well! If we search in our free local papers, we'll be able to find events taking place throughout the summer that cost nothing! They are always advertising things for youngsters to do during the holidays! They know parents need to keep their children entertained!" This thought came to Jules instantaneously as an idea they could use.

114

"That's a good idea!" His mum agreed. "Well considered, Jules!" It brought a smile to his mum's face.

However, the truth was as they both parted, Mum to go upstairs to the bathroom and shower and Jules to go back in to the living room to watch television, how were they going to cope with those two and their antics once they had arrived. Last year when the two of them came over, they managed to create chaos and disaster where ever they went over the course of their stay. Hence, both were wondering, what would they get up to this time.

Jules was further thinking over how they had often played tricks on him. He was under the impression before they arrived last year, that they would be kind and fun to be with. However, when they did arrive, he had a real shock. They were as opposite to that as could be. Maybe, as opposite as black and white. That is not to say that they were not loveable and good companions but they were playing tricks continually on their English cousin and getting him in to all sorts of trouble.

And one thing for sure, is that Jules never got in to trouble at home, at school or when he was out and about normally. Yet, when the twins arrived, this ability to stay out of trouble seemed for him to go out of the window. What was worse, was this time he didn't even have his Uncle Gideon there to help him to stand up to their antics and, in return, play tricks on them.

"Perhaps, they have changed!" He kidded himself. "Perhaps, they have matured to become a well-behaved boy and girl! It might be possible they have learnt from last year's events and will not be any trouble this time. They both could be kind, considerate and helpful. Perhaps, I am worrying without any real reason!"

Yet, even Jules could not bring himself to believe that. It would be far too much for the twins to have changed so within the space of a year. He did not feel it was in their character either.

"They are what they are!" He concluded in the end.

"You'll have to help me get the sleeping arrangements sorted out in your bedroom again! We'll do it later!" His mum called down from upstairs.

"Oh no!" He had forgotten how the last time they were there, one of the twins had ended up on his bed and the other on the fold-away bed. While he was relegated to the sleeping bag.

He thought to himself, "This time I will tell them that I'm keeping my own bed. They can have the fold-up bed and sleeping bag on the floor!" He nodded to himself determined not to let the same happen again this year.

*****

Police Sergeant Muddle was determined to catch the thief who his colleagues had been unable to apprehend for a long, long time now. This was his big chance. He would get a recommendation if he caught him and the elusive criminal was finally brought to justice.

The ruddy faced officer after chasing this clever foe was certain he had him trapped in the garden. He was so sure, if he kept on searching and searching in to every far corner of the greenery he would find him. There was no way he could have got over the wall to escape. Moreover, there was no way he could have sneaked out the gate. The officer was far too vigilant for that to happen.

Remember, he was a sergeant no less!

"He must be here!" He took his helmet off and scratched his head in dismay. "He couldn't escape without me seeing him!" So he continued the search. Looking in places where even he knew it was humanly impossible to hide for he had to be somewhere. His torch light flashing high and low in a desperate effort to find the elusive thief.

It was then there was a mighty splash as his foot went in to the pond. He had spotted the pond when he entered the garden but with his focus being on the robber he had forgotten about it. He was so busy looking in every other direction but down that he stumbled straight in to it.

As he tumbled, he fell over on his side. What was worse, he had put the whistle in his mouth a few moments earlier to free his hands. In the confusion, he gave accidently some very loud and long blasts in to the whistle. Within moments, many local householders, even though it was late at night, were at their windows trying to ascertain what on earth was going on.

This time, even the owner of the garden looked down to see what was happening. It was then he saw the torchlight in his own yard. He knew he had to go down and investigate. Quickly, he pulled on his clothes.

Police Sergeant Muddle had by now pulled himself out of the pond and found that he was tangled up in a protective netting that ran right over the pond. In frustration he tugged at the slender threads to try and untangle himself. Not aware he was pulling out the ground pegs that held it fast over the water.

"What on earth is this all for?" He wondered as he untangled himself and began to lay it out on the grass.

It was at this point a heron, who the police officer had disturbed from its night sleep on the nearby lake with his whistling, was alerted. The bird began to fly over to investigate what was going on. It seemed to work out quite quickly that the splashing water sound was coming from the pond.

Further, it knew there were some excellent tasting carp in that pond. Carp it would love to eat. However, the fish eater had been unable to get at them due to the diligence of the house owner who carefully kept his fish safe with a protective net over the water. The very protective net that the sergeant had now pulled off.

It was while the officer had his back to the pond and desperately attempting to deal with the tangled netting all about him, that the secretive bird landed quietly on the border of the water. Within a moment, it had stepped in to the water and managed to identify where the carp were. Its long beak was soon swallowing them down one by one.

The police sergeant, on hearing a rather strange gulping sound being made behind him, turned to see in his torchlight a very satisfied looking heron staring back at him. Taking off, its wings made a lot more noise than when it arrived but that can only be expected after all the extra weight it was carrying with the fish it had eaten.

"What the...!" Was all the sergeant could say as the grey hunting bird flew over his head and back to the lake it had been resting on for the night. Content with its unexpected late night meal.

By now the owner of the house had opened the door and was making his way out with his torch.

"Hello! What on earth is going on here?" He asked.

There before him was Police Sergeant Muddle looking quite wet through. It was impossible not to notice the pieces of lily pads stuck to different parts of his body and a protective net still clinging around one foot that he had been unable to disentangle. The house owner also just caught sight of the last flaps of the heron's wings as it flew out of the garden.

"My carp!" Was his immediate thought. His torch went down to the pond to search for them. The shock on his face told the whole story. "They've gone! The heron has eaten them!"

He looked at the police officer in dismay. Somehow knowing this was his fault and expecting some kind of logical answer.

"Um! It was like this!" He was about to tell this very angry householder the story of events when his police telephone rang.

"Hold on a moment!" he said to the house owner, who having rushed to get dressed looked a bit like an upside down, inside out, peg full of clothes himself. Yet, in truth, for the policeman, he was more than pleased the telephone call came when it did. For he had no idea how he was going to explain to the man facing him about what had happened to his prized carp.

"Sergeant Muddle, we need you to go in search of some stolen hair!" Came the message over his phone.

Even the police officer's eyes shot wide open in surprise.

"Stolen hair?" He asked.

"Yes! We have had some more cases of stolen hair reported and we need your help immediately! Please report back to the station!" The phone operator stated.

"I am sorry about your carp, sir!" Apologised the apologetic officer. "I'm afraid I was pursuing a highly dangerous criminal in to your garden and I was in the process of searching for him! I can only apologise for the bird taking your fish but your net was not well pegged down I am afraid!"

Before the bemused man could reply the policeman continued.

"You must excuse me, sir, for I have another important case to deal with!" With that the man in blue made a hasty retreat to get back to his police station as soon as possible. Leaving one perplexed householder standing saddened and shocked at what had happened.

*****

The hair eater soon fell asleep in his lair after his night's hunting. There was a real contented smile sat on his bulging face as he lay there. He had some more hair stacked beside him from his travels. These he would have as a snack when he woke up. That would do him until his next night jaunt in to the streets above.

There was very little wind around at that moment in time and this seemed to increase the smell he was exuding. Even the rats were now moving further down the sewer tunnels to escape the obnoxious smell he was giving off. Yet, the beast itself rolled over from side to side as he slept, dreaming wonderful dreams of eating people's hair.

Of course, this increasing smell had a knock-on effect for those above the sewers. Although the town people had almost accepted the fact that the smell came from the explosion at the pickle factory as they had been told by the mayor, the water company itself was not so confident.

Their own olfactory meters told them a different story. These very technical machines led them each time back to the sewers. Hence, they were wanting to explore the possibility that down there was a blockage somewhere. They believed it could be that which was causing the sewerage to back up and create this horrendous smell across the town.

It was for this reason they felt obliged to send some men in to the sewers and explore. To see if they could pinpoint a problem. Of course, it was the water company's responsibility to maintain an effective sewerage system so that was what they must do.

They knew that if the sewers were eventually found to be the cause of the smell and they had done nothing, all hell would break loose. Questions would be asked as to how they could allow that to happen and then not deal with it. Hence, they were hoping to solve the problem, that is, if there was a problem in the sewers, prior to fingers being pointed at themselves.

However, for the company, the problem was no workers wanted to go down in to the sewers! Rumours had been spreading for quite a while about a creature living down there. A gruesome creature who ate anybody who went in to its underworld. When the management had tried to force its work teams to enter this nether region, they were met with teams going off sick. Or, reports being filed by teams that had supposedly gone down there but had not. They said they checked the system and there was no problem down there at all. This was even though the management rightly guessed, they had only poked their heads through the drain cover to have a look and nothing more. Alternatively, another team had returned, as quick as it went in and were rushed off to hospital. After they had been overcome by the obnoxious smell.

What could the water company do? It was a potential problem that was not going to go away.

Well, the management decided finally to offer one team a huge bonus to go in and check the sewer system for them. Additionally, there was the added compensation of an extra week off work afterwards plus increased pension payments being made.

This team would be provided with specialised breathing apparatus, satellite trackers and ropes so they could quickly find their way back out. The team, the management focused on, to do this task were a brave lot who had undertaken difficult tasks for them before and always proved successful. The water company had a lot of faith in them. They needed to.

The team had been pretty clever though. They knew no other team would do that job. The job with big whispers about big mysteries down there. Hence, they had asked for more and more benefits, until they felt they could not squeeze anything more out of the company and then agreed to undertake it.

At last, the time had come for the brave team to undertake the search of the sewer system. They stood at the removed hood entrance and looked down in to it. They were wondering what lie ahead for them. Once their oxygen masks were in place and they could all hear each other on their joint communication system they started to enter the depths of the world below.

They turned on their powerful torchlights and started to follow the direction that their olfactory meters were getting the stronger readings from. The stench getting more powerful with each step they made. It smelled like a pool of sickness wrapped up in baby's poo. The machines were actually beeping almost continually by the time they reached the lair of the hair eater.

It was at this point they were expecting to find a huge blockage of sewerage. This, they expected, would then have to be unblocked by them. Not a very nice job but one they could do. So, it came as a surprise, when they entered the space that was the creature's lair to discover there was no blockage at all. Not one!

Furthermore, this huge sewer cavern they were in was not down on the map they had been given. They looked at each other as to how could it be there. These maps were meant to be an accurate picture of the sewerage system. So how could this cavern not be included.

"Wow! This is an amazing cavern!" One of the workmen said over his communicator for the others to hear. It was like discovering a city on the moon. "Look at the size of it!"

"I kind of remember my dad, who used to work on the sewerage system, saying there was a huge cavern where they would go and relax. A cavern that the bosses above were totally unaware about. This must be it!"

The leader of the group soon moved his interest on to the fact that this seemed to be the epicentre of the smell. He looked around and couldn't work out how that could be. There was no sewerage blockage of any kind there. He was beginning to think their machines were not working properly or having a day's holiday.

"I can't see a problem here at all!" He called out to the others. He was about to suggest to his men they explore the tunnels there abouts when he saw some sort of movement in the far corner. They had all seen the dark bulge at the side of the cave but had assumed it was a part of the structure of the walls. But as his torch focused on the bulge at the side he began to realise it was moving up and down as if it was breathing in and out! But how could a wall breathe in and out.

He was about to say to his colleagues what is that over there? When the dark bulge rolled over. The hair eater had been disturbed by these interlopers. The creature opened its enormous eyes to be confronted by the bright torch light aimed straight at it.

In fear the hair eater made the most frightening of sounds. More in fear for itself than aggression. At the same time, it opened its mouth wide as it screamed and showed it's array of long pointed white teeth.

All the team were watching as the hair eater turned, looked at them and then made this outrageous sound that nearly deafened them. They looked in to those wide, open white eyes. They looked at his sharp, enormous teeth and they knew what they had to do. There was only one thing they could do!

"Aghhhh!" One cried out, but which one it was difficult to say. They all turned and scrambled back through the sewers at a sewer record speed.

They were up the stairwell and back out in to the open air within an incredible short period of time. The managers who were waiting there for their return, stood back surprised as they came out of the manhole at such a pace. They almost shot out of the hole like bullets from a gun. They were further surprised when the team slammed the cover shut over its entrance before they stopped to take in a much-needed deep breath.

"What did you see?" One manager asked as their team started to take off their underground equipment.

"Was there a problem?" Another wanted to know as the team looked at each other.

They looked at each other in disbelief. Not sure how to tell their bosses what they had seen and unsure whether they would be believed.

One by one they sat on the floor by their vehicle and shook their heads in shock.

"I am never going down in to that sewer again!" One of them said as he sat down next to his colleagues. He held his head in fear at what he had observed.

"You are never going to believe what we saw down there!" The leader of the team finally said to the gathered bosses.

*****

Robin Biggs, the local TV reporter for the area, was looking in to the stories about people losing their hair overnight.

"I woke up and all my hair had disappeared. Just like that!" One elderly gentleman commented.

Robin Biggs had seen him walking through the town as bald as a new born baby and asked him whether he was a victim of hair loss during the night.

"My wife is always complaining about it being too long so I thought she had chopped it all off during the night! But she denies that!" He smiled. "Anyway, it means I won't need a haircut for quite a while!"

"Aren't you feeling the cold with your head hairless?" Robin asked.

"Oh! Yes! But I've got a woolly cap in my pocket if it gets too cold!"

The TV presenter then introduced to his audience the locally renowned psychologist, Doctor Anderson. The doctor was a professor at the nearby university. The reporter was going to ask him to give his opinion on what he thought had happened to the people's hair.

"No one seems to be able to explain how the hair disappears over night!" He mentioned to the psychologist. "They go to bed with a full crop of hair on their head and wake up in the morning with it all gone. There is no sign of hair on the floor or the bed and they haven't felt a thing. Yet, their hair has disappeared! And this is happening not only in one part of the town or to one type of person. The hair that disappears belongs to very different people at very different ages. It all seems rather odd don't you think, doctor. Have you got any solution to this problem or have any idea as to what is happening?"

"Um! Yes! Well, I believe, it's all to do with sleep-walking!"

"Sleep-walking?" Robin Biggs looked as stunned as a frozen partridge in the fridge-freezer at this response. It was not what he was expecting. He had never heard of that suggestion before. It came as bit of a surprise. "Can you explain how it could be possibly due to sleep-walking?"

"Um... Yes! Well, I believe, what is happening is these people are waking up in a highly self-hypnotised state during the night. This is due to the mass media coverage lately about hair disappearing while people sleep. They are then cutting all of their own hair off in a similar fashion to that which they have heard or read about. After doing the deed they then sleep-walk back to their bed. Of course, they wake up in the morning with having no memory of what they had done. I believe these people's own subconscious is deeply worried about them losing their own hair. Hence, this is driving them in to a sleepwalking hypnotic state whereby unconsciously they cut off their hair without any ability to recall what they had done or why!"

"That's interesting!" The TV presenter replied but was not too sure he believed this version of events. "But doctor wouldn't the hair be somewhere in the house if they cut it off themselves? And isn't it odd no family member heard them getting up and doing the deed?"

"Um… Yes! Well, I believe, that the heart of the problem lies in the fact that in the original hair loss case there was no trace of hair the following morning. Hence, each following case has tried to replicate the exact same circumstances as the first one. Therefore, there will never be any evidence of what happened or where the hair is! People's subconsciousness ensures there is not!" The professor took a moment to continue his train of thought. "Um…yes! Well! This is so characteristic of so many cases of mass hysteria that there is no doubt that my theory has to be correct!"

"But what about the vast range of people who have come up with the same thing happening to them? Almost every one of them, doctor, has no history of sleep-walking, self-harming, drug or alcohol problems or any other conditions that might cause them to cut off their own hair during the night!"

"Um … Yes! Well, I believe, these people's subconscious concerns are very deep rooted. As deep as a coal mine. There seems no reason to suggest they had to have previous mental issues before. However, for some reason these previous disappearances of hair overnight seems to have had a profound effect on them. Of course, they have no memory of what they have done, how they did it and why they did it. It is interesting to note that their subconscious was even clever enough to ensure that all those around them were fast asleep at the time they did it and had no idea what they were up to!"

"Your explanation is most interesting, Doctor Anderson, and will no doubt help us to unravel why it is happening!" Yet, even the TV reporter himself shook his head in utter surprise at the doctor's interpretation of why people's hair was disappearing.

"And Doctor have you any thoughts on the strange smell that is reaching right across the town and causing a problem for us all? Do you support the view that the source of it was the explosion at the pickle factory as the mayor has so vociferously indicated?"

"Well! Yes! Um, I believe, if we look at the supermarket sales of garlic and onions over the last few weeks we will see there has been a huge rise in these strong-smelling vegetables being sold."

Once again, Robin Biggs, could only look at him in surprise. This seemed such a very different reason to anything he had heard proposed before.

"But how can this horrendous smell be connected to the higher increase in the sales of garlic and onions?" He knew he had to ask the question. It was his job.

"Yes! Well! Um, I believe, as people are eating more onions and garlic, these strong smells are escaping from their homes and entering the local air all about us. Hence, the awful smell we have to put up with."

"Right! Thank you, Doctor Anderson! Your insight has been most useful!" The TV reported shook his head in disbelief at what he had heard in the interview. It was not what he was expecting. But then when interviewing Doctor Anderson it never was.

*****

No one seemed to be that concerned about the growing cloud formations above the town. England is famous for the way the weather changes quickly and how the sky can look quite spectacular at times. The fact that a cloud seemed to stay still above the town went unnoticed. It was as if passing clouds were a permanent fixture in the sky at that moment in time. People were too busy with getting on with their lives to notice the unmoving cloud.

What they did not know and, not even the puddle hoppers beneath their puddles realised, was that the clouds above them were full of small creatures who were on a mission. A mission that would affect the whole town. Yes, you are right, the cloud jumpers had arrived. Their long travels were over and they commenced to prepare for the coming revenge they wanted to inflict upon their adversaries below.

No one noticed as they jumped from cloud to cloud with their usual grace and ease. Undertaking various tasks that needed to be completed before their awaited plans below could commence. They landed so gently and with much dexterity on the soft texture of the clouds, it was as if they were landing on a soft cushioned carpet. Picking off pieces of cloud to eat as and when they were peckish as they set about their allotted tasks.

A large group of cloud jumpers were working under the guidance of Castor, their warrior chief, who was leading this assault on the puddle hoppers. All remembering what they considered was the bad treatment they had received by their nearest relations below. It had never been forgotten.

The cloud jumpers believed it was time for revenge. Their revenge. It would also give them a chance to get some more workers for their cloud-making. Not surprisingly the number of children working for them had been dwindling.

Furthermore, no one below seemed to notice the long, sinuous, almost invisible cloud ropes that began to hang down from above the town. They were almost like long spider webs floating in the sky. In this way the cloud jumpers began to prepare for the evil deeds they would undertake in the coming days.

These plotters were being extra careful to keep an eye open to avoid people and, of course, their arch rivals, the puddle hoppers. They wanted to keep their presence a secret for as long as they could. Trying not to let the cat out of the bag until they were ready.

Yet, if you had a very good telescope and looked up on the edge of one of the clouds you might be able to manage to see three bluish, greyish faces looking down at you. Of course, they were the three evil puddle hoppers. They still had not fully found their cloud feet and felt quite insecure in trusting the cloud's soft surface. It did not help when they looked down at the earth below that it seemed such a long way off. However, they were getting more confident with their cloud legs day by day.

Chapter 9

The moment came when the twin's airplane took off and they were finally up in to the air. Australia gave a big sigh of relief as the troublesome two left. The continent had a few weeks of peace. Fortunately, for the two travelling children the third seat next to them was still empty. Whether that was due to luck or whoever was meant to sit there had decided to find another seat in the cabin rather than be stuck next to two children. Children who they thought would probably want to be going to the toilet all the time and shouting.

So, Seth and Bronwyn came up with a plan. They decided they did not want to keep the roo hidden in the rucksack for the whole journey. It was not even certain if the young creature would be willing to stay cooped up in such a small space for such a long period anyway. Hence, they both moved over a seat each so the one by the window was free. Seth brought the roo out of the rucksack and they both gave it an enormous hug followed by a bit of dried fruit to eat. Then Bronwyn sat the animal in the now vacant window seat next to them both.

"What can we do Sis to disguise the roo? How are we going to make him look like a child!" Seth looked a bit perplexed as to how they could succeed in this part of their plan.

"Why don't we put my baseball cap on him and a blanket over his body! So, he looks like a child asleep!"

"Blow me down Sis that's a brain stormer!"

They got the cap out of the bag and placed it on top of his head. The roo did not seem to mind it being there. In fact, he seemed to use his paws to slightly adjust it. The animal appeared to be taking part in their attempt to disguise him.

Was it possible it even understood what was happening?

"That looks brill!" Bronwyn smiled at their new friend in his hat.

They then put the cabin sleeping blanket over the top of him. It covered his whole body up to his nose that was just peeking out.

"Wow! You'd never know he was not a nipper! Would ya!" Seth raved.

"Noop! Looks good to me, broth!"

Even the roo seemed to be content with his lot. He put his head on the seat arm as still as could be and seemed to be resting. Bronwyn carefully stroked his shoulder to reassure him. To which the roo seemed to respond and begin to really relax with his two new found friends.

Yet, their plan was about to be tested. The flight attendant was making her way along the aisle checking everybody was okay now the airplane was up in the air. This was going to be a very long flight for one and all.

When the flight attendant arrived at the two children plus the roo sitting in their three seats, she did a double take. Then another. For she had been the one who had helped the twins to their seats and asked whether they wanted their backpacks going in to the locker above.

"That's funny!" She looked a bit out of sorts.

The twins looked up at her, pretending to be a bit surprised.

"What d'yer mean, Miss?" Asked Seth.

"Well, I could have sworn there was only two of you when you boarded. Now there are three children sitting in this row? I must be imagining things!" She kept on looking at the three of them a bit confused by what she was seeing. You could see her continually counting one, two, three and not believing what she saw.

"Ah! No!" Seth stepped in with confidence. "There were three of us! You probably didn't notice our brother who followed on behind you!" He was trying to bluff his way through this.

"Yeah! He is always dragging behind!" Bronwyn followed suit. "He's bit of a real slow coach! We are always having to wait for him! A real pain!" She smiled sweetly at the flight attendant to try and get on her good side.

Finally, the flight attendant seemed to accept the fact that she was wrong. Yet, when she did look more carefully at the third child sitting in the window seat she was a bit surprised by what she saw.

"He's certainly got some strange looking features your brother?" she said.

"Yeah! Mum and Dad always say he isn't going to win any best-looking children competition prizes!" Seth joked.

"He's got such a long nose?" The flight attendant added.

"Well, he keeps pulling it, I'm afraid! We don't know why!" Bronwyn quickly came up with a reason no matter how irrational.

"And his ears?"

"That's due to his liking Mickey Mouse!" Seth stated.

"Mickey Mouse?" The lady above them was astounded by this comment.

"Yeah! He loves Mickey Mouse and wants to have the same ears as the Disney character! So, he keeps pulling on them! He's silly!"

"Oh! He is really odd!" The flight attendant looked a bit confused by what they had said. But, there again, she had met some rather strange passengers in her time in that job. Hence, she quickly accepted their rather strange responses to her questions.

They were probably lucky she did not have the best eye-sight in the world either. She had put off going to get her eyes tested for weeks. Using the excuse that she would get it done the week after and, of course, the week after never came.

"Is your brother okay?" She posed the question.

"Okay! What d'yer mean?" Seth replied trying to pretend that it was rather a silly question.

"Well! He looks rather unwell and his face. It looks a sort of a brown colour as if he has got some sort of sickness." She added.

"Ah! That's because he don't like flying!" Bronwyn retorted quickly.

"Yeah! He always goes queasy when he's on a plane! Real pain our brother!" Seth continued to try to convince the flight attendant that this was their brother and he was just suffering from a bit of flight sickness.

"You don't think he's going to be sick, do you?" If the truth be told, when she had to deal with someone being sick, it turned her stomach over and made her want to vomit as well! Hence, she was hoping she would not have to deal with a child being sick.

"No way!" Bronwyn almost laughed. Pretending of course. "He'll be fine in a while. A bit of a nap and watching a bit of TV and he'll be as right as rain!"

"Well, if you are sure!" She was not convinced but decided she still had a lot of work to do. There was a need for her to be getting on. So, it was best to leave things as they were. The three children did not seem to be causing any problem. They appeared to be happy so best not to upset what doesn't need to be upset!

Throughout this discussion between the twins and the flight attendant, the roo had sat there as still as a Greek marble statue in a museum. You would have thought he was asleep. It was as if the roo knew they were talking about him. Moreover, it was as if the young kangaroo realised that if it began to move around or reveal itself to be an animal that would be the end of its attempted escape from the zoo.

So, the young creature seemed to be happy to follow what his two new friends wanted him to do and keep up the pretence. It was as if he knew this was his way out of his previous caged life. Somehow, it seemed as if he was even joining in by pretending to be a young human being. Moreover, he seemed to be quite enjoying the game the three of them were playing.

It was not too long before the trolleys arrived with the evening meals. The twins were ready to stuff themselves silly with food. They soon worked out that they would end up with a third plate full of food. Those who were serving were bound to give a meal to the roo. Hence, that would be an extra meal for them. Their stomachs roared with success.

"What would you like chicken, pasta or vegetarian?" The flight attendant, but now, a waitress asked. She was still looking at the brother sitting in the window seat with a slight suspicion.

"Chicken!" Both twins answered.

"And what about your brother!"

Fortunately, he was looking down as if he was asleep. So, the request as to what the supposed brother would eat was answered immediately by the twins.

"Oh! He will have chicken as well! He likes chicken!" Seth beamed. Knowing this would be extra food for both of them and feeling quite pleased with himself.

Once the flight attendant had moved on, they opened up the young kangaroo's meal and took out the chicken and anything else they thought their animal friend would not eat before passing over the remainder to the roo.

The roo set about using its paws to pick up and eat the vegetables and fruit. The way it was eating the food it must have been pretty hungry. He was making such a sucking noise that the lady and gentleman in front of him both looked behind at one point with a look of disgust on their faces. Obviously, thinking to themselves, a child should have better manners than to make such noises as that while eating.

Yet, the twins were making just as much noise as their friend as they gorged themselves on their own meals. Then came the joy of sharing the remainder of the third one between them. You could tell they were content by the happy look on both of their faces. They sat back after finishing the meals with a smile as wide as the Mississippi river. Even the roo, having watched them sit back, sat back himself in a similar way. It was as if he was copying them. This made both the twins laugh.

"Bringing the roo with us was a real banker of an idea!" Seth said.

"Yeah! He's real good fun!" Bronwyn agreed.

After everybody had completed the meal the staff on board the plane cleared everything away. Once those chores were complete, the lights in the craft were dimmed so that everybody could go to sleep. The air hostesses made their way to their own sleeping quarters to try and get as much sleep as they could. In a few hours, they would have to commence their duties again for the remainder of the flight.

Soon everyone on the flight to England was trying to get some sleep. It is never easy trying to get to sleep on board an airplane but with the lights dimmed and the window shutters down, people were soon trying to escape in to their own private worlds. This included the twins who were very tired by now. Even though they had no intention of going to sleep, their eyes were soon closing and they were joining the rest of the passengers and air crew in the land of nod.

Only one person was definitely not asleep on the aircraft. Well, they weren't really a person were they. Of course, it was the roo. He looked at his two friends and saw they were both happily snoozing with broad smiles on their faces. Hence, the small creature took the opportunity to jump over them with a single kangaroo leap and land in the aisle. It was going to take the chance to explore its surroundings while everyone slept. Perhaps, it was even hoping to find the odd eucalyptus tree full of leaves!

The happy mammal was able to bounce along the corridor without any obstacle stopping him. He was loving the freedom. Everyone was in a comfortable sleeping position in their seat, leaving the aisle clear for him. Some passengers were curled up in balls, others had pulled the blanket over their heads while a few leaned right back in their seat and were stretched out full. The snorers were the ones who broke the silence, although, some were louder than others. It certainly did not sound like a church choir.

As the roo bounced along he was able to smell some of the food that people had sitting on their fold-away tables. At times, he even used his paws to grab some of it to eat. When these people wake up, they would be surprised to find their food missing. No doubt, they would blame the person sitting next to them for taking the food they had left there for later.

The roo made his way down the plane, bouncing along quite joyfully. Sometimes, he was almost hitting the ceiling as he enjoyed this freedom that he had not had for quite a while. Being cooped up in a small bag was quite a discomfort for a creature that was used to roaming wide open spaces.

Of course, as he made his way down the plane, some sleeping passengers would turn over in their sleep and momentarily half-open their eyes and see to their astonishment a kangaroo bouncing along. Not surprisingly, they believed it was part of their dream and turned over to go back to sleep.

When they later woke up, they would tell their companions that they had this strange dream about a kangaroo bouncing along the aisle of the plane while everybody else slept. Of course, nobody was ever going to believe them. I mean, would you believe it?

With a few smaller hops the creature found itself in the first-class compartment. Of course, this was a perfect place for a young kangaroo as there was a lot more table space and, hence, people tended to leave a lot more food lying around. Food that a small roo would really like to indulge in. The small biped soon found it had a real liking for chocolate bars. With a few paw and teeth movements it was easy for it to unwrap the chocolate and eat the contents.

*****

"Hey! Seth wakes up, mate!"

"Urgh! What's the problem Sis?" Seth was far, far away in bongo land in his deep sleep. It was not only a surprise for him to be woken up but it was also a surprise for him to wake up and find himself sitting on a plane. It took him a few minutes to remember where he was and why he was there.

"The roo! Seth! It's gone walkabout!" His sister looked worried.

"What roo? What do you mean gone walkabout? Where?" Then it came back to him about how they had sneaked the young creature on to the plane unnoticed. "Hot crocodiles! We better go find it, Sis!" he said rubbing his eyes that did not really want to open or stay open for that matter.

They unbuckled their safety belts and commenced to get themselves moving along the aisle. Looking in both directions to see if they could spot their friend who had disappeared. Yet, he was not to be found.

"Where the heck could it be mate?" Seth puzzled.

As they went along they looked in to every row of sleeping passengers to try and see if the roo had somehow got itself in to one of them.

Little did they know, that by now the roo was amongst the ladies Australian cricket team. As you can guess, he was searching for food. Further, it is not hard for you to imagine there were many among the cricketers who were really good at snoring. What can you expect from such a great sporting team! Snoring was obviously their second sport.

As their mascot ate up the abandoned food left on their tables, the roo noticed the wicket-keeper who had been very friendly to him while the photo was being taken. The stopper had even taken the time to stroke and talk to him as the camera snapped away. Hence, the animal was soon returning the compliment with his paw stroking the player's face.

It must have tickled her as the wicket-keeper laughed while still in her sleep before eventually turning her face around to sleep facing the other way. This made the mascot do the same again. Once more, the cricket player smiled and turned her head back to where it was before. Her hand rubbing her nose where the roo had tickled it.

"There he is bro!" Bronwyn whispered and pointed him out to her brother.

"Crickey! We better get to him quick before he wakes that cricket player up! The way he's tickling that girl's nose, he's going to wake her up and the girl will think she's in a TV reality show!"

"Come on bro!" The sister pulled her brother along after her further down the aisle where, fortunately for them, everyone was still asleep.

Seth put his arms around their small friend and hugged him. As he released the animal, the boy put his finger up to his mouth to let the creature know he must not make a sound. Immediately, the roo lost interest in the wicket-keeper and commenced to snuggle up to Seth.

The cricket player seemed to be soon back in to her own sleep rhythm. It was as if nothing was going to wake her up anyway as she carried on snoring happily. Tucking her head in to the pillow for better comfort.

Bronwyn saw one of their cricket bats lying between her feet. She picked it up, studied it for a few moments and then tucked it under her arm. She had an idea for that cricket bat and the cricket ball next to it.

"What y'er doing?" The brother asked.

"Well! These guys have got a lot of bats and balls, I reckon they won't miss these. We can give it to Jules as a present! What d'yer think!"

"Spot on, Sis! We said we wanted to give him something didn't we! Now we have it!" The two twins both did high-fives to each other. While the roo looked on unsure what was happening.

The three passengers made their way back to the seats allotted to them. Ensuring they did not wake anyone up on the way. They realised if they had woken anyone it would be difficult to explain away a kangaroo being on the plane.

Once again, ensconced in their seats, with safety belts on they all began to fall asleep. This time though Bronwyn had tied a line of string to her animal companion, so that he could not get up and go walkabout as if he was in the Australian outback. However, even their marsupial friend fell asleep quickly, curled up in his ball. When he did, it was easy to see how everybody would assume he was just a small boy getting a bit of a rest.

As passengers woke up after having a number of hours of sleep and the air hostesses got back to work serving breakfast a number of those rubbing their eyes could be heard to say, "Do you know what, I could have sworn I saw a kangaroo hopping along the aisle in the night!"

"Don't be daft! It was a part of your dream!" They were told. "Ha! A kangaroo indeed! Next you'll be seeing pink elephants crawling up the wall! You had probably a glass of wine too much before you went to sleep!"

*****

Once the plane had landed at Heathrow the twins squeezed the roo back in to the backpack! He didn't seem to mind. It was as if it was a game to him. A lovely warm place to curl up in and have another sleep.

"Hey! Where is your brother?" The air hostess who had administered to their needs on the flight asked as they were leaving the plane.

"Oh! Him!" Replied Seth. "He's somewhere behind us!"

"Yeah! He's always slow and late! Got spiders in his britches!" Bronwyn added.

"Okay! Have a lovely stay in England you two!" Their flight attendant smiled at them. Thinking to herself what lovely innocent children. If only she knew!

Once out of the plane's door they rushed along the walkways just in case the air hostess on the plane wondered why their brother had not got off the plane after them.

They got through passport control quickly as they were classed as only young. The same thing happened again at customs where they were ushered through in to the airport lounge as if they were celebrities with no searching of bags at all. Right through the airport, everyone was wishing them a lovely time while in England and trying to ensure they got dealt with without delay. Fortunately, no one even attempted to check their backpacks! That could have been a disaster if they had.

When they got in to the airport lounge, the ladies Australian cricket team were already in the area and having their photographs taken. They were being asked endless questions by the inquisitive media who were there to greet them at the start of their tour.

Chapter 10

At the local Parkside Primary School in Boreham Wood, Mrs. Catterhorn, the Deputy Head Teacher, was sorting out the PE lessons for the day. There has been quite a bit of rain recently and a lot of classes wanted to get out and enjoy the finer weather while it lasted.

"Mrs. Caldwell! I suggest you take your class out first and then Mrs. Stacey can take her class out afterwards." Mrs. Catterhorn pinned the time-table up on the staffroom noticeboard and then got herself a well-deserved cup of coffee.

"That's good! It means we can do our PE before we start the day's class lessons and it won't disrupt us during the rest of the day." Mrs. Caldwell seemed to be happy with this arrangement.

"And can you leave the PE equipment out for me as well!" Mrs. Stacey added. "It will save time not having to get it all out again as well as put it away."

"Of course!" With that Mrs. Caldwell went away to start getting the class ready for their PE lesson.

When they got outside, Mrs. Caldwell soon had the children doing small group sessions with bean bags, bats and balls, skittles, quoits and the larger apparatus. She allowed the children ten minutes on each activity before they moved on to the next.

While watching the children performing their selected activities and helping one or two who were struggling, she decided that she could perhaps get a group running and catching hoops as she had noticed a few children were struggling to run and control smaller apparatus.

With this in mind she went in to the PE shed which was right next to where the children were doing their activities. She was in the process of getting out the hoops which were stored right at the back of the shed and putting them by the door ready to take out.

Over the few minutes she was in there, the children outside seemed to get quieter and quieter. But she thought no more about it as she emerged from the depths of the back of the shed, picked up the hoops she had gathered and came out to set up this new activity for the children.

"Children I want you …" Mrs. Caldwell was stopped in her tracks. There was not a child on the playground. She began to think perhaps they had moved further around behind the school building so she could not see them. But none were there either.

"Where have they gone?" She asked herself. "Perhaps, they have all gone back inside the classroom for some reason!"

It was the only conclusion she could reach. Her own logic not being able to explain any other reason for their sudden disappearance.

It was then she noticed some of the children's shoes sat next to puddles in the middle of the playground!

"Oh no!" She was alarmed. Remembering what had happened last year. Even though no one ever believed the school's staff about the creatures and the puddles. The teachers at the school still knew what had occurred. "Oh! No!" She repeated in horror.

Mrs. Caldwell rushed back in to her classroom and as she expected there was not a child there either. She rushed to the hall, thinking the Head Teacher may have called the children in there for some reason. However, that was empty as well. It was at that point she spotted, Mrs. Catterhorn in the staffroom and went to explain to her that she had lost her class of children while they were doing PE!

"Don't be silly! A whole class can't have disappeared!" Her superior brushed her statement aside. Forgetting what had happened a year ago when almost all the children disappeared.

"Mrs. Catterhorn, I have searched the school and they can't be found. I had only popped my head in to the PE shed for a few moments. It was impossible for them to all disappear in those few moments."

It was then that Mrs. Stacey rushed in looking just as horrified as Mrs. Caldwell.

"Mrs. Catterhorn, Mrs. Catterhorn, my whole class has disappeared!"

"You as well!" A shocked Deputy Head Teacher looked at them with dismay.

"I had taken the children outside for PE and went back in to the classroom quickly to get my whistle that I had forgotten. When I came back out, they had all disappeared! It can't happen. They can't be there one minute, then all disappear the next."

"Well! The same thing happened to me! So, it can happen!" Mrs. Caldwell could only concur with her colleague about the children disappearing.

"The funny thing is Mrs. Catterhorn is that there are some shoes lying beside puddles on the playground! I wonder if …." Mrs. Stacey was about to say if it was the puddle hoppers!

"No! It couldn't be! Don't say that!" Their superior looked horrified at her two fellow teachers.

"You know how we were mocked and belittled for saying what happened in the puddles last year. We don't want the same thing to happen again do we!"

"But what else can it be?" Mrs. Caldwell gasped.

"No one believed us before! They said we had made it all up!" The Deputy Head Teacher looked perplexed.

"The school's governors wanted to sack all of us for gross negligence! We can't have that happen again."

"Mrs. Catterhorn! Mrs. Catterhorn! My class has disappeared!" In to the staffroom rushed Mr. Duckett, the class teacher, who was next in line to take his class out for PE. He had a very similar story to tell.

*****

"The town seems to be experiencing another odd phenomenon this summer with children disappearing again as they did last year!" The local reporter, Robin Biggs, was as much surprised and shocked as everybody else in the community. "We are, once again, picking up stories of children disappearing without a trace all over the town." His filmed report stated.

"Ben, my son, was playing football in the street with five of our neighbours' children." A mum told him. "I was watching them from the kitchen window. I went over to the cupboard to get some teabags to make a cuppa, when I returned and looked outside at where they had been there was nobody there. All six children had gone. I thought they had gone in to one of the other neighbours' houses to get a cold drink or something. Yet, when I checked at each of those houses, the children were not there either! They seemed to have totally disappeared!"

"Was there nothing at all left behind by the children?" The reporter asked.

"Just the ball and next to a puddle was one of the children's shoes!"

"That is strange!" The TV reporter gazed at his guest. "If you remember last year, many of those abducted talked about the fact they were imprisoned in puddles! Of course, the story was considered too far-fetched. Yet, a shoe left by the puddle, does seem to be a bit of a coincidence and it is the only clue we seem to have!"

"There is a similar story of children playing on the play equipment at Allerton Road Recreation Ground! Mrs. Hughes was one of the mums there! Mrs. Hughes can you explain to us what happened?"

"Us mums were chatting away while the children were playing their games on the apparatus. There was a lot of laughing and whooping. When it suddenly stopped! When we all looked over to the play equipment where the children had been no one was there! The children had all disappeared! We searched and searched all around but we could not find any of them!"

"Were there no signs of what had happened to them?" The confused TV reporter asked.

"Only a couple of single shoes belonging to the children lying by a puddle! That is all!"

"A shoe by a puddle! This seems to be happening at each case of children disappearing!"

"You don't think it is possible it was true about last year?" Mrs Hughes posed the fearful question.

"What do you mean?" The intrepid television reporter asked. Yet, in reality knowing exactly what she meant by her question.

"I mean it could be true that the children were kidnapped last year and held hostages down in the puddles by small creatures as they stated! That is before they all suddenly returned!"

"I am sure that's not the case!" Robin Biggs could see the fear of this speculation in her eyes. "The stories about that happening were all proved to be untrue. If you remember, the eminent Doctor Anderson demonstrated how it was only a case of mass hysteria that had taken place." The mum had an unsure look on her face.

"But viewers we are hearing of another case coming through on the line." The reporter held his ear-piece to show that he was picking up a new item of news. "We are going straight over to our local Parkside Primary School for some more disturbing news about children disappearing."

"Hello, I do believe I have got Mrs, Catterhorn, the Deputy Head Teacher, on the line!"

"Hello! Robin! You have!"

"You were one of the schools worst hit last year with children disappearing if I remember right!"

"We were! You are right!" She added with conviction.

"Can you tell us what has happened now at your school!"

"I am afraid we have lost almost all the children again! They have disappeared without a trace. It was a PE day for every class and every time the children went out to do their PE lesson, the children disappeared. Every teacher said the children were there one minute and the next minute they had gone. The police are searching the area at this very moment to try to find out where they have all vanished to!"

"We know the children didn't turn up for days last year so this time is there any clues as to what happened to them?"

"Well, none at all, except an odd shoe was left here or there by a puddle!"

"What again!" The reporter gasped. "This is becoming a running theme with the children disappearing that shoes are being left next to puddles. It is interesting that we have no record of any person seeing any of the children disappear or hearing anything. How can this be happening. It doesn't make any sense. What is going on?"

Mrs. Catterhorn was not too keen to once more talk about the creatures who live in puddles as she got herself in to great trouble last year. So, she was far more cautious in her reply this time.

"Well! I remember a lot of those who disappeared last year talked about being held captive in puddles but their stories were increasingly considered to be incredulous." She stated cleverly. Careful not to say what she really thought.

"Well, Mrs. Catterhorn, let's hope that the police can soon come up with a solution as to why all these children are disappearing again as we are hearing about more and more cases here in the office. It is becoming quite overwhelming!"

You could tell Robin Biggs was struggling to keep up with events, as his earpiece was red hot with stories of more and more children vanishing without a trace. Yet, in almost every case the only clue was the odd shoe left by a puddle.

*****

Jules was at home and listening to the news on the television, when the stories about children disappearing became 'breaking news' items. At first, he thought nothing of it as he set about preparing vegetables for their evening meal. This was another job he was doing to help his mother.

He was well aware how exhausted she was by the time she returned from this new job. It was not difficult to notice, she was coming home far more stressed than she was in the other job at the pickle factory. Yet, they both knew she couldn't leave this new job. The fact was they needed the money.

However, it was not long before he hooked on to what was being said on the news channel. Some worried parents and teachers were soon mentioning their children were disappearing and that the only clue left behind was the odd shoe by a puddle. Otherwise, there was no other indication as to what had happened and the children seemed to have disappeared in to thin air.

It was surprising this time, that no adults had been taken either. He soon picked up how, Robin Biggs, the TV reporter, was linking it to last year's disappearances in the town. Jules began to worry about what was going on! It surely could not be his friends, the puddle hoppers, doing such deeds. They would never do such a thing he was certain.

He was aware too, that if the disappearances of these children were linked to puddles once more, there was a chance that people would begin to reconsider what happened last year. Perhaps, they would start to give the stories about creatures and puddles more credence. That would be a real problem for his puddle friends.

If people started to seriously consider the possibility, there may be creatures living in the puddles around the town, they could begin to look out for them. Then the next thing to happen may be that someone would spot a puddle hopper entering or leaving a puddle. In the past, they would normally brush it aside.

Saying to themselves, "It's probably a bird," "It's a small animal" or "It's a moving shadow."

Yet, this could change. It would not be long before they blamed the puddle hoppers for the missing children. They would see them as some sort of threat.

This was all looking rather miserable for his small friends.

"Surely it can't be the puddle hoppers!" Jules said to himself. "They would never do anything like that. Why would they? They want to live peacefully with people!" You could see him mulling over this strange situation.

"Could it be some other puddle hoppers, like the three who came last year, have arrived in the town and they are taking the children away?" He pondered. He was sure there had to be another reason.

Once Jules had done as much as he could to help his mum around the house and prepare for that night's meal, he decided he needed to go and talk to Prok. He might know something about what was happening. He didn't like going over there as it might attract unwanted attention to the tribe but this seemed to be an exceptional reason.

The television news reports seemed to be suggesting somehow the puddle hoppers were linked to these events. Moreover, he realised that if the puddle hoppers did not know what was happening then it was wise for Jules to warn them about it. For there could be major repercussions for his friends. If human beings found out about their existence and started to link them to the disappearing children goodness knows what people might do.

*****

Luce was on the field collecting moss for those who were too elderly in the community to collect it for themselves. She knew that many of the elders liked their moss particularly moist and thick. Hence, she was wandering further away from the Gateshead Road field where her people lived.

She had made her way along the hedges almost up towards the top of Aycliffe Road. Keeping close to the thick bushes, she was able to ensure she was not observed by any people who happened to be wandering nearby.

Humming to herself, she was happy and enjoying the moment. She knew where to look for the moist, thick moss she was after. Carefully lifting up branches and leaves to get to the variety she wanted. This was a walk she had done many times before. It made a lovely pleasant afternoon out for her.

She had told her parents where she was going and they were happy for her to go. Everybody in the tribe knew she was a very sensible puddle hopper and had done this many times before. It was nothing new. A reminder to take care was enough they felt to say to her.

It was then Luce heard the light brush of something against the branches around her. She thought it an odd sound. It was like her own intuition telling her quickly that something strange was happening. Immediately, she stopped looking for moss, stood up and began to look about her. She was soon startled by what she saw.

"Ha! Ha! Who have we got here then Rik!" It was one of the three returned evil puddle hoppers. He seemed to be enjoying the moment.

Not that Luce realised who they were as she looked at the three creatures facing her. At first, seeing they were three puddle hoppers, she assumed that it must be three fellow members of her own community. Nonetheless, she was soon flummoxed when she realised she did not recognise them. She was sure she knew everyone in the tribe but not these. So, who were these three standing in front of her?

She had not directly met the three evil puddle hoppers last year and so had no idea what they looked like. So, it never even crossed her mind that this is who it could be. Why should it be them anyway! As far as she was aware, and the rest of the tribe were concerned, those three evil creatures had been returned to the Alaskan permafrost to remain their permanently frozen and would never be seen again.

"Who are you three?" She questioned. Not recognising that she was in any danger. "I don't think I've seen you in the tribal home?" She looked them up and down hoping to find that she somehow knew them but had forgotten.

"Ha! She doesn't recognise us!" Trid mocked. "Here we are, three of her own kind, and she doesn't even recognise us! How disappointing! What do you think Sur!"

"Not good enough!" Sur came very close to her and pulled on her cheek. "Here we are! Come all this way especially to see her and she doesn't know us at all!"

"Should I know you?" She was beginning to think that she should know them from the way they were talking to her.

"Well! We're going to get to know you quite well! Don't you think Trid!" Rak laughed.

At this point all three laughed and gathered around her so she felt quite hemmed in. As a matter of fact, she was hemmed in and there was no way she was going to escape from them.

Already, Luce was beginning to feel frightened. Very frightened in fact. They were not acting at all in a friendly way. The way they were mocking her and coming close with a threatening air was beginning to really worry her.

"What do you mean you're going to get to know me quite well!" She looked bemused. "I don't understand what you mean by that!"

"Let's just say we have plans for you!" Trid touched her by putting his hand on her shoulder. It was an attempt to intimate her. "Plans we are not too sure you will be pleased with! But you'll get to like them one way or the other!" He laughed as if a hyena had taken over his throat.

"I am not too sure I know what you mean! And I don't think I want to know what you mean!" She was truly frightened by now. These were not like any puddle hoppers she had ever met before. "I think I need to get back to the rest of the tribe!"

She made an attempt to squeeze past them and make her way back to the community's puddles. However, every attempt she made to get past the three of them was baulked. She found herself hemmed in with the three puddle hoppers looking at her with evil intent.

"I don't think little miss puddle hopper you are going anywhere. I think you need to come with us. And that is not back to your home. We have other plans for you." Rak continued with a snigger.

"Yes, you may not be going back to your tribe for a long, long-time sweetie!" Surr giggled.

"We need to start teaching your tribe a lesson. A lesson they won't forget after what they have done to us! Don't we!" Trid looked at his two colleagues.

Who both agreed whole-heartedly with their compatriot.

Luce was by now absolutely terrified. It was beginning to dawn on her who these three could possibly be. They were the three evil characters from last year. Yet, how were they back? It did not make sense. Yet, one thing she knew was that she was in great danger. What had they got planned for her?

It crossed her mind that she needed to get back and warn the rest of her people that these three evil fellow creatures had returned. Furthermore, they were back and intent on revenge against them. Yet, how was she going to escape their clutches. Escape seemed impossible.

"Please let me go!" She started to plead with them. "I promise I won't tell anybody about you being here! I just need to get home. They will be worried where I am!" With that she started to cry.

"Oh! She cries as well!" Sur giggled again. "I like it when little puddle hoppers cry! It makes it so much more fun!"

"She might as well have a good cry now for she won't be able to cry much when we take her to where she's going!" Rak added.

"What do you mean? Where are you taking me?" She tried to back away from them in fear but there was nowhere to back away too. They had surrounded her.

She hadn't thought about how they had suddenly arrived all around her. If she had, she would have realised it did not make sense because she was being so careful in studying every direction to see if any human beings were about. Surely, in these sweeps she had undertaken she would have spotted the three puddle hoppers coming her way. Yet, she had not! How was it possible they were suddenly next to her. She was about to find out.

"Here! Tie this around her waist!" Trid gave the cloud rope to Rak while he held her tight.

"What are you doing?" She looked down puzzled as Rak completed tying the knot on the very light but strong cloud cord.

"You'll find out!" Giggled Surr.

"But we were meant to only collect children?" Rak mentioned. "What will they say when we bring this puddle hopper girl up on to the cloud?"

"They won't say anything! They'll see we have taken her for ourselves!" Rak abruptly replied. "We need to get revenge on the puddle hoppers below too! They know that! She'll be useful when we start to set up our own tribe very far away from here."

"I think we should take her whole tribe and drop them in to the ocean!" Surr snarled. "After what they let those humans do to us last year! To think they even helped them. Against their own kind too! They're not fit to call themselves puddle hoppers!"

All this terrified Lace even more.

"Right! Let's get her up there!" Rak called out.

With a tug on their very thin cloud ropes, the three of them plus their hostage, Lace, commenced to make their way up to the clouds. At first, it was with an almighty jolt. Particularly for Lace, who was stunned by this sudden upwards motion. It was down to her three captives to steady her as they rose up higher. It was strange for her, as her feet left the ground and she almost began to float in the air.

But there was no doubt she could feel the rope around her waist pulling her ever upwards. Yet, the rope was so thin you could hardly see it. There was such a lightness to the cord, it did not seem possible that it could hold anyone's weight!

Now she understood how the three evil puddle hoppers had appeared around her so suddenly and without any warning. They had arrived on this gossamer-like rope. It was like trying to see a fisherman's line between his rod and the sea as you walk past but you never can as it is far too thin.

Lace couldn't believe what was happening to her as she was pulled further and further up in to the sky.

"Where are you taking me! What is happening!" She cried in trepidation as to why she was being lifted up in to the sky. She did not understand what was going on. It all seemed like a bad dream.

Higher and higher they went. The cord around her waist holding her tight and secure as they neared the clouds above. The other three holding on to her as they rose up. Ensuring she did not try to escape from them. Not that that would have been very clever as she was likely to fall to her death at that point.

The ground below was getting so far away. Everything below was getting smaller and smaller as if they were becoming toy models in a shop window. The four of them swayed a bit in the breeze but nothing stopped their advance up in to the clouds.

What the three kidnappers did not notice as they surrounded Lace and started to tie the cloud rope around her was that her small pet mouse slipped away. The mouse ran down her leg and away without them even realising its presence. The small creature commenced to make its way back to the tribe's home.

*****

Jules arrived at the road besides the puddle hopper's homeland. He did a thorough check all around him to ensure no one was watching before he ventured in to the field where his friends lived. Looking across the field it was almost impossible to believe that a tribe of unknown creatures lived beneath the puddles that looked so innocent and still.

Puddles that looked like any other puddle you came across on your daily travels. Jules often found himself looking in to puddles as he passed them by and wondered if there was a puddle hopper in there looking up at him.

By the time he had reached the huge puddle that never seemed to dry up, Prok was coming out of the puddle to greet him. The tribe clearly knew who was around their home and tracked them while they were in the vicinity.

"Another visit from my good friend!" Prok smiled and sat down beside the puddle to greet him. "It's good to see you again. We don't see you almost for a year and here you are again. Twice within a very short time!"

"I am pleased to see you Prok but, at the same time, I come with a few concerns you may or may not know about!"

Prok could see by Jules's face that he was worried about something. He knew Jules would not come to the tribe's home unless it was absolutely necessary.

"You better come below so we can speak without having to be wary of other people observing us."

Jules nodded and he knew what he had to do. Prok waved for him to step in to the puddle and Jules accepted the offer. As soon as his foot hit the water, he was sucked down in to the underworld below. Once more, finding himself in the huge cavern where the puddle hoppers lived.

Jules followed Prok over to where his father, the chief, was sitting with a group of elders. They, again, greeted him as a respectful friend. Very few humans were allowed in to this alternative world as trusted friends but Jules was one of the few.

"Father, Jules says he has a worrying concern for us!"

"Let us hear what he has to say!" His father invited Jules to sit down with him. "You are welcome as a friend of the tribe. Speak freely, Jules, so we can understand what the problem is!"

Jules began to explain to the chief, Prok and a group of elders gathered there about the TV news reports he had been listening to. Telling them about the children disappearing again as they had done last year and how the odd shoe was being left by puddles around the town. He explained how he was wondering if the tribe knew anything about what was going on. Further, he told them how these reports were beginning to be linked back to last year's disappearances. He explained that he was worried that the puddle hoppers could end up being blamed for these latest children disappearing.

When he had finished telling them his worries, he waited to hear their reply. For a while, the elders discussed it in great detail in their own high-pitched language. At times, looking at Jules with concern. Of course, he had no idea what this all meant.

After a long consultation the chief turned towards the boy and started to give their considered reply.

"Jules! We believe that our very distant cousins who live a very different lifestyle to us and behave in a far less moralistic way have returned to this town. We think they are intent on doing harm to your people and our people."

Jules gave a puzzled look to the chief. He had no idea there could be even more puddle hoppers in the world. But if you think about it why not! Why would there only be puddle hoppers in this small town.

The chief began to explain. "You see, puddle hoppers became separated right across the world many thousands of years ago, like human beings were by oceans separating continents. As you can imagine each tribe began to live in very different ways from the others. Changing to survive in the very different habitats they found themselves in."

"One of these tribes, Jules, took to living in the clouds. We call them the cloud jumpers, as they have the ability to jump from one cloud to the next as well as having the skill to use twisted cloud rope that you can hardly see to make excursions up and down to the earth below. Like us, they have remained almost unknown to human beings."

"You mean they live in the clouds above us?" This was startling news to the boy. Who would ever have thought that creatures could be living in those clouds right above our heads.

"Yes! Yet, although, they have not been really a major problem to mankind, to us puddle hoppers they have been at loggerheads as far back as we can remember. They take our youngsters and, I must add as well, your human children too. They then use these captive children to make special cloud homes they can travel through the sky with."

Jules took in a deep breath of shock. He had never imagined when he went there he was going to hear such an astonishing story.

"Yes, sadly," Continued the leader of this tribe. "They want to take these young people and puddle hoppers and put them to work in their cloud-making factories. Of course, we try to stop their kidnapping and, hence, it has ended up with us being their foes. We believe their behaviour is totally unacceptable!"

"And do you think it is them. They have returned and they are the ones taking the children?" The boy probed. Trying to make sense of what they were telling him.

"Yes! We do. Some of our own people have seen them using the very thin cloud lines to go up and down from the clouds to the earth. We have spotted them up there in the clouds as well." He paused before continuing. "I am afraid it appears a very dangerous time for our young people and yours."

"They seem to be taking such large numbers of children this time! This has never happened before and we are unsure why." Prok interrupted his father.

"But why would they leave just an odd shoe by puddles if they are taking the children up in to the clouds?" Jules had not worked this one out in his head yet.

"Us, elders, have been discussing that very point, Jules!" He looked seriously at the tribe's friend. "We believe they wish us to get the blame for stealing the children!"

There was a look of horror on Jules's face as at long last he began to realise the likely implications of what was happening.

"In other words!" Jules commenced. "If people's stories from last year are re-examined, in the light of the children disappearing this year, they will give more credence to those who said they were held captive in puddles. Although, last year, such ideas were ignored and people said it was all due to some sort of mass hypnosis. Now they may begin to believe them. And once they begin to blame the puddle hoppers for the children's disappearance, it would not be long before the humans began to see you as evil creatures. The worry is they would then start to attack you in fear and retribution."

"I think you are beginning to see what horrifying tricks the cloud jumpers might be up to, my friend!" Even the chief was looking worried at this point. He realised his tribe could be in danger of extermination unless something could be done to stop the cloud jumpers game plan.

"But how would they know about last year?" The thought crossed Jules's mind. "Were they up there watching us?"

"We were not aware of their presence but they could have been. In the light of recent events, they probably were here. They may have decided to keep out of sight during the days when the three evil puddle hoppers were causing so much trouble. They may have wanted to see how things worked out for us and whether we could survive the probable human backlash."

"And now they are going to use what happened last year against us!" Prok shook his head in anger.

It was then that both Prok and Jules heard the little squeaks coming from the side where the young puddle hopper was sitting. Both looked down to see the mouse was clawing at Prok's side. It was as if the mouse was trying to catch his attention which, of course, he was.

Jules did not understand the significance of this at first. He smiled as Prok picked up the mouse in quite a different mood to his friend. Prok looked perturbed and fretful as he held the mouse up to his face. It was as if he was trying to get the mouse to talk to him.

"Is something wrong?" The guest asked.

"The mouse belongs to Lace!" He continued to stroke it. "She never goes anywhere without it! Something must have happened to her!" There was real concern in his voice. He looked at his father and the other elders, who were by now, themselves beginning to be alarmed. They were aware also how she took the little pet everywhere with her. It was quite a joke amongst the puddle hopper community.

"She went out searching for moss for those who can't get out themselves!" The chief's son added.

"We must send out a search party!" The leader stated. "Let's not jump to conclusions. Let us try to find her and establish the facts!"

With that the chief turned to his advisers and they were soon in a high-pitched discussion. From this Jules was sidelined.

*****

As soon as Lace arrived on the cloud, her hands were tied with cloud string and she was pushed along across the cloud by her three captors. The three of them seemed to be very comfortable on the clouds now. It was as if they were cloud jumpers themselves. Their confidence on being on the cloud had developed quickly over the last few days.

Soon Lace was led in to a space within the cloud itself. Each space was like a white-coated room. The sight almost made her cry for she knew she had become their prisoner. Furthermore, even though she was being held captive herself, she could now see many children there also. Tied up in neat little rows. It was as if they were slaves aboard a slave ship bound for the Americas.

Many were crying for mothers and fathers as well as the fact that they wanted to go home. Not that it mattered to the cloud jumpers who set about their business around them. Just beyond the children, they reached another white room where she was told to sit and they bound her up like the children she had just seen. There was no escape.

Lace was beginning to think she would never see her home or her own tribe again. It appeared these three cruel puddle hoppers were intent on taking her away with them. She was not to join the children at the cloud-making factory.

They wanted her for themselves.

Chapter 11

"Mum, there are a lot of people standing at our front gate!" Jules noticed as he looked out of his bedroom window. "Some of them have cameras. I think they are reporters!" He noticed many of them had paper and pen or were on their telephones.

His mum opened the downstairs window curtains at the front of the house to be confronted by the same picture. It could only be the press. She had no idea why they were there or what they wanted. But she felt it could not be good.

Opening the curtains, seems to have signalled to the reporters that they could now legitimately knock at her door and ask her questions.

She heard the first knock at the door and naively opened it. Whether she thought it was a neighbour, a postman or a delivery man who knows, but it did not cross her mind it would be one of the newspaper reporters wanting to interview her.

"Can I help you?" She looked at the reporter mystified as to why he was at her door.

"The mayor has reported that he believes you sabotaged his factory because you are a spy from a far eastern country. That it was an attempted espionage! Have you anything to say to that?"

"Me! A spy! Espionage! Has he lost his head!" Was all she could respond. This was so bizarre it was beyond being farcical.

"Yes! The mayor explained that in reality he makes ammunition for the army at the factory and was undertaking a very top-secret order at the time. Your actions will greatly delay his delivery times and he suggests that was your aim. Would you like to reply to that?" The reporter was saying this as if he really believed it to be true and a good story. For that was what he was after was a good story. "He states he did not realise at the time that you were working for a foreign country and your only reason for being in the job was because you had been ordered to stop production of the much needed ammunition by the armed forces. Would you like to respond, Constance, to his statement! Have you got anything to say for yourself!'

"But he only makes pickles from onions there! That is all he does! He doesn't make ammunition for the army that's all nonsense!"

"Ah! But as it is top secret what his company was making then it would be obvious to hide it under the guise of making something normal like pickles! Isn't that true, Constance!"

"That could be true! But believe me, all the time I was there, I only ever was involved in making pickles and that was all!" Jules' mum was beginning to get frustrated. By now there were a group of journalists standing around her and the photographers were taking photos with their flashes going off all the time. Poor Constance was being blinded by them as she stood there. Of course, she had no experience of how to handle the press and they were making the most of it.

"But, perhaps, you were making pickles, while the real workers, elsewhere in the factory were making ammunition. Your job was part of the elaborate deception. Yet, as a spy you knew what was really going on there. Hence, you took your time to plan the operation to blow up the factory as required by the foreign government you work for."

"Come on!" She gasped in disbelief. "Next you will be saying, I'm Mrs. James Bond! This is total fantasy! I know every bit of that factory inside out. It's not that big! And I know everyone in there. None of them are working on ammunition! Everybody is only working on making pickles to be sold! Just pickles! Nothing but pickles! Talk to any of his employees and they will tell you! I think the mayor is losing his mind or something!"

"But Mrs. Appleyard, the mayor says that you were heard speaking in a foreign language. Possibly Chinese!" Another reporter added.

"What! I can't speak any other language but English and only English! If someone told him they heard me speaking in a foreign language, they must have mistaken my mumbling and grumbling at having to work at such a horrid place for a foreign language! And what is more, the explosion was an accident!

That was all! I think the mayor is trying to get a bigger insurance cheque if you ask me! As well as put all the blame on me rather than his pickling machine!"

With that she slammed the door closed as the reporters continued to try to ask her more questions about events on the day of the explosion. She could not believe that these highly intelligent newspaper men were believing such idiocy that was being put about by the mayor.

*****

A few hours later a black car arrived outside the house and the journalists were all moved to the side by the local police officers. When the path to the house was clear, the man on the backseat of this very auspicious looking car got a nod from a very senior looking police officer he could get out.

You straight away felt there was something special about this man getting out of the car. He looked important wearing his dark glasses and carrying a briefcase. His suit was dark and he was wearing a grenadier officer's tie. His shoes had been cleaned that morning and his face looked suitably serious to fit his presentation. The local police chief nodded to him at which house he was to go to and then watched him make his way up the garden path to the front door.

He knocked a few times but Jules's mum was reluctant to open the door. At first believing him to be just another journalist wanting a story. It was only when she peeped out the window and realised that the crowd of newspaper journalists had been moved back and it was the police who were stopping them entering the garden that she thought she had better open the door.

"Hello, Mrs. Appleyard, I assume?" The man in his dark glasses and suit asked. He must have been in his thirties and had well-groomed hair. Yet, a rather ambiguous smile. One you were not too sure if it was a friendly one or not.

"Yes?"

"I would like to ask you a few questions if possible. I am from M15 and it would appear there is some questions about your actions at Mr. Brian's factory that may need answering."

Constance could not believe it. The country's security forces were now involved. It seemed so silly when it was only an accident that had happened at the pickle factory.

"Come in!"

He must have noticed the frustration in her voice.

She led the very important looking man in to the living room. Jules remained upstairs, out of the way, wondering what was going on.

"If I understand this correctly, Mrs. Appleyard, Mr. Brian believes you are a foreign spy who blew up his factory to stop ammunition being made for the army?"

Constance nodded, flabbergasted by his statement.

"Of course, I have checked your police records and any other piece of information I can find on you and I can find no connection with you and any sort of espionage! Nor are there any such links to extremist groups!"

"I know!" She felt quite relieved at what his searches had discovered! She knew it was all preposterous. She had no such ridiculous connections to any foreign country or hostile extremist groups. "Look, I'm afraid he's making all of this up! I think it is to try and get a good pay out from the insurance company or something! It's madness! Total madness! I am no spy! I never blew up his factory! It was a total accident due to faulty equipment!"

"Well! We have to look in to these matters I am afraid! I can find no record of ammunition being made on the site either. It seems to be just pickles are being made there as you suggest."

"Yes! Yes! Thank goodness someone is seeing sense at last!" She felt quite relieved at everything this MI5 officer was saying. He had seemed to have looked up the facts.

"I don't think there is any need for me to take this matter any further but as MI4 passed this matter on to me to check out, I will now pass the matter on to MI6 to check it out as well!"

"MI6? What do you mean? Can't you just tell them it's utter nonsense!" She exclaimed.

"I'm afraid not, Mrs. Appleyard. They will not allow me to do that! Each department has to investigate the matter for itself and then pass it on to the next department!"

"Well how many more departments need to review it before the security services realise that none of it is true?"

"Ah! I am afraid I am not at liberty to tell you that! It's top secret of course! But there are quite a number of departments who will need to check this matter before the final okay is given!"

The lady sitting opposite him could only look at him in despair.

"Well! What am I to do in the meantime! With the press hounding me. The police wanting to send me to trial! My life is in ruins!"

"Once our investigations are all completed, I am sure the press and police will fall in line with our findings!" He smiled at her.

"Well! How long will that take?" She pleaded.

"A good question, Mrs, Applegate. It can be any time from six weeks to two years!"

With that the MI5 officer got up and made his way out, thanking her for her time and disappeared in to his very big black car.

The police were the next to knock on the door.

"Morning, Mrs. Appleyard, we would like you to accompany us down to the police station for a chat!"

"But I have already told you everything about the explosion at the pickle factory!"

"Yes! But we have some more questions for you now! The mayor has been making further statements on the matter. Hence, I am afraid we will need to discuss these new revelations with you. So put on your coat and shoes and let's get going!" The police officer gave her no smile or any sign of human warmth as he tried to hurry her along.

Once again, at the police station, Jules's mum had to put up with a torrid rush of quick-fire questions that were very far from the truth. The mayor had made a further statement saying that it was her who had been kidnapping the local children on behalf of the foreign country she worked for. She was then getting them sent to that country as cheap child labour.

All this was difficult to defend against, especially as she could not afford a lawyer. In truth, there was no evidence to prove anything against her except that she had accidently made a faulty machine explode in the pickle factory.

How was she meant to defend herself against such ludicrous accusations that her boss was making.

*****

"Now after hearing what your boss, Mr. Brian, has been saying about the explosion and Constance Appleyard's part in it, was there anything you noticed about her that might have suggested to you that she was working for a foreign government?" The intrepid local reporter, Robin Biggs, was now on to this story. It was an attempt to try and get a reaction from one of Constance's co-workers at the factory. He was after a scoop.

"Well! Now you have put it that way! Perhaps, Mr. Brian was right about her. I mean these foreign spies are very good at hiding their true identities and doing their sabotage unnoticed. It is just what they are like when you see them in a spy movie on TV isn't it. You would never know they were a spy, would you!"

"Do you think she could have pretended to be friends with you. While her sole intention was really to infiltrate the factory and start the explosion!"

"Ohh! I never looked at it that way! She was certainly very friendly! I mean that could have been her intention, couldn't it!"

"Have you ever heard her speaking in a foreign language?" The TV journalist continued to question her. His bosses back at the TV studio's centre pushing him to get more information. "A slip, maybe. She would have been trying to hide her real identity and country of origin, there is no doubt."

"Come to think of it, now you mention it, there were times when I couldn't understand a word she was saying. I thought that was down to the noise of the machines in the pickle factory, but it could well be that she was talking in a foreign language!"

"And do you think that the factory was making ammunition for the army? Let's be honest, you were working there and would probably know whether or not, production of such items was taking place. And Mr. Brian, the owner, has already stated that the factory was making military produce. Not just pickles. That is why he believes the factory had been infiltrated by Constance. She was a spy and sent there to stop production at any cost."

"Yes! The factory was a strange place to work. Although we were making pickles at our end of the workshop, goodness knows, what they were getting up to at the other end. They were always a strange lot over the other side of the building. They could have been doing anything!"

"Well, ladies and gentlemen, this does seem to suggest there is a reason to look further in to Constance Appleyard's actions on that day at the factory. What, at first, seemed like an innocent accident is now turning in to an international incident. We do seem, possibly, to have our own case of a foreign spy working in one of local factories. Moreover, their clear intention was to halt production of military hardware at any cost. No doubt we shall be hearing more about this case in the near future." He looked sternly back in to the camera. "That is all for now, from your roving local reporter, Robin Biggs!"

*****

Jules's mum had arrived home exhausted and stunned after another visit to the police station. There they had interrogated her as if she was a master criminal or a crazed terrorist. The questioning was undertaken by a senior officer, who specialised in cross-examination. He had been brought down especially from London to do the interview. In the interview, one question followed another question with no time in between.

They had asked her if she would like a solicitor present. Yet, there was no way she could afford such expensive people. Where would she get the money! All she could hope for, is that by telling the truth, they would eventually see she was innocent and Mr. Brian was making it all up for his own reasons.

She sat down on the big armchair in their living room and took in a deep breath to try and take it all in what was happening to her. Jules was busy in the kitchen making her a cup of tea and a sandwich as they had not given her a thing to eat or drink since she entered the police station many hours ago.

Then, when they had completed their examination of her, they left her to find her own way home. Even though she was dazed and slightly confused by it all. Her son could see that she was not her normal self and in his usual supportive way was doing all he could to help.

The reporters had all disappeared after she was taken to the police station. So, once again, their home was returned to its usual serenity. A place that was quiet and still where nothing ever happened. Well, occasionally it did but not very often!

Jules heard a car pulling up outside their home as he was in the kitchen. He assumed that the car would be for a neighbour. So, he carried on making a cup of tea for his mum.

A few minutes later there was a knock at the door.

"Not more reporters!" Was his mum's first reaction.

"What do they want now? Don't tell me your boss has been making up more stories about you!" You could tell Jules was as frustrated as his mother by these ongoing ludicrous allegations. "I'll go and answer the door!" He smiled before his mum got up. He knew she needed to rest and recuperate.

He was nearly knocked back off his feet when he saw his two cousins standing there in front of him. Both Jules and his mum had forgotten they were due as everything else that had happened that day had taken their full attention. "Bronwyn! Seth!" he said in a state of shock! "It's great to see you again!"

"Blimey! Cobber! We thought you were never going to answer the door mate!" Seth smiled.

By now Jules's mum had made her way to the door. She had heard Jules say the twin's names and remembered they were due to arrive. So, with haste she rushed through to greet her nephew and niece.

She was soon hugging them and greeting them as if they were her own children. If nothing else, their arrival had taken her mind totally off all that had been happening with the pickle factory.

She could now focus on these two youngsters who were to be her guests and let the ongoing case with the police be pushed to the back of her mind. They all sat in the living room and chatted for there was an awful lot to catch up with. For it was almost a year since they had parted.

"And how are your mum and dad?" Constance asked the twins.

"Oh! They're good!" Seth answered. "They've got lots of barbies over the next few weeks with work mates!"

"I think they'll be pleased to have a break from us two!" Bronwyn added.

"But it's great to be back in Boreham Wood with you two! We really missed it here, mate!" Seth looked around him with a warmth remembering last year's stay.

I am not too sure what Jules and his mum were both thinking at that moment. It was unclear whether they were remembering the previous twins visit in the same light as their two present guests were.

As the conversation continued, Bronwyn became awfully quiet. There was a reason for that. She had to focus on a little ear followed by the rest of the head that popped out of the backpack she had in front of her. The young kangaroo had been in the rucksack for quite a while. He wanted, obviously, to see where they were and what was going on.

The girl tried to hide roo's head by putting her leg in front of the bag. This hid him just enough to stop him being seen. Next, she attempted to try and push him back in to the bag unnoticed by the two facing her. This proved difficult as he was busy looking around the part of the room he could see.

The twins had decided not to mention anything about the roo in their rucksack. They felt sure their aunt would have their new friend taken to a zoo straight away. Yet, both children had grown to like him and wanted to keep him with them. Hence, they were hoping to keep its presence a secret. There was no doubt that was going to be a very difficult task.

"Isn't it lovely to see both of your cousins again, Jules!" His mum beamed.

"We had such a lovely time with you both last year!"

Jules thought to himself, "I think you are forgetting a lot of things that happened while they were here, mother."

"Yes! It's wonderful to have you two back again!" He carried on. Wondering what on earth Bronwyn was up to as she seemed to be continuously pushing something back down in to her bag. But the twins were the twins!

"No news from your Uncle Gideon then?" Seth asked his aunt and cousin.

While he was asking the question, Bronwyn finally succeeded in getting the roo right back down in to the knapsack. It was as if she was trying to place a very large woolly jumper in to a very small space as she pushed and shoved. At last, she sat back up looking relaxed. Yet, she was wise enough this time to keep her backpack hidden behind her leg. So those facing her could not see if the roo started to shift about occasionally.

"Now, why don't you two go upstairs and get yourselves settled in to Jules' room."

"Have we got the same arrangements as last year?"

"Yes!" She replied without thinking.

Jules looked at her aghast, wondering how she could say that. He wanted the bed to sleep in this year.

The twins nodded to each other and started to collect their bags to go upstairs to the room they were going to share with Jules. While he could only watch worried what he would find upstairs when he eventually got up there. After they had both, so called, "settled in!"

When they had disappeared upstairs, Jules and his mum made their way in to the kitchen. Each having the same idea as the other. They went to the cupboard where the money was kept. There was an area designated for his mum's and his own savings boxes.

"Where do you think we ought to put these money boxes?" Jules asked his mum. Both remembering what had happened last year. "I know let's try hiding them in the pantry!" "That's a good idea!" Her son agreed.

Finally, they both settled on a place for their money boxes at the back of the pantry where they believed the twins, who last year stole all their money, would never find them.

"That will do!" His mum nodded.

"They are making a lot of noise up there?" His mum noted. Obviously, Jules never made any sort of sound in his own room. He was as quiet as a mouse walking on a tightrope normally. "I wonder what they are up to!" She puzzled. "Probably, both are a bit lively after sitting still on that plane for so long!" She concluded.

At that point, Jules decided to get up to his bedroom as quickly as he could. He dreaded to think what they could be up to, making such a racket. He ran up those stairs as if he was late for the departing Eurostar train from London to Paris. He wanted to ensure they left everything in his room as it was and that he got the bed. His own bed. Somehow, he doubted that would happen.

They both could hear Jules coming up the stairs.

"Let's put roo under the bed before cous gets here!" Bronwyn exclaimed.

Seth nodded in agreement.

Yet, as they turned towards the small kangaroo they were horrified to see it was eating carrots. They both were puzzled as to how the roo had gotten hold of carrots. When with total horror they realised it was eating the models their cousin had carved out of carrot. Models he had placed proudly on display on the sideboard.

Jules had reached the bedroom door as they finally got their secret roo hidden under the bed. Both raised their fingers to their mouths to say "sshhh!" to the unknown guest. Hoping he would remain still and quiet.

"Watcha Cous! We've got the beds! If that's all right with ya! Same as last year mate!" Bronwyn grinned.

"We knew you gave them to us last year and would want to do the same this buckaroo year!" Seth added. "Real good of ya, mate!"

In the few minutes that Jules and his mum had been in the kitchen trying to find another hiding place for their money savings, the twins had managed to remove his pyjamas from the bed and put them on the sleeping bag. Now one of them had his bed. While the other had the comfortable fold-up bed.

Poor Jules had ended up with the sleeping bag again. Their clothes were by now all laid out neatly on the top of what they considered their beds as if it was a fashion show. Once again, Jules had missed out on securing his own place of sleep for the length of their stay. He was demoted to the sleeping bag again.

There was a really dejected look on Jules's face as he contemplated the fact that he was going to spend the next few weeks again in a sleeping bag on the very hard floor. While those two slept in reasonable comfort. Still, it was too late to do anything about it. Once again, he just had to accept it.

"No! That'll be fine! It will be okay!" His face cracked a reasonable looking smile in return but it was a real, real struggle.

"Thanks, mate!" Bronwyn tapped his shoulder in gratitude. "You're a great cous!"

"By the way mate, we got you this!" Seth brought out from his case the Australian cricket bat and ball. The ones they had managed to take from the wicket-keeper as she slept on the plane when they were searching for the escaped roo. "Thought yer might like them as a pressy, mate!"

Seth handed his cousin the shining, lovely smelling cricket bat and the cherry red hard ball. They looked like they had only recently come out of the sports shop.

"They were given to us by one of the ladies Australian cricket team who was on the same airplane as us, Jules! Can yer believe it, mate!" Bronwyn told a little white lie and winked at her brother.

"Wow! Thanks! It's great!" Jules was truly stunned as he looked at this almost new cricket bat and ball. "You say they are from the ladies Australian cricket team! Don't you think you should keep them for yourselves! It is such a valuable gift!" He was so pleased with his present that he was even beginning to forgive them for taking his bed and leaving him the sleeping bag on the hard floor.

"No way, mate!" Seth intervened. "We want to give it to you as a pressy! You're such a great cous to us!"

"That is so kind!" He glared at his new gifts with joy. It was such a great present. One he would cherish for years to come. Getting a gift from his cousins last year was a first, for he had never received a gift from any one bar his own mother of course.

"You know! I've never played cricket!" He confessed to his cousins. "I have watched it on the tele but never had a go!"

"You've never played the greatest sport in the world, mate!" Seth looked shocked. "Well! It's lucky Sis and I are here. We can teach yer the game!"

"Yeah! We'll make a cricketer of yer!" Bronwyn put a reassuring hand on his shoulder.

The smell of freshly cut willow from the wooden cricket bat filled their bedroom. It was such an exciting but smoothing smell.

Yet, there was another smell in the room. An odd smell. Jules had noticed it when he entered. At that point, the cricket bat and ball were in the case. So, the strong smell of his presents did not hide the more over-riding one that had pervaded this bedroom when he first entered.

His nose went in the air again to try to figure out what it was.

Suddenly, the twins panicked. They realised their cousin was sniffing the air. They concluded perhaps he could smell the roo under the bed. For on entering the room, they had decided to let it have a bit of a run around. In an instant the roo was bouncing all over the place enjoying his freedom after being cooped up for so long in that tiny backpack.

These were the noisy sounds Jules' mum had heard in the kitchen coming from above. Kangaroos were never meant to be still or confined! The two children left it to run around for a while, realising it needed to let off steam and do some exercising. It is true the room was a bit small and the marsupial did keep bouncing into and off the walls like a rubber ball but it was doing itself no harm.

"That's odd? Where have my carrot models gone?" Suddenly it dawned on their cousin they were no longer on the sideboard where he had so proudly arranged them.

"Ah! Those! Right!" Seth looked at Bronwyn as if to say, "How can we explain this?"

"Yes! Well! What happened cous was we accidently knocked them over. Blimey mate, we did not want to upset you. So, we were hoping you would not notice. They were smashed up real bad and we were going to make new ones that looked exactly the same cous. Then we were going to replace them." Bronwyn made it all up on the spur of the moment to try and somehow appease Jules!

"Yeah! Mate! That's dead right!" Seth agreed. "We are so sorry, it was a big, big accident and we were hoping to replace them before you realised. But now, you know, we can only say sorry, mate!"

Jules was so disappointed. He had made those carrot characters and was hoping the twins would be impressed with his artistic work! Unfortunately, it seemed to him as if the twins were up to their old tricks again with the carrot characters being broken and then disappearing. It was rather odd though to say the least. Yet, he was used to everything to do with the twins being odd. And if the twins were going to be up to their old tricks, he wondered what kind of holiday it was going to be like this time.

All night, whenever, Jules woke up he could have sworn he heard a strange sound. It was as if there was someone else in the room who was asleep and snoring. In the end, he convinced himself that the sound must be something to do with one of the twins and the way they slept. He was sure it was coming from somewhere close to them. Perhaps, one of them, had a double snore or one of their stomachs was rumbling all night as they were still hungry.

Jules was first down for breakfast with the twins following close behind him.

"Did you twins sleep okay?" His mum asked.

"Sleep! We were like two full-up crocodiles asleep on the beach at Darwin. It was great!" Seth barked.

"By the way, Jules, we left a book on the bed you might enjoy!"

"Hey! That's good of you! First a cricket bat and ball and now a book! You are so kind!"

"That's really kind of your cousins, Jules, why don't you go up and take a look at it!"

"Okay!" Jules was intrigued to know what book they had bought him. Hence, he was soon running up the stairs to enter the bedroom.

It never crossed his mind, that it was a bit strange that they had left the bedroom door slightly ajar. It never crossed his mind he could be walking in to a trap. His thoughts were so focused on the chance of getting a new book as a present.

Forgetting what the twins were like, he pushed the door to the bedroom open and took one step in. It was just enough space for the water bomb the twins had made to fall on him from above the door and burst. Whether it was luck or well planned, it is difficult to know, as the water from the water bomb exploded all over Jules so he was soaked from head to foot.

He stood there drenched through.

"The twins have arrived!" He thought to himself.

"You've changed your clothes!" His mum commented as he came back down for breakfast.

"Yes!" He gave a look of annoyance to the twins as they rolled about laughing. It had taken him quite a while to clear up the water from the floor that had fallen about him. His clothes he had decided to hide until his mum had gone to work. Then he would put them outside on the washing line to dry off. "I realised it was going to be a bit warmer than I thought so I decided to change and put on some lighter clothing!"

While he made his speech to his mum as he was sitting down, the twins were covering up their mouths to hide their own laughter.

It was surprising that Constance had not noticed their giggling. Yet, she was so focused on getting breakfast for the three teenagers and thinking about getting herself ready for work. The obvious reason for Jules changing his clothing escaped her.

"Now Jules, I've been thinking!" His mum looked her son in the eye.

"Okay!" He looked at her uncertain as to what she was about to say.

"Well! The twins may like you to take them down to the new shopping-centre that has just opened. You could show them around!" She smiled sweetly at him. "They could probably do with a lazy day at a slower pace to recover from their long journey. Come to think of it they are still probably recovering from their jet lag!"

Jules mulled it over for a moment and thought that could be a good idea. The three of them would be able to wander around the new shopping-centre in a relaxed way. Maybe, some people he knew would see him with his cousins. How proud he would be to say to them, "Yes! These are my cousins from Australia!"

The twins looked at him waiting for a reply. They were beginning to get a bit worried he might say, "No" due to his being upset about the water bomb.

"Yes! That's a really good idea!" He replied finally. A smile crept across his face as he looked at the twins. "I think they will enjoy a slow, lazy day of recovery!"

"That sounds buckaroo, cous!" Seth tapped him on the arm in agreement.

"It will be good to look around the Brit shops again as well!" The truth was Bronwyn liked shopping.

*****

After Jules's mum had said her farewells and hoped they had a fun day in town, she began to focus on the hard day's graft that lay ahead for her. Moreover, her thoughts zoomed in on the accusations Mr. Brian was making about her due to the explosion at the pickle factory. Straight away, at having such ideas, she began to get upset and feel rather gloomy about it all.

The future did not look good for her. The thoughts went whirling around and around in her mind as she commenced her journey to work. For a short while, with the twin's arrival it had taken such matters off her mind. Now they were back. Back with a vengeance.

While Jules was busy doing some housework downstairs, the twins were upstairs plotting as usual.

"Let's take the roo with us, Sis! He won't be any problem, I'm rip sure." He looked at the cute fella with a friendly eye. "You won't be a problem will you mate!" Stroking the young creature as if it was a new puppy.

"Let's stick it in the backpack then, Seth!" She replied. "There were no problems with it at the airport and on the plane. It seemed to be quiet all night as well. So, it should be able to sit still and quiet in the bag I reckon while we go around the shops!"

They commenced to speak to the roo as if it was a small child. A child who understood every word they were saying. Hence, they started to explain how they were taking it in to town and it must remain out of sight in the rucksack.

"It's a chance for you to get out and get some air, mate! Instead of being stuck in this small room!" Seth carried on stroking it.

"And remember to keep still in the bag!" Bronwyn reiterated looking it in the eye.

Both seemed to be under the impression this young kangaroo would be able to do exactly what it had been told.

At that point Jules came in to the room and was a bit surprised how they suddenly seemed to both tense up for some reason and go quiet. It was as if he was intruding on something. A secret between the both of them he was not meant to know about. They both stood up suddenly and made a fuss over the backpack before putting it on Seth's back. He thought no more about it as he searched for his socks in the drawer.

"We'll meet you downstairs in the hall Jules!" Bronwyn said.

"Yeah! Mate! We're ready. Ready to go as a work pony in a tin mine!" Seth supported her.

"Okay! Won't be long!" Their host replied.

When the twins got downstairs, they spent a few moments whispering to each other before disappearing in to the kitchen. Very quietly, you could hear the gentle movement of jars and boxes being moved about. Yet, it was not noisy enough for Jules who was still upstairs in the bedroom to be aware of what was going on down there.

"Come on cous!" Bronwyn called up. "We're ready!"

"I'm here!" Jules came running downstairs. The small group were soon closing the front door behind them as they departed.

*****

At the shopping-centre the twins were in their element. Rushing here and rushing there. It was as if they did not have any shops in Adelaide. Both of them seemed to be really interested in the fashion stores, especially Bronwyn. And as other teenagers passed by, they were really keen to look at what they were wearing. Asking Jules if that was the latest fashion or not.

Not being able to afford to keep up with fashion trends, their cousin found all of that quite difficult. He had no choice but to confess he was not too sure if something was fashionable or not. Fashion not being his thing.

At one store Bronwyn decided to try on a t-shirt. She put her backpack down on the floor while she went in to the changing room to put it on. It seemed for a moment she had totally forgotten about a certain small creature in the rucksack. At the same time, the two boys were elsewhere busy looking at the sportswear.

They took no notice of what Bronwyn was up to and where she had put her bag down. Especially, Seth who should have been looking out for the young kangaroo when the bag was on the ground. But it seemed he had forgotten about the young animal they had with them!

Jules was amazed at the amount of money the two twins had to spend. "Their parents must have given them a lot of money to come over to England with!" He thought.

"They seem to have enough money to buy lots of different clothes. How lucky they are!"

He could only watch in admiration while they spent the money on new items in the shops. If only he could have done the same. It never crossed his mind that the money may have come from a bit closer to home. He thought his mum and he had hidden their savings really well having learnt from what the twins did last year. Or, at least, they thought they had hidden it well enough!

While Bronwyn was in the changing room, the roo popped it's head out of the rucksack. It could not work out why the walking movement it had got used to had stopped. It became concerned as to what was happening. A bit alarmed that it may have been deserted.

Once, its head was out of the rucksack, it could see that the twins were not around. This began to worry the young creature. Yet, there were a lot of strangers around. Strangers who seemed to be getting closer and closer. Yet, the two people he wanted to see were nowhere to be seen.

The roo decided to explore this new environment it found itself in. Squeezing the rest of its body out of the backpack. After a few flexing of stiff muscles, it made its first leap across the showroom of the shop. No one seemed to notice. But as it began to knock over displays of clothes and its strong tail whipped around and felled mannequins or stands, it caused people to look in its direction.

Yet, by the time the shoppers had looked to see what was happening, the small creature had moved away to another part of the store at lightning speed. Leaving the onlookers puzzled as to what had occurred. Why were clothes, stands and mannequins lying on the floor.

It was a small boy who first noticed the young kangaroo leaping around the store floor.

"Mum, I think I can see a kangaroo!" He smiled with glee. Giving the creature a wave.

"Nonsense! Kangaroos only live in Australia! And that's a place very far away from here!"

Yet, a few moments later, she screeched in shock, at seeing that it was a kangaroo who was leaping around the store. Here son was right. "There's a kangaroo leaping around your store!" She called over to a sales assistant who was standing a few feet away and wondered what was going on.

The sales assistant smiled in jest at first. But her eyes nearly popped out of her head when she saw it as well!

Soon there were a number of sales staff frantically trying to capture the small renegade creature as it leapt about the huge space causing more and more damage. It was always that bit too fast for the sales personnel. It managed to keep a few feet between them and itself as it hopped around. Unfortunately, the room was taking a bit of a battering with a wild roo and its whipping tail running loose.

It continued to knock over anything that got in its way. Each time the sales assistants thought they had cornered it, the creature leapt away with a mighty jump. The marsupial was too fast, too nimble and, obviously, too clever for them.

It wasn't long before the roo had escaped in to the thoroughfare of the shopping-centre. Shoppers were soon dodging out of the way of this hopping whirlwind as it ran in panic from one end of the covered area to the other. Sometimes going in and out of shops on its way. One can only guess that it was searching for its two friends.

The shopping-centre's security guard were particularly peeved as it evaded them. They tried all sorts of ploys to capture the beast. Each one of them came to a miserable failure as the roo foiled them time and time again. It was as if the creature understood that it was being hunted down and there was a need for it to escape.

It wasn't long before a tannoy message was to be heard.

"I am afraid we appear to have a kangaroo leaping around the shopping centre. So, until we have captured it, please can we ask customers to enter in to the shops. With the store doors closed on to the thoroughfare you should be safe. Hopefully, our security staff will not take too long in capturing the creature. We are sorry for any inconvenience this may cause."

Bronwyn was unaware the roo had escaped from her bag. She was still admiring herself in the mirror of the changing room in the t-shirt. So, it came as a shock to hear that a kangaroo was jumping around the shopping-centre over the tannoy. Immediately, she knew it could only be their roo. "It must have got out of the bag," she thought with horror. She rushed over to where she had left the bag and was not surprised to see it was now empty. The kangaroo had gone.

Seth and Jules, at that moment, were enjoying a computer game in the gaming shop. With earphones on, they were unaware of the chaos taking place in the boulevard outside the shop they were in.

It was only when the tannoy interrupted their game to explain what was happening outside that they became aware. The speaker cutting in on their game channel. It was at that point Seth realised it could only be one particular kangaroo they were talking about. It had to be their kangaroo.

"A wild kangaroo here in our shopping-centre! That's a bit weird?" Jules shook his head in surprise. "How did a kangaroo get here, of all places?"

"Yer, does seem a bit odd, mate." Seth smiled at his cousin. Yet, in truth, he was more than aware as to how the kangaroo had arrived there. But he did not want to let on to his cousin.

"Hey! That's odd, isn't it!" Jules smiled to himself. "You two arrive from Australia and the next day a kangaroo is spotted in the shopping-centre where you are visiting! What a coincidence!"

"Sure is, mate!" Seth took a great gulp and hoped that their cousin did not put two and two together and make four.

With great haste, he told his cousin to carry on playing the computer game while he popped out and told Bronwyn where they were.

Seth and Bronwyn arrived in the middle of the boulevard at the same time. They looked aghast at each other. The empty backpack in her hand told the story. "I only put the roo down for a mo'. One mo! I wanted to try on a t-shirt. The next mo' he was gone. Gone as fast as a jack rabbit down a sandy hole!" She fretted.

"Well, let's see if we can get him ourselves before those security guards do! Come on Sis!"

The two of them were soon running in the direction from where they could hear shouting. They assumed that was where the kangaroo must be.

When they arrived at that point, they could see the officials were looking inside a shop for the elusive creature. While both of them could observe the roo was actually on the opposite side of the thoroughfare to where they were searching.

They could see the small marsupial was sitting eating an apple. Someone must have dropped it in their hurry to get to safety inside a shop. Not another soul was to be seen on the boulevard. This was the twin's chance. Perhaps, it would be their only chance to get their friend back before he was caught by the security staff.

"Quick! Come on! We should be able to get the roo back in to our backpack without being seen with a bit of luck!" Seth whispered.

They both scurried along trying to remain undetected by the security team until they reached the young kangaroo. Fortunately, the creature did not try to get away from them. He even seemed pleased to see them. Bronwyn held out her hand and he came to her.

Seth started stroking his back to calm it down and they were able to put it back in the rucksack very quietly. Both kept an eye on the security guards on the other side of the building who had not seen what they were up to. Hence, the twins sighed with relief they had not been observed. Bronwyn put the now heavier bag on her back again and they started to make their way back to Jules.

"Hey! What are you two doing here? Everybody was meant to get off the boulevard and inside a shop!" A guard spotted them as they came around the corner.

"Oh! Is that why the place is so empty!" Bronwyn pretended to shake her head in surprise as if she did not know what was going on.

"We heard something on the old tannoy mate but couldn't understand it! We only just arrived from Australia yesterday!" Seth tried to explain.

"Um! You haven't seen a kangaroo running around have you?" He looked at them suspiciously.

"A kangaroo? No way mate! Didn't think you got them here in England!" Bronwyn tried to look confused. She was desperately hoping the roo in her rucksack was going to be very still. Not try to poke its head out at that moment!

"We don't! But there has been one hopping around the shopping centre!"

"Tell you what mate! See that fella over there!" Seth pointed at Jules, who was making his way down the boulevard. He was coming to see what had happened to his two cousins. His computer game had finished and he was wondering where they were.

"You mean him!" The security guard pointed at Jules.

"Yeah! That's him! Well, I saw him prancing around wearing a kangaroo suit. He threw that suit away in a bin only a little while ago! You don't think people thought he was a real kangaroo, do yer?" Seth was struggling to stop himself from laughing.

"Is that right! I shall go and have serious words with that young man! He's probably caused a lot of panic here with his prank!" The security guard shook his head in anger at the young man walking towards the three of them. "I think he is in going to be in a bit of trouble and thank you for helping! I hope you have a lovely stay in England both of you!"

With that the twins made a sharp exit in the opposite direction to which Jules was coming from. He watched them walk away and wondered why they were doing that. Surely, they had seen him.

"Oh! Well! Perhaps, they hadn't seen me!" He reflected on why they were walking away from him.

"Oi! You! I want to have a word with you!" The man in charge of security called over to the boy approaching him.

"Me?" Jules looked at him surprised. There was even a bigger surprise yet to come.

"I suppose you think that was funny! Do you realise you frightened a lot of people and closed down the entire shopping-centre with your stupid prank! I can tell you the owners of this place are not going to be pleased with you when they find out what you did! I don't want to see you in this shopping-centre again! Do you hear me! You are banned from it!" The security guard was wagging his finger in front of Jules's face in anger.

Jules was shocked! What was going on? What had he done wrong? What prank? He had been only playing a computer game in the gaming shop.

He walked away with a real dejected look on his face. He could get no answer from the security guard as to what he was supposed to have done.

He just kept on replying, "You know very well young man what you did!"

Then it twigged with Jules. He began to wonder if this had anything to do with the twins. Getting him in to trouble again! What had they done this time!

*****

The twins were the first to arrive home before Jules. They were loaded with shopping bags full of things they had bought themselves. You could hear the bags rustling as they walked through the door. Both of their hands were holding the heavy bags. It was easy to see how heavy they were, as their shoulders were slumped forwards and the palms on their hands were red with sores.

"Hello! You two!" Their aunt who had only moments before arrived back from work. She looked them both up and down. "You look like you've had a good day shopping! Those bags look really heavy with things you have bought!"

"Yeah! We had a great day, thanks, Aunt!" Bronwyn replied with a great big smile.

"Yeah! We bought lots of things!" Seth was as excited with his purchases as his sister. "We'll look like young Brits now we've got the right fashionable clothes to wear!"

"I'll show you some of the clothes I've bought Aunt if you'd like to see them. We don't want to look out of place while we're staying here!" Bronwyn added. "Oh! I'm sure you both wouldn't! But it's lovely that you've got new clothes for your time here!" She was so pleased they had a lovely first day. Then she realised that Jules had not arrived back with them.

"And Jules? Is he with you?"

"Ah! He got held up at the shopping-centre. He was talking to one of the security guards. He seems to know everybody, our cous! But he'll be back in a short while!" Seth quickly came up with an answer.

By the time the twins had put the bags on the table, Jules walked through the kitchen door.

"Hello Jules!" His mum smiled at him. "Well done! The twins seemed to have had a lovely day at the new shopping-centre with you!"

He looked at the twins with daggers in his eyes. They looked at him with sniggers on their lips.

"Yes! I think they have had a great first day!" Jules replied with tight lips hiding his obvious anger.

*****

"Ohhh! Nooo!" Jules's mum screeched in the kitchen.

Jules quickly ran downstairs to find out what had happened. He had only gone upstairs a few moments earlier and was about to go in to his bedroom. The twins had gone up a few minutes before him loaded down with their shopping bags. Jules could hear those bags being rustled as they took out one item after another that they had bought in town.

"What's wrong mum?" He gasped as he reached the kitchen. Looking around for some sort of catastrophe!

His mum was at the kitchen pantry and looking inside at something he could not at first observe. Yet, it only took him a few seconds to work it out what had probably happened. He quickly feared the worst.

"Oh no!" He joined her with a similar look of horror as he looked inside the pantry. Both were shocked at what they saw. They saw their money jars were empty. All the money they had been saving over the year had disappeared. For his mum it was money for food and the bills. While for Jules it was his savings for his mum's birthday and Christmas presents. How could they do that!

Both knew immediately who had taken the money for it was not the first time. Perhaps, they should have been even more cautious. They knew what the twins were like! One thing for sure it would mean it was going to be a hard financial struggle for mother and son alike for the coming months. Furthermore, it did not help that Constance was in a precarious position with her job at present. Not that the twins were aware of any of that. In Australia they were used to having money readily available at home.

No wonder the twins had such a lovely time at the new shopping-centre with all that money they had to spend. It was Jules and his mum's money! They both agreed not to say anything to the twins! What could they say without blaming them outright! From now on they would keep their savings in the bank while the twins were staying there.

Jules was making his way back upstairs as the twins were coming down.

"Everything alright mate?" Seth asked.

"Yes! Thanks!" Jules nodded his head but would have liked to have said a lot of very different things to "yes."

They were both giggling and Jules was beginning to recognise that when they giggled like that, they had been up to something. He began to worry what they had done in his room. He entered it very cautiously, ensuring there was no water bombs waiting for him. He looked about very suspiciously to see if he could spot anything that did not look right. Was there anything out of place. He did not trust the twins at the moment. They were so full of mischief like young gremlins on the rampage.

Yet, no matter how hard he looked he could not see anything out of place. He even checked his sleeping bag to make sure they had not put anything in there. It was then, he thought he heard some rustling coming from one of their bags over in the corner where the twins had put everything belonging to them.

He was going to investigate what the noise was when he stopped himself on route. For he noticed that his Second World War airplanes that he had made out of airfix had been moved about. They were now sitting right on the very edge of the set of drawers. However, as he went to pick one of them up to move it back, it would not budge.

"That's odd?" He quizzed. Wondering why it was stuck fast!

It was then he realised that the twins had glued it down on to the set of drawers. Moreover, they had done the same to all his model planes. So that was what they had been up to! He knew there was something. While he was dealing with trying to unstick the airplanes, he totally forgot about the rustling noise that was coming from one of their bags.

Instead, he began to wonder if the twins were going to be like this for the whole duration of their time staying with them! If so, he would have to be on his guard. Double guard! Perhaps, even triple guard!

Chapter 12

Jules woke up and stretched. He was still getting used to spending the night in the sleeping bag on the floor and his body had not yet fully adapted. Hence, he was waking up quite stiff from the hardness of the ground and he found stretching helped his body get rid of some of that stiffness.

He stood up and looked over at the twins asleep. One in his bed and one on the fold-up bed. They were fast asleep. The jet lag was still having an effect on them after travelling from Australia. Both were finding they were getting tired quite early in the evenings.

Then when they went to bed, they wanted to sleep late on in to the morning. It was a similar thing that had happened last year, Jules was certain that eventually they would get in to the normal routine of going to sleep and getting up as we do in this country. It would just take time.

When he looked down at Bronwyn's bed, he had to do a double take. He could have sworn there was another head on the pillow beside hers. At first, he thought she had a teddy bear cuddled up to her. It looked so sweet. Then this other head moved slightly. He jumped back in surprise. There was no doubt that the second head was alive.

Jules's next thought, was that perhaps Seth had slept in the same bed as his sister overnight. Yet, when he looked in to Seth's bed, you could see his head on his own pillow. He was fast asleep as well. How could there be a third head?

"Pssst!" He whispered to the third unexplained head.

"Hello! Are you a friend of the twins?" All he could think of was that they had asked a friend to stay overnight. A friend that they had met up with yesterday.

"But that was very odd," he thought to himself. He had been with them most of the day. In the evening they had watched television together and had gone to bed at the same time? So when would they have had a chance to meet a friend without him being there?

Surely, they would have told him about this friend and the fact he or she was going to stay the night. They would have asked his mum's permission, he was sure as well. Then he thought, perhaps, this friend had arrived after Jules had gone to sleep. Perhaps, he had slept right through all the commotion of this friend arriving. That made some sort of sense. Yet, he was surprised, if that was the case, all that noise did not wake him up.

The head moved again and looked at him. But the head said nothing. Jules thought to himself, "Their friend certainly doesn't look that well! He or she looks quite grey!" But he put it down to looking at this friend in the half-light with the curtains closed.

"Hi! I didn't see you arrive last night!" Jules continued to speak to the twins' friend.

The head just bobbed about in the half-light. Looking at him and then burying itself quickly in to the pillow.

"Are you Australian as well? From Adelaide?" He waited for an answer but none was forthcoming.

The head continued to bob about on the pillow. But there was no answer to Jules's questions. It was as if he was being ignored.

In the end, Jules gave up and thought he would talk to the twins about their friend when they got up. He felt certain they would introduce him as their cousin when they did. He wondered whether his mum knew about the friend staying with them or not. However, he decided to go and wash.

Jules was washing his face when he happened to look in the mirror. To his surprise, he thought he saw a kangaroo in the bathroom doorway. He wiped the soap out of his eyes as quick as he could and looked again. There was nothing there now.

"Blimey!" He thought. "I really am beginning to see things!"

He wiped his face on the towel and was about to commence cleaning his teeth when standing right next to him on a chair was a real kangaroo. It was looking him right in the eye. At first, he stood back in utter surprise and took a double take.

When he had convinced himself that it really was a kangaroo standing next to him and looking him in the face, he began to put two and two together and realise it was this creature that was in the bed next to Bronwyn. It had not been another person at all but a very small kangaroo.

The kangaroo started to drink the water in the wash basin. Obviously, it was thirsty after a night's sleep and without thinking about how odd all this was, Jules started to put more water in to the sink for the animal to drink.

"So you're thirsty are you! Have those twins been giving you enough to drink!" He asked the creature as he stroked it gently and admired its short, soft fur. "But the question is how on earth did you get here? I bet those twins have got something to do with it!"

After finishing his ablutions, he returned to the bedroom with the kangaroo and decided he had enough reason to wake up his cousins.

"Hi, you guys, it's time to wake up!" He called loud enough. His mum was downstairs and would not hear what he had to talk to them about. He assumed that she did not know about this third Australian visitor in the house.

The twins woke up, yawned, and rubbed their eyes. You could tell they were not too pleased at having been woken up. It seemed to be taking a few moments for them to work out where they were and how they had got there. You got the feeling they were expecting to wake up and find themselves in their beds at home in Adelaide. Yet, they were working it out between yawns.

"What's up cous?" Seth was the first to focus on their cousin. "I was truly in to dreaming about eating a barbie at that point, mate!"

"Um! I found this in the bathroom with me!"

Both twins looked at the small kangaroo standing next to Jules.

"Ah! Yeah! Well mate! We expected you'd come across him eventually!" Seth added.

"It is a kangaroo isn't it?" He asked.

"Yeah! But...it's only a baby roo!" Bronwyn replied.

"How on earth have you ended up with a roo!" He looked at them astounded.

Hence, they began to tell him the story of how they ended up with the roo in their rucksack. Of course, they laid it on thick about how the zoo keeper was being cruel to this poor creature and how the roo was more than pleased to go with them. They explained that there was no trouble with the young animal on the plane or at either airport.

"He's such a good roo, mate. I think we should keep it a kind of secret from yer ma though!" Seth concluded. "She may not be a bubble of hot joy to have a wild Australian marsupial running around in her house! Yer know what mums are like!"

"I don't know if we should tell her or not." Replied an unsure Jules. "But I don't know how we can keep such a big creature as this a secret to tell you the truth!"

"But let's try, Cous!" Bronwyn looked sad at the thought of losing their friend and she answered with suitable triste in her voice. "I would hate to see roo being taken away from us and put in a Brit zoo. He would then be returned to that horrible grizzly bear of a zoo keeper! That wouldn't be right."

"Yeah! Mate! He likes being with us and he's been no problem at all!" Seth smiled at their cousin. "I reckon he'll go under the radar with your ma!"

Although, Jules was not too convinced, he decided to go along with their wish. "Well, let's keep it a secret from mum for now! But we may need to talk about it again later."

"Fair do, mate!" Both of his cousins agreed.

It wasn't long before Jules found that the roo had worked out how to open the fridge door. It was there he found it helping itself to the carrots from the salad department. The three of them had to buy some new carrots before Jules's mum returned home. Then another day the celery and cucumber disappeared. As far as food was concerned, the roo was always one step ahead of them.

One morning before going to work, Constance was downstairs going in to the kitchen when she was passing the stairwell. When she looked up the stairs, she thought she saw a movement. She looked up and nearly jumped out of her skin as she thought she saw a kangaroo hopping in to Jules's bedroom.

"I know I've been under a lot of stress at the moment with work and this court case but seeing a kangaroo hopping about the house is very worrying! Perhaps, I need to go and see the doctor!" She touched her forehead to ensure she did not have some sort of high temperature.

It was not long before the roo learnt to undo the outside kitchen door with its paw by pulling it down and then inwards. In the garden it discovered a place full of wonderful smells for a young roo to explore. It was soon eating all the flower heads, as well as the sweet potatoes.

It loved the fresh grass and anything that had green vegetation like the carrots or potatoes. Of course, the twins and Jules were always just too late to stop the roo feasting on the magnificence of this outside utopia.

"Ahh! Where have all my flowers gone!" Was the first thing that Constance noticed when she went in to the garden after work. "And where are all the vegetables I was growing! There's nothing left but very short grass! Everything else has disappeared!"

It had all gone as well! She was quite right. It was like a squadron of locusts had spent the day there before moving on.

She looked on totally bemused. "It was all there this morning! I watered everything!" She shook her head in disbelief. "And the grass! It's been totally cut right down to the earth!"

By now Jules and his two cousins had arrived in the garden. They were expecting this scenario to happen but had not quite worked out how they were going to deal with it among themselves.

"Yes!" Said Jules, "I cut the grass earlier on!"

"No!" said Bronwyn looking at her cousin sternly. "It was those sheep, Aunt!"

"Sheep?" Jules's mum looked at Bronwyn with astonishment. "How on earth did sheep get in to the garden?"

"Yes! Well! Yer see! It's my fault, Aunt!" Seth tried to look contrite. "And I really apologise, but I left the back gate open and some sheep got in and ate everything including the grass!" He gave a look to Jules, as if to say you better go along with this. "We didn't realise what was happening until it was too late and had to shoo them out! I'm so sorry Aunt!" He lowered his head in shame.

"Sheep! I didn't even know we had sheep around here!" Constance shook her head in surprise.

"Ah! Well!" The twins had not realised that you do not get sheep passing through a small English town near London. Of course, there was loads of them in and around Adelaide. So, they thought it would be the same in England. So once again the three of them had to think on their feet.

"Yes! It was really unfortunate but a poor old farmer was walking his dotty sheep down this road to market. They became upset at the noise and some got away from him and his collie. Sad to say, Aunt, your back gate was open due to me and in they came!"

"Yes! Very unfortunate!" Jules added.

He did not like to lie to his mum but the twins had come up with this story so he decided he had no choice but to go along with it. Yet, he knew he wanted to talk to them later about telling her the truth. There was no doubt in his mind that she was going to find out sooner or later about what had really happened.

You cannot keep a kangaroo in the house and not expect it to be discovered. Especially, one, that has a tendency to jump about so much and wander.

"Well of all the strangest of stories!" Constance shook her head in disbelief. "Who would have thought that sheep would ever get in to the back garden and do such damage. I would certainly like to have a word with that farmer!"

*****

In one sense, it was as if Jules knew the twins were going to come back that summer. For in Brook Park, during the early spring, the council had put up a new adventure course for youngsters to use as part of their endeavour to keep children fit and healthy. The course included a sky walkway, swinging from rope-to-rope, climbing over walls with grips, crawling under netting, climbing through tunnels and sliding down metallised slopes. Since their instalment, he had worked very hard on his timings to go around the adventure course.

He wanted to be able to beat the twins going round the course, that is, if they turned up that summer. Over time, he managed to get his time down to a very fast and respectful ten minutes. He felt confident if the twins came that year they would struggle to match his speed. His intention was they would see how skilful he had become at tackling the course. Both would be impressed by their cousin.

"And while we're at the park, mate! We can give you your first cricket bat and ball lesson!" Bronwyn had not forgotten their promise to teach him how to play cricket.

"That's true Sis! I'd forgotten about that! Buckeroo!" Seth added. "That'll be darn great, cous!"

Jules wasn't too sure about that, remembering how they had given him his first boomerang lesson last time they were in England. Yet, he smiled appreciatively anyway.

When they got to the park, the twins were suitably wowed by the new adventure course and dead keen to give it a try.

"Let me show you the way I go around!" He stated to them. Pulling back on their over-zealous desire to just get on there and have a go. He explained that he had worked out a course around the equipment and timed himself on it.

"How long does it take you to get round, mate?" Seth quizzed. He could not wait to give it a go.

"I am down to ten minutes at the moment." The local boy said with bucket loads of pride.

"Okay! You lead!" Bronwyn agreed, seeing that Jules was keen to show them what he could do on there.

So, for their first attempt of going around the adventure course, they followed their cousin as he had requested. Listening to his advice on what to do and where to go one after the other. Each twin taking note of what he said and how he did it.

"You say you can do it in ten minutes?" Seth asked as if it was a challenge.

"That's a real good time cous!" Bronwyn sounded supportive of her cousin.

"You time us, then cous! And we'll see how long it takes us Aussies!" Seth was really up for the challenge. But we knew he would be.

Jules felt quite confident as they set off. He felt sure his existing record would stand the test of time against them. He watched them go and even he had to admit they could move fast. They seemed to motivate each other. One never allowing the other to get too far ahead. It was as if it was a challenge for one twin to keep up with the other.

As they passed one obstacle after another, Jules began to have a look of horror on his face. They were not only beating the times he had set up to every obstacle but they were smashing the time he had set for the whole course. After spending months of doing the course and improving his time only by seconds over a long period, they seemed to be already beating his existing record at their first attempt.

"Well! That's a real tough course yer set, mate!" Seth was laying on the floor looking up at his cousin. "I'm wack-er-rooed!"

"I need to rest a mo too!" Bronwyn added. "What was our time like then cous?" She lay on the ground next to her brother and looked up at him.

Jules was too busy biting his tongue in sheer disbelief. How could they both do it. They had never done the course before.

They both looked at him waiting for his reply.

"I don't know how you did it but you've done it in eight minutes! That's two minutes faster than me! And I've been practising on the course for months!" He was truly stunned. "What do you two drink, rocket fuel!" He gasped.

"Well, I reckon we can even do it faster once we've got the hang of it!" Bronwyn shrugged her shoulders as if the time they had achieved was nothing really.

"Yeah! Perhaps next time mate, we'll give it a proper go!" Seth conjured up a comment that left Jules thinking how on earth could he ever cut his time to match theirs!

"Yeah! Hey! We've brought the bat and ball, so let's give you your first cricket lesson!"

Both twins were quickly upright and picking up the bat and the ball. Leading Jules to an area where it was flat enough and grassier enough to play a game of cricket.

They had brought a cardboard box to use as a wicket. They had found it at the back of Leeming Road shops and carried it with them to the park.

They did not have to go over the rules too much for Jules. He had seen the game being played on television and had a rough idea of the rules and what to do. Seth and Bronwyn spent some time showing him how to stand when batting and then showing him how to bowl.

"Let me demonstrate to you, mate!" Bronwyn urged. She took the bat. "Bowl me a good 'un bro!" She called up the other end of the wicket where Seth stood.

When he bowled her a ball, she managed to hit it right to where Jules was standing as a fielder. He only just caught it in his stomach. He went a kind of raspberry red.

"Get the idea?" She asked him.

Jules nodded his head. Even though he was feeling a bit nervous about the whole thing.

"Right, you give it a go now, cous." She gave him the bat and went to take up the position of fielder. "Remember, keep your eye on the ball and when you bring the bat through, try to really whack it! That's how you can make a lot of runs! You never know you may end up playing for England in Adelaide!"

"Are you ready Pommie!" Seth teased his cousin.

Jules nodded his head and Seth bowled him a medium paced ball. He did not want to do it too fast or with too much spin for Jules on his very first ball.

Yet, Jules watched the ball intensely as it came down the wicket and he brought the bat through from behind as Bronwyn had showed him. He must have caught the ball just right. For soon it was sailing up in to the air with both twins and Jules watching it with surprise but also admiration.

"Blimey, mate, look at that one go! It's a real corker!" Seth praised him. "First ball too!"

What they did not know was that the park-keeper, sadly, the same one who last year took a hit on the head with a boomerang from Jules, was heading over to pick up some rubbish that had been dropped. He hated to see rubbish on his precious park's grass. If only he had seen who had dropped it, he would have given them a lecture on litter.

The park-keeper was in the process of putting the litter in his rubbish bag, when he thought he heard something whistling through the air. He looked about him to try to work out what it was. While at the same time the three who had been playing cricket were so busy ball watching they never bothered to work out exactly where it was going to land.

Well, not until it was too late. Suddenly, they worked out where the cricket ball was heading. The look of horror crept over all three faces.

Especially, when they realised, who this person was who was going to be on the receiving end of where the ball was going to land.

"Bang!" The ball landed right on his forehead. There was no doubt that he would be having a huge bump there in a while. It knocked him off his feet and he took a few minutes to sit back up, rub his forehead and then try to work out what had happened. Finally, his eyes fell on the cricket ball. Next, he began to search around for who could have possibly hit it.

By the time his eyes landed on Jules, the twins had disappeared in to the safety of the bushes and were making their escape home. Leaving their cousin to face the music once more.

After rubbing his eyes in surprise! The park-keeper by now had worked out who the culprit was. Furthermore, he soon realised that it was the same boy who had hit him with a boomerang almost a year ago.

"You!" The man in his very official uniform stood up and called out. "You again!"

Jules looked around him, hoping this time to get support from his cousins. Only to find that they had, once again, disappeared like swallows after an English summer. Leaving him to face a very irate looking park-keeper.

After another stern lecture from the park-keeper, Jules found himself banned once more from the park. He was told in no uncertain terms he was a menace to society. No apology seemed to be enough for the official whose bump on the forehead, Jules watched growing bigger and bigger as he spoke.

*****

Constance was already in the kitchen preparing the meal after getting home from work. She realised that while the twins were staying with them, Jules would not be able to help her in the same way he normally did. He was going to be too engrossed in trying to entertain them. And she could see, how difficult that was going to be with their ferociously inquisitive natures.

"Hello Bronwyn and Seth!" She greeted them as they came in to the kitchen.

"Had a good day, then?"

"Brill!" Bronwyn answered.

"What have you been up to?" She resumed her normally daily questioning.

They started to explain the day's events and what they had been up to.

"Where is Jules?" His mum asked. Realising that he had not come in with the twins. She thought he would enter soon after them but he had not. Perhaps, there were things he had to deal with in the garden before he came in she began to think. However, he had not appeared.

"Yeah!" The twins looked at each other and wondered what they could say to cover up what had happened.

"We were at the park and Jules decided to spend some time talking to the park-keeper! He seems to get on with him! So, we thought we'd make our way home!" Bronwyn made up the story.

"Yeah! Seems to get on real well with that guy! They seemed to get on together like two black widow spiders meeting each other in a corner of a house!" Seth continued with the storyline.

"I remember you telling me before how he got on well with the park-keeper. That boy seems to get on with everybody! I think everybody likes him! He has such a way about him!" She smiled contented that her son seemed to have such good social skills.

It was at this point Jules walked through the door with the bat and ball. He stared at the twins with a really blistering look as if to say, "And what happened to you two! You left me right in it again!"

"Jules! At long last! Did you have a lovely chat with the park-keeper!" His mum smiled as she looked at him.

He looked at the twins first and then back to his mum. "A really lovely chat mum!" Was all he could say.

*****

"We can't get out!" Came the cry from a puddle hopper who wanted to leave the cavern beneath the puddle to go and get some moss to eat. He had woken up and seen the sun shining through the puddle and decided to take a gentle stroll around the field to find some moss rich in early morning moisture to eat.

"Don't be silly, of course, we can get out!" One of his friends laughed. Thinking his friend was making up some sort of joke.

But when they both looked up and out of the puddle there was a very fine mesh across it. They pushed and pushed against the fine thread but it was like lines of steel that criss-crossed above them and no matter how they tried they could not budge it. They were imprisoned in their own homes.

Soon all the puddle hoppers were waking up to the same dilemma. All were trying desperately to get out of their homes where they had somehow become imprisoned. Yet, it was all to no avail. They were firmly entrapped in their caverns beneath the puddles where they lived.

"What are we going to do!" One of the female puddle hoppers asked. "How are we going to get food to feed ourselves!"

This was a question many of those who were now finding themselves trapped were asking with some trepidation.

"I'm sure we'll think of something!" The chief of the puddle hoppers replied as he sat down to talk to his close advisors on how this had happened and who could have done it. Moreover, what were they going to do about it.

If only they had known that during the night the cloud jumpers had quietly descended from their cloud home to put in place a major part of their plan. They had weaved together the fine cloud threads in to a dense rope until it became as strong as steel.

Using this strong rope, they had then set about sealing every puddle where the puddle hoppers lived in the town. So, it was not possible now for any puddle hopper to escape from their puddle homes. They were trapped inside. Their cloud cousins had inter-weaved the strong rope across each of the puddles and tied them fast down on each side.

This clever plan had been suggested by the three evil puddle hoppers. They knew that if the cloud jumpers were to succeed in stealing the children, they would need to ensure that the puddle hoppers were safely out the way and unable to interfere in what they were doing.

Otherwise, the three evil puddle hoppers were certain their nicer brethren would attempt to save the children and thwart their distant cousins attempts at kidnapping such a large number of them. Now with the puddle hoppers securely entrapped they could start the next stage of their plan without any interference.

Moreover, the three fellow evil puddle hoppers wanted sweet revenge on these fellow creatures following what they had done to them last year. They wanted to ensure that the people of the town would blame the creatures living beneath the puddles for these deeds.

They wanted men to either wipe them out or at least drive them away from their homes. As they looked down from the clouds they laughed at the success of their plan so far. The puddle hoppers were truly unable to escape and could only look up in horror as their distant cousins stole more and more children without any interference.

*****

Soon the cloud jumpers next stage of the plan was in full swing with the three evil puddle hoppers helping. They were sliding down their silken ropes in numbers and finding children to take above and imprison with ease. They were able to tie them at the waist with cloud rope and pull them up in to the cloud before anyone below saw or knew what had happened. The plan was working perfectly.

Each time they would leave one of the children's shoes by a puddle. It was a clue to suggest that it was the puddle hoppers who were doing this dastardly deed. Even if people did not want to believe in these creatures' existence up until then, when they started to link the shoes with the puddles, they would soon change their minds. It would not be long after that, before they would commence to blame the puddle hoppers for what was happening. The people in their anger would then start to plan what they were going to do about it.

The schools were almost empty as the children were disappearing up in to the clouds. The teachers were all blaming each other for allowing their pupils to vanish. Each asking the other where the children had gone and how could they vaporise in to thin air. It did not make sense. The police and firemen were at their wits end trying to find out where the children had disappeared to. They searched all the buildings in the town and the nearby countryside but, of course, all to no avail. The children had somehow gone without any real trace, bar the shoes left by puddles across the town.

The inside of the cloud was becoming more and more full with their captives. It was not a very nice sight to see either. Nearly all of whom seemed to be crying or had cried. Even though their captors threatened them with beatings if they did not stop. This made no difference, the children would only continue to cry. They wanted to return home. Not that it had any effect on their captors, for it only fell on deaf ears. The cloud jumpers had plans for the children and were not to be persuaded otherwise.

The tethers holding the children inside the cloud were secure enough to hold them fast. After a number of days the children were beginning to find they could eat the fluffy clouds given to them by their captors. Although, it never seemed to fill them up. It managed to ensure they had a meal that kept the body fit and well.

All the children cuddled up to each other in fear. Those a little older offered comfort to the younger ones and kept on repeating the mantra, "We are sure that our mums and dads will soon come and save us!"

Lace in the next room was in a similar dilemma. She feared what her three captors had in store for her. She realised her only hope was if Prok and her fellow puddle hoppers could make a rescue attempt before the cloud jumpers and their three evil friends started to take them away.

*****

"The disappearance of the children in our town remains a big mystery that, at the moment, is unsolved." Robin Biggs, the local TV reporter was still broadcasting about the children disappearing. It was the main story.

"The town's council, our local police force, supporting agencies and many town's folk have been searching high and low to try to find out where the children have disappeared to. But all to no avail. The only clues, are still the shoes left by children next to the puddles across the town. Those children who are left are being carefully guarded by not only their families but by the police themselves. Here I have a small group of children I have gathered from the nearby homes to try to find out from them what they think has happened to their friends."

The camera turns to look at the children, who try to smile at the camera but find it difficult as they are obviously very worried about their lost mates. Then the camera reverted back to the TV presenter with his ever-big smile.

"Their parents have kindly agreed to them coming over here to Meadow Park and talking to me on this matter. I am keen to see if they can give us an insight in to what has happened to the children who have disappeared. Let's start with Michael Dalton, who goes to Parkside Primary School and find out from him if he saw anything."

The TV news reporter turned around with the microphone in his hand to face the children he had collected to talk to. The camera zoomed over to pick up the children. The problem was the children were no longer there. To the full horror of the TV reporter and the camera man they had disappeared. Within that short period of time they had gone. If they had only looked up, they would have seen them disappearing in to the clouds above.

*****

"Pssst!" A quiet voice called from behind a bush.

Jules was in the garden by himself. Probably enjoying a few moments of tranquillity from the intense needs of the twins who were now back in his life. He had forgotten how demanding they were on his time and patience. He enjoyed having them around but they were difficult at times in many ways.

The twins, at that moment in time, were upstairs with the roo trying to get him to dress up as a school boy with a cap, shirt and tie, trousers and shoes on. The poor creature was not keen. However, they were. They both believed they would be able to pass the young kangaroo off as a small school boy in the town, if only they could get him to wear the old clothes of Jules.

"Psssst!" There was the sound again.

Jules turned towards the bush and saw Prok, the young puddle hopper, sat behind the bush in the garden.

"What are doing here Prok?" He was more than surprised to see his young puddle hopper friend.

"I need to talk to you!"

Jules looked around to check no one was about and then disappeared behind the garden shed to be with Prok. It was a place where they could talk in peace. He was uncertain whether Prok knew the twins were back from Australia. He may have seen or heard them while he was waiting for Jules.

"Did you find Lace?" Was his first thought on seeing Prok. When he had departed from the puddle hopper's cavern he had assumed a search would soon find her and bring her back to the tribe's home. Jules thought she had wandered a bit too far away and the mouse had just leapt out of the pocket and got left behind.

"No!" Came the reply. There was a deep concern in Prok's voice.

Jules looked at him realising there was a problem.

"But I think I know what's happened to her!" Prok continued. "It's far worse than you can imagine!"

"Oh no!" Jules gasped. "Tell me, what is it!"

"I better start with what happened last night!"

Prok began to tell his friend how he had gone out again to search for Lace and heard some rustling and whispering of voices speaking in their language. He decided to hide. Not too sure who it could be. For most puddle hoppers tend to be home by the time night falls. He thought it further strange that the voices had an odd lilt. He had to really concentrate to understand what they were saying. It took him a bit of time to remember where he had heard the lilt before.

In horror he remembered it was the cloud jumpers! He knew they were usually up to no good and he wondered what they could be doing. But by the time he had got back to his tribe's home in Gateshead Road, the cloud jumpers had been and put the very strong cloud rope across the puddles. Of course, Prok had tried to remove the cloud ropes but to no avail. They were far too strong.

While his tribe were all trapped inside with no escape.

"But why would the cloud jumpers do that?" Jules seemed confused.

Prok commenced to remind him of what his father had told him about them. How they were a bad tribe set on doing evil deeds. How they were always trying to take human children and young puddle hoppers as captives to work in their cloud workshops.

However, he explained he was unsure why they seemed to be taking such large numbers of children at the moment. Far more than usual. Hence, he believed, they had imprisoned his tribe in their caverns to stop them interfering in what they were doing. Then he added with horror, he believed they had taken Lace as well.

"Lace? Why her? I don't think she's a very young puddle hopper?"

Prok continued to explain to his friend it did not make any sense to him either.

"We have to do something!" Jules felt enraged at what was happening and wanted to help his friend get Luce back as well.

"There is even worse I am afraid!" Prok shook his head in disbelief.

"Worse! How could that be?" Jules looked at his friend astounded that there could be worse still to come.

"Yes! I believe the three evil puddle hoppers who were here last year are back!"

"But how can that be? Gabriel, my uncle, took them away frozen in boxes. He was going to inter them in Alaska again. It's impossible for them to be back here!" Jules found it difficult to accept what Prok was saying. He could not imagine Gabriel failing them.

"I know!" His friend added. "I could not believe it at first. But I am sure it was them I saw sliding down cloud ropes and helping the cloud jumpers lay the steel-like ropes over the caverns. I couldn't stop them. There was far too many for me to do anything about it."

"Well! What are we going to do, Prok! We have got to do something!" Jules added aghast. Looking at his friend for some sort of idea how they could deal with this problem.

They decided to go beneath the cloud where all this dastardly action was taking place. Their intention was to try to spy on the cloud jumpers from below. It was an attempt to try and see what they were up to. In this way, they were hoping they could formulate a plan to help all those entrapped above escape. Prok lead Jules to a little wooded area besides the park where many children had disappeared. They could observe what was happening from there.

"Look! That is the cloud the cloud jumpers are using to hold the stolen children and Lace in!"

Jules looked up and could see in the centre of the surrounding small clouds there was a huge ball of white. He felt sure that must be the one Prok was referring to. When you looked up, you realised that particular cloud did not move. Even though the wind was moving clouds either side of it. Moreover, you began to observe that cloud was quite low in comparison to the others. Yet, not too close to the earth to catch the attention of anybody down below.

"Look!" Prok pointed to some children being tied up with cloud string so thin you could hardly see it, a little further away in the park.

It was the first time Jules had seen the cloud jumpers and he was surprised how they were like white versions of the puddle hoppers themselves. These kidnappers were nervously looking around for people. In an attempt to make sure their evil deeds would remain unobserved and a secret. They were unaware that Prok had escaped their attempts to imprison all puddle hoppers. Hence, there was still one who knew what they were up to and could try to stop them.

"Come on! We have got to stop them taking those children!" Jules was up and running towards the group of cloud jumpers with the captured children.

Calling out to them. "Hey you! Leave those children alone!"

The cloud jumpers turned towards the advancing teenager and the accompanying puddle hopper. They must have been surprised as after a few words to each other, they abandoned the idea of taking the children with them and started to make their own way back up to the clouds. Throwing cloud balls down at the two who had interrupted their nefarious act.

Jules and Prok dodged the cloud balls as they landed around them. But Prok could not resist picking them up and in return throwing them back at the disappearing villains.

Jules soon joined him and he was quite astounded to find the cloud balls were so light. When you threw them, they shot through the air with considerable force and accuracy. From below they were able to hit the ascending creatures and hear the accompanying cry of pain from their success.

The two avengers were then able to release the children from their cloud ropes and send them back off to their homes. Telling them to stay there and not go outside for their own safety.

Chapter 13

Constance was laying down on the couch in the living room having a quiet moment. The twins and Jules had gone to the shops to get her some items for the evening meal. She was worried that Seth and Bronwyn may have found some more money in the house with the intention of spending it in the shop as they were so keen to go! She had so little money now, it was a worry how the next bill was going to be paid. Let alone think about the future.

To make matters worse, she was expecting a letter from the police asking her to attend a court hearing. She felt certain that Mr. Brian had somehow managed to ensure she would end up taking the full blame for the explosion at the factory. It didn't help that her new job was not a pleasant one. It was like working in a cess-pit. Everything seemed to be going wrong in her life and no way of fixing it. She felt helpless and a victim of dire circumstances. And all this was closing in on her. She was certain there was worse to come.

Her thoughts were interrupted by a knock at the door.

In her present mood she feared the worse. She even considered not opening it. "Let who is ever there go away and leave me alone."

Yet, whoever it was knocked at the door again. And then again. They seemed determined to get an answer.

She knew she could not ignore it. It was not in her nature. So up she got and went to answer.

"Gideon!"

"Constance!"

They both hugged each other at being reunited. Both, so relieved to see the other. Yet, they didn't realise for very different reasons.

"I have missed you so much! And we haven't heard from you at all! I sent you letters but never got a reply. I became very worried. But wait! What are you doing here?" His sister-in-law could not contain herself. If there was a way out of her mess, then Gideon would be the one she felt who would be able to help her. He had that magic ability to turn things around.

"It's great to see you too! I've missed you and Jules so much. I am so glad to be back! It's like returning home!"

"But why didn't you answer my letters?"

Gideon commenced to explain with great sadness about how he had been sent to work at a forward drilling camp right in the north of Alaska all by himself. How, in his isolation, her letters had not been forwarded on to him. He, further, told her how his letters, the ones he wrote to her, in a similar way, had not been sent.

He said how horrified he was when he returned back to the Head Office to discover his letters and hers were all still sitting there. Again, he was shocked to find the money he had asked his office to forward to Constance and Jules had not been sent at all. No matter how furious he was, there was little he could do about it he explained. It was too late.

"And I can only apologise now! The oil company I work for really let me down!" He shook his head in shame. "I hope you can forgive me!"

"It doesn't matter. It was not your fault. So why are you here?" Constance was still trying to put Gideon's turning up unannounced in to some sort of context. Of course, it was a really pleasant surprise to see him but there was no warning of his coming. Yet, she was conscious of the fact that he may be able to offer her some real valuable support at that moment in time. A time when so much was going wrong in her life. Support she could really do with.

"I must admit the money and letters are not the only reason for me returning!" His face took on a more serious look. "The three evil puddle hoppers have somehow escaped! I have no idea how but they have! And I fear they will be on their way back here for some reason! So, as I still have a lot of holiday time available, I decided to come here and make sure you and Jules are safe from those three evil characters. Moreover, I want to take the opportunity to apologise to you face-to-face about not replying to your letters or forwarding any money. That was terrible! I hope you will both forgive me. Of course, while I am here, if you are happy with it, I would like to spend some time with you both again! Not only did I enjoy my time here last summer but I can take the opportunity to try to find out if those three evil puddle hoppers are around. And if they are, what are they up to!"

"Gideon! That's wonderful! We loved your company last year. I know both of us could not want for anything else this summer. It was so good having you here last year with us! But it's not such good news about the three puddle hoppers though. I just hope they don't turn up here."

"It's great to be back!" He smiled.

"You'll be pleased to hear that the twins are back here as well!"

There was a look of surprise on her brother-in-law's face as he recalled all they had got up to last year. How they had nearly caused a catastrophe with the three evil puddle hoppers. Yet, as he began to think about it, he decided there was a need to show a sense of forgiveness towards them. He hoped they both had learnt a valuable lesson from last year's events.

"I think that's good news!" He cautiously responded. "How's Jules getting on with them! Last year they were always playing tricks on him?"

"Well, they still are! But he enjoys having them here all the same. Two children of his own age to do things with. His own cousins. And he's getting better at holding his own with them. At least, I think he is!" Both laughed.

Within a few hours, Gideon had transferred some large sums of money across in to his sister-in-law's bank account. Immediately, that relieved Constance of one of her ever-growing worries. Gideon will never know how relieved she was. There was now enough money in her account to pay off the growing debts, pay for some bills coming up and not have to worry about getting food to eat. Constance, of course, said that he did not have to do that. Even though she knew she was desperate for the funds and he would never accept her "No!"

"I want to give it to you both! This is like my home now. You two are my only family!" He reassured her.

It was not long before Constance was explaining to him about the explosion at the pickle factory and how the owner was pinning the blame on her. She told him how she was due to appear in court accused of causing the explosion soon.

Moreover, in addition to that, she was being accused by the owner of being a spy for a foreign power who had made her do it. Her boss had stated not only did his business prepare pickles for sale but they also made ammunition for the country's army. She was sure that was utter nonsense.

"He sounds a real nasty bit of work your boss!" Gideon offered support. "I think we will need to deal with him!"

There was still a lot she had to tell him. She went on to explain about how a MI5 officer had been to the house to find out if she was a foreign spy. In the end he assured her that not only was she not a spy for a foreign country but the factory had no military connection either. She told him how the M15 agent and her both agreed the boss's stories were totally unfounded.

Yet, the MI5 officer admitted he was unable to put the police right on this matter. He explained that all the other security departments at Whitehall needed to assure themselves she was not connected to a foreign power in any way as well. Only then would they correct the misinformation being given out by her boss to the media.

"This gets more absurd as you go on! And the police and the media are buying all this rubbish?"

She nodded her head in dismay. At long last she had someone who would listen to her side of the story and see how unfair it all was. Someone who would be on her side.

Still, not finished, she explained about how she could not find another job in the town as Stanley Brian was, also, the mayor. After the explosion he had put it about that she was a bad worker. So, no one in the town would give her a job. Yet, somehow, ironically, she had found a job with his own brother who also has a factory.

His factory was always short of workers as no one wanted to work there. Hence, they would take on almost anybody as the conditions were so awful. She went on to explain how shocked she was about this new place where she was now working. For they were taking food that had been disregarded or left for weeks, repackaging it and selling it as fresh.

"Are you sure you are talking about Boreham Wood?"

She nodded in exasperation.

"It sounds more like something from the days of a Victorian industrial town."

*****

"Aghh!" Jules yelped in his bedroom.

The twins giggled at each other downstairs in the living room where they were sitting with Gideon.

"Have you two played another trick on my nephew?" He asked.

"No!" They replied in unison and tried to look innocent. Giving him a look, as if to say, we would never lie. Though Gideon was sure it was the case they were lying.

A few moments later, Jules appeared in the doorway, looking knives at the twins and holding his hand that was red raw. The mouse trap they had put in his rucksack had done its job.

"Hey you two, I forgot to tell you I have a present for you!" Gideon smiled at the twins.

He had given Jules his present earlier on. Yet, of course, he had not expected the twins to be staying with Constance and his nephew when he arrived. So, he had ordered something special on line for them.

"You have!" Both twins jumped up with joy. "Where is it!"

"I will get it for you later. I put it by the bed in Jules's mum's room." He knew

they would not be able to wait.

Before he had even finished his sentence the twins had made an excuse to leave the room and were rushing up the stairs like Formula One cars in a race.

"Uncle Gideon we need to speak!" Jules looked seriously at his uncle.

"Okay! It sounds important, Jules!" His uncle looked across at him.

"It is! Very important!" His nephew looked as if he had the world on his shoulders. "Perhaps, we can do it later in the garden!"

"Sure! If you wish!" Gideon was now fascinated to find out what the problem was. He wondered why they had to meet in the garden. "Can it wait that long?"

"Not really!" Came the reply. "But I need to speak to you alone!"

At that point something was happening upstairs that took over from their discussion.

"Ow! That hurt!" Was repeated twice.

Jules looked at his uncle and wondered what had happened to the twins.

"That will teach them!" He laughed. "I knew they could not stop themselves from going in to your mum's room to get their presents."

"What did you do?" Jules asked. A smile creeping on his face. An ally at long last against those twins and their ongoing tricks.

"Not a lot!" He smiled back.

A few moments later the twins arrived back in the living room. They were not looking very pleased with themselves. Their faces were looking very red and battered. Jules wondered what his uncle had done. Nonetheless, he was really pleased.

"Did you find your presents?" He smiled. "I hope you like them!"

"Thanks, mate! They're great!" said Seth with what seemed a sore mouth.

They both seemed to be finding it difficult to walk as well. It was as if the stuffing had been knocked out of them.

Overnight, Gideon had ordered two boxing punch bags on springs for the twins so they both could let off steam. He thought it might help with their bad behaviour. Fortunately, the equipment had arrived very early that morning so both teenagers were still asleep and unaware anything had come.

After a bit of consideration, the uncle decided to set up the two punch bags in his room in such a way that they would bounce up and hit the twins if they entered the room without his permission. He guessed rightly that Jules would never enter the room without his agreement. But the twins, they were a different matter. A very different matter.

After last year, when they sneaked in to his room and stole the frozen evil puddle hoppers he wanted to stop such a thing happening again. Hence, he had sprung the punch bags right back. Tied them by string to the door handle. Thereby, if any one entered the room without permission, both punch bags would spring up and hit who ever had come in to the room uninvited right in the face.

Of course, the twins walked right in to his trap. Once they had opened the door and rushed in, they were greeted with a full blow to the face by their own new punch bags. In shock they were knocked off their feet and ended up sat in the doorway stunned. Contemplating that, perhaps, they should have waited as Gideon had suggested.

"By the way," Gideon added. "I hope it reminds you two to keep out of Jules's mum's room while I am staying in it. I remember what happened last year very well!" He gave the twins a stern look.

While, the look on their faces suggested that a lesson had been learnt. They would stay out of there in the future. They both looked quite sheepish behind their very red sore faces.

*****

Gideon left the house later in the morning with the intention of trying to help Constance. He knew she was innocent and somehow, he had to prove it. Thinking about it over night he had come to the conclusion that his answers probably lay in the burnt-out factory itself. So that was going to be his first port of call.

On arriving there, he was stunned that a lot of building workers were already clearing away rubble from the damaged part of the site. While in another part of the factory repair work was commencing.

"Hey you! What you doing here!" Some sort of site manager approached him as Gideon entered through the factory gates.

Gideon wondered how best to answer him and secure his entry. He had to get in to the site if he was going to help Constance. But as it worked out he did not have to worry on that score.

"Are you that insurance assessor?" The grumpy manager in his white building site hat asked. "We weren't expecting you until tomorrow!"

"Well! You know how it is!" Gideon decided this was his way in. "Wires get crossed and I am sure I put down that I was coming today!"

"Okay! No problem!" The site officer seemed happy that he was there. "Hopefully, it means our building firm will get paid earlier as well! Here, put this protective hat on your head and wear this official site visitor badge. I'll leave you to get on with it then!"

And so, he did. Gideon could not believe his luck for he now had free rein of the site.

It wasn't long before he tracked down the cause of the fire and where his sister-in-law worked in the pickle factory. He looked at what remained of the piece of machinery that had caused the blaze, carefully studying it from all sides. To his surprise he found a notice stuck on the back of the machine right out of sight. This slip was from the Department of Health and Safety.

It had somehow managed not to get destroyed by the explosion and ensuing fire. This clearly stated that the machine had been condemned a full year ago and should not have been used in the workplace at all. The health and safety office had considered it far too dangerous until it had been properly maintained and repaired.

Gideon took a photo of the notice before carrying on. He made his way in to the factory office. There was no one there and to his surprise the filing cabinets were unlocked. They were fire proof ones and so nothing inside them had been damaged. Hence, he was able to rummage through all the firm's business documents at his leisure undisturbed.

It was not long before he came across what he was looking for. There were letters going back over the last five years from the company who serviced the machinery in the factory. They stated categorically, they were very worried all the equipment in the factory had not been annually serviced by them for a number of years.

Moreover, it needed to be done immediately for safety reasons. Each letter pointed out the machinery could become quite dangerous unless they were serviced and checked as required by the Department of Health and Safety. In each of these letters the servicing company stated they would take no responsibility for any accidents that might occur unless the machines were serviced immediately.

Yet, each letter went unheeded by Mr. Brian. Nothing had been done. Gideon took photos of each of the documents. He knew he had some strong evidence to support his sister-in-law's case against her boss.

Having gathered the evidence he required, Gideon began to make his way out of the factory. He stopped at the site manager's office to hand in the safety helmet and the official visitor's badge he had been given.

"I hope you got all the information you required?" Asked the grumpy official. "Don't want any delays in paying up do we!"

"More than enough! Thanks!" His visitor smiled back as he started to leave the site.

*****

Later on, Jules slipped in to the garden with his uncle to have the quiet talk he had requested earlier. The boy knew he needed this wise man's help again. This was another huge problem that had hit the town. One, that somehow had to be resolved. He was hoping his uncle was the man who would be able to do that.

"You said you wanted to have a chat with me about something quietly? And I think I need to tell you something as well!" His uncle added. Little did either know it was going to be about the same thing.

"Hold on a minute!" He urged Gideon as he turned to the puddle in the grass. "Prok! Are you there?" He called out.

Within a moment the young puddle hopper was standing next to the two of them.

"Prok!" The older man was surprised to see him come out of the puddle in the garden. "What are you doing here!"

Jules and Prok began to tell Gideon about all that had happened recently in the town. When they mentioned the return of the three evil puddle hoppers, Gideon's face lit up in horror. It was just as he feared. The reason he had returned.

"I guessed this is where they would be!" The oil explorer explained how he had buried those evil creatures back where he had found them the previous year. Much deeper down too. Unfortunately, he was then sent far to the north in search of oil, Hence, he could not keep an eye on their burial site. Yet, on his return from the north, to his horror, they had gone. Their boxes had been dug up and they removed. "You, know, I had a hunch they would somehow get back here. They would want to seek revenge."

"They seem to be working together with the cloud jumpers. Each working with the other to achieve their own evil ends!" Prok stated. "We have to do something!"

Of course, Gideon had never heard of the cloud jumpers before and was surprised when Prok explained who they were and where they lived.

"So it's logical to think those three escaped from their internment with the help of the cloud jumpers. I wonder how they knew they were there?" He thought for a moment and then came up to the obvious conclusion.

"Somehow, I guess they must have followed me there when I left here! I had no idea I was being followed. And now you tell me, they've imprisoned all the puddle hoppers in their homes, taken Lace up in to the clouds where they live and are kidnapping children to use in their cloud workshops!" Gideon pondered over all that was going on.

It was a lot! An awful lot. When he arrived back in this English town, he did not expect to be facing such a huge problem.

"I agree with both of you we've got to stop them. What is worse, in some way, I feel responsible for what has happened. Perhaps, I should have been more cautious than I was when we were interring those three evil creatures!"

"But you had no idea you were being followed by the cloud jumpers, Uncle. Where ever you buried them, no doubt, they would have been watching from the clouds above!" His nephew tried to reassure him, there was no way he could have prevented what happened.

"What do you think we should do?" Prok asked. Hoping this knowledgeable, clever, older human being would come up with a plan.

"In the morning I think we need to go and look at where these cloud jumpers are living. We should try to work out where Lace and the children are being held prisoners. Then we need to see how your tribe have been sealed in the puddles, so we can have a think about how we can possibly get them out." Gideon replied.

The other two nodded in agreement.

"There is one other thing." Jules remembered before they parted.

Gideon looked at him as if to say, "There is more!"

"The twins have brought a young kangaroo with them from Australia!"

His uncle looked at him as if he had been knocked over with a giant cricket bat.

"A roo?" Came the shocked reply.

And with that, Jules commenced to tell his uncle all about the roo. How it was being kept secretly up in their bedroom and his mother still knew nothing about it. He explained the reason they had not told her was that all three were afraid she may have it taken away to a zoo.

"So not only do we have the two "trick-mad" twins in the house but a young roo that no one is meant to know about. How on earth are you going to keep a baby kangaroo a secret. I have no idea!" He gasped. Gideon could not believe what he had heard. There again, anything about the twins and what they got up to would never surprise him.

*****

The next morning, Gideon, Jules and Prok set out to see where the cloud jumpers had established their base above the town. Prok moving from shadow to shadow. Little did they know the twins had decided to take the roo to the park that morning as well. They were going to let him have a little bit of a free run. The twins had been delayed from going to the park as Bronwyn could not find her shoes.

Their clothes were spread out all over Jules's room. It was impossible to walk around without standing on top of something belonging to them. They seemed to throw things on to the floor and leave them there. Every so often Jules or his mum would have a clear up but, in the end, often they gave up. It seemed impossible to know where to put all the twins' things.

"Look Sis! There goes Gabriel and Jules!" Seth called out to his sister from the bedroom window.

"Hey! Blimey mate! And they've got a puddle hopper with them!" His sister sounded quite excited at seeing one again.

Neither of the twins had seen any of the creatures since their return. They had not even had a chance to mention them to their cousin either. Not that they weren't interested in finding out about the creatures they had such adventures with last year because they were. Extremely so. But the young kangaroo had taken up so much of their time since arriving.

"Wonder where they're going bruv?" She tried to think.

"Well Sis! Jules and Gideon were pretty darned secretive last night. I was sure they went out in to the garden to chat. I could hear them gibbering on out there like a couple of old copper pots boiling over." Her brother added.

"I got a feeling Seth, there's something going on here mate! Aunt said that Gideon wasn't due to come here this summer? But he has turned up like a gecko hiding from the rain in the bathroom! And why would they be going off with a puddle hopper? We know that we are all meant to keep their existence a secret. Yet, there is one of them. Then there is the mystery of all those children disappearing in the town on the local news. It's a bit of a mystery wrapped up in a bigger, fatter mystery, if you ask me."

The girl from Australia was trying to put everything together and come up with an answer as to what was going on but not having much luck.

"I reckon we ought to follow them. Sis. A bit like Sherlock Holmes with his magnifying glass to find out what they are up to." Seth urged.

And so, they did. Keeping far enough back not to be noticed. This 'following others' lark was something that came to the two of them like learning to ride skate boards. They truly loved the idea that they were pursuing others who were totally unaware of their presence. Of course, the kangaroo was with them too! Hidden in the backpack. They were still intending to take it to the park afterwards for a runaround.

*****

"Jumping mud slugs! Why have they stopped there and hidden behind that bush? Do they think they are aborigines hunting a wild dingo or something." Seth couldn't work out what the three of them they had been following were up to.

"They seem to be looking up at something?" Bronwyn puzzled.

It didn't seem to make any sense. Why would they hide behind a bush in the park and look up in to the sky. It seemed absurd to say the least.

What they didn't know and couldn't see were the cloud jumpers going up and down from the cloud above on the cloud ropes. Cloud ropes that were almost invisible except to the most discerning eye.

*****

"Look!" Said Prok. "They are still stealing children and taking them up in to the cloud."

So, the three watched as some more children were being transported up to the cloud where they would be imprisoned. The cloud jumpers almost looked invisible against the sky and clouds. So, it was easy to see how they were doing their evil deeds almost unobserved.

"There! Look!" Called out Jules. "It's one of those three evil puddle hoppers!"

"I see him!" Hissed his uncle who wanted to go right over there and pull the creature down from his cloud rope. But he knew that would not be a very wise thing to do. He could end up as much a captive as Lace and the children.

"We will have to think of a plan to get up on to the cloud and rescue the children and Lace!" Gideon concluded. "And it will have to be quick because I can't think they will stay around for much longer. They must have a lot of children in the cloud by now. That is if the news reports are right!"

"You're right Uncle!" Jules agreed. "Do you think you can come up with a plan?"

"I have to!" Was his short reply.

"Let's go and have a look at the cloud ropes they have imprisoned your tribe with in their homes, Prok. We will need to get them released first if we want to have any chance of succeeding against the cloud jumpers and their three notorious allies."

The three cautiously moved on. Carefully keeping an eye on the cloud hoppers so they were not observed departing. They made their way along the brook to Gateshead Road. Here, Gideon was able to look at the steel-like cloud cables that went across the puddles and were imprisoning all the puddle hoppers. He knew he had to find a way to cut those cables loose and free the tribe.

Gideon tried pulling the steel-like cloud ropes up with all of his strength, which was quite considerable, but to no avail. They were far to strong and were not going to be budged by a man. He wondered whether a metal cutter could do it. He had brought one with him that he had found in his late brother's tools chest still in the garden shed. Yet, when he tried to cut through it, the cutter could make no head way. In fact, its teeth were going blunt.

"I'll have to come up with something else! This is not going to work!" The older man shook his head in despair. He was hoping the metal blade would cut through the steel-like cloud but it did not. At this point he began to realise this was going to be harder than he thought.

*****

Once, Gideon, Jules and Prok had moved away from the bush and began to follow the beck, the twins went over to see why they had stopped there. As far as they could make out there was nothing worth stopping for. It seemed a bit odd to the two of them. The twins were craving for excitement and adventure as they had enjoyed last year. Yet, at the moment, those they had pursued and hoped would provide some, were not providing any.

"There isn't nothing here, Sis!" Seth growled as if it had been a waste of time following those three.

"Yeah! Sleeping koala bears! Come on let's keep following them. They may come up with something interesting for us!" Bronwyn was still enjoying the pursuit. It was fun following people who did not know they were being followed.

Both twins stood up and wandered in to the middle of Brook Park, unaware they were right below the main place where the cloud jumpers operated their ropes for going up and down from the cloud.

They had not noticed the ropes that were so slight and no thicker than a fishermen's line. That is until they were lassoed and being hoisted up before they knew what was going on.

"What the...!" But it was too late, they were surrounded by cloud jumpers and rising in to the cloud itself. They had been captured.

The young kangaroo, on hearing all this high-pitched talking from the cloud jumpers, poked its head out of the backpack and in fear leapt back down on to the earth below. The cloud jumpers were obviously surprised at the sudden appearance of this strange looking creature. A creature which they had never seen the like before. It stunned them as what to do.

"Get it!" Ventor shouted to the others around him. "Don't let that creature escape!"

Hastily, one of the other cloud jumpers threw a cloud rope around the roo with the intention of pulling him up in to the cloud. Yet, he had not expected the young creature to bounce in to the air as high as the ascending group with the twins and butt him.

"Hey! What's going on!" Shouted Ventor as he grabbed the end of the cloud rope around the creature. In so doing he found himself looking the roo in the face as it flew up right next to him. He was stunned that a creature could jump that high in to the sky. Of course, he had never heard of kangaroos or had any idea what they could do. In surprise and shock, he let go of his end of the cloud rope that was tied around this strange animal's waist and, by doing so, set it free.

The cloud rope was still tied around the kangaroo like an elf's belt as the twins were rising up towards the cloud. Of course, with the cloud belt, this allowed it to bounce up and gain extra height. In this way it was able to leap in to the air and be right next to the captors and his two friends. It looked like the small creature was going to try to release them.

But the small marsupial soon found itself being attacked by far too many cloud jumpers to achieve that. Hence, the young kangaroo only managed to escape many grasping hands by luck and leap back down to earth and safety. It could only watch in frustration as the twins disappeared from sight.

*****

"Look! It's the twin's young kangaroo!" Jules saw the creature over by the brook as they were returning home from the puddle hoppers' home. "I wonder what it's doing over there by itself?"

"More to the point where are the twins?" Gideon quizzed.

"It's got some cloud rope around it's waist!" Prok observed.

As they came up to the roo, it did not run away. It recognised Jules and appeared to want him to help it in some way. This whole country would be foreign to this southern hemisphere animal. Not that it had any real freedom while in Australia where it had lived in a zoo up until very recently.

"We better take it home with us!" Said Jules. "It probably escaped from the twins!"

Prok and Gideon looked at each other. They were both coming up with the same answer as to what had really happened to the two of them.

"I'm afraid that is highly unlikely, Jules." His uncle explained. "I am afraid I think they have been captured by the cloud jumpers! They must have thought the twins were younger than they are and taken them up to the cloud like all the other children. Goodness knows what plans they've got lined up for them all."

"It looks like they tried to capture the baby kangaroo as well and failed." Prok added pointing to the cloud string tied around it's waist.

It was then the young creature took a leap in to the air.

"Wow! Look at how high he can jump with the cloud string around him!" Prok shouted in delight. It was giving the roo an extra lightness to reach unexpected heights.

"Look the roo can almost leap as high as the clouds!" Jules exclaimed in wonder.

"We better grab him and pull him down! Before he bounces right away from us!" Gideon grabbed the light lead and held it fast.

Desolated, at the loss of the twins, the four of them made their way back to Jules's house. Trying to think how they were going to save everyone captured by the cloud jumpers. At the same time, Gideon and Jules had no idea as to how they were going to explain the twin's disappearance to their aunt.

Who, so far, had been unaware of what has been going on in the town with the cloud jumpers. They believed she had enough to contend with at the moment.

They did not want to add to her troubles.

Chapter 14

Everyone clapped and waved their Union Jack flags when Prince Willie and his daughter Princess Charlie arrived at Campions House on top of the hill overlooking the flatter plain in which Boreham Wood sat. They were greeted by the mayor and his wife, with her latest wig on.

At first, they were led through the grand Edwardian house to the lovely colourful, long garden at the back. The two royals were there to attend a garden party for local children who need help in some way. The prince was hoping his presence would raise money for the cause and, of course, give it much needed publicity.

There in front of them lay a feast. Princess Charlie's eyes lit up with excitement as she would soon be able to choose what she wanted to eat from that wonderful display of food. Her stomach was already saying, "Let me at it!" There were tables full of cream and fancy cakes and the most sumptuous savouries of every sort you can imagine.

The sandwiches were stacked high in carefully structured towers. The joy to her, was that it was often the case, being a princess she got to choose her plate of goodies to eat before anybody else. No wonder she loved being a princess.

"We hope you will open the festivities by cutting the ribbon your royal highness!" The mayor bowed lowly to Prince Wille as he offered him the scissors to cut the fine golden material before him.

The prince duly gave a praiseworthy speech on the good work the charity was doing. Stating how he was so impressed with the time and effort everyone involved was putting in. He commended them on how they had helped so many local children who, for whatever reason, were struggling in many different ways. Eventually, before he bored everyone silly, he concluded, "I, hereby, declare this garden party open" and cut the golden tape.

When the prince had cut the ribbon, another chorus of cheers went up and the obligatory flag waving followed. He led his daughter through the crowds either side of them in to the middle of the blossoming garden.

"Now would you kindly do us the great honour of being the first to take your choice of what to eat from these splendid tables of food the town's folk have kindly donated and prepared for the occasion." The Mayoress curtseyed again. Careful not to let her wig slip.

"No! Let the children come and get their plates of food before the princess and myself! This occasion is for and about them." The prince urged.

He could see all the children waiting there with their little Union Jakes. Their eyes nearly popped out with joy when they heard what he said. Each one ready to leap in first.

Nonetheless, his own daughter, Princess Charlie, looked up at her dad in utter despair. She was so looking forward to having first choice of all that lovely food. Now she had to wait until all the other children had tucked in. She looked in horror as her favourite cakes and savouries were all disappearing. When her father eventually said she could join the other children to fill her plate up, she was soon there with her elbows flying like those who were there before her.

Of course, she managed to get some of the food she liked. To be honest, by that point, none of the children realised the princess was now amongst them. They were all too busy focusing on getting their own delicious food amongst the flying elbows.

It was not long before the adults were sitting at tables and talking over afternoon tea about the charity and its work. While the children, who were present, including the princess, even though she was dressed in a very fine silk dress, were playing catch with a ball.

The prince was keeping an eye on her even as he chatted away. He had developed the royal skill well. So, he was able to sound very interested in what people were saying to him, as well as praise their work and effort at the right moment, yet, at the same time, watch his lively off-spring.

Prince Willie was thinking to himself as he watched her trying to catch the ball, "Do you know, we will have to work on her "catching ball" skills. She has dropped the ball every time it has been thrown to her!" Both her royal parents were keen on sport.

However, this time, when the ball was thrown to her and she dropped it, the ball bounced off in to the woods at the side of the lawn. Without hesitation, Princess Charlie was running into the undergrowth to catch up with the ball and bring it back. In a moment she had disappeared behind the initial trees and was soon lost to the sight of her father, who had been watching what had been happening.

*****

"She'll do nicely!" Smiled Trud, one of the evil puddle hoppers, as the princess ran right in to his arms.

They had seen the children in the garden and had been hiding in the woods to see if they could get one of them. Little did they know it would be a princess they would capture.

Princess Charlie looked in horror at these three strange creatures who were standing around her. Within a moment they were tying something around her waist.

"What are you doing?" She asked.

"Well! Young girl! We think you better come with us! We have some other little friends you might like to join!" Rak giggled.

"But I need to get back to my dad! He's waiting for me." She was almost in tears as they held her tight. Stopping her from returning to her father.

"I wouldn't worry about that little girl!" Chuckled Surr as he started to lift the princess up in to the air with the three of them holding her.

"Where am I going?" She cried out in vain. Quite astonished as her feet began to lift off the ground.

"Don't you worry about that! We'll look after you!" Trud stated.

"We'll do that alright!" Rak giggled some more as the four of them rose higher and higher up towards a passing cloud.

*****

It seemed that Princess Charlie had been in the wood for quite a long time retrieving the ball. Even the security guards attached to the two royals were

214

beginning to wonder what had happened to her. You could see them beginning to talk to each other on their two-way radios. Almost immediately, the one nearest the wood started to make his way in to it to search for her.

It wasn't long before he could find no trace of the princess and was on his two-way radio to his colleagues. There was a bit of panic in his voice by then. You could see his colleagues rushing over to help in the search. While Prince Willie's own personal bodyguard moved closer to him as concern grew this could be a threat to both the royals.

Prince Willie had seen his daughter go in to the wood for the ball and he had become more and more agitated as she did not reappear. He was about to rush over there and commence his own search for his daughter, when to his great horror, he saw her rising up in to the air. She was rising higher and higher on what seemed like nothing.

How could that be happening he wondered to himself. It was a few seconds before he could distinguish the three puddle hoppers from the background and see them stealing his daughter. Yet, no way could he see the strong, thin threads that were pulling them up to the cloud until he really looked very closely. You almost needed a microscope to see them.

"We have to stop them!" He called to his bodyguard and pointed up to where Princess Charlie was now rising up in to the sky with the three strange looking creatures. Presumably, it was assumed, she was being kidnapped.

The bodyguard wondered what was going on but his eyes followed to where the prince was pointing. Where he was soon able to pick out Princess Charlie and her three captors rising higher in to the sky. He quickly alerted his fellow security officers who, in turn, all looked up in horror.

But what could they do? They could not fire a shot at the kidnappers in case they hit the princess herself. They could only watch in horror as she disappeared up on to a passing cloud.

Prince Willie saw his daughter disappear on to the cloud and then watched as her kidnappers forced her to join them leaping across the clouds moving through the sky. They were getting further away from where he was on the ground.

"Quick! We have to follow them!" Prince Willie caught the arm of his personal bodyguard and they both started running towards their official car parked still outside the front of the house.

His chauffeur was sitting with his feet up on the dashboard reading the newspaper. He was not expecting the prince back for quite a while. These occasions normally took a few hours. There was bound to be a lot of commotion from the gathered crowd when the prince and his daughter were on their way back. This would give him plenty of notice, or, so he thought, to prepare himself for departure.

Suddenly, the side and back door to the royal car burst open. The chauffeur was stunned to see that it was the prince who jumped in the seat next to him. Moreover, he had a very worried looking face. While the personal detective scrambled in the back.

"We have to go now! I'll tell you what direction to take! Turn left on to the road!" He yelled at the chauffeur who was still in a state of shock. The prince had never spoken to him like that before. He was normally so calm and polite. He had never sat in the front with his chauffeur either.

The driver immediately threw his newspaper down, put his cap on, started the car and was heading on to the road as ordered within a moment.

He had no idea what was happening but just obeyed orders. It was obvious it was urgent.

"There they go!" The prince cried out, looking up at the clouds and watching the three evil puddle hoppers leaping with the captive princess from cloud to cloud. "Turn left! Turn left! Here!"

The chauffeur was not sure if the prince had lost his mind as he kept looking up in to the sky and saying, "There they are!" Before giving him the direction he needed to take. It all sounded quite bizarre but he knew it was important for him to keep driving as directed. Although, he couldn't see a thing in the sky.

"They seemed to have stopped at that big cloud!" The bodyguard called out as he looked up from his rear seated window. "They've disappeared right in to it. It doesn't make sense?"

"You know that cloud seems really close to the ground! How odd!" The prince puzzled over what he was looking at.

"Look! If you observe very carefully, you can see other creatures going up in to it!" His bodyguard pointed out to his royal highness.

"Yes! You are right! I have no idea what's going on!" The prince looked up totally flummoxed. "How on earth are they almost flying up in to the air and walking on clouds. It doesn't seem possible? But they are doing it and what is worse is they have my daughter!" You could tell he was angry but very frightened for his daughter at the same time. One thing for sure, was the prince was a man of action and had already decided on a plan.

"Right! I want you to stay here and keep an eye on them," he said to the bodyguard. "While I go and get my helicopter! I am going up there to get my daughter back!"

"But it may not be safe, sir!" His companion suggested. "And my orders are to stay with you and protect you!" Of course, that was his official job. If he let the prince go off without him and something happened to the prince he would be in big trouble and likely to lose his job.

"Blow! Your orders!" The prince raged. "I will ensure you don't lose your job! I need you here to keep an eye on my daughter just in case they start jumping away on to other clouds. Then you can follow them and report back to me!"

His stare at the bodyguard was very determined and forceful. The police officer knew he had no option but to obey. Anyway, you have to obey a prince don't you.

"Keep your radio on and me up to date with what is going on here!" The prince said to the bodyguard who was by now getting out of the car ready to do his part in watching what was happening to the princess.

"Okay driver, get me to Elstree Airport and to my helicopter as quick as you can!" he said forcefully to his chauffeur.

With that they drove off very fast and were breaking the speed limits. This, they felt was reasonable, given the gravity of the situation they were in. It was more than likely no police officer would book them for speeding once they were aware it was the prince and the urgency of the prince's mission anyway.

Chapter 15

"Hello sister-in-law!" Gideon greeted her as she came in from work. He tried to make sure his greeting was full of cheer as he could see that she not only looked very tired but quite down in the doldrums. He wondered what he could do to cheer her up.

"I'll get you a lovely cup of tea! You rest your legs up on the couch now and I'll bring it through to you!"

"You don't have to do that Gideon!" She replied. "I've got lots to do!"

"Exactly, you can't carry on like this! You need to take a rest and have a lovely cup of tea before you even think about doing anything else!" While he was saying that he was leading her in to the sitting room and gently placing her on the settee.

"That's very kind of you, I'm sure!" She smiled at him. In a sense she was pleased he had forced her to sit and relax. That was something she would not let herself do if she was alone. Even though she was very tired she would force herself to get on with all that had to be done at home. At least, now it meant she had to have a break.

When the elderly man brought in the tea for both of them, he gave her an official looking letter as well. It was from the local courthouse so he feared the worst for her after what she had told him about the impending court case.

On opening it, "Oh! No!" She blurted out in sheer frustration.

"What's up?" He asked.

"The local court is requesting my presence on Friday. It is about the explosion they say I caused at the pickle factory. Where they will consider whether the case shall go forward to a criminal court or not." She sank in to her seat absolutely destroyed.

"They are bound to find me guilty! What is going to happen to Jules and the house! What is going to happen to all the ongoing bills we have to pay! Oh! Gideon! I am terrified!" Tears were swelling up in her eyes.

"Hey! Don't you worry yourself. I am sure everything is going to turn out fine! And I am here to help you now! We'll sort this out together!" He tried to reassure her.

He knew it was time for him to do something. He had to try and get Constance off the hook. For too long now, this so-called mayor had been able to put the cause of the explosion at Constance's feet. By doing this, Gideon was sure, he was keeping the true blame for how and why it happened from himself.

*****

Gideon was shown in to the interrogation room at the police station while he waited for Inspector Alan Shepherd, who was in charge of the case against Constance to arrive. To be truthful, the police officer in charge, had not done as much delving in to the case as he should have done. To him it seemed a simple 'open and shut' case.

He certainly did not want to get on the wrong side of the mayor that was for sure. This very important man in the town could make things very awkward for him, his career and the whole of the local police force if the case did not go according to how this very important man in the town wanted.

"I hear you may have some new evidence on the explosion at the pickle factory, Mr. Appleyard?" He stated as he entered the room.

"I think I do!" Smiled the determined looking brother-in-law.

"Well! It appears a very simple "open and closed" case to me, Mr. Appleyard!" He smirked, as if there was nothing that was going to change his mind. Especially, if it was from an unknown member of the public.

"Well, I think you need to carefully look at these photos I've taken! I think once you've seen them you may have to rethink your approach to this case, Inspector."

"Oh! Right!" For the first time the police officer opposite him looked a bit more concerned.

The visitor then showed the inspector the evidence he had gathered on the case. At the same time, you could tell Gideon was thinking if they had done their job properly they would have found this information out for themselves. The stunned policeman was taking notes as they chatted and getting his interlocutor to promise to send him copies of the photos he was being shown. Each one seemed to shook the police officer more and more. This was vital evidence that had not been uncovered before.

"You are quite right, Mr. Appleyard, this puts a very different complexion on the case!" He looked a bit embarrassed at this latest information. "I think Mr. Brian has a lot of questions to answer and I look forward to talking to him about it. I think we can immediately stop the case against your sister-in-law going ahead. It is obvious, or, so it appears to me, she has been wrongly accused. What is more, it looks like she has been vindictively pursued by the factory owner through the media as the one to blame. Obviously, it appears his reason was to deflect blame away from himself."

"I'm glad you see the evidence is quite conclusive in proving where the guilt lies and are now going to put the matter right. My sister-in-law has suffered terribly at the hands of this corrupt man!" Gideon shook his head in despair.

"It would help her considerably also, if you could ensure that his further accusation against her, of causing the bad smell in the town due to the explosion, is strongly rebuked as well. The smell and the explosion are not related in any way. Yet, Mr. Brian's constant media attacks keep stating they are. They have caused her to suffer much at the hands of many angry citizens in the town who he has unfairly wound up about the matter."

"I will do that certainly. But, tell me, Mr. Appleyard, how can you be so certain this horrendous smell is not related to the explosion?"

Gideon got out his chemical analysing machine and showed it to the inspector. It was the same one he used at work to help analyse the chemical makeup of gases in the air. It was useful in his search for oil. He showed the officer the chemical make-up of the air in the town. It proved that it in no way could the smell be due to an explosion at a pickle factory. The chemical composition for it was all wrong!

"Well, that is really interesting! Thank you again! I will ensure that those accusations are strongly rebuffed in the local media news. I can assure you that

I shall be bringing Mr. Brian in for questioning in the next few hours and he can expect quite a rigorous time. Is that it or is there anything else that you can help us with!"

"Well there is one other thing!"

Gideon began to tell him that he might want to pursue where Mr. Brian was getting his onions from as his claim that they were locally fresh was certainly untrue. He mentioned this to the inspector, as he knew this would lead to where they really were coming from. The hope was that this further investigation would bring Grunswick Brian and his factory under the microscope as well.

Gideon explained Mr. Brian's brother was using onions that were not fresh as stated. The ones he was using were being sold as scrap by other food suppliers. These same onions, one brother was buying cheap, re-packing them and falsely stating they were locally farm fresh before selling them on to the other brother.

"This sounds very interesting, Mr. Appleyard! And I can assure you I will be following this up!" The police inspector could already see the feather in his cap for getting to the bottom of the real reason for the pickle factory explosion.

Then, on top of that, uncovering the corrupt nature of the mayor's very business. The word 'promotion' was already going around his brain in big, red, bright letters. He could see himself as a commander. "You have been most helpful and I cannot thank you enough!"

Inspector Alan Shepherd, promised to ensure the court of justice withdrew their request for Constance to attend the forthcoming hearing. He stated, he was going to telephone her personally, apologise to her for the accusation that had been found untrue and tell her they were now pursuing other evidence and lines of inquiry.

With this success behind him, Gideon next went to the Department of Health and Safety. Here, he again showed them his evidence. They were totally horrified at what had been going on in the pickle factory as well as at his brother's onion business. It was decided by them to suspend immediately any sales from both businesses until these allegations had been properly investigated.

If it proved true, and the evidence clearly suggested it was, both would be taken to court for purveying food dangerous to health, giving the public false information, providing dangerous working conditions for their staff as well as breaking health and safety rules in the work premises. Gideon was informed there may be even other possible accusations to follow. Yet, to him that sounded more than enough.

"We will be sending Mr. Brian a letter right away with a copy to his insurance company notifying them of his lack of servicing of equipment. Equipment, he was obliged to maintain. It will also state that this will be followed up by likely court action." The Health and Safety Officer continued.

"I will add that I will be going to his brother's factory as well. I will personally be leading the inspection team for a thorough search as to what is happening there. We intend to go through their paperwork very carefully. You can rest assured, Mr. Appleyard, if we find what you allege is true, he will be receiving a strongly worded letter from us also. It will clearly tell him of the court action that is likely to follow."

"That is really good news!" Gideon knew he had achieved exactly what he had set out to do. Constance would now be vindicated. While both the mayor and his brother were rightly going to be dealt with. He knew, if nothing else, he had achieved one success upon his return to Boreham Wood.

*****

"Would you believe it!" Constance beamed with delight as her brother-in-law walked in the door after most of the day he had spent trying to prove her innocence.

"What's happened?" He pretended he did not know. Although he could guess.

"Police Inspector Alan Shepherd has telephoned and apologised that I had been pursued for the crime of the explosion at the pickle factory. He stated new evidence has emerged that I was not to blame and he would be pursuing a new trail of inquiry."

"That's amazing!" He added and they hugged each other in joy. "Quite right too!"

"And then when I was watching the local news. I was stunned as it showed the same police inspector taking Mr. Brian, the mayor, who has been so cruelly blaming me, in for questioning on the explosion! Can you believe it? That is not all. For then the same police inspector made a statement to say that our previous suspect is no longer considered in any way connected with the case.

Furthermore, he added that the smell that is about the town and had been blamed on the explosion at the pickle factory had nothing to do with it at all. I was dumbfounded. People have been horrible to me for so long. Blaming me for the smell and now I have been proved innocent. It is all so amazing! Everything seems to have changed within a few hours!" She looked so relieved. "You know Gideon it is such a weight off my shoulders!"

"That's good!" He smiled contented. Knowing his day's work had achieved exactly what he wanted it to achieve. Yet. he knew now he had a bigger problem to deal with. The cloud jumpers!

*****

"Are you sure it is me who should be going down in to these sewers looking for this monster? I know nothing about sewers. Wouldn't it be better for one of your own men to go down there?" Sergeant Muddle looked frightened as he sat on the edge of the sewer entrance, straightening his very important police helmet. The smell that was about the town seemed to get much worse as he bent his head down over and in to the sewage entrance. He withdrew it quickly to take in some cleaner, fresher air. Yet, even that was not much better.

It had been decided that he was the one who should go down in to the sewer system and seek out this creature. "This was not an issue for the sewer business," they told him. This was a matter for the local police officer in the area to sort out.

"No! You're just the man for it!" His superintendent assured him. "If you come across any one or thing, you can arrest them in the name of the law!"

The manager of the sewer works in the town nodded his head in agreement. In no way did he want to go down there himself. He also knew none of his teams would go down there either after what happened to the previous team who entered that underworld. Their account of events had spread quickly amongst all the sewer workers and it was not a job any of them wanted to undertake now.

Of course, the sewer manager had tried to bribe various teams again with even bigger bonuses to go down and find this monster. Yet, all to no avail. He had tried to scare them by saying they would be sacked if they did not go down there! Once again, all to no avail.

His work force said they would rather lose their jobs than be eaten by a wild creature lurking in the sewer system. He had tried offering promotion to anyone, if they went down there but no one would bite. What is the use of having promotion, if we are dead, is all they replied with fear written in their eyes.

So, it was all down to Sergeant Muddle. His own superintendent had authorised it. His boss had said, "We maintain law and order not only on the ground but above and below it as well, sergeant. If anyone is breaking the Queen's law down in those sewers, then they should be apprehended. We know our work is not conventional at times and this seems to be one of those cases. Go and do your duty!"

Yet, the sergeant had heard the rumours about a monster living down in the sewers from those who had gone down there as well. He had grown up in the town and knew lots of people thereabouts. Because of the very nature of his job, they often told him of the gossip of who had done or seen what. In this case, the gossip was clear.

No sewer worker would venture down in to the sewers. They were terrified of the wild creature that had been seen down there. It was supposed to have great big teeth and a frightening roar. A creature as tall as a grizzly bear and just as ferocious. A creature, he may soon be facing.

But what could he do? He had been ordered to go down there, so go down he must! He was a sergeant in the Queen's police force and, hence, needed to show he was a leader of men. Brave and courageous.

"Good luck!" The sewer teams around him smiled. He could tell they were under the impression he would not be coming back. Their supportive smile hid the real comment they wanted to say which was a combination of "we're grateful it's you and not us going down there" mixed with "you are brave." Yet, they could not see the policeman's hands shaking in fear.

"You'll be fine! If you cannot arrest the creature for being a public nuisance then just take a photo of it. This will enable us to know what we are dealing with. Oh! By the way, see if you can manage to communicate with it that would be useful. It will help us in the future!" The works manager of the sewerage company was being quite relaxed about what lay ahead for this brave soul going down there. Perhaps, he was trying to give the police officer a sense of 'there is nothing really to worry yourself about' type of confidence. I am not too sure he was succeeding though if that was the case.

Slowly, the unwilling adventurer lowered himself down in to the sewage system with the torch in one hand and camera in the other. The olfactory machine hang about his neck. That would allow him to locate the source of the smell and, hence, where the monster was. Of course, if there was one. The manager of the sewage works had shown him how to use the machine for detecting the source of the smell. It should guide him right to the problem.

When he reached the bottom of the ladder, he was standing in the sewerage itself. Luckily, he had put his wellington boots on. He seemed to be at a crossroads in the underground system and had no idea which way to go. His torch caught one or two rats scurrying away from its light as it focused on them.

He did not like rats too much. There again not many people do. And it sent a shiver up his spine. Yet, he knew there was no going back for him, he had to continue his exploration of the sewers and try to locate this terrible creature as requested.

The olfactory machine indicated in which direction the smell was strongest. So, he began to follow the huge main drain with the raw sewage running down it. After each step the stench in the air became more rancid and the taste on his lips became sicklier. He wanted to turn and leave this horrible place but knew he had a duty to perform.

"For Queen and Country," he repeated to himself. The machine took him around a few more bends and was beginning to register nearly eighty per cent. His own nose was telling him he was getting close as well. He took a mighty gulp because he realised that if there was a monster down there, he was getting very close to meeting it.

It would have been far more sensible for Sergeant Muddle to have worn a proper work man's hard hat rather than his police one. It did not help that the rather tall helmet kept on being knocked from side to side as the tunnel was not very high in places. To tell you the truth, it was becoming a bit of a nuisance for him. As he turned a corner in the huge drain, the police helmet hit a lower iron bar that was hanging down from the ceiling.

To his dismay, it fell off his head and in to the running sewerage. He quickly retrieved it and stood up straight to put it back on his head without thinking. Unfortunately, as he stood up straight, his head hit the protruding iron rod with a real thump. The same iron rod that the hat had originally hit. He was knocked out. He crumpled up in a ball on the edge of the running sewerage. Luckily, his head had landed beside the wall of the sewer and away from the sewerage itself.

Before becoming knocked out, as Sergeant Muddle was so close to the huge cavern where the hair eater lived, the creature had picked up on his human smell. It realised a man from the world above was coming his way.

"Umm! What do he be wanting?" The hair eater asked himself. He decided to go and investigate who was coming towards his home.

It was then the hair eater found the sergeant knocked out on the side of the sewer channel.

"Hmm! He not be dead. Must be he sleeping! Funny time he be sleeping!" The sewer monster smelled him. "Um! I like the smell of him hair! It make me lovely snack!"

And he could not resist it. Within a moment the hair eater was gobbling up the policeman's hair and leaving him as bald as a plucked corn eating chicken ready to cook.

"That be lovely! He had delicious hair for me! Um! Me like!" The hair monster then left the man lying in the sewer system and made its way back to his lair.

It was not long after, that the sergeant came to.

"Oh! That hurts!" He thought as he held his throbbing forehead. "I need to keep my head low in future! I must have knocked myself out!"

He placed the police helmet back on his head and from then on, kept very low. He had no idea at that point that all his hair had gone. He did have a strange feeling about his head but put that down to the knock he had received.

Unfortunately, as he gathered up all the bits he had dropped when he knocked himself out, he realised he had lost the olfactory counter in the sewerage channel somewhere. After a lot of fishing around in the sludge he found it but it was not working. Obviously, the filthy water had got in to its inner parts and now it was as useless as a candle without a wick.

"Damn that!" The frustrated policeman uttered.

Being the trusty sergeant he was, he decided he would go on without the olfactory machine and make a thorough search of the surrounding sewer system. He knew from his last reading that the source of the smell was very close. Hence, the monster, if there was one, was very close too. So, he spent a long time using his torch to search the drains all around him.

Yet, in none of the directions he went did he find this supposed hair eater's cavern. After a few hours he decided that he had been everywhere where the source of the smell could have been coming from but found no such monster. Although, without the olfactory machine he had come very close to the cavern he never discovered it's actual whereabouts.

But what he did find, was places where the sewerage itself had built up and was causing a blockage. This he assumed must be the source of where the terrible smell was coming from.

"They were making that up about a monster! Typical! There is no cavern there either! Those workers were just scaring everybody." Sergeant Muddle assured himself. "I would have come across it by now if there was a cavern here!" Yet, he had missed the creature. Not by far, mind you, but he had missed it.

The brave sergeant on this basis decided to make his way back to the sewer entrance and tell those waiting above for him the news that no monster existed. The awful smell came from just the build-up of sewerage in the drain system. Now the monster theory had been disproved, the workers could return to clear it all up.

Once his head popped out of the sewer entrance there was a buzz of excitement from those gathered around awaiting his return. That is if he did return. Many had their doubts.

Finally, after getting himself out, he had a drink of water from the flask that was handed to him and stretched his back to its full length. It felt so good after being crouched for so long in those tunnels.

The crowd of sewer officials were getting impatient to find out what he had seen. What had happened.

"Did you see the monster?"

"What was it like?"

"Did it attack you?"

"There is no monster!" He smiled with confidence. "I searched high and low in the sewers but I could find no monster. What I could find though, where those awful smells are the strongest, is built up sewerage blocking the system that needs to be cleared."

"Ha! I knew it!" The manager of the sewer works huffed! "They've been making it all up! The lazy so-and-so's just did not want to go down there!"

You could tell that all the gathered workers around the manager and the sergeant were stunned by his findings. Some of them had seen the creature. They were about to say, "We know what we saw!" when the police officer started to take his helmet off to wipe the sweat from his brow.

"Sorry lads!" He let out a deep breath. "But I could find no evidence whatever to support what you say! I searched and searched to no avail! I was unable to find your monster anywhere!" He wanted that to be the end of the matter.

Yet, there was a sudden gasp of surprise as his police helmet was finally removed. They could all see that Sergeant Muddle was now totally bald. Not a hair remained on his head. All were aware that he had gone down in to the sewer system with a full head of hair and now it was all gone!

The sergeant was not too sure why the whole crowd was looking at him with such a gasp of shock and horror. He could not work out why they were all looking at the top of his head in particular. Of course, he could not see up there and was uncertain what the attraction was.

"What has happened to your hair?" A worker finally asked him as the others were still staring up at his bald head in a state of shock.

The sergeant felt the top of his head. He could not believe it was so smooth.

Then he realised why it was so smooth.

"My hair it's all gone!" He shouted out in total shock.

*****

"Me be hungry for more hair! Me like hair! Me want hair!" The hair eater's stack of hair in his cavern was now all gone. He needed to go back up to the surface and find more heads to feed on. It was alright snacking on spiders' webs but it was not as nutritious as human hair and did not have such a juicy taste either for this creature of the deep.

When dark had fallen, the cover to the sewer was quietly lifted off and moved to one side again. Out from the opening came the long sinuous arms of the creature from the depths below. The long clogged up hair covering his head with two glowing white eyes looked from side to side to be sure no one was about.

Before long, he slid himself out from the sewer entrance and was soon moving in to the nearby garden with its long shadows. A place where he could hide himself. There he would be able to put his sensitive nose up high and smell the air. Smell the air for tasty hair.

Every time he breathed the horrendous stench from his mouth spilled out in to the evening and spread further afield like a pungent mushroom cloud. So, if anyone was around, they would have soon been putting their hands over their noses in disgust and asking themselves what was that awful smell.

When the creature was sure there no person was around, he began to raise his very effective nose in to the air to smell for tasty hair. Hair that he could eat and enjoy.

"Lots of lovely hair me smell!" He licked his hairy lips with joy. "Umm! But no children? Why no children? Always children! Me like soft hair of children!" The hair eater did not know about the cloud jumpers and what they had been doing. "Me have to find sumptuous person with hair! Me smell good hair! Much tasty hair all about me!"

His nose wandered from one direction to the next as he toyed with where to start his evening adventures.

"That one smells really nice!" His eyes nearly popped out. "That is yummy! It different to others! Um! Me like that one! Me go there!"

The hair eater began to follow the trail of the scent, little realising it was leading him right to the head of Gideon. The reason this man's hair smelled so different was the Alaskan wilderness that still clung to his hair no matter how many washes he had undergone!

"Yum! Me smell all sorts of wild plants and animals on hair! It smells like nature itself." He licked his lips in anticipation. "Me can't wait for his hair! Um! So good!"

The hair eater was careful as he slinked along the shadows, every few metres putting his nose in the air to ensure he was still on the right course to get to where the smell was coming from. The hair that he was so looking forward to.

Finally, he climbed over Jules's and his mum's wall and disappeared in to the hedge. Here, he listened for the sounds all around him. Was there any one around? Could he hear anybody talking in the house? All seemed very quiet.

He could just make out the sound of people sleeping and someone snoring. His next task was to find a way in to the house so he could get to his next victim. The smell of this Alaskan hair was getting stronger and stronger. It was overwhelming him with his desire to eat it.

"Me want this hair! It smells good!" He repeated to himself as the taste lingered on his lips. Encouraging him to move ever closer to this ever-enticing smell that drew him in.

He could not believe his luck when he found a window open right where the smell was at its strongest. He knew this was the room that was the source of this wonderful odour.

"Me be there soon! Yummy!" He smiled in anticipation.

The hair eater was soon silently slipping up the side of the wall and through the open window. His years of doing this, meant he was able to do it without making a sound. If you were watching, you would only see the dark figure move in equal time to the wind that was moving the trees and other vegetation and so think nothing of it.

It was not long before the hair eater was curled up in a corner of the room as if it was only a mere shadow. His eyes popped wide open in delight for he could see his meal now but before advancing over to it, he wanted to ensure the person was fast asleep and likely to remain so. The creature, as still as the shadow he was in, allowed his nose to feast on the hair in preparation for the meal he was about to enjoy.

When the hair eater was certain that Gideon was fast asleep and unlikely to wake up, the monster slowly and carefully made his way over to the sleeping head. This he had done so many times before. Within moments, the hair monster was smelling his hair and going in to the full nine stages of ecstasy. His eyes were getting wider and wider as his teeth began to reveal themselves.

They revealed themselves not as part of a pleasant smile but, as belonging to a rapturous, strong carnivorous hair eater. Teeth that were ready to do their duty. Glee was written all over his face at the thought of what was to come!

As we know most people would carry on sleeping as the hair eater set about his deed but Gideon having spent so long in the wilds of Alaska had a sort of seventh sense to danger. Hence, the nearness of this creature, the warmth it radiated and the gross malignant smell it gave off with its breath were soon sending alarm bells to his otherwise very relaxed brain.

The creature normally had the ability to sooth and calm the person whose hair he was gorging on. Sending them into an even deeper world of sleep. Often the person would even have a sweet smile on their face. Unaware of what was happening millimetres above on their head.

Nonetheless, Gideon was different to most people. Years of living among polar bears had made him far more vigilant. Alerted, his eyes opened and were confronted by the creature who was about to start eating his hair. The hair monster was so confident this eating would go like any other, he was taking his time to fully enjoy its rich fragrance before his first bite.

"Lushly! Yum! This is lushly! Me enjoy!" The monster whispered to himself unaware in the changing of the breathing of his intended victim.

Gideon grabbed the monster around its neck in one swift movement and had it pinned down on the ground before the hairy monster knew what had happened. This had never occurred before. It had always been successful in getting people's hair. So, the creature was stunned that someone had woken up and overcame him before he knew what was happening.

He had been so successful for so long, it was likely the hair monster was not being as cautious as he should have been. If it had been more alert, it probably would have recognised the change in the breathing of Gideon, felt his eyes opening and the sudden intake of breath as he was faced with the hair monster who was not the most handsome of creatures. But for the hair monster the price of his negligence had been paid now. It had been caught! What would happen to him!

"So, you are the one who has been going around eating everybody's hair!" Gideon looked down at the creature with his hands around its neck. Below him, the hair eater dare not move. Looking up at him with those big, open pearl white eyes. Horrified at what the future might hold now it had been caught.

"Me do no harm! Me only eat hair! Nice hair! Me hurt no one!" The creature looked at him pleadingly. The hair eater could speak a kind of English but not too well. It had obviously picked up some words over the years of listening to the people who lived above ground speaking. People who were unaware that there was a hairy monster nearby listening.

"That's true! But you're certainly frightening the life out of them!" Its captor continued. "Why do you do it?"

"Me eat hair! It lovely! Gives me goodness! Me mean no harm!" The creature hoped he could convince this person holding him down that he was no harm to anyone. "Me like people's lovely hair!" It smiled with the thought of eating someone's hair.

"Well! We're going to have to come up with some sort of compromise my friend. We can't have you crawling around people's homes in the middle of the night and stealing their hair. It won't be long before someone dies of a heart-attack or something!" The man holding the creature looked deep in to his attacker's eyes trying to get some sort of idea as to a way forward. He wondered how on earth this creature and the surrounding people could live in mutual coexistence.

The hair monster looked a very strong creature and Gideon wondered what he could tie him up with. He could not hold him down for ever and he needed to find a solution to the problem of the hair monster and people's hair. It could not go on with him eating such meals in the middle of the night that was for sure.

He remembered the cloud jumper's steel-like cloud rope that was around the roo. He had managed to get some of the rope away from the roo to study it. He wanted to try and find a way to remove it from the top of the puddle hoppers' caverns. He was sure by releasing these small creatures, they would soon find a way to get the better of their near cousins in the sky.

Using the pieces of cloud rope he had, the man tied it around the wrists and ankles of the creature so it could not get away. This would give Gideon the time to consider what was best to be done with this bizarre animal he found next to his bed.

Gideon decided to let the hair monster stay tied up on the floor, while he tried to get some much-needed sleep before morning arrived. He would then take the opportunity to discuss with his sister-in-law, Jules and Prok as what would be the best thing to do with this very odd creature that had turned up in his bedroom.

The tired man was about to close his eyes and return to his sleep when he heard some crunching noises that brought him back to full alertness. Gideon opened his eyes and looked down to see what the captured creature was up to. To his utter shock, the creature had eaten through the cloud ropes around his feet. It was about to start on the cloud rope that was holding its hands tightly. Then the creature would have been able to make its escape.

"Well! That didn't do the trick!" His captor got up and found some old-fashioned rope to use. This time he tied the creature's hands behind his back. Next, he pulled his ankles up to the wrists at his rear to tie them there as well. With the rope tied behind him there was no way the creature could get at it to gnaw its way through.

"This should hold you for now! I am sorry it's not more comfortable. But I think tomorrow my friend, I have discovered a great way how you can help us!"

"You let me go! Me do no one no harm! Me go far away. Go somewhere else to live! You me can trust!" The hair monster pleaded.

"I am very sorry my friend! But we need your help tomorrow! And we really need to work out how you can feed without causing so much of a fracas!"

Gideon at last began to fall asleep. The creature lying next to his bed on the floor unable to escape.

In the morning Gideon introduced this extraordinary animal to Jules and Prok. The young kangaroo after smelling the creature decided it was best to keep well away. Taking an apple to eat, it disappeared in to the garden. While, Jules's mum had already gone off to work.

Gideon soon explained that the source of all the hair going missing was down to this hair eating creature. Moreover, the source of the awful smell about the town seemed to be emanating from this sewer creature as well.

Prok explained that he and his tribe were totally unaware of this animal living down in the sewers. Although, he explained that there had been puddle hoppers who had said they had seen a creature moving in the shadows when they were out for some reason in the dark of night. Now they would soon all know who the creature was and what it got up to.

The hair eater was sat on the floor between his three captors looking as contrite as a robin with its feathers all fluffed out on a Christmas card portraying innocence. It was as if he would never harm a soul. If anything, it looked quite frightened and timid sat there.

It seemed that this animal would never be a danger to any other creature that is besides eating hair. There was no doubt it was strong and, by all accounts, had a loud roar but, otherwise, it appeared to be a rather gentle giant. A gentle giant who disliked attention. Mind you, it was a shame about the smell.

"Well! We should be able to find a way for this hair eater to live alongside us humans and puddle hoppers without him having to break into people's homes in the middle of the night and frightening them nearly to death!" Jules was sure his uncle was right. He was already thinking of hair-saloons and the hair they cut off their customers. Perhaps, this unwanted hair could be passed on to the hair monster to eat.

"We need to consider if we should involve the local authority in our planning about what to do about with the hair monster!" His uncle stated.

"They are eventually going to find out about this creature living in their sewers. It may be a good time now. The town can then decide how best to coexist with this new addition to the area. I am sure he could be useful in some other way besides disposing of unwanted human hair. Maybe, he could help with cleaning the sewer system!"

"That makes a lot of sense!" Prok agreed.

The poor hair monster sat listening to his captors talking. All he wanted, was to be set free so he could get back in to the safety of the sewers. However, that was not going to happen. But what was going to happen to him was the question. "But there is better news!" The older man gave his two young friends a smile.

"What is that?" Jules seemed astounded at this further statement.

There was not been much good news around as far as he could see. After all, children were still being kidnapped, the twins had been more than likely kidnapped, they had a hair eating monster on their hands, the cloud jumpers were still up to their nefarious deeds in the town aided by the three evil puddle hoppers and, not least, the puddle hoppers, who were going to be vital in sorting out a lot of these problems, were still imprisoned in their homes. Where was the good news he wondered.

"Well! I have discovered that our friend here can help us in a very useful way!" With that Gideon pointed down at the creature who now looked up at him in great surprise.

"How can he help us with these problems?" Prok was intrigued.

"Last night, I bound him up with some cloud rope that I had taken from the ones they had tied around the roo. I discovered, a short time after, the hair eater was eating the cloud rope to try to make his escape!" Jules's uncle beamed with delight.

However, it took a few moments for the meaning of this discovery to sink in with Jules and Prok. Yet, it eventually did.

"You mean he can eat the steel-like cloud ropes that are imprisoning all my tribe!" Prok began to realise the implication.

"Yes, my friend! I think he will be able to!"

"Brilliant! If we get the puddle hoppers freed, they will be able to help us to get everybody held prisoners back from the cloud jumpers!" Jules clapped his hands in joy.

*****

It wasn't long before the hair eater had eaten away all the steel-like cloud ropes over the puddles and set the puddle hoppers free. Although, the humans would not be so happy with this new arrival in their town, the puddle hoppers were delighted with their new friend. He was straight away welcomed in to their homes with great honour.

Once the hair monster had completed his task, the small group who accompanied him were soon heading down below in to the great cavern at Gateshead Road to discuss with the elders, the events that had taken place over the last few days. They needed to come up with a plan. A plan to deal with the cloud jumpers!

Prok was greeted with many warm hugs and kisses by the tribe for his part in their release, especially from his proud father, the chief.

"Well done, Son!" There was great relief on his father's face. He realised the danger they were all in if they had been unable to escape from the puddles that held them captive. It could have been a catastrophe.

"And thank you both! Once again! You have helped us deal with a difficult problem!" The chief turned to his son's accompanying friends. "But who is this?" He approached the hair eater and touched him warmly. "I am aware it is down to this fellow creature that we are all free! We owe you much and can't thank you enough my friend!" He took the hair eater's hand, shook it warmly and with much sincerity.

Jules explained the story surrounding the hair eater and how he had been eating people's hair in the middle of the night. Much to the town's dismay. No one really knew who was doing it and why! It was at this point Gideon, took over and explained how he had captured the hair eating creature as he tried to eat his hair. After which, there followed a long debate on how they could all live in peace and harmony with this new addition to the town.

It was not long before they got down to discussing the real problem they were all facing. How to deal with the cloud jumpers and the re-released three evil puddle hoppers who were undertaking such wicked deeds in cahoots with each other. All agreed they had to be stopped and plans had to be made to release everybody who was being held hostage in the cloud.

Chapter 16

"Remember not a sound from anybody!" The chief of the puddle hoppers whispered as a large army of his fellows plus Gideon, Jules, the hairy eater and the roo followed him up to the cloud lines hanging down to the ground from their base above.

They were hoping for a surprise attack on their distant relations as a way to get up on to the clouds. They believed the cloud jumpers were still under the impression the puddle hoppers were safely imprisoned beneath their puddles. If the cloud jumpers realised their close relatives had escaped from their detention then they would have been a lot more vigilant. Much thought had been given over to how best to release the children, Lace and the twins.

Eventually, it was decided to try to secure the cloud lines as a means to get up to the clouds and confront the cloud jumpers. Otherwise, all the sky people would have to do, is pull up their cloud lines and move away. There would be very little those below could do then. The puddle hoppers needed to explain to Gideon and Jules that by having some cloud about them they would be able to walk on the clouds and not fall through.

Soon some of the puddle hoppers were climbing up the cloud lines. Their cloud belts around them. They were near to reaching the cloud itself when a cloud jumper, unfortunately, spotted them. A high-pitched squeal was soon heard. He was calling his fellow cloud jumpers to come and help him stop the attack that was about to take place.

Immediately, the cloud people knew there was an urgent need to pull up the cloud lines and stop more attackers getting up the ropes. This was their best hope of defence. If they could pull up the cloud lines, they could stop the attack in its tracks.

"Alarm! Alarm! We are under attack from the puddle hoppers! They have escaped their imprisonment! And they are climbing the cloud lines! Help! We have to stop them!"

A puddle hopper by this time had reached the top of the cloud line and was already tackling the cloud jumper who had raised the alarm. This gave valuable moments for a lot more puddle hoppers to reach the cloud from the lines they were climbing. This initial team of attackers were then ready to help fend off the cloud jumpers who were likewise rushing out from inside the cloud to try and drive their foes back down the ropes whence they came.

Soon those puddle hoppers who were up on the cloud were fighting hand to hand with the cloud jumpers. The attackers would not budge an inch backwards though. They knew how important it was to hold fast. This attack depended on them staying put. If they lost the initiative, the cloud jumpers were likely to escape. They had to keep these defenders away from the cloud lines.

This would allow them to get more of their attackers up the ropes and help defend their newly claimed toe-hold on the cloud. Of course, their foes were just as determined to drive the attackers back down. The cloud jumpers could then raise the cloud lines so no more enemies could get up to their quite formidable stronghold in the sky. The next few minutes would be vital as to who would come out on top.

All the time this fight was raging, more and more puddle hoppers were streaming up the cloud lines. Desperate to help their colleagues. From below they could hear the struggle taking place above and knew how important it was to win this battle. Yet, their determination was being equally matched by the cloud jumpers themselves. They were arriving from inside the cloud in numbers to help defend their home. They were aware they had to be as equally motivated as their distant cousins from below to win or they would be overrun.

Those on the ground below commenced to make cloud balls from pieces of cloud that were tumbling down from the fighting above. Once, squeezed tight, the cloud balls became hardened missiles that gave anyone it hit a real thump. By employing a puddle hopper already up on the cloud to catch the hard cloud balls they threw up, they were able to make quite a substantial pile of weaponry on their toe-hold section of the cloud.

This was then being used to constantly bombard their determined foe with a rally of cloud shot that was able to knock them off their feet and send them hurling backwards. Hence, stopping them from taking part in any more fighting for a while. Thus, gaining the attackers more valuable time to get a greater number of puddle hoppers up there. Bit by bit the area the attackers were holding on the cloud was increasing.

It was plain to see this additional armoury of cloud balls that were being thrown at their foe was helping to hold back large numbers of the cloud jumpers from joining the fighting. The defenders had to continuously dodge and duck to avoid being hit by one of these very hard missiles.

It was at this point that Jules's mum was returning home from work when she came across the battle that was taking place by the brook in the park.

"What on earth is going on here?" She was stunned.

Of course, she was well aware of the existence of the puddle hoppers. Moreover, she could see they were throwing white balls up in to the cloud. But she had no idea why they were doing that? Up on the cloud she could make out there was fighting taking place between puddle hoppers and what seemed like creatures very similar to themselves but lighter in colour. Yet, once again, what this was all about she had no idea.

It was then she spotted Jules and Gideon among those on the ground. They were part of the team who were throwing cloud balls up on to the cloud. This seemed very strange to her to say the least. Yet, after last year, she was willing to accept, sometimes, bizarre things do happen in their town. Moreover, with the present one involving Gideon and Jules, this did not surprise her in the least. They seem to get themselves involved in all sorts of strange situations.

"Hey!" She was suddenly held fast by the three evil puddle hoppers whom she recognised straight away.

"You three evil creatures! We thought Gideon had frozen and buried you for all time!" She yelled in horror at seeing them again. Her attempt to try and get loose from them was proving useless.

"Ha! If only!" Trud smirked. "We are not so easy to get rid of, I'm afraid! And we remember you from last year! You might come in handy! Jules's mum!"

"Yes! We're back!" Rak raged. "And we want some revenge after what your son and that Gideon did to us!"

The three evil creatures were securing some children to a cloud line to pull them up and so attached one to her as well. All this was taking place well away from the battle that was being waged further along near the brook. No one had seemed to have noticed the cloud lines further down the stream that were now being employed by the three evil puddle hoppers.

When the puddle hoppers started their attack on the cloud jumpers, the three fellow evil creatures had been elsewhere attempting to get more children for the cloud jumpers to take with them to their cloud-making island. Hence, having been caught out, they were now trying to return to the cloud for their own safety and to join in its defence. They knew if they were caught on the ground they would be in great danger from their own kind.

Within a single cackle of a witch's laugh, the three evil puddle hoppers were lifting the children, Jules's mum and themselves up in to the air. The children with them already starting to sob as the ground beneath them fell away and they were raised up to this other cloud world that existed above.

"Help!" Constance bellowed aloud. Hoping Gabriel and Jules would hear her but she realised they may be too far away. Yet, it was worth a try. The battle raging above may make it a bit too noisy for her voice to travel that far and be heard.

However, Jules recognised his mother's voice straight away. Even only as a whisper and from that distance he knew who it was. He turned to see her being hoisted up in to the sky by those three evil puddle hoppers that had caused so much trouble last year. They were again repeating their dastardly acts.

"Mum!" He called out but it was too late.

"So, you are the ones who have been taking these poor, innocent children! I should have guessed." Constance snarled at her three kidnappers as they reached the cloud.

"Ha! And we are having a lot of fun getting our own back on your people!" Surr gloated.

"And now we have Jules's mother! This is an extra bonus we were not expecting! This is really working out well! Our revenge is getting sweeter and sweeter!" Rak laughed aloud.

The battle was ferocious a little further away from where the three evil puddle hoppers arrived with their hostages. They watched their allies fighting the enemy of them both. They were desperate to get over there and help them. Yet, they needed to deal with the children and Jules's mother first. Then they could join in the fight.

All this time, more and more puddle hoppers were reaching the cloud and joining in the struggle. It must be said, there were still a large number of cloud jumpers arriving from inside the cloud as well to try to help defend their home. At that point, there seemed to be no one clearly winning the battle. Although, the attackers were certainly pushing back the defenders from the cloud lines as time went on.

This was due to the fact that with each new puddle hopper that arrived, more space had to be found on the cloud for him to stand. Hence, the cloud jumpers were forced back a little bit more by each new arrival. Not only were the puddle hoppers getting more and more numbers in strength on to their foe's home territory but this slow gaining of ground seemed to be putting them in an ever stronger position.

*****

Now it so happened, on the same day as this battle was taking place, the whole ladies Australian cricket team had been to the television studios in Brook Road. You may be surprised to hear this was not too far away from where the battle was taking place. They were there for an interview with the television's sports editor about the upcoming match. An audience was present and, in due course, they answered questions about themselves before departing on their team coach. They needed to get to Manchester for the next day's game.

Some of the ladies Australian cricket team's players felt they needed to stretch their legs after being cooped up in the hot studio for so long. It was at the point they were passing Brook Park. A few members of the team decided to ask the driver to stop for a while. Of course, they had no idea a major confrontation was taking place there.

"Hey mate," they said to the driver. "Can we stretch these old walking sticks of ours! We've been sitting in that stuffy old pommie studio for so long, a mother emu could have laid a whole nest-full of its huge eggs in that time!"

He agreed and so they all got out and began to take in the fresh air and stretch themselves.

"Hey! What's happening over there, mate?" The opening batswoman was the first to see the fracas taking place not far from where they were all standing.

"Don't know mate! Looks like some sort of 'argie-bargie' going on if you ask me!" Came the fast bowler's reply.

"They seem to be throwing those white things up in to the air!" The wicketkeeper said with a look of surprise in her eye.

"Yeah! Look up there mates! Can you see those funny creatures fighting on the clouds! Am I seeing things or what?" The spin bowler had her hand over her eyes to protect them from the sun as she looked up.

"Hey! I reckon you're right mate. Let's shifty on over there and find out what's going on shall we?" The opening batswoman was by now intrigued.

Soon the whole team was making their way over to where the battle was taking place.

"These are bloody strange looking creatures throwing those white fluff balls up at the clouds?" The fast bowler looked at the puddle hoppers unsure what or who they were. She had never seen anything like them before.

"Hey! Up there on the cloud! Look! There's some up there too. See them! I don't get it mate, how comes they aren't falling through all that fluffy stuff!" The wicket-keeper could not work out how they were defying the laws of gravity as humans know it.

"Hey! Let me eat rat's legs! Look over there! There's a small kangaroo!" The spin bowler spotted the roo. "Blimey mate he can jump better than the roos in Aus! He almost reached the cloud with that leap! He could enter the Olympics if you ask me!"

"Hey! Fella! What's going on here then?" The Captain of the team asked Gideon. "And who are these strange looking guys with ya, mate?"

Gideon explained about how the cloud jumpers were the ones who had been stealing the children from the local town. Their intention was to take them away and keep them in captivity. Even the ladies Australian cricket team had heard on the news about the disappearing children.

"We can't have that, mate!" Her Deputy Captain shook her head.

"And you say, these creatures here, who are trying to help us get the children back, are called puddle hoppers. Strange name that's for sure! And you say, they've come across their evil cousins before and know they are hell-bent on doing mischief. That isn't good!"

"So, what are you trying to do, mate?" The fast bowler asked Gideon. "Get up on the clouds and release the children? And if yer don't mind me asking mate, how comes they don't just fall through the cloud?"

Gideon explained to the team about how the cloud jumpers ate clouds and are so light they can live and walk on the clouds with no problem. While, others, like humans and puddle hoppers need to use the cloud rolled up as string and tied around our waists to stay up on the cloud. He explained how these cloud belts act like a sort of balloon air bag. Jules' uncle then showed them the thin cloud lines that went up to the cloud. Pointing out how strong they were. "Not only does it allow the cloud jumpers to go up and down from the clouds but we are using them to help us to get up to their base in the clouds and release their captives."

The cricket team in their green blazers watched on in amazement.

"We haven't heard of anything like this in Oz! It's as odd as watching a platypus swimming!" Their spinner shook her head stunned by it all.

"Hey! I think we can help here, mate!" The Captain smiled.

She had a quick word with the rest of the team and soon they were all rushing back to the coach. They got the driver to drive over to where the action was taking place and then told him to open his underneath luggage compartment. Here was all of the team's cricket equipment.

"Right ladies! Let's do it!" The Captain called out. They all did high-fives!

Instantly, some members of the team stood ready with cricket bats in hand, while others began to pick up pieces of cloud littered on the floor and squash them in to balls. Those with the cloud balls then began to bowl them at one of the players who had a cricket bat. Next, there was a heavy thud, as the batswoman, hit the cloud ball so hard it shot up in to the air. It shot up in to the air with a lot more speed than any of those throwing them could and with far more accuracy too. The cricket team obviously had the ability to whack the ball directly on to the cloud above and hit an evil cloud jumper with almost every shot. Moreover, it was with such velocity that those who were hit were in great pain and had to fall back away from the action. It was like having red hot cannon balls being fired at them on a battlefield.

"Brilliant!" Gideon praised them. "That's just what we need! You are like the much-needed artillery field guns in a war. Keep it up ladies!"

"They're retreating!" Jules called out. "Thanks to the ladies Australian cricket team. You have got them on the run. Keep it up team!"

Cloud ball after cloud ball was bowled and then hit ferociously with the cricket bat. These balls were being struck with such accuracy of batting, the cloud jumpers were being knocked off their feet. Some, were in such a severe state of shock, they were being forced to run away and desert the battle.

"You know team, this is great practice for the upcoming match against the poms!" The spin bowler laughed with her colleagues.

"Yeah! Sure beats sitting in a studio full of stiffs!" The wicket-keeper giggled.

More and more puddle hoppers were getting on to the cloud with ease at this point. This was giving them a growing advantage. There was little concern that the lines which went down to the ground would be recaptured by the cloud jumpers now.

Some continued to try and reach them and stop the numbers of attackers increasing. However, it was in vain. For their opponents were finally getting the upper hand. The skills and accuracy of the ladies Australian cricket team with the cloud balls had been substantial in ensuring victory.

Chapter 17

While the battle for the part of the cloud surrounding where the lines went to the ground was still raging vigorously, the buzz of a helicopter could be heard getting closer and closer to where the fighting was taking place. From a small dot on the far horizon, the craft grew bigger and bigger until the sound of the engines were extremely loud and the rotation of its blades caused quite a downward moving air current.

Prince Willie had arrived to try and get his kidnapped daughter back. His chauffeur, who was a helicopter pilot himself, had been brought along sensibly by the prince as well. He would need him to fly the machine while he attempted the rescue. The prince was surprised to see a full-scale battle taking place as he neared. He thought he was the only one aware of these creatures living on the clouds.

Obviously, this was not the case. This made him only fear more for his daughter. Yet, when he saw what was going on, he soon realised he not only had to try to save Princess Charlie but there was the need for him to help those fighting the cloud jumpers too.

Very adroitly, the prince guided the flying machine until it was hovering right next to the cloud.

"You take over!" He yelled at his chauffeur and gave him the controls. "I'm going to jump on to the cloud and try to save Princess Charlie. When I come back with her, I want you to take her to safety while I help the others overcome these kidnapping brutes! Don't worry! I will call you back to the cloud when I am ready to leave here! But your priority is to get Princess Charlie to safety at all costs. Then return as quick as you can when I call you!"

The chauffeur nodded that he fully understood and the prince made his way over to the door. When the prince looked over at those fighting the cloud jumpers, he soon realised they all had pieces of cloud tied around their waist.

From the helicopter, he reached out, rolled some up and tied it around his own waist.

Then without hesitation the prince leapt on to the cloud. The cloud around his mid-drift gave him the buoyancy and lightness he needed to stay on the cloud and not fall through. He gave a sigh of relief and was now ready to start the search for his missing daughter. At this stage leaving the fighting to others.

However, immediately, two cloud jumpers attacked this new comer who had landed on their cloud. Of course, they had no idea he was a prince as much as they did not realise they had a princess down below. They attempted to tie him up with cloud rope and pin him down.

Yet, the prince was a lot stronger than they were. He was soon throwing them off himself so they bounced across the cloud. Both were soon skidding towards the edge and only stopped themselves falling off the cloud by grabbing the very end section.

The prince looked about him to see where he could possibly find his daughter. He knew she had to be there somewhere but the question was where. He then spotted some of the defenders coming in and out of the cloud through what looked like an opening.

He pushed a few more defenders out of the way as he made his way over to it. He was soon inside and having to push aside cloud jumper after cloud jumper who were a lot lighter and smaller than he was. Gradually, he forced himself further and further in to this very strange white world.

"Get out of my way!" He yelled! "Where is my daughter?" He grabbed one of the small creatures around him and pinned him against the cloud. Sadly, he had picked on one of the cloud jumpers who did not know the human language.

"Charlie!" The prince called out in despair. "Are you here somewhere! Charlie!"

"Daddy!" A timid voice replied back. "I'm here!"

A voice, of course, he recognised immediately. He straight away started to push aside more cloud jumpers who tried to stand in his way as he made his way to where the voice had come from. Soon another large white room started to appear in front of him. To his surprise, he could see that there were many bodies placed around the outside of the huge room.

At first, he could not work out who they were. Yet, as he got nearer he began to realise to his horror that these bodies all belonged to children and some of the strange blue creatures he saw fighting on the cloud above. Even more shocking to him was that they were all sat in a row and tied by cloud lines to the wall.

"What on earth is happening here?" He looked at the scene before him with utter horror. "This must be all those missing children! Who would do such a horrendous thing. Why would they have all these children chained up?"

"Daddy!" Called Princess Charlie again. "I'm here!"

He straight away heard where the voice had come from and ran over to his daughter. He could not help but give her a really big hug before attempting to undo the cloud rope that held her. It was useless. He could not untie it.

"It won't break!" He yelped in frustration. Wanting to set her free and get her out of that dismal place.

Realising he was not going to be able to release his daughter, he went over to what seemed like a guard. The guard was still coming around after the prince had thrown him up against the wall as he entered the room.

He pulled the guard over to his daughter and in a very threatening way said, "Release her!" He then put his hands around the cloud jumper's throat as a threatening gesture. "Or else!"

The guard did not understand the man's words for he could not speak English either, but he certainly understood what he was threatening to do.

Hence, the cloud jumper quickly released the girl who hugged her father. "Daddy, you saved me! They were going to take me away!"

"They were never going to take you away from me, Charlie, I would never let them do that!"

Prince Willie was about to order the same guard to start to release the other children when a group of cloud jumpers appeared at the door. It was obvious their intention was to overpower this man who had penetrated so deep in to the cloud itself.

The prince knew he would not be able to overcome this strong force of defenders before him by himself. His only hope was to try and get his daughter to safety first, before helping the other attackers overcome the cloud jumpers and set the children free.

He picked up Charlie and took another exit he had spotted out the corner of his eye. Of course, he had no idea where it went, but it was his only hope. He was soon pursued by the defenders, who were far nimbler going through these corridors than he was.

Looking behind he could see they were catching up with him fast. Just in time the prince, carrying the princess, emerged through an entrance on to the cloud. The chasing group were about to grab him when he leapt for the safety of the helicopter and landed inside its open door.

He turned ready to push off any of these small creatures who had followed him. Yet, when he looked behind him, he could see none of them had pursued him on the helicopter. They had decided to stay wisely on the cloud. From there they looked at him with a snake and its venom in their eyes.

"I want you to go with Hugh, our chauffeur, to safety while I try to help save the other children!" he said to his daughter who nodded that she understood.

"Right take Princess Charlie to safety and I will call you when I need you!" He shouted to Hugh. Whether Hugh heard him or not with the helicopter engine being so loud and the prince not having a microphone connection is unclear but he knew exactly what his boss wanted him to do.

He nodded, as the prince jumped back on to the cloud, landing with such force, he managed to knock over the whole contingent of cloud jumpers who had been chasing him. This gave him the opportunity to rush over to join the puddle hoppers in the ongoing fight.

Chapter 18

Looking up from the ground, Gideon, Jules, Prok, his father the chief of the tribe and the other elders could see clearly that the puddle hoppers were pushing back their detested foe. The lines to the clouds seemed secure from danger. Hence, allowing more and more puddle hoppers to get on to the cloud and strengthen the numbers fighting above. A foe who seemed to be retreating further and further back.

"I'm going to go up there!" called Gideon.

It was clear he wanted to be in the thick of the battle. There was no doubt his considerable bulk would be useful in pushing back the much smaller cloud people. He was soon on the cloud line and pulling himself up to the cloud. Jules watched, as within an instant on reaching the cloud, his uncle was involved in the fighting. Throwing off the cloud jumpers who tried to pull him over and tie him up with their cloud rope.

"Come on!" Yelled Jules, going over to the roo and climbing on his back. "You know you can jump as high as the cloud. With my guidance you will be useful fighting those cloud jumpers. We will be able to jump right over the top of them and attack them from the back!"

The roo seemed to understand what was expected of him and leapt high up in to the air with Jules on his back. This time he rose up in to the sky but was just short of the cloud. Landing again back on the ground. Probably due to the extra weight of Jules.

"Come on you can do it!" Jules encouraged the young kangaroo. "One more try!"

With that the roo jumped up in to the air once more. But this time he landed on the cloud itself. Fortunately, he landed at a spot where no fighting was taking place. Also, it was right behind the cloud jumpers themselves. They were totally unaware of the sudden appearance of this new enemy behind them.

"Did you see that roo jump, mate! It went as high in to the air as a pancake being thrown from a frying pan on pancake day!" The wicket-keeper smiled. "Good old roo! Go get 'em roo!"

"You know what, mate, that roo looks a lot like our mascot back in Aus? Do you remember it?" The fast bowler had an amazed look on her face as she tried to work out how could that possibly be.

"Do yer know, I reckon you could be right, mate. Blimey, how'd he get here! Kind of odd things going on around here and all! Sends a rugrat on hot coals up your spine!" The spin bowler looked amazed as well.

By now the ladies Australian cricket team had stopped their bombardment. Tired out with exhaustion. Their job well done. They could see the puddle hoppers pushing the cloud jumpers back further and further. A great cheer went up from them when they saw the prince jump in to the fray and help the puddle hoppers.

"We got to be going ladies!" The coach driver called across to the cricket team. He had not been taking much notice of what they had been up to. He was more concerned with the water temperature in his luxury coach. "You've got to be at Old Trafford by early evening! And the match starts tomorrow! I'll lose my job if you are late!"

"Blimey! He's right mate, we better be going! I think we've done our bit to help! Don't you!" The Captain looked quite pleased with herself.

"That's a shame, mate! This has been pretty brilliant!" The opening batswoman was so enjoying it. "Not often do we get the chance for our batting and bowling to actually help save real lives!"

With that the ladies Australian team said their goodbyes and received great thanks from the chief of the puddle hoppers. Who explained they may have failed in this fight without the use of their extra fire power.

"We just hope those kids are all right!" The Captain shook the little blue creature's hand as they boarded the coach and made their way off to Manchester for the next day's game.

*****

Jules tugged the roo and with one leap they were in amongst the fighting. Attacking from behind. This was a great shock to the cloud jumpers who did not expect them to be there. The young fighter, had his cricket bat with him and was soon walloping the defending creatures who were in his way. Stunned and hurt they fell away from the fight. Creating more gaps in their defending wall.

At the same time the three evil puddle hoppers had secured the children and Jules's mum who they had recently captured. They were now ready to join the fray. The three of them were more than aware that if the cloud jumpers and themselves lost this battle there would be a good chance they would be recaptured. And if they were recaptured, it would probably be the case they would more than likely be re-interned in their boxes and frozen.

Hence, the consequences of losing were horrifying to the three of them. Especially, if you compare it against the rosy future being offered to them by their fellow conspirators. If they won, they would be able to live in reasonable comfort in a place of their choice. Yet, this very wonderful future they hoped for was now under a great threat.

The three new defenders were soon fighting their fellow creatures. They seemed to have had a lot of experience fighting and were getting the better of every duel they were in. Even though the attackers were more than keen to overcome the three creatures who had brought their kind in to such disrepute.

No matter how hard they tried, they found in each one-to-one match they were out manoeuvred by their three evil opponents. It said a lot about the type of life the three of them had lived up until then. They were even making in-roads in to the puddle hoppers defence and getting nearer to the cloud lines. This was encouraging the cloud jumpers! There was hope yet!

However, eventually, the three evil creatures found themselves pitted against the prince himself. He recognised them straight away as his daughter's kidnappers. This was going to be his opportunity to make them aware how he felt about what they had done. It was not going to be pleasant. Next to him, lined up were Gideon with Jules and his roo. There was anger at what these three escaped creatures had done written all over their faces.

Even the three evil defenders gulped at who they were facing. They could see how determined they looked for revenge upon the three of them. Yet, the three evil characters gave a good account of themselves in the ensuing fight.

Both hurting and making all of their three giant foes stumble or fall back at times. However, in the end, they were no match for their determined combatants, who overcame the three of them.

Gideon, after they were overpowered, took the opportunity to tie them up with cloud rope.

"You three have caused enough problems!" He stared angrily at them. "There will be certainly no escape for you this time, I can assure you! I'll make sure of that!"

The cloud jumpers realised they had lost. The puddle hoppers had now fought their way to the entrances to the interior of the cloud itself. There seemed little more to defend.

"We have lost!" Castor, their chief, called out in his high-pitched voice for his warriors to hear. "We have to retreat or suffer being captured and endure the humiliation they will heap upon us! Yet, if we leave the cloud and our home now, we can live to fight another day against these irksome puddle hoppers and their nuisance friends."

"You look pleased with yourselves, puddle hoppers, but we shall return and have our revenge. You have not seen the last of us!" Castor's councillor, Kloxon, snarled at those facing him.

"You tricked us this time but we will be more careful next time we come! And be assured, puddle hoppers, we will come back!" Celeste, the leader's wife raged.

With that the cloud jumpers were all running from their foe. Abandoning their cloud home. Finding any way they could to escape in a hasty, unorderly retreat from the pursuing puddle hoppers. They were soon leaping from one cloud to the next away from where the vicious battle had taken place. Off to seek refuge where ever they could find it after their defeat.

They would soon get back to their island. Another cloud to use would be there waiting for them. Another cloud they could use to fly across the skies. It's true, it was a long trek back now. However, what was more devastating to them was the loss of all the children they had captured over the last few days. Children who were going to bring a new energy and life to their cloud workshop.

The existing children who had been there for such a long time were getting too tired and their output was falling. However, if the cloud jumpers put it in to context, they were not too worried, for they knew they could find another town, with other children to replace those who need replacing. It was only a matter of time. It was not the end of the world.

A great cheer went up amongst those above and below as the cloud jumpers turned and started running away and leaping across clouds. They realised at last they had achieved the hard fought for victory they so wanted.

Of course, there was much congratulating taking place, while at the same time others tended to broken bones, wounds and abrasions. It had been a harsh and cruel battle but victory was theirs.

"Can someone explain to me who those awful creatures were who kidnapped my daughter?" Prince Willie at last had the chance to ask the question. A question that had been on his mind since the moment she had disappeared. Of course, he had not had time to ask it before and it had not even been his priority. His priority was to get his daughter back. Then ask the questions after.

Gideon took the moment to introduce the prince to the chief of the puddle hoppers and ensured that the small creature was aware that the prince was heir to the kingdom above where they lived. He explained to the prince who the puddle hoppers were and where they lived. Telling him how the secrecy about their existence was paramount to their safety and future. Immediately, the prince assured them of his own silence and support. He said how well they had fought that day against such a determined enemy.

And thanked them for their help in securing the return of his own daughter as well as all the other children. Moreover, he assured them if they ever needed his help in the future, they could be certain he would be there to offer all the necessary support they required. He also assured them that now he knew of their existence he would ensure their tribe's homes would become an area of significant importance and remain left alone. His desire was that they would be able to live undisturbed from those above ground.

"Now I have to make my farewells, sadly!" He explained with regret. "I have an important engagement with the Queen and our guest, the President of the United States, tonight at Buckingham Palace. I am sure I can leave those poor children interred inside the cloud to be freed by your good selves. And if there are any problems let me know and I shall ensure they are sorted out immediately."

The prince telephoned his chauffeur, who, within a few moments, arrived with the helicopter. The royal leapt aboard the craft, waved his goodbyes and the rotary machine flew off in the direction of the Palace gardens in London.

Gideon, Jules and the puddle hoppers made their way down inside the cloud.

The white corridors were eerily quiet now the cruel inhabitants had all ran off.

Hence, they soon heard the calls and cries from where the children were.

"This way!" Gideon called and those following him all speeded up as well. The noise from the children became louder as they reached the great hall where they were all imprisoned. At its entrance, the group all stopped and looked in horror at the scene that lay before them. All those children tied up, sitting huddled in total fear at what lay ahead of them in the future. That is, if the cloud jumpers had got their way.

"Get the hair monster up here!" Yelled Gideon. "He'll soon get all these cloud ropes off the children and set them free!"

"We're going to free you!" Jules shouted across the hall to ensure each child could hear him. "You are all going home!"

Another great cheer went up! Yet, many children still carried on crying and would until they were returned home safely. Their stress was so easy to see. For many, the whole situation had been overwhelming and they wanted their mums, their dads and their home.

"Mother!" called Jules. "Bronwyn! Seth! Lace!" He wondered where they were as he could not see them within the great white hall.

"We're here!" Came the joint reply.

Jules rushed through to a smaller side chamber and there they all were! Beaming with joy at being rescued at last.

"What took yer so long, mate?" Seth jested. "I'm getting pretty stiff sitting here like an unwanted sausage six weeks out of date!"

"We just had one or two cloud jumpers and evil puddle hoppers to deal with!" Jules replied with a smile.

"Me do good! Um!" The hair eater smiled as he ate cloud rope after cloud rope. Obviously, the cloud ropes did not taste anywhere near as lovely as the hair he enjoyed eating but it was food. Hence, he munched quite happily on the ropes as he released child after child and the small group in the side chamber.

"Thank you!" Gideon said gratefully to the hair eater. "You have done very well! But we have to think how we are going to stop you raiding people's hair in the middle of the night! People won't put up with that!"

Once everybody was back on the ground and the puddle hoppers had disappeared from the park, Gideon commenced making arrangements for the children to be returned back to their homes. It was not long before parents were arriving with tears of joy in their eyes to collect their loved ones.

Of course, they were asking many questions about how their children had been found in Brook Park? The parents were sure this whole area had been searched and searched again and again without any sign of them being there before.

Gideon fended off the questions with, "I am sure that all will be revealed on another day. Now just enjoy the return of your child!"

This, the parents, were more than pleased to accept as they made their way home with their returned loved one wrapped up in the warmest of hugs.

Chapter 19

"And then we were tied up with pieces of cloud and put in a big empty white space in the cloud itself. So, we couldn't escape. It was horrible!" One child described his ordeal to Robin Biggs, the TV reporter.

"And there were lots of us children in there. Most were crying or wanted their mums or dads! Not me though! You should have heard them! What a racket." Another child joined in with her views.

"Yeah! And these creatures that live in the clouds were really nasty to us. They kept telling us to shut up crying as we were never going home again!" Another who spoke still had a wobble of fear in his voice.

"And can you tell us what these creatures looked like?" The TV reporter was questioning them as to what happened after they disappeared.

"Yeah! They were all white and short and funny looking with pointed ears!" One tried to describe their captors.

"You should have seen them, they were quite shiny and their skin was smooth like." Another remembered with fright in his eyes.

"And they had protruding eyes that looked right through you as if you meant nothing to them!" This girl held her hands up to her eyes to show the reporter what she meant.

"Their faces were all narrow and they had funny tufts of white or grey hair on top of their heads! They looked as if they were from out of space or something!" One of them added.

"And some spoke English but when they spoke to each other it was in this really strange high-pitched sound that went right through you! They terrified me! They were horrible!" Another girl remembered.

"Thank you, boys and girls! You've given us a really good description of what you remember." The TV reporter looked at them as if he was not too convinced. As if it was a bit too far-fetched for such a thing to happen.

"Well! What do you make of this, Doctor Anderson?" He asked the psychologist who often appeared on this local news channel to give his views on any events the news team felt he could help the audience better understand. "You have to admit it does sound a bit strange? Creatures living in clouds? Again, we hear mention of the small, blue creatures as well. Children talk about how these blue small creatures helped them escape. Just as they did last year? All the children say they were kidnapped and held prisoners inside a cloud? How could that be? And all the children talk of being taken up to the cloud on cloud lines and then tied up with cloud ropes? Surely, this sounds far too outrageous to be true, Doctor?"

"Well! Um! Yes! It is quite amazing isn't it! The children in this town certainly have a great imagination. If you remember, it was only a year ago they were telling us they had been sucked down in to puddles and held captives there." The Doctor chuckled as he said it. Throwing obvious disdain upon the children's statements.

The TV reporter was only too happy to chuckle with him.

"Well! Um! Yes! I believe we have got to remember, these children received a lot of attention from adults last year when they mentioned they had been sucked in to puddles. It would not surprise me, if, once again, by talking about being lifted up in to the clouds and then imprisoned by these cloud creatures they believe they have found a way to gain the adults' attention they so crave."

"So, you believe they are making all of this up, Doctor Anderson?" Robin Biggs asked his guest on the news channel.

"Um! Yes! Well, I believe, it is the same syndrome as last year. In that there is a collective, mass hypnosis taking place amongst these children. There is no doubt they fully believe what they saw and what they say. Yet, who started it and how it spread is difficult for us to get to the bottom of. It may be one child is the initiator for last year's and this year's similar mass hypnosis. However, we must remember they are children with children's imaginations and they are all truly convinced what they say happened did happen. And there lies the root of the problem!"

"Are you not convinced then, Doctor?" The TV reporter was prompted to ask by his editor in his ear-piece. "If it is all made up as you suggest, how is it best we deal with the children?"

"Well! Um! Yes! Let us be realistic. For we are living in a real world of science and fact. How can creatures be living on the clouds? How absurd! How can they leap from cloud to cloud and climb down lines made from cloud? How absurd! Us, adults have to be rational. Use our logic and common sense in this matter. We must realise it is totally inconceivable such things could have happened." The Doctor looked in to the camera seriously.

"You believe it is all made up then, Doctor!"

"Um! Yes! Well, I believe the children have been involved in making a gigantic hoax upon the town's adults! How much this is due to their consciousness or sub consciousness, it will take time to work out. It may be worth us all remembering that a similar problem could arise again next year. The children have realised it is a good way to draw attention to themselves and may attempt to try it again. For it is attention they, obviously, very earnestly crave."

"Thank you, Doctor Anderson, for your wonderful insight once more!" The reporter turned to face the camera. "Once again, according to the doctor, it does seem more than likely the town has been tricked by their own children. There does seem to be an oddness, to say the least, about their disappearance and what they say subsequently happened to them. I am sure we will be hearing a lot more about this story over the coming weeks. This is Robin Biggs, your local reporter, handing back to the studio."

*****

"Blimey, Jules mate, that doctor on the TV of yours is a real duffer!" Bronwyn shook her head. "How comes the mums and dads don't believe their kids?"

"Good question, Bronwyn!" Jules shrugged his shoulders. "But if it helps us keep where the puddle hoppers live a secret I'm happy to go along with it!"

"Guess you're dead dingo right there, Cous!" Seth slapped him on the shoulders. "Sleeping possums, we don't want the whereabouts of the puddle hoppers found out! That would be a real Bunsen burner disaster!"

"And it's great we haven't seen any of those cloud jumpers since they were driven away!" Gideon reminded everyone. "The puddle hoppers have checked the clouds for days now and assure me they have left. They don't think we'll be seeing them for a long, long time! They have had their noses well and truly bloodied."

"Thank goodness!" His sister-in-law sighed. "It was bad enough with those three evil characters around, let alone a whole host of evil cloud jumpers wanting to take the town's children away."

"Will they go and take children from other towns next?" Jules asked.

"I reckon they will try!" His uncle replied with frustration. "They seem hellbent on keeping their cloud workshop going according to the three evil puddle hoppers when they were interrogated by their own kind. They reckon they use the children to make the clouds they live on out of a refined cloud material they put together! It would be nice to be able to stop them using children in this terrible way! I will have to think about that for a while. See if I can find a way to help those poor children already stolen from their homes and being maltreated!"

"I dread to think what would have happened if they had taken so many children away from this town! There would have been more tears shed than water that flows down the River Thames in a week!" Constance added grateful they did not succeed in what they set out to do.

*****

"We have some breaking news for you. This has just come in from the local courthouse." Robin Biggs appeared on the screen. "Robin what have you got for us?"

"Well, Mr. Brian and his brother, Grunswick, have both been found guilty by the jury. The judge has announced he will pass sentence on them later in the month!"

A big cheer went up in the Appleyard's household with Constance leading it. Things had been certainly turned around since Gideon had arrived back at the house. He had paid all the outstanding bills, given her and Jules a huge amount of money to deal with future bills and expenses. Stated he wanted them to consider him as part of the household now.

This they were both excited about. The three of them were all very close. He was offering to pick up most of the household bills from now on if Constance was in agreement. This was a great relief to Constance. Who would not have to worry about such things in the future.

On top of all that, the court case against Jules's mum had been dropped. Grunswick's horrendous factory where she had been working had been closed down. Yet, this lack of income from her work at his factory was no longer of importance due to Gideon's financial support. There was further news that new owners were taking over at the pickle factory from Mr. Brian.

Now he was going to be indisposed for quite a while with a likely prison sentence, he had decided to sell the business. And to Constance's great delight, the first thing the new owners did, was to invite all the workers who wished to come back to work there when the factory reopened the chance to receive full-pay each week until then.

Yet, the greatest satisfaction of all for Jules's mum, came from the fact that she had been temporarily elected Mayor of Boreham Wood following the conviction of Mr. Brian. People in the town, felt so ashamed and aggrieved with themselves as to how they had treated her. Even though they knew she was such a lovely person and could never have done such a thing. Hence, it was agreed to award her the interim role until a new mayor was elected.

So, there she sat at home with her new gold chain of office around her neck. She was enjoying being picked up in a Rolls Royce each day and driven down to the town hall. Now she was being asked to sign important documents, to give her opinions on town matters and lead council meetings.

There were also the many functions she had to attend. Ones, where she would take along, while they were still there that is, the twins and Gideon as well as Jules. The twins were elated, as the events were always full of fantastic food and even though they had to put up with a lot of dull speeches it was always worth it because of what they got to eat.

*****

The sewage company were more than delighted to keep the knowledge about the existence of the hair eater a secret as suggested by Gideon and the new mayor. As long as the creature stopped taking people's hair to eat in the middle of the night and gave up frightening the workers who had to go down in to the sewer system.

It was agreed that the sewage company would buy up all the hair from the local hair-dressing salons each day and give it over to the hair eater to eat at his leisure. He agreed that he would no longer go and terrorise people by stealing their hair while they slept. Furthermore, he would leave the workers who came in to the sewers alone. In fact, it was agreed that due to the hair being provided, the hair eater would help clean out any large build-up of sewerage. What was more, he was making quite a lot of friends among those workers who started to venture down there. Once they realised he was not a man-eating monster. Of course, they were also sworn to secrecy about his presence.

*****

"Right this time I will make sure they do not escape!" Gideon had once more refrozen the three evil puddle hoppers and placed them in cannisters ready to take back to Alaska with him.

"Are you sure!" His sister-in-law looked at him with quite a disbelieving eye. "We don't want those three evil creatures turning up again next year!"

"I will be extra careful. I promise you, Constance!" The man tried to look as reassuring as he could after having one attempt at reburying them fail. "I shall ensure there is not a cloud in the sky, a puddle on the ground or a creature on the horizon when I bury them. This time there will be no mistake!"

"That's good news!" Jules added. "They do seem to cause a lot of trouble around here when they are about!"

"We aren't so sure, Jules, mate!" Seth shook his head. "It's been real blooming exciting both summers we've come over. And those three little guys, they really get things happening, don't they!"

"Yeah!" Bronwyn added to her brother's comments. "Don't get any excitement like this buckeroo summer back in Adelaide!"

"It's all as quiet as snails asleep in their shells down there, mate!" Seth added.

"Well, these little devils are coming with me back to Alaska and you will never see them again, I can assure you!" Jules's uncle tried to ensure that everyone there got the message. There would be no mistakes this time. "So, twins, I don't know what you are going to do for excitement next summer because there won't be the three evil puddle hoppers here!"

"And it's a real shame you had to send our little roo back to Oz with the ladies Aussie cricket team! We'll fair dinkum miss him mate!" Bronwyn looked sad at his departure.

"I am afraid, we had no choice in the matter!" Gideon tried to make the twins aware of what they had done and why." The zoo keepers in Adelaide were beginning to ask big questions about where the young kangaroo was. It could have got you in to a lot of trouble when you got back home. You were lucky, the ladies Australian cricket team were only too pleased to take it back with them and say it had somehow slipped in to one of the team bags."

"Fair dinkum! I suppose!" Seth agreed. "I like that they promised to make sure the little critter and it's roo mum will be released in to the outback."

"That's great news!" Jules smiled. "He was a great help against those cloud jumpers. It is lucky kangaroos can't talk as it would have quite a story to tell."

"Yeah! I reckon I have never seen a roo cowboy before either, Jules!" Seth joked. Remembering how Jules had been riding on the back of the young kangaroo on the cloud. "You were like John Wayne in a cowboy movie, mate!"

Everyone laughed.

*****

"Ow!" Jules screeched in total shock.

"Are you all right, Jules?" His mum called out in to the garden where she knew he was. She had sent him out there to put some of the leftovers from the meal in to the bin. The twins had left quite a lot on their plate that night which was quite unusual for them. They had then darted off upstairs at top speed. So instead of asking them both to put the waste in the outside bin she had to rely on her ever-dependable son to do the task.

"Yes! Mum! I'm fine!"

She may have noticed a slight note of irritation in his voice though.

Not that he was fine really.

You see the twins had been up to their tricks as usual. This time they had managed to put a spring device at the bottom of the green waste bin. It was the bin where all the food waste was kept ready to be collected and recycled. I think you can imagine what was going to happen!

As Jules lifted up the cover to the green bin to put in the waste food from the twins, it released a catch for the spring inside the bin to leap upwards with a great velocity. Thus, it sent days of food waste, which was quite considerable, flying in to the air. And when it flew out of the bin, it fell naturally all over the person who was standing right next to it. Of course, that person who happened to be standing right next to the bin was Jules.

To add to his humiliation, the twins had been watching everything unfold from the upstairs bedroom window where they were rolling about in laughter at their trick's considerable success. Seeing their cousin covered from head to toe in foul-smelling food waste they thought was a real treat.

They left it to their cousin to clear up the mess in the garden while they got on with packing as it was time for them to go home. Their holiday was coming to an end.

Not that Jules let them get it all their own way!

It was not long after he had finished clearing up the mess in the garden he heard the twins gasping for cool air and rushing down the stairs to get a glass of water. He smiled to himself knowing what had happened.

"These are as hot as a midday sandy beach in Adelaide!" Yelled Bronwyn.

"Get me some water! Before I fry an ostrich egg on my tongue!" Puffed Seth.

"Sweet revenge!" Their cousin said to himself still brushing off some waste food from the trousers he was wearing.

For Jules had been to the local toy shop and bought some trick sweets. On the packet it said the contents were all different flavours boiled sweets. Some were lemon, some were strawberry, others were black current or raspberry.

Yet, the trick was in the fact they were all very hot sweets that burnt your tongue.

Moreover, that uncomfortable burning heat would remain for quite a considerable time afterwards. Jules knew if he left the packet lying beside his sleeping bag, they would spot it and eat some of them. It was in their DNA. All he had to do was wait and he would hear them leaping about with hot pokers in their mouths and gasping for cold water.

*****

Gideon was the first to leave. On the front doorstep waiting for his taxi stood the twins, Jules and his mother.

"Now you are sure you've got them secure this time!" Jules smiled at him.

"And remember to check for clouds when you bury them!" His mum added.

"Don't worry, they are secure and I'll scour the horizon for any clouds or anything that moves! I think I have learnt a lesson!" The traveller nodded.

"And thank you for your help again with so many things!" His mum said sincerely. "From monies, to helping with my work and dealing with the cloud jumpers! You always seem to help resolve all the problems!"

"And this time I have put in place a bank order to pay you so much a month! Hopefully, that will help you both out! And if there is anything you need you must let me know! And remember I'm coming back next summer!" He smiled. "And this time I will ensure that we can keep in touch over the year!"

"Promise!" Jules added.

"Promise! Nephew!" He added.

"What about us, cobber! Can we come back next year!" Asked Seth. "We don't want to miss out on the excitement! We don't get excitement like that back in old Adelaide!"

"I hope there won't be any excitement next year!" Jules' mum said with a sigh. "The last two years have been more than enough, thank you!"

"Ah! Aunt! Don't be like that! It's brill all that happens here!" Bronwyn hugged her with joy. "It's like being in an adventure story in a book!"

"Anyway, you know you are both welcome back here any time! Excitement or not!" She concluded. "Isn't that right, Jules!"

"That would be fantastic!" Jules beamed. "I will be looking forward to you two and Uncle Gideon coming back next summer!"

He knew the thought of them all arriving again next year would help keep him buoyed up right through those cold winter months. It was something to really look forward to. He could not believe that when those three arrived exciting things tended to follow. The twins and Uncle Gideon seem to go together with trouble like rhubarb and custard. He could not wait.

Eventually, the taxi arrived and the final farewells to Gideon were made.

Next it was the twins turn to leave. It was easy to tell they did not want to go. Going home for them meant dealing with the problems they had left behind. These ranged from working out their future schooling, to what friends did they still have left and not forgetting trying to deal with a very irate local community. All, who it seemed, wanted the twins to behave well. Of course, we know that was not going to happen.

"Thanks for everything both of yer!" Bronwyn hugged her aunt and cousin and would not let go. "You can't believe how exciting it's been for us! Wackeroo!"

"Trouble is, mate! No one ever believes us when we get home and tell them what's happened! They think we made it all up!" Seth shook his head in despair.

"And it's all been exciting as riding a kangaroo!"

"Well, you both know you are welcome here any time! We love having you!" Their kind aunt stated. And I think she probably meant it. Yet, there may have been fingers crossed behind her back. Fingers crossed that we could not see when she said it.

When the taxi arrived, the final kisses and hugs were given before the twins departed. This time without the roo. Well, as far as Jules and his mum were aware!

"It's going to be so quiet around here again!" Jules flopped in a chair after their departure. "I will really miss having those three around. It's like being caught up in a whirlwind, inside a hurricane and under a tornado when they are here!" He smiled remembering the last few weeks and what had happened. It had been such fun.

On the mantlepiece his mum found an envelope from Gideon with a cheque for a lot of money. She knew, thank goodness, they would not have to struggle over this coming winter as they had last year.

Gideon said he felt this was his home now and wanted to be a part of their lives! His actions were proving to be as good as his words. And both his sister-in-law and nephew wanted him to be very much involved in their lives as well.

They liked him and he was now a fully pledged member of their family.

"Ahhh!" The screech came from Jules's mum as she entered the kitchen!

"What is it, mum!" Jules called out as he rushed in to the kitchen after her to find out what had happened.

The twins had done it again! This time they had made four painted papier-mâché cloud jumpers and left them looking in the kitchen window. They looked so real. It was as if they were about to come inside and kidnap Jules's mother. Hence, her yelp when she entered the kitchen.

"Those twins!" She laughed. Seeing the funny side of it. "They are quite impossible!"

"They certainly keep us on our toes when they are around!" Jules agreed. "It's difficult to keep one step ahead of them!"

"I'm not sure we ever do!" His mum sighed. "But they are lovely and I miss them when they have gone!"

*****

Jules was on his way to see the puddle hoppers when he saw the old lady he had not seen for weeks. She was waiting to cross the road with her shopping bag. He was making his way over to speak to her when he spotted the same three thugs who had attacked her before. They were coming from the opposite direction and getting nearer to her.

He feared for the worse and started to walk a bit faster to reach her before they did. Jules was worried the three of them would want to take their revenge out on the old lady. She had been the cause of the motorcycle gang confronting them. Yet, as both he and they got closer to her, he could see that not only were they walking with severe limps but they each had an arm in plaster.

As he got even a bit more closer he could even distinguish they each had black eyes and bruising around their fat lips. Obviously, the motorcycle gang had not just warned the three thugs to leave little old ladies alone in the future but backed it up with a physical thumping.

Hence, Jules was surprised they were going anywhere near the little old lady again. You would think they would fear a repeat of what happened to them before.

What he had not realised was they had not seen the little old lady ahead of them. Once they did, they quickly changed direction and started to hobble back from whence they came. Obviously, afraid that even by getting too close to her may cause them to have a problem with the Hawker Hunter motorcycle gang again. A problem they did not want. They had learnt their lesson.

"Hello!" Jules greeted her.

"Oh! Hello Jules! It's lovely to see you again!" She turned and looked up in to his face. "You do look well!"

"Shall I help you across the road and home with this shopping?" He was always kind.

"Oh! That's very kind of you, dear! You can help me across the road if you like, as the traffic goes so fast these days! But this bag has hardly anything in it and is very light so I can manage it all the way home!"

"Okay!" Jules smiled. He then helped her cross the road when the flow of the traffic had ceased.

"That was kind of you, dearie!" She touched his hand in gratitude.

Jules felt a warm feeling go right through his body as she touched him. A warmth that made him glow inside.

"Have you had a lovely summer?" She asked.

"Well! I thought it was going to be quite quiet and boring but do you know what it has been really exciting and unusual! It's a bit like last year! Suddenly these amazing things started to happen! Who needs to go on holiday when there are such exciting things happening here at home. It is as if the holiday has come to me!" He found himself talking with great joy at how his summer had turned out! "So, you know what, I think I've had a lovely summer, thank you!"

"That's good, dearie!" She smiled and nodded with satisfaction. "And it's lovely to see you again! But I better leave you now as I know you're going somewhere important!"

"Yes, I am!" He replied and wondered how she knew that. "Are you sure you will be able to manage getting home by yourself though?"

"I'll be fine this time, dearie!" She touched his hand again in kindness. "Just you go off and see your little friends!"

Once again, he felt that warmth from her hand surge through him. Then it crossed his mind and he was left puzzled, "How does she know I'm going to see some small friends?"

As he walked off he turned around to look at her. To his surprise she was not there. She had somehow disappeared.

"That's odd," he said to himself. "How could she disappear so suddenly. She was walking away from me very slowly only a few moments ago and now she has gone!"

*****

The field was already fenced off at Gateshead Road where the puddle hoppers lived. Prince Willie was as good as his word. He had bought the whole area and had it designated as an area of special significance to remain untouched in the future. He had given this area to a charitable trust to look after. There was a proviso that stated it must always be kept exactly as it is now and be left to nature.

The local community scratched their heads as to why this plot of land that was just a few cow fields had been designated such a special place. To them it did not make sense. However, they were pleased to have such a special place in their vicinity. Another small piece of land saved from urbanisation.

Jules had been given a special key so that he could enter through the new security gates that had been erected at the edge of the field where the puddle hoppers lived when he wanted. The charitable trust had agreed that he would be on their board to monitor all discussions about this special area. Of course, this was done at Prince Willie's insistence.

After re-locking the gate, the young man made his was over to the puddle where the main tribe of puddle hoppers lived. Things had changed so he did not have to worry, as he had to in the past, about being observed by passing people. The whole area was sealed off now.

Before he even reached the puddle, Prok and Lace came out to greet their friend.

"It is good to see you again, Jules!" Prok laughed.

"How are you after your imprisonment by the cloud jumpers, Lace?" Jules asked.

"It took me quite a while to get over the horror of what those three evil creatures were intending to do with me. But with Prok and my family's help I think I'm getting there now, thanks Jules!"

"It must have been awful!" said Jules in sympathy.

"You were very brave!" Prok added.

"I wonder how all those children who suffered the same experience as you are holding up? It won't help that their parents won't believe a single word they say about what happened!"

"Yes, I worry for them too!" She shook her head in concern. "We all got quite close, tied up by those cloud jumpers. Even though I was in the next room, we could still talk to each other. As you can imagine we shared many fears of what we thought lie ahead for us. All fearing the worst."

"Do you think the cloud jumpers will come back?" Jules asked Prok.

"My father and the elders believe they will but not for quite a while!" Prok replied.

"Next time, we will be ready for them when they do return! I think we have learnt we have to keep an eye on the clouds above us in the future. It seems they are bound to be annoyed with us for stopping their dastardly deeds once more. At some point they will want to seek some kind of revenge! Hence, we will need to be alert and ready."

"I wonder where they have gone? Whether they have returned back to their base to get a new cloud home? Or do you think they have gone to another town to try and get more children?" Jules rued.

"One thing is for sure where ever they go it is bound to be bad news!"

"I dread to think!" Lace said with real feeling. "They appear so cruel!"

"It is amazing that you are distantly related cousins, yet, so different!" Jules mused.

"Yet, not even all puddle hoppers are all good, Jules. Look at the three evil ones Gideon is taking back to Alaska with him to bury. And I am sorry to say, we both know, not all human beings are good either," Lace added.

"Yes, I suppose you are right there, Lace!" Jules agreed.

"It's wonderful now this area has been fenced off and we no longer have people wandering across the fields!" Prok added.

"Yes, the prince has done you proud. I know he was very grateful when he realised the role you played in helping to save those kidnapped children as well as his own daughter! And when he discovered where you lived and how precarious your home had become, I think he was determined to help secure your future," Jules agreed.

"Well! He seems to have done that. And he seemed a really good man too!" Prok smiled.

"Well, I suppose I better be going." Jules smiled. "It has been another exciting summer!"

Printed in Great Britain
by Amazon

40206883R00150